BIRTH OF A DARK NATION

RASHID DARDEN

OLD GOLD SOUL PRESS
WASHINGTON, DC

Old Gold Soul Press
Washington, DC

www.rashiddarden.com
www.oldgoldsoul.com

Birth of a Dark Nation is a work of fiction. Any references to real people (living, dead, or undead), events, establishments, organizations, or locales are intended to give the fiction a sense of reality and authenticity. Other names, characters, and incidents are either the product of the author's imagination or are used fictitiously.

First Edition

ISBN 10: 0-9765986-6-3
ISBN 13: 978-0-9765986-6-4

BIRTH OF A DARK NATION
is dedicated to the life and memory of

ADEJIMI SHOPADE

ACKNOWLEDGEMENTS

My gratitude goes to God, first and foremost, then my family, in the blood and in the spirit.

To my loyal readers who have made the leap with me from contemporary fiction to stories of the paranormal, I thank you for supporting me from the beginning. You have believed in me even when I wasn't sure I believed in myself.

Rhaema Friday, you have been a blessing to me in my time of need. Thank you for saving this project. Thank you to my copyeditor Elizabeth Collins and to my review panel Nikki Butler, Lana Johnson, Latoya Mitchell, and Trenile Tillman.

Thank you to the team who made the cover happen: designer Charlis Foster, who brought my vision to life in ways I couldn't imagine; my brother Coy Lindsay and my friend Zac Yorke for providing faces to match the story; and to Teri Greene and Christopher Akinbuwa for being in-person assistance and for being soundboards to the emerging ideas. Thanks also to Neil Wade, Gavin ML Fletcher, and D'Mario McDonald for their coaching and feedback.

Thank you to my friends Steven Allwood, Demetrius Beynum, Anthony Bowman, Elizabeth Khalil, Zun Lee, Lydia Obasi-Hills, and Michael Myers II for their various assistance throughout the writing of this novel.

This book could not have happened without Indiegogo and the generosity of so many people who stepped up to the plate when it was time. Those people are: Tony Lamair Burks II, Teresa Weber, Carmen Cardenas, Andre Robinson, Erin Cribbs, Geoff Riggins, Williams Ricks, LaJwanne Louis, Lindsay Kendrick, Tab Robinson, Will Saunders, Cassie Jeon, Jayson J. Phillips, Pontip Rasavong, Shari Hunt, Tremaine White.

Gil Shannon, Jr., Mario Camacho, Josephine Bias Robinson, Scott Purnell-Saunders, Emily Shaffer, Aaron Mitchell, Alexander Parks, Amanda Hicks, Jamie C. Stewart, Sara Matz, Devin Cunningham, Danielle Hunter, Erin Marie Meadors, Jason E. Livingston, Criscilla Stafford, Robert J. Donigian, Robin Robinson, Chanta Cobb, Krista Robertson, Delphinia

Brown and Jamie Sykes, Duane Edwards, Tiffany Lezama, Carly Kocurek, Edwina King, Elyshe Voorhees, Elyssa Brecher, Harrison Beacher, Jason Williams, Jarrett Beck, Latoya M. Mitchell, Monica Segura, Raina Fields, Rhaema Friday, Sarah Reilly, Yarnell Culler-Dogbe, Zoila Primo, Terredell Burroughs, Denise Monty, Desmond Patton, Bernard Bazemore.

Frederick Davis, Takima Jones, Angela Stepancic, Danielle Barrios, Lorri G., Samantha Kerr, Allison Poole, Chris Hill, Mary Garvey, Ayana K. Domingo, Michael Brown, Christopher R. Brient, Andrea Robinson, Charles Murray, Douglas Franklin, M. L. Ward, Elizabeth Louis, Alex Trivette, Heather Graham, Crystal Taylor, Danita Brooks, Jeanné Isler, Jeri Ogden, Joseph Alexander, C. Lorenzo Johnston, Ken Alston, Cheyanne Keene, Lakisha Odlum, Lenore Matthews, Mekea H., Michelle Freeman, Marie Preston, Rodney Frank, Robert Barrow, Sandie Bumbray, Storme Gray, Symya Williams, Tiffany White, Monique Eddleton, Christy Chukwu, Donnetta Butler, Jordyne Blaise.

Cicely Garrett, Zaid A. Zaid, Jennifer Samson, malik m.l. williams, Nickay Penado, Omar McCrimmon, Kimya Moore, Erika Gunter, Angel Brown, Moises Mendoza, Brandon Jay McLaren, Cashana Morrison, Chris Moore, David Carus, Liz Burr, Carolyn Ricks-Lakey, Dana Baylous, Erica Cannon, Linda Madison, Gary Chyi, Ivan Land, Jr., John Foster, Kathleen McDaniel, Katherine Steadwell, Latoya Hankins, Linda Finder, Marcus Felder, Marllana Whitaker, Maya Zimmerman, Mike Ramsey, Muhammad Salaam, Olivia Sawyer, Tracy Joseph, Patrick Higgins, Raven Moore, Courtney Beale. And special thanks to those supporters who declined public acknowledgement, and all those readers who gave whatever they could to help make this happen!

My Indiegogo campaign could not have happened without the assistance of Joe and Sheela Alexander, Tony Burks, Lana Johnson, Omari Aarons, Muhammad Salaam, Jennifer Gormley, and Geoff Riggins.

To all of my teachers everywhere, but particularly the following teachers from Georgetown University, here on earth or in Heaven, I owe this to you: Keith Fort, Stephanie Vermeychuk, Angelyn Mitchell, Dennis Williams, Tod Linafelt, Joseph Murphy, Maurice Jackson, and Adam Rothman.

Finally, God bless you, Brandon Elliot, wherever you are.

Birth of a Dark Nation

Prologue

Good Friday

By design and by choice, he had the sort of look that was unmemorable. He had the skill of disappearing in a crowd and turning invisible while standing by himself on the corner of Rhode Island Avenue. Like a chameleon, he became part of the scenery, unnoticed by anyone who walked by him. His was an invisible life.

Discretion was paramount to his survival. There would be no need for anyone to remember the not-too-short, not-too-tall, brown skinned young man of 18 to 30 years old. His face was not meant to be picked out of a line-up. To be recognized would be suicide. The length of his hair would have betrayed him, had black men and dreadlocks not gone together like peanut butter and jelly in the early years of the 21st century in Washington, DC. If the '90s were known for bald black rappers and R&B crooners, the trend was ultimately reversed by a fusion of hip-hop and Caribbean culture that marinated in DC's multiple generations of political and aesthetic resistance, with a side of mambo sauce for good measure. Black hair was beautiful and men embraced their locks like the crowns they were meant to be.

It was a good time to emerge from the shadows. He could let his locks descend from his head like they did hundreds of years ago when they were free. And he could walk among the people without fear for the first time in a long time.

He had a meeting with the big man at St. Augustine's Catholic Church, a huge urban cathedral on 15th and V Streets, near the epicenter of DC's campaign of gentrification. For as many years as he had quietly lived in DC, it had been quite some time since he'd been in a church. It just wasn't his scene. He had to go out and purchase a blazer and necktie just for the occasion.

He pulled his dreadlocks back with a rubber band and kept his look nondescript. He looked up the tall spires of St. Augustine's reaching to heaven and entered the sanctuary.

He counted three pews from the back and took a seat, clasping his hands in front of him as if in prayer. St. Augustine's stayed open until midnight on Good Friday for the faithful to quietly pray and reflect on the significance of the day. It was around 11:15 p.m.

By 11:30, he was joined on his pew by an old friend, another average-sized, average-looking black guy in his 30s or 40s. His dreadlocks cascaded down his back and hit his waist.

"Aragbaye," the friend said.

"Welcome back to DC, Babarinde," he said. They shook hands and smiled. They vaguely resembled each other with their subtly handsome features; not quite brothers, but definitely from the same place. Aragbaye looked around and then clasped his hands again. Babarinde did the same.

"How long are you here?" Aragbaye asked.

"Only for as long as I need to be. I'm heading to Union Station as soon as I leave here."

"I wish you could stay longer. DC has changed a lot since the last time you were here."

"I know. I saw the new convention center. Never even saw the old one. And an elected mayor? Who knew?"

"I knew."

"You probably had something to do with it," Babarinde joked.

Aragbaye chuckled. "Maybe."

They sat in silence for a few more moments.

"I know this isn't a social call," Aragbaye said.

"You're right. It isn't. I came here to tell you something important."

"I'm listening."

"The new dawn is coming."

Aragbaye held his breath.

"When?"

"I'm not sure. But soon."

"So…what do you want me to do?"

Babarinde handed his friend a thick folder.

"The man in this folder…he's your responsibility now."

Aragbaye carefully opened up the folder. On the left was an eight by ten photo of a handsome man who was about thirty years old. It looked like a simple portrait, as though for a passport or maybe for his job. Black polo shirt. Dark skin. Close cropped hair. Extra meat on his bones. Good looking.

"My responsibility, huh?" Aragbaye repeated.

"Know him. Keep him safe."

"Who is he?"

"It's all in there. His name is Justin Kena."

"But who is he to us?"

Babarinde stood up.

"He's 'The Key.' Our people will see the new dawn because of him. That's all you need to know. Be well, brother."

Babarinde left the church. Aragbaye took another glance at the folder.

"Justin Kena. This should be interesting."

Easter Sunday

He decided…
He decided…
He decided to die…

"Turn that music down," he growled. "It's giving me a headache."

The radio softly whined gospel music in the cozy, dark room with the four-poster bed. His stately wife glided over to the clock radio and turned it off entirely.

"Well you didn't have to turn it all the way off," he said snidely.

"I know you hate it."

"I don't hate it. It just…doesn't ring true to me."

His wife sighed. As her husband paced, she sat at the foot of the bed, gazing at their prisoner: a beautiful, young, bound and gagged black man with long dreadlocks, naked from the waist up, wide-eyed with unbridled fury.

"I never thought we'd capture one of them," he said. "They're so few in number. So strong. So fast."

"So smart," his wife added. "To live among them all these years and never get discovered."

"We'll do that again. Sasha!" he barked at his servant.

"Yes, sir?"

"Did you draw his blood?"

"Yes, sir. The vials for the week are downstairs, in the vault, waiting for pick-up."

"Did he put up much of a fight?"

"Yes, sir. But Malcolm and Andre restrained him."

"Very good," he said. "You'll do this every other day until otherwise instructed. He'll get used to the routine." He walked toward his wife and exhaled. "As long as we keep this one alive, we'll figure out how they do it."

"He'll never talk. His kind is defiant."

"His DNA will talk for him," the husband said, addressing the angry young man on the bed. "And then we won't have any more use for you."

"Come to bed, darling. It's almost sunrise."

The man and his wife calmly but quickly left the room. The servants were left to tend to the patient before the sun rose.

The brown haired white woman and the dark black man smoothed out the wrinkles in the sheets and tightened the restraints on the prisoner's hands and feet.

"This is supposed to be one of their high holy days, too," Andre said.

"You know a lot about them," Sasha replied.

"Yeah. I make them my business."

The man in bondage stirred. His eyes softened and pleaded for mercy. His breaths were rapid.

"Poor thing," she said.

"I've got the morphine."

He found a vein and injected the ordinarily deadly dose of morphine deep into the prisoner's body. The prisoner tried to scream, emitting only sickening muffled wails from behind the gag. The prisoner's skin healed itself shortly after the injection was done. In only a few moments, his eyes fluttered closed.

"This should have him out for the day," Andre said. He removed the gag from the prisoner's mouth.

"Let's go," Sasha said.

"Wait," he said. He reached into his pocket and produced a strand of green and white beads. He carefully placed them under the prisoner's pillow.

"Stay strong, brother," he whispered.

They left, turning endless locks on the other side of the door. As the sun came up over Rock Creek Park, the prisoner felt the thinnest of rays pierce the shade of the sole window in the room. Sunlight slashed all the way across the room, almost touching his hand. He knew it was there, but he was too weak to grasp it.

Part One:
The Seduction of Justin Kena

ONE DAY IN JUNE

I was always the first person in the office because I didn't want to have to walk past the other idiots I worked with. It was much better on me and everyone else if I just came in first, unlocked everything, and settled into my little corner of Magdalene House without having to worry myself with small talk. On paper, we were a social service organization for HIV positive women. In reality, we were the place that social workers went to die.

I was their IT manager, which meant I had to show old ladies how to reboot their computers and empty their spam folders.

Thirty years old, a computer science degree from Syracuse, and this is where I was. Trapped.

Magdalene House was located in the Northeast quadrant of DC, in a neighborhood which hadn't decided yet whether it would be sleepy and suburban or gritty and blighted. Rhode Island Avenue had storefront churches and liquor stores dotting each corner, with Chinese food carry outs and beauty salons in between.

There weren't many trees in this neighborhood, at least not on the main street. Just bare sidewalks. In the summer months, there were always pockets of kids and young adults loitering about. They were loud, but usually harmless.

Magdalene House was located just off Rhode Island Avenue, on 22nd Street. But in contrast to Rhode Island Avenue's bustle, 22nd Street was quiet, tree-lined, and purely residential. The row houses were short, wide, and spacious. The yards were small in the front, but always well-manicured. This was not the type of neighborhood that had neighbors who didn't give a damn about appearances. And just because they were in "the hood" didn't mean they were poor, or couldn't afford to maintain their homes.

So, even though Magdalene House was nestled in an area of Ward 5 that was no stranger to prostitutes and drug dealers, it was still clear that if they wandered into the residences on 22nd Street, they would not be welcome (unless, of course, they were visiting their own grandparents).

DC was weird that way. The city was nothing at all like Hamilton, the small New York town where I grew up.

Between 8 a.m. and 10 a.m., I was the only one at work. The official hours of the office were 10 a.m. to 6 p.m., but since I didn't provide any direct service to clients, I could work an earlier shift and be home in time for the evening news.

I didn't hate my entire office, though. Over the years, I had made two good friends there: Steve and Cissy.

Steven Waller was a tall, slim man in his early fifties with a bald head and a gray beard. He had a soft, raspy voice like Harry Belafonte. You couldn't tell him that he wasn't still pimpin' after all these years. His eyes seemed to twinkle when he talked. That twinkle wasn't enough to blind his two ex-wives to his cat-daddy ways, so he was resigned to enjoying himself on the singles scene once more.

Cecilia Flint had been known as Cissy among her friends and family for most of her forty years. She was short and buxom with curly blond hair that often fell into her eyes. She had a husband and a daughter at home and she took no shit from them or anyone else in her immediate vicinity.

About two and a half hours into the day, Cissy and Steve would usually stroll in at the same time, either with breakfast to share or with car keys in hand, eager to take a short trip to a diner or coffee shop.

This time, Steve brought the breakfast, which was good because Cissy was always trying to sneak some healthy shit into the mix, as if we really gave a damn. Steve knew what I really liked.

"Scrambled eggs with cheese, home fries, grits, and bacon, like you like it," he announced, putting my Styrofoam container in front of me.

"Perfect," I said. "How much I owe you?" Steve put his hand up, closed his eyes, and vigorously shook his head.

"Thanks, man!" I smiled. We did that for each other all the time. Sometimes it would be my turn; sometimes it was Steve or Cissy. We dug into our food and immediately began our gripe session. We sat in Cissy's office, which was adorned with photos of her husband and daughter.

"So what's new?" I asked.

"Well, I tried to go to a conference in Nashville, but Ernie said no," Cissy huffed.

"Figures," I said.

"I don't know why he won't let us be great. Seems like no matter where I work, the wrong people are in charge," Steve said.

"Does he even have a degree?" Cissy asked.

"His resume says so," Steve said.

"I'm sure he bought one from someplace. There are diploma mills all over the internet," I theorized.

"God, I hate this place! I wish the economy wasn't so bad; I would leave today," Steve said.

"But the clients are worth it," Cissy said firmly.

"I can't believe the board is okay with this guy," I said.

"They're all his friends. They'll never fire him," Steve said.

"So what are we going to do?" I asked. Cissy shrugged.

"You can do computer work anywhere. You tell me what you're going to do."

"I don't know, Cissy. I just want to work someplace where I can make a difference."

"You've been here almost four years now. What difference have you made? I mean you basically back up the servers. How does that help women with AIDS?"

"Damn, Cissy."

"I'm not trying to be mean, honey. But you are still young and have a lot of good ideas. You don't have to work here if you don't want to. You've got a lot of executive leadership potential."

"She's right," Steve added. "You've got some of the best ideas in the building, but Ernie's dumb ass…"

"I'm starting to think Ernie's last name is 'dumb ass' for real," I said.

"Might as well be. We are up shit's creek here and nobody is doing anything about it."

I shrugged.

"Well, let me know when y'all have a plan together. I'll support it." I stood up to leave Cissy's office.

"That's it?" Steve asked.

"I don't know what else I can do. We're all stuck in crappy jobs at a mediocre organization with a shitty boss and a negligent board of directors. What can I do other than apply for a new job?"

"It makes me sad that this place has robbed you of your passion."

"Passion?" I laughed. "Don't worry about me. I'm going to be okay. But if y'all will excuse me, I'm going to run to Dollar General and get me a soda. Want anything?"

My coworkers shook their heads. I headed out the door and jogged across the street during a rare break in the heavy Rhode Island Avenue traffic.

This dude who I saw from time to time was sitting on the steps of the Masonic hall, casually looking in my direction. I had conditioned myself not to notice the boys on the street. Even after four years, I wasn't as comfortable in Woodridge as I was in my little corner of Uptown, where I'd lived since moving to DC. I kept my distance.

It was hot. I hated the summer with a passion. I'd gained so much weight since college and it seemed like the summer heat made me more aware of myself. Sweat rolled off my neck and down my chest, pausing at my stomach as if to mock its ever-expanding roundness.

I had never been a small guy, but the preceding few years had been incredibly sedentary for me. I really needed to join a gym, but I was afraid that the moment I did so, I'd lose my job and then not be able to afford it.

Excuses.

I just didn't feel like doing anything about it.

I bought my Sprite Zero and exited the store. I could see the profile of the guy sitting in front of the Masonic hall more clearly. He had on a light gray t-shirt with a plain black book bag, jean shorts, plain black tennis shoes, and short white socks. His long dreadlocks came past his broad, strong shoulders. His face was a living dichotomy: the roundness of his cheeks made him appear youthful and innocent, but his eyes were somehow old beyond his years, and his eyebrows and nose converged into acute angles, making me unsure whether he was truly sinister or just born looking suspicious.

He saw me looking.

"Aye, I got some music. Got some DVDs," he announced.

"What?" I asked, stopping in front of his stoop.

"I got some music… Old school hip-hop, go-go, R&B. Whatever you want. And some movies. Got that comedy shit, shit that's in theaters now. I got you."

This nigga was trying to sell me bootleg merchandise. I hadn't been hit up by a bootleg man in years. With all the ways to get free music on the Internet–legally or not–I was taken aback by his offer.

I looked at his face and time stopped. Now that I could see him full on, I saw the depths of his beauty. He wasn't plain at all, nor was he sinister. He had impossibly dark eyes and a smooth, dark brown face. His dreadlocks crowned him perfectly.

"I don't need any music," I said, suddenly full of confidence. "But I'll tell you what–find me some movies that are stronger than an R rating, and we can talk."

He looked at me quizzically.

"Oh…you mean you want some of them nasty movies? Some triple X?"

"Yeah. Sure."

"I gotchu. Where you be at?"

"I work across the street at Magdalene."

"Aight bet. I'ma be back through here with some flicks on Friday, aight?"

"Bet," I replied. I jogged back across the busy street.

What was I doing? Did I really just arrange for my friendly neighborhood bootleg man to bring me some X-rated movies in front of my job?

Yes. I did.

He was kind of cute though. Might be nice to see him again. And I was somewhat of a connoisseur of pornography, so why not? Straight, gay, whatever—I just liked porn. Not like there was much else to do with my free time.

Toward the end of the day, I got notification of an event I had put on my calendar. The Syracuse alumni chapter in DC was putting on another one of their happy hours downtown. I didn't really want to go, but I didn't have any reason not to. Maybe I could do some networking or something. Or maybe find a dude.

I looked very much like an IT professional that evening. Navy blue polo shirt and khaki pants. Nothing special. I looked like everybody else coming from work on the train I took to get to Gallery Place.

I exited the train right by the humongous Chinatown arch extending over H Street. Chinatown is like a tiny version of Times Square. Lights and LED signs blink all over the place and the streets are clogged with tourists toting digital SLR cameras they never take off automatic mode.

The happy hour was at this Spanish tapas place. A tall, bald white guy dressed in his best business casual with an Orangemen button on his shirt shook my hand and asked me when I graduated. I told him and he smiled, noting that he'd never seen me at a function before. I said I normally didn't come, but I figure I might as well see what it was all about. He smirked.

The Syracuse folk had an area in the back sectioned off with orange balloons. I sat at the furthest corner table and looked at the "Syracuse Specials," as they were called. I ordered some kind of apple and walnut salad and something with scallops. They were cheap.

I didn't really feel like talking, but I forced myself to make sounds come out of my mouth when the white people I didn't know asked me questions they didn't care about.

Computer science, when asked my major.

For about eight years, when asked how long I'd lived in DC.

Yes, I remembered Tasha-Lynn Williams, the African American president of the Student Association and the only other black student they personally knew.

No, I didn't know where she was now.

No, I didn't know where any of the basketball players ended up.

I hurriedly downed my first and second beers and contemplated a third micro-plate of Spanish food.

Just when I thought the evening couldn't get any more vapid, in strolled the hosts from BET's 106 and Park.

Okay, not really. But it was just as bad.

I never connected closely with my African American classmates at 'Cuse. I mean sure, I had my close friends and suitemates. But I wasn't that dude who joined the Black Student Alliance or waged protests. That was fine for some. I just wanted to graduate, play some video games, and maybe smoke a little weed.

But these other people, the ones who put on full faces of makeup and carried leather satchels just to go to class, had morphed into a shiny black buppy class that did happy hours and brunch and spent money they couldn't afford on galas for causes they didn't care about, just in the name of being seen.

These were not my kind of people.

"Hey Justin man, how you doing!"

"Long time no see!"

"Where you been?"

"You still work in the nonprofit sector? Oh."

"You need to come visit my spot on U Street!"

"Come to our ski trip!"

"Come to homecoming!"

Yes, because the first thing of my to do list would be to spend more time with people who judged my blackness based on how well I could keep up with them financially, whether my political beliefs were the same as theirs, and whether I talked like them.

To hell with all that. I was going home.

I made up some excuse about having to feed a dog that I didn't have and I jetted out of there without having exchanged a single business card. That was quite alright with me.

The bus would get me home just as quick as the train would, without any transfers, so without hesitation, I hopped on the northbound Georgia Avenue bus to take me back uptown.

The sun had already set and it was pretty dark by the time I got to Georgia and Kennedy. I couldn't believe I had wasted so much time at that stupid happy hour. All I wanted to do now was take off my work clothes, eat some real food, watch television, and go to sleep.

The bus let me off at the liquor store and I walked toward my apartment.

The street was empty, which was odd for Kennedy Street at any time of day. Suddenly, the path to my apartment building felt miles long rather than blocks, and I could hear a pin drop.

I looked to my left; nothing. I looked to my right; still nothing. I quickened my pace.

There was a rustling in the bushes next to me. I turned sharply to face them, but saw nothing. I walked quicker.

My heart began to race and I coughed. My mouth was dry. I needed water immediately.

I heard more rustling and I turned around. Nobody was there. I ran.

My hands shook. I reached in my pocket for my keys.

Finally, I reached my doorway amid what sounded like thousands of dry leaves shaking around me. I fumbled with the key for a second, but finally got it in the door. I ran up the stairs to the third floor and again fumbled with the locks on my old, blue metal door.

I got the door open, slammed it behind me, locked both locks, and ran to my bathroom. I closed the bathroom door, locked it, and ran the water in the sink.

I sat on the toilet lid and tried to catch my breath. Both of my hands still shook. I grabbed a cup, filled it with water, and sipped.

Slowly, I regained control of my nerves. There was nothing out there that could have harmed me, but I was deathly afraid, like the world was going to end; like the two covers of a book were closing in on me and I was trapped in the middle.

I'd never had a panic attack before, but later, when I looked up the symptoms, I convinced myself that's what had happened.

June

We leaned on the edge of the reception desk, the only two people in the office.

"Why are we even open on Fridays?" I asked Steve.

"Man, I don't know. And why am I the only case manager here on Fridays?"

"We suck."

I had already run every scan known to man on the server. Everything was fine. The website had been updated from top to bottom. Ernie was out on another vacation. The office was quiet.

"I bet you're gonna have a client try to come in at 4:30 to get some services," I said nonchalantly to Steve.

"Fuck you, nigga. I hope you get a virus on your hard drive."

I laughed.

"Where Ernie at this time?" I asked Steve.

"Some place in Canada. Like Toronto. Some shit."

I shook my head just as the doorbell rang.

Steve and I walked to the other side of the reception desk, where even Lana was gone for the day. It was 4 p.m.

Steve looked at the black and white image on the security monitor.

"Can I help you?" he asked through the intercom.

"Yeah, uh… I'm lookin' for dude that work here. Uh… I don't know his name. He jive brown skin, a li'l thick."

Steve was puzzled. "Is he talking about you?"

"Let me look at this dude," I said. I went to the monitor and could tell immediately who it was by his stance.

"Oh, that's that dude from the other day. Buzz him in."

"The bootleg man?" Steve asked. I nodded. "Oh lawd. We finna have the bootleg man all up and through here."

I smiled. Steve buzzed the dude in and he walked straightaway to the reception area.

"What's up man?" I said.

"Chillin'. You good?" he asked.

"Yeah man, I'm good. I'm sorry I didn't introduce myself last time. My name is Justin. Justin Kena."

"Dante," he replied. I stretched my hand out to his and he accepted my handshake.

"This is my coworker, Steve. He's a case manager." They shook hands.

"What a case manager do?" Dante asked.

Steve glanced at me.

"A case manager is like a social worker that helps people get the things they need or are entitled to. It's like somebody who helps people that can't help themselves because they don't have a network or support."

"Oh, okay." Dante put his book bag on the reception desk and unzipped it. "You a case manager, too?"

"Nah, I do computers," I answered.

"What kind of place is this?" Dante neatly arranged his white envelopes of DVDs on the desk while he listened.

"Magdalene House basically provides housing for women with HIV," I replied.

"Oh, okay. That makes sense."

"So what kinda flicks you got?" Steve asked.

"Well, your man here tried to play me earlier this week, tommbout he ain't want no G-rated movies up in this camp. So I got a whole bunch of that good shit fo' dat ass. I got that
Pinky, Jada Fire…some Cherokee…"

"Damn man, you weren't playing!" Steve exclaimed. He pawed at the disks, picking them up to look closer at the titles.

"That's cool," I said. "But do you have any Brian Pumper?"

"B. Pumper? Hell yeah!" Dante dug deeper into his bag and pulled out two disks. "Phatty Rhymes & Dimes…and Black Ass Master. Here you go man."

He placed them in my hand. I raised my eyebrow.

"He's good," I told Steve.

"Man, I knew not to come half-steppin' when you said you wanted some flicks."

"How much?" Steve said.

"One for five. Buy two, get one free."

"What's 'The Candy Shop' about?" I asked.

"Oh, that's all girls," Dante said. I wrinkled my nose.

"I don't know if you could tell, but I like dudes," I said, pushing 'Candy Shop' back toward him. "So anything you get with Brian Pumper, Mr. Marcus, or Lex Steele–we good. Anything, really. But it's gotta be some dicks involved."

Steve laughed and Dante was unfazed.

"I gotcha," he said. "Well take these two B. Pumpers and this jont right here—Mr. Marcus is in that one. And I will throw in an extra one for your boy."

"That's a deal," I said, peeling a ten off my slim wad of cash. "Whatchu want, Steve?"

"Yeah… I'll go ahead and take that Candy Shop."

"Nasty bastard," I said with a smile. I gave Dante my ten and he placed the DVDs in my hand. For a split second, our fingers touched.

"Enjoy the movies man," he said. Steve immediately took his out of my hand and ran back to his desk.

"Your man really likes his flicks, huh?" Dante asked, zipping up his bag.

"Yeah man, I guess we both do." As he slung his bag on his back, our eyes met for a moment.

"Aight man, I'm out," Dante said. He abruptly turned around and headed toward the door. I followed him.

"Thanks for coming by," I said. "You know, I didn't really think I'd see you again."

"Why you think that?" He placed his hand on the handle of the front door.

"I mean, you know… I never really saw you around here before."

His hand left the door handle.

"I live on Thayer Street. A block from the Masonic hall. I lived there for a while."

"I didn't realize that."

"Justin's the name, right?" I nodded. "Well, Justin, let me give you some advice. If you take your head out of the clouds and, you know, actually look around sometimes, at the things right there in front of your face, the people, maybe you'll notice a whole lot of things you been missin' out on."

"I didn't mean to offend you, man."

"I ain't offended," he said, opening the doorway to the porch. The summer heat spilled into the foyer.

"And I ain't mad that I been out there for a few months and the first time you looked in my eyes is when you saw that I had pornos."

My dark skin blushed.

"But that don't mean nothing. Now I know you. And now I'll speak. And I hope you do the same."

I nodded and extended my hand to him. He smiled, exposing perfectly white teeth contrasting sharply with his deep brown skin.

"I'll do that. Thanks for coming by, Dante," I said.

"My pleasure," he said, firmly shaking my hand and then walking away. His jean shorts sagged slightly and his blue boxer shorts peeked out.

I stared at him through the glass door until he disappeared around the corner.

Steve walked up next to me.

"Uh…so… Dante, huh?" he asked.

"I mean, whatever. He's cute," I said, avoiding Steve's gaze.

"He aight," Steve said.

"I mean yeah, he's not like super fine or anything."

"You like him."

"No I don't."

"Yesssss yoooooou doooooo."

"I don't know him. I only just found out his name."

"Nigga, you are about to skip down the street singing show tunes, I can see it in your eyes."

"Shut up."

"Just be careful. This dude is a corner boy. If he'll sell bootlegs to a stranger, you know he's reckless. You got too much to lose messin' around with a boy like that."

"Dude, I don't like him."

"Okay man. I gotcha."

Steve walked back to his desk while I walked upstairs to my office. I sat down in my chair, adjusted the back, and reclined. As I stared at the ceiling, I made an admission to myself.

Fuck. I *am* attracted to this dude.

June

Even though I hadn't had a panic attack since the night of the happy hour, I decided to drive to and from work every day afterward. And on each day, I noticed Dante. He wasn't always just posted up at the corner. Sometimes he'd be walking to the Dollar General or the carryout. Sometimes he'd be waiting at the bus stop to head to parts unknown. And, of course, there were the days that he'd be sitting out in the shade of the Masonic hall, selling his bootleg movies and music.

What he said had resonated with me. I was usually too wrapped up in my own thoughts to notice anything going on around me. I didn't used to be that way, but the past few years at Magdalene House seemed to suck the life right out of me. I'd become reclusive and detached from social life. The few friends I had from college were scattered across the country and I hadn't managed to make new ones. In fact, I wasn't even sure how to make friends outside of work.

I knew my mom was worried about me. I made sure I spoke to her every Sunday night, after dinner and before 60 Minutes. She and my dad were enjoying the retired life but always made sure I was doing okay.

They knew I was gay. They were fine with it. My four older siblings had already begun to give them grandchildren, so nobody was upset that I probably wouldn't. At least not the old fashioned way.

I never caused my family any problems. Syracuse was a breeze for me. And nobody so much as batted an eyelash when I left Hamilton, New York, to come down to DC to work. I was responsible. I was *good.*

My mom worried if my goodness prevented me from taking romantic risks. She loved me and wanted me to be happy, but she didn't quite understand just how hard it was to meet quality guys, even in a city as gay and as black as DC. Men didn't seem to get me. They didn't seem to be attracted to me. So, I suppose I made the decision to stop being hurt and start focusing on me. My career. My small little corner of this world.

I knew my mom wanted more for me, but as long as I stayed out of trouble, there wasn't much she could do to make me want more for myself than I already had.

At least I had a job and a handsome guy to look forward to seeing a few days out of the week, even if it was just a wave in the air across Rhode Island Avenue.

I didn't know him. I didn't even have his phone number. But it was nice to meet somebody new.

As I sat down for our semi-regular staff meeting, I positioned myself at the far end of the room so I could see out the window.

"New seat?" Steve asked. I smirked. He looked out the window and saw that Dante was on his regular spot directly across the street.

"Lawd," he said. I shrugged. Ernie, our bumbling executive director, sat down and began the meeting.

Magdalene House was the kind of organization that attracted two types of employees. First, you had the ones who were claimed to be passionate about the cause itself–women living with HIV. My boss Ernie fit in that category, as did the majority of case managers. While their passion was admirable, it didn't always translate into best practices. I learned that one couldn't govern or manage a nonprofit based on emotion. It takes a delicate balance of knowledge, skills, policy, and good, sound business practices. They were hired based on passion years ago. Now? They were just taking up space.

Magdalene House was known for none of that. That made it challenging for the second, business-savvy group of people, employees like Steve, Cissy, and me to excel in our fields. Although Steve was a case manager and did have a passion for helping people, he held a master's degree in social work and often had a hard time understanding why our data collection and case management practices were so archaic. It was almost criminal how poorly records were kept. And that affected Cissy's job in development, too. Whenever a grant proposal had to be written which specifically asked for hard numbers, she had no choice but to guess the figures.

So the day-to-day work got done because of a love for the clients and their plight, but important work like grant proposals, operations, and leadership got short shrift because, really, nobody was in charge. Nobody worth a damn.

Ernie had been executive director for years, hired by friends on the board of directors who just needed somebody to keep the organization running day-to-day. By the time I got there, Magdalene House was already in the middle of a very slow decline.

Steve was the first to notice. Even though the formal records were spotty, he saw that the caseloads for all the case managers were slowly dropping off. The clients weren't dying. They were just finding other places to receive housing and the other services we provided. Younger, shinier nonprofits were opening up their doors across town, and even though they did the same things we did, the clients were wooed away by the newness and the incentives of the other organizations. I couldn't be mad at them, either. With the private foundation money the new organizations were receiving, they were able to give their clients cool things for loyalty, like an Amazon gift card for six months of keeping appointments. Steve tried to introduce a similar incentive program, but Ernie wasn't having it. Magdalene couldn't afford that, he said.

Cissy then began to see that Ernie wasn't giving her as much to do, and that he hired contractors to handle the government grants. It was obvious to everyone that Ernie was giving his own cronies work to do while slowly, but surely, taking away Cissy's responsibilities. She was basically relegated to writing appeal letters and trying to plan special events.

Finally, I realized that all the external projects that I used to assist on had been cut. No more volunteer recruitment, no more supervising interns. Just running virus scans, downloading software, and ordering new equipment. The salary was adequate, but it was clear that Ernie was controlling us by taking away responsibilities.

"I've got some bad news," Ernie began at our regular staff meeting. "We were denied funding for capital improvements on the house. We've got to wait another year before we can improve the HVAC system."

The room grumbled.

"I know, I know… It's tough."

He always said, "It's tough," as though that were an actual answer to any questions we had.

"But we've got to keep moving forward as a team."

"I have a question…" I began. "It seems like we haven't been winning these major grants lately. Is there anything we can do to fortify this process? You know…as a team?"

"Not really," Ernie responded. "It's totally a political process. They already know who they want to give the grants to from the outset. We just have to keep trying."

Cissy tried her hardest not to roll her eyes at Ernie. We knew he was feeding us bullshit.

The meeting continued much like a Charlie Brown special, with echoes of French horns standing in for the voices of my coworkers. The program staff was ignorant to the major issues. Except for Steve, they wasted time in meetings telling stories about clients rather than focusing on the hard data and contributing ideas toward a long-range plan. Luckily, it was Friday again, and I'd be home soon enough.

Around 4:30 p.m., Ernie had left for the day, and the rest of my coworkers slowly tiptoed out. Before I knew it, I was in the building alone. I turned out the light in the attic and walked down the steep stairs to the second floor. I went to each small room, closed the blinds, and turned the lights out. As I did the same for Ernie's office, I mused that his desk was too junky to ever find anything incriminating on it.

I locked the door to the second floor and continued down to the main level. Somebody–probably Steve–had already locked the big brown door to the reception area, leaving me to just turn on the security system and lock the front door of the building as I left.

As I did that, I felt a light tap against my back, then a second. I turned around and saw Dante down the sidewalk, lightly throwing small pebbles at me. One hit me in the chest.

"Nigga, what are you doing?" I asked, brushing away the dust that the pebble had left on my red polo shirt.

"Nothin', man. Just messin' with you."

"Don't you have some movies to sell?" I asked him as I walked off our porch and onto the sidewalk.

"Always man," he said, giving me dap. "But I just wanted to come by and see the homie. See what's good with you."

"I'm okay. Ready to get out of here." I started walking in the direction of my car.

"You got some place to be?" he asked me.

"Just home. Gonna order some food and chill out."

"It's just you? No kids?"

"Nigga, you know I'm gay."

"Yeah, I know. That don't mean you ain't got a family."

"Well, I don't. It's just me."

"Oh, okay," he said. He stopped walking. I paused along with him.

"What's up?" I asked.

"If all you gonna do is go home…I mean…you ain't gotta go home to kick it."

"Where else I'ma go?"

"You wanna come to my crib?"

"Your place? I don't know about that, man."

"Come on, I'm just across the street and up the block."

"I don't know, Dante. Like tonight? Like right now?"

"Yeah, right now. Come on." He started walking back up the street.

I followed him and stopped at the corner.

"Dante, maybe we can hang out another day. I'm really tired and—"

"Will you stop trippin' and come on across the street? All we're going to do is order some food and kick it. You act like I'ma rape and murder you or something. Shit, I'm hungry too, nigga. Damn."

"Well…okay," I said. Spending an hour or two at his place wouldn't be the worst way to spend my Friday evening. And I'd only be a block from my car if I needed to make a quick getaway. Not that I would need to.

I caught up to him at the corner across the street. As we walked up Thayer Street, we passed a few kids skateboarding down the street. Where I grew up, skateboarding was for angry white kids. On the avenue, it was just another way for black boys to get around.

The houses on Thayer Street were all designed slightly differently. Though most were square and compact with small front yards, some had vinyl siding and others had brick facades. While some had fully enclosed porches that were filled to the brim with junk, others had no porch to speak of.

Dante's house was near the corner. There was no actual house on the corner–it was a vacant lot. Because I could see the front and the side of Dante's house, I could tell that it was much larger than I originally thought it would be. It was three stories tall, like the Magdalene office. I assumed that the third floor must have been a full attic like ours was.

"This is the crib," Dante said.

"All this is yours?" I asked.

"Yup," he replied. "Used to belong to my cousin."

"I see y'all are keeping it in the family." He opened the door and let me in.

The house was simply decorated on the inside, with a brass wall clock and matching sconces on either side adorning the far wall where the sofa sat. The carpet was thick beneath my feet. The place itself smelled… old. Not bad. Just old.

"Have a seat," he said. I thanked him and sat on the sofa, picking up the remote control from a small coffee table and turning on the television. I turned it to the channel nine news.

"Make yourself at home," he quipped.

"Thanks," I replied sarcastically. "I just don't like to miss the news."

As he disappeared into the kitchen, I could hear him opening up the refrigerator. Annette Mitchell was on television reporting on some sort of scandal in city hall, as if that was anything new in DC.

"I don't watch a lot of TV," he said, emerging with two cans of Diet Pepsi.

"Word? I love it. I like being entertained. Music, sports, movies, all that."

"That's what's up," he said, passing me a drink.

"Thank you," I said, popping open the can. "So what do you like to do?"

"I dunno, just chill I guess." He sat on the opposite end of the couch from me.

"What's a day in your life like?"

"Why you got so many questions?"

I laughed.

"You do realize we just met last week, and the extent of our relationship is me buying your bootlegs?"

"Why you act so saditty, yo?"

"Saditty? Are you kidding me? I'm just trying to get to know you better, dawg. You seem like a cool dude, but I'm starting to rethink that."

Now he laughed.

"You feisty."

"Damn right I am." I sipped my Diet Pepsi. He chugged his and burped.

"'Scuse me," he said.

I burped in response. Loudly.

"Nigga, you nasty!"

"Whatever. I already farted on your couch."

He laughed hard. I smirked.

"Aight nigga, I'm no good at this, but here goes," he began. "I live a real simple life. This my family house. We had it a long time. Right now, it's just me living here. I ain't go to college or nothin' like that. And yeah, I be sellin' movies and shit to pay bills. I'm good at it. But I'm good at whatever I feel like doin'. I don't want you to think I'm just some scrub, you know?"

"I don't think that," I said.

"Yeah, you do. Look at your body language."

I looked down at myself and saw what he meant: my arms were folded and my legs were turned away from him. I looked like I didn't want to be there.

"You're observant," I said sheepishly. I uncrossed my arms and faced him more.

"Yeah, I notice shit," he said. "So how long you been at Magdalene?"

"About four years. The money is okay, but the work sucks. I sit in front of a computer all day."

"I see. So you sit in front of a computer all day then come home and sit in front of a TV all night."

"I mean, you make it sound like a bad thing," I smiled.

"It's whatever. I just like taking walks sometimes. You know, be out in the air and shit."

"That's cool," I said. I sipped some more Pepsi until it was gone.

"That don't sound like your kind of thing."

"It's cool. Dante, I gotta be honest with you."

"What's up?"

"I don't know what I'm doing here. I don't know what you're into. I ain't been on no date in years. I'm just-"

"Whoa, dude… Slow down. You getting all hype for nothing. I just want to spend some time with you, yo."

"Why?"

"Because you fine as shit, nigga damn. And you seem jive smart. And on the real? Ain't no nigga ever step to me so bold like you did. I mean shit, what gay niggas you know gonna cop some straight porn? If you don't think that's hot, then you need to get it together."

"You think it's hot that I like straight porn?"

"Hell yeah. You know what that says to me? That you don't have no boundaries like a lot of these niggas out here. You down for whatever."

"Nobody's ever accused me of that before," I laughed.

"First time for everything, right? Now just relax. We gone order some food, watch some TV like you like, and get to know each other and shit. You say this new for you, well it's new for me too. A nigga wanna get shit right the first time, ya dig?"

I nodded. And blushed a little bit. This dude was different. I liked it.

We ordered some General Tso's chicken and vegetable fried rice and watched the rest of the news with a few awkward interruptions for "getting to know you" types of questions. By the time the food arrived, the ice had finally been broken, and I felt free to delve a little deeper.

"So, you ever get worried about getting in trouble for selling your movies?" I asked. I savored each bite of the spicy chicken dish.

"Not really. Po-pos ain't thinking about nothing less than weed. Bootlegging shit ain't hurting nobody. Niggas in the hood ain't got no money for shit no way, so these studios ain't missing no loot." He shoveled a helping of rice into his mouth.

"That's true. And plus, the Internet practically put shit you want right in your lap."

"Yeah, true that."

"You ever thought about using USB drives for movies instead of CDs and DVDs?"

"How dat work?"

"Like, say you sell your…clients, I guess…sell them a USB drive for cheap, and then whenever they want something new, you upload it to their drive from a laptop or something."

"That could work. But I still gotta have discs for the niggas that ain't got no computers."

"True," I said. "I guess you got this under control, you don't need my advice."

"I like how you think, though."

"Thank you man. Hey, you ever thought about doing a job that, you know, has benefits?"

"Like a nine to five?"

"Yeah."

"You hiring?"

"No."

"Then no."

"Damn, just like that?"

"I got my income man, I'm good. For now at least. And I got some experience doing construction and shit like that. Landscaping. Even worked on a trash truck for a little bit. But I'm good right now. I can pay my bills."

"I feel you. It's cool."

"What about you?"

"What about me?"

"I get the feelin' you ain't into yo job all like that, either. When you gonna move on?"

"You hiring?"

"Naw."

"Then I'm good." I winked.

"You funny."

We talked more, about a lot, but at the same time, nothing big at all. It was nice just getting to know the basics from somebody who was so simple and uncomplicated. He was just a dude making his own way. Nothing special.

But he was very handsome, and even through the thick DC slang and accent, I could tell he was also very smart. He had a way with words that was intriguing.

By no means am I saying that he was beneath me, or that I was better than him in any way. All I am saying is that he was different from anybody else I had ever had an interest in. He shared things without saying them explicitly and provoked me without being spiteful.

He was cool. And I could tell he felt the same way about me.

We talked so long into the night that I fell asleep right there on the sofa. Like a perfect gentleman, he put a blanket over me and walked up the stairs, letting me sleep alone.

Although I slept rather fitfully, plagued by dreams that I couldn't remember once I woke up in the morning, I still woke with a sense that I was in a safe place, with someone who cared about me just up the stairs.

Happy Hour

Cissy did her best to cultivate donors for Magdalene House. Her latest venture was a happy hour at a venue on U Street. The corridor had once been a burned out strip where no business would thrive, but with the addition of a metro station, the once dead street became something of a young professional hotspot in DC.

Steve and I committed to helping Cissy man the event when the rest of the staff shied away. It didn't surprise us. When it came to the staff, they didn't do anything beyond regular work hours unless something was in it for them.

The three of us walked up to the venue with its soft neon lights and tiny windows that were too high to peer into, in stark contrast to the other lounges and restaurants on U Street which practically invited the public in through their wide windows.

"Aye... Is it true this place is a swinger's club after ten?" Steve asked.

Cissy remained silent.

"Oh my God, it's true!" I exclaimed. "You got us doing a fund-raiser at a swinger's club!?"

"Listen, I don't care what they do after we leave. All I know is that the owner is letting us use this place for free."

"That's what's up," Steve said. "Well, hopefully, this will be a huge success."

Despite Steve's hopes, the happy hour wasn't much of a success. It wasn't exactly a flop, but only about ten people came through, and most were Cissy's friends. I sat at the table next to Steve, collecting donations and logging them on Cissy's laptop while she made small talk with people she'd obviously already known for years.

All of our promotion on Facebook and Twitter meant nothing at the end of the day. Magdalene House just wasn't the kind of place that would get its fundraising success doing happy hours. Magdalene didn't have enough political cachet for the vapid DC buppies to even consider supporting us. To them, and to many, we were the equivalent of a mom-and-pop store trying to compete with Target.

I felt bad for Cissy, who smiled through the entire evening, even after it became apparent that Ernie wasn't going to bother to show up. Her friends didn't stay long, and only one or two actually bought a drink. Most just dropped off their donations and left within 20 minutes.

As we packed up our promotional materials four hours later, a young Asian woman came into the bar, dressed in all black. Her black hair was full and bouncy, with one blond streak just right of the center of her head.

"Oh, hello! You must be from the Magdalene group, right?"

"Yes, we are," I smiled. "We were just packing up."

"Oh, I'm sorry I missed you guys. My name is Chiyoko. I'm the bartender for the late night crowd."

"I'm Justin," I said, shaking her hand firmly. It was slightly cold.

"Oh, sorry about that," she laughed, noticing my reaction. "I've got bad circulation, so my hands are always cold!"

"Not a problem," I smiled. "This is Cissy, she's the director of development. And this is Steve."

"Pleased to meet you," he said. He was practically salivating over the young woman.

"You guys are welcome to stay as my guests, if you want. That is, you know, if you're into the clientele here."

"Maybe next time," Cissy said quickly. "I've got to get home to my kid."

"Same here," I said. Steve looked at me from the corner of his eye.

"I think I'll stay," he said. "Watch you work for a little while."

"Fine with me," Chiyoko laughed. She then turned her attention to Cissy. "Oh yeah, I was hoping to give you this. I was going to mail it if I didn't catch you here."

She dug deep into her purse and pulled out a wallet. She peeled a hundred dollar bill off of a stack of bills and handed it to Cissy.

"Here you go. I read up on Magdalene House when the boss said you would be having an event here, and I just wanted to support."

"Wow!" Cissy exclaimed. "Thank you so much! Would you like a receipt?"

Chiyoko threw a hand up and shook her head vigorously. "Please, take it. It's the least I could do."

Cissy took the bill and gave Chiyoko a hug.

"Thank you so, so much."

Chiyoko smiled back.

"Have a good evening. It was nice meeting both of you. And as for you, Mr. Steve, let me fix you a drink. Bloody Mary?"

"Works for me!" Steve said excitedly. As they disappeared back into the bowels of the club, Steve turned around and gave Cissy and me a thumbs-up sign. We laughed and left the club.

"That Steve. What are we gonna do with him?" I wondered aloud.

"Pray. Women are his Achilles' heel."

"Where are you parked?" I asked.

"Right here. Got really lucky finding a space. Are you okay getting home?"

"Oh yeah, I'll be fine. I'm parked a few blocks down. See you at work tomorrow!"

I began walking down 13th Street in the direction of my car. I laughed to myself again as I thought about Steve and his new friend, Chiyoko. He was one smooth player, even at 50.

The street felt still. No wind blew, no cars moved, and everything felt oppressively immobile. My car seemed miles away and the muscles in my chest began to contract and tighten over my lungs.

No, not again.

I felt like the world was going to end if I didn't get to my car right then and there. The rustling noises began again and I picked up my pace. I reached into my pocket and tried to get a grasp on my keys but my hand kept shaking and sweating.

I looked around. No one was there. But I knew somebody was. Somebody had to be.

I broke into a sprint, finally getting my keys in my hand. My car was in sight, and if I could just get inside, everything would be okay.

I ran, sweat falling off my brow, stopping only when I got to the car door. I hit the auto-unlock button, threw the door open, and hurled myself inside. I slammed the door shut and stuck the key in the ignition. I turned the volume up on the radio and tried to forget that I was panicking. In the passenger seat was a bottle of water—I grabbed it, fidgeted with the cap, and finally got the bottle to my lips.

I finally began to calm down in the safety of my car.

"This shit has got to stop," I thought.

CARNIVAL

It was way too early to be awake on a Saturday morning, but these were the things we did for the guys we liked.

"You lived in DC this long and ain't never been to Carnival? Shit, you live *two blocks* from Georgia Ave and you ain't *never* been to Carnival? Whatchu got against Carnival?" he asked me that week.

"I ain't got nothing against Carnival!" I said. "I just…never made a point to go before."

"Well, we going."

I stood on Georgia Avenue and Kennedy Street in front of a pink and black brick building, in the oppressive heat of the early morning. The building had been a barbecue place once, but it was now a Chinese carry out.

It was also the landmark where I'd met Dante so that we could enjoy the DC Caribbean Carnival. It was to be our first date, even though we had spent practically every day together for the past two weeks. One day, he might surprise me with lunch from the carryout. Another day, if the weather was cool enough, we would walk around the block and just talk. And of course, some days I would just spend the evening with him watching television and talking.

I was digging him. So it was no big deal when he asked me if I would go to Carnival with him. I only lived two blocks from the start of the parade route, so I might as well step on down the street and watch it with him.

He got off the bus on Kennedy Street and I smiled slightly, not wanting to show the world how deeply I was attracted to him. As usual, he was wearing a crisp white sleeveless t-shirt, but today he was wearing faded green camouflage shorts. A red, white, and black bandana pulled his long dreadlocks back.

"Nice bandana," I said, giving him dap as he approached me.

"Thanks. Representin' Trinidad today."

"Looks good. I'm representing the tiny nation of Kena Island. Population one."

"You crazy," he said. "Hey, we goin' up this way today, Georgia and Missouri."

"Is that the best spot to see the parade?"

"See it? I said we're gonna be in it."

"What the hell?" I said, stopping in my tracks. "As hot as it is out here, you want us to walk in the parade? I'm not dressed for this shit man."

"It's fine, the weather ain't that bad, and you don't need to do nothin' special. I know the band. We good."

"Dante, I don't know," I said.

"Aight, just walk with me to this little park. We'll check it out. If you don't wanna do it, we can just watch. But we gotta hurry, the shit is about to start."

He got some pep in his step and started jogging up Georgia Avenue to where it met Missouri. There was a park there where all the bands were assembling. For DC Carnival, a band wasn't just musicians; it included huge flatbed trucks with enormous speakers as well as dozens of dancers. Some of the bands had elaborate costumes with feathers and sequins. I had seen pictures of folks I went to college with who had gone to real Carnivals down in the islands. They were off the chain.

DC Carnival was smaller, but still shaping up to be a lot of fun. On this hill were hundreds of dancers assembled and waiting to march with their bands down Georgia Avenue. Dante led me down the other side of the hill to the band furthest away from everyone else. These dancers were not wearing specific costumes at all, but instead were doused head to toe in blood red body paint.

"This is the Cold Blooded Band," he explained. He took his shirt off and wiped the sweat from his forehead with it. It was my first time seeing his naked torso and I enjoyed the view. Every inch of his chest looked like it had been carved from mahogany.

"Yeah, looks creepy," I replied. As I walked closer to the dancers, rather than looking ominous and scary, they actually all had smiles on their faces. I could tell that this was a friendly group by the way the laughed and carried on around each other.

"So, where do the non-bloody folks line up?" I asked.

Ignoring me, Dante introduced me to a friend of his.

"Justin, this is Kenny. He's with Cold Blooded." Kenny was a tall man with cornrows and caramel colored skin. He was 6 and a half feet easy and had shoulders wider than most small houses.

"Nice to meet you, Justin," he said in a deep bass. "Stand over there, please."

I backed up a few paces as he directed and Dante stood next to me.

"Clear!" Kenny shouted.

Suddenly, I was drenched with red paint from head to toe.

"Son of a bitch!" I immediately took my shirt off to rub the paint from my face, when another torrent of red paint doused me. Now I looked unrecognizable from the rest of the dancers.

I looked over to my left and saw that Dante was also covered in the paint, even to the tips of his dreadlocks. The volunteers kicked us out of the station and told us that if we waited in the sun, the paint would be dry before we knew it.

"Dude, I can't believe you set me up like that! I don't want to be in a damn parade all day, and I for damn sure don't want to be in this damn body paint!"

"Hey… I just wanted to do something fun and spontaneous with you," he said quietly. "I'm sorry I ain't ask you first."

I leered at him and then looked away. I was pissed. I was inclined to just walk back over the hill and go home.

"Don't go," he said. It was almost as if he had read my mind.

"I ain't going anywhere. I just better goddamn well enjoy this fucking parade."

His white teeth shined through the red paint as he smiled.

"You will," he said.

After standing in the sun for about twenty minutes, the paint had indeed mostly dried, just in time for the band to wind up and the soca music to start playing.

I hated to admit it at the time, but I really did end up having a great time. I hadn't heard good soca since I was in college. To hear it live and in a band of a hundred people was on another level all together. As soon as we began moving down Georgia Avenue, I forgot how pissed off I was at Dante.

It was hot. Yet we danced all the way down Georgia Avenue, grinding and winding away. The sweat broke through our body paint and made flesh colored trails down our bodies. I didn't even realize until four blocks down the parade route that I was naked from the waist up. I did not have the same kind of body that Dante did. I was about a forty in the waist and curvy in places I should have been angular. In short, I probably looked like somebody's crazy pot-bellied uncle out there. Panic slowly crept over me.

I stopped dancing and started walking. I tried to imagine that I was invisible and would somehow disappear entirely.

Noticing how my demeanor had changed, Dante, who previously was swept up in the music, came back down to earth to reassure me.

"You know you look good, right?" he said earnestly.

"Whatever," I said. I didn't truly believe him.

"Seriously." He slapped me on the back and prodded me into dancing again.

Did I mention it was hot? We walked and we marched and we

danced and we walked and we marched and we ran (when there was an unforeseen gap in the parade) and we danced some more. I swear I sweated off ten pounds that day.

We finally ended up at Banneker Field, across from Howard University, for the big Caribbean festival after the parade was over. I was exhausted and hungry, yet Dante seemed to have even more energy. We got some Jamaican patties and ate them on the bleachers.

"Aren't these supposed to have beef? Where's the beef?" I asked.

"Oh, I got vegetable. You know I don't eat meat, right?"

"Yeah, I noticed. But *I* like beef though! I guess I'll live though." I smiled.

"You having fun?" he asked me, as we watched the revelers dance in front of the big stage and continued to bake in the sun hours later.

"Yeah, I am," I said through a still-red smile on my face. "I kind of want to go home and shower, though."

"Yeah, me too," he said. We had spent hours on the parade route and just kicking it at the festival but I didn't really want the day to end.

"Hey… Why don't we go to my place?"

"But I'm still all red and sticky," he said. His dark brown eyes gleamed in the sun as he spoke.

"You can shower there," I said.

"Word?"

"Yeah man, you shouldn't have to catch the bus all the way across town like that."

"We gotta catch the bus to Kennedy," he countered.

"Well, I was just offering," I said. "And you haven't seen my place yet."

"You inviting me over?"

"Yeah."

"You sure?"

"Yes! See, now you actin' silly." I stood up and began walking to the trashcans and the exit.

"You comin'?" I asked. He stood up and followed me off the field.

As the parade had been long over, Georgia Avenue was now open to traffic again. We waited about ten minutes before one of the big 70-route buses came up the street. We paid our fare, but only after the driver told us we "bet not" sit down in his seats. We stood up for the ten-minute ride up the street, laughing the whole way.

Soon, we were at Kennedy Street. I thanked the driver and we started walking the few blocks back to my apartment. There were no rustles in the bushes this time around. I couldn't believe I had been so frightened of nothing on the nights I'd had my panic attacks.

I noticed at this point that Dante and I very rarely made small talk. When we did have conversations, they were thorough. Robust. But when there was down time, we sort of just…looked at each other. Sometimes, I smiled. Sometimes, he shrugged. Most times, there was just this sense of peace. It was only in that moment that I found it to be strange. To be around someone so often and to say so little, but to feel so at ease, was a new feeling for me, indeed.

"You good?" he asked, as though he read my thoughts in that instant.

"I'm good. My apartment building is on the next corner. The big yellow one."

Kennedy Street was similar to Rhode Island Avenue, with its liquor stores and beauty salons, but my street also had more residential properties. One side of my street had Mexican and Ethiopian restaurants with a row of five houses in between them. My side of the street had two big yellow brick buildings. They were three story apartments, each with around twelve units. The buildings were on opposite corners of the block and an unbroken row of two story houses filled out the space between them.

"This is it," I said. I took my keys from my pocket and unlocked the front door. There was no security system in this old building, just a Plexiglas door in a metal frame. I walked up the stairs to the third floor and Dante followed me.

"This is an old building," he said, as he looked around the hallway. We had a black and white tiled floor and institutional-looking blue walls that seemed to come straight from a 1940s-era hospital.

"Yeah, it is. We don't even have central air, man. I've got to leave one of my units on while I'm out just to make sure shit doesn't literally melt in this heat."

I opened my door and the heat from the living room hit us.

"And this is clearly not the room where I keep the air on," I joked. He paused and looked around my space. It wasn't anything to write home about. I'd guess that the 42-inch flat screen television was the most interesting thing in the room. I really needed to invest in some curtains, as the metal blinds—even when closed—were doing nothing to keep the heat out. Nor were the hardwood floors.

To my surprise, he wasn't interested in the TV, or my CD collection, or even my DVDs, which had their own small shelving system.

Instead, he made a beeline to the small, framed photos on my wall. He inspected each one carefully.

"This yo fam?" he asked.

"Yup, I can point them out later. Let me show you the bathroom now and get that shower going."

I led him down the hallway toward my room but stopped short at the linen closet. I grabbed spare towels and washcloths and held on to them. I then turned the corner and entered my bathroom, turning on the light and ensuring that there was enough soap and shampoo there for him.

"I think you got everything now," I said, turning to leave. He grabbed my arm.

I turned back around.

"What's up?"

"I don't have everything I need," he said.

"Oh," I said softly. He pulled me close to him and looked down at my body, still caked with blood-red body paint and stained with sweat. Neither of us had put our shirts back on.

"You look so fuckin' good," he said.

"Thank you. Your body is amazing."

"Thank you." He grabbed my face, closed his eyes, and kissed me on the lips.

I held him at his sides and kissed him back. I felt like a brittle doll made out of clay. Our bodies rubbing against each other through the dried body paint felt unnatural.

"I'll start your shower," I said. I let him go and turned on the hot water, then the cold, then the showerhead.

"Thank you," he said. I turned my head as he began to take off his shorts. I began to wash my hands (which I should have done before touching the clean towels–dummy) and I looked at myself in the mirror. I was a fright. Too bad we didn't take any pictures.

"Justin."

"Yeah?"

"Whatchu waitin' for?"

I looked at Dante, who had stepped into the shower and had leaned back to look at me through the side of the curtain.

"I'm not waiting for anything," I said. I was confused by his comment.

"Then why you not in here with me?"

"You want me to shower with you?"

"Yeah...please."

"Aight," I said, nodding. I slowly dropped my shorts to the floor next to his and climbed in behind him in the shower. I couldn't help it—seeing his thin, narrow body in the shower directly in front of mine gave me an instant erection. The red paint rolled off his body under the force of the water, leaving behind dark, brown, and wet muscle.

He backed up onto me, rubbing his ass on my erection. I hugged him from behind and rested my chin on his shoulder, next to his still-red dreadlocks. I didn't realize until that moment that I was actually taller than him. I was taller and I was bigger. The entire time, I had the physical advantage against him. For what reason would I have to be remotely intimidated by him, as I often felt?

I knew why. His personality was six feet tall. His masculine aggressiveness commanded a room, or a park, or whatever space he inhabited at that moment. Whatever he even remotely suggested felt like a demand to me. And I was totally smitten by him.

He grinded his ass on my erection and asked me if I liked it. I did. I told him so. He grinded on me harder. My arms embraced him from behind and traveled down his torso. I cupped his erection and was pleasantly surprised at its length and its girth.

"Justin," he moaned.

"Yeah," I whispered in his ear.

"Can you help me wash this red shit out of my hair?"

"No doubt," I said. I grabbed the shampoo from the caddy in my shower and squirted copious amounts in my hands. I rubbed them together and then started working it into his long locs. He took the shampoo from me and did the same until his head was a massive mushroom of white foam. He closed his eyes and relaxed while I took my time scratching his scalp and working the dye out of the locs.

I stood back and let him rinse the suds from his head until the last remnants of the red dye drained down the tub and the water was clear. Dante wiped the water out of his eyes and faced me, his erection still rock hard.

"Let's…uh…" I began.

"Finish up in here?" he asked.

"Yeah… Expeditiously."

We lathered up and scrubbed vigorously, making sure every last bit of dye was off our bodies. He turned the water off and I hopped out first, grabbing towels and tossing them to him, one for his hair and another for his body. There was still one left for me.

Before I was even the least bit dry, he began kissing me again. He threw his towel onto the hallway floor and I led him into my bedroom. I fell into my bed and Dante pushed me down, his mouth barely leaving me.

"Justin," he said, in between kisses to my face and neck.

"Yeah, man?" I said back. He stopped and stared deeply into my eyes.

"You smell…so…fucking…good!"

He kissed me on my lips, and then my neck, inhaling deeply.

That's weird, I chuckled to myself.

"Zestfully clean, baby," I said. We flipped over and his still damp dreadlocks made a halo around his head on the bed.

"Justin," he said again.

"Yeah?" I looked into his eyes.

"I want you," he said.

"I want you, too," I smiled.

"I want you to fuck me. Right now."

"I want to fuck you right now," I repeated. I spread his legs and lifted them over my shoulders as he held on to my sides.

"Wait, I need to go get a condom and lube," I said, letting his legs slide down.

"You don't need a condom," he replied. "Just lube."

"I don't need a condom," I repeated without thinking. "Just lube."

I reached in my drawer and grabbed the tube of lube as well as a handful of condoms. I shook my head. What was I thinking?

"I always use condoms, babe. Don't know what I was thinking." I unrolled the Magnum onto my erection, smoothed some lube over it, and rubbed some into Dante's hole.

When I looked into his eyes, he looked puzzled.

"You okay?" I asked.

"Yeah. I'm good. Now fuck me."

I slowly slid my penis inside his tight hole. He let out a slow growl as I adjusted myself inside him. He grabbed onto me tightly.

"Goddamn, you so big," he said. I grinned on the outside but was high-fiving myself on the inside.

We fucked for a really, really long time. Dante was full of tricks, from the reverse cowboy to some shit I'd never done that must have looked like a giant crab. I worked that ass like there wasn't going to be a tomorrow.

It all came back to my favorite position though: face-to-face with me on top. Those final few thrusts were magical. We looked at each other eye to eye the whole time until I came inside him (and safely in my condom). At the precise time that my body spurt my kids out, he shivered and came in white torrents on his own chest, completely untouched by me or his own hands.

I felt like a king. I'd never made anyone come just by fucking. It typically didn't work like that between men except in pornos. But hell, if it worked for Dante, it for damn sure worked for me.

Shortly after it was over, I fell asleep. Dante crawled next to me and dozed off as well.

Moments later, or maybe even an hour, I couldn't tell, I was awakened to Dante kissing my neck passionately, over and over in the same spot. It felt good at first, then it started to hurt.

"Dante," I said, caressing his hair. He continued kissing and biting my neck.

"Dante," I said again. He bit harder.

"Dante, stop it," I said, pulling away sharply.

"Oh… My bad," he said. I looked at him once more. He looked genuinely sorry and I immediately felt bad.

"It's okay," I said. "Just started to hurt a little."

"I won't hurt you again," he said. "I'm sorry."

"I said it's okay," I reiterated. I pulled him next to me and continued caressing his still damp hair.

He was a weird one, but I liked him. I never expected to be in this much control of him in the bedroom, but it was an arrangement I could learn to love.

Resignation

So, Cissy quit.

We really should have seen it coming, especially with the slap in the face that was Ernie's absence at the happy hour. Though it did raise a few hundred dollars—more money than we would have received without it.

Steve and I were upstairs in my office bullshitting when it happened. I could hear Cissy raising her shrill voice first, then Ernie's deep bass rising in volume. Steve's eyes grew big and we both tiptoed toward the stairs to hear the argument better.

"Oh, that's rich!" Cissy shouted. "You expected me to work miracles when you won't even show me the fucking budget? Why won't you or LaJwanne coming off that information?"

"That's LaJwanne's domain as the finance director, not yours."

"The *budget*, Ernie? Really? I can't see the budget?"

"I don't need to show you the budget for what I need you to do."

"I am the director of development! I am not only supposed to know the budget, I'm supposed to be able to tell you whether or not we can even reach the goals you set. This is a leadership position and we're supposed to collaborate on these things. Now how in the hell do you expect me to raise those kinds of dollars in the next fiscal year?"

"That's not my problem, sweetie. I've already taken the load off your plate by getting grant writers for the government grants. You're supposed to be out here making the relationships."

"How many dossiers have I researched for you? How many of Washington's richest people have I created profiles for? You know where these people are. I've given you practically everything but their social security numbers, but you won't do the work! You won't follow through! You come to work—sometimes—and just sit in your office all day doing nothing, expecting the money to just rain down from heaven. I can't do everything, Ernie."

"Then maybe you need to find another line of work. You only have one directive in this office and that's to raise money. And I've given you a lot of freedom to do that, but I can see that you can't."

"Now wait just a goddamn minute. I've busted my ass for this organization for the better part of a decade. You can't tell me I don't know development. If there's one fucking thing I know about the nonprofit sector, it's development."

"Watch your mouth."

"No, you watch your mouth. I am tired of this shit, tired of it! I am sick of working for a talentless, uncreative, unconnected, lazy executive director who won't do the minimum that the job requires. And I'm tired of you giving away these contracts to grant writers who are your friends and aren't nearly qualified to do what's required. Ernie? I quit. I quit this fucking job so hard."

"Alright then, peace be with you."

"And peace be with you, you lazy bastard. And by the way? Your breath smells like ass."

I hollered. Steve hollered. Ernie surely heard us. We hurried down the stairs to see Ernie retreating into his office and slamming the door. Cissy had an empty cardboard box and threw her personal effects into it. Tears were streaming down her face.

"Wait, this is for real?" I asked. Cissy nodded and Steve immediately went to her. She sobbed while he held her.

"I just can't do it anymore," she wailed. "He just…won't let any of us be great. We could be doing so much here…"

"I know, I know," Steve comforted her. "It's okay."

He stroked Cissy's hair as she wiped her eyes.

"But what are you gonna do now?" I asked. Cissy shrugged.

"I don't know. But anything's got to be better than this. Justin, promise me that you won't get stuck here. Steve and I, we're no spring chickens anymore. But you? I know you have it in you to be more than your job title. Go back to school, get a master's. Find an executive leadership program. Something. But don't stay here. This is a dead end."

I nodded vigorously.

Steve and I helped Cissy to her car. I didn't know what else to say other than goodbye. It all happened so fast.

"Well champ, that leaves us. The only two people at Magdalene with any goddamn sense."

"This is crazy," I said. "It's just been us against the world for so long. I can't believe she's gone."

"Life is more than a paycheck, Justin. You know that."

I nodded. Steve and I stood on the porch in silence for a few minutes. A Metrobus stopped in front of the Masonic hall across the street. Once it pulled off, I saw Dante walking toward Thayer Street. He glanced over at me, kept walking, then stopped and glanced again. He raised his hand in the air and smiled. I forced a smile and a wave back. He beamed.

My life was filled with constants like paychecks and bills, but I had taken for granted that the sector in which I worked could change at the drop of a dime. I began this work because I cared about people. I didn't want to be a cog in a machine. I wanted to use my expertise to somehow change the sector for the better. But I was stuck, just like everyone else around me. The only way out was to get unstuck; to realize that the only constant could be change itself.

Cissy was gone. Steve and I were left behind to pretend as though she never existed, still concealing from Ernie that we held him in little esteem, even while we knew in our hearts that he was doing his hardest to topple the organization from the inside. We couldn't prove it, and now his biggest critic had taken herself out of the game. We couldn't trust the board of the directors to do the right thing.

It was just me, Steve, and our paychecks until we found something better.

"You okay, my dude?" Steve asked, as I watched Dante turn the corner and disappear up the street.

"We gotta do better, man," I said. "All this is changing around us."

"How we gonna do better?" he asked.

"I dunno. Stop being complacent. Start fighting."

"Fighting for what? The clients? The best we can do for them is send them someplace else."

"Fight for something better than what we got. I don't know. That's all I got…right now."

Steve touched my shoulder and rubbed it, nodding with understanding.

Something sparked in me that day, the beginnings of an epiphany. That I was meant for more than the life I was living. Somehow, I was going to figure out what was next.

I walked to Dante's house after work, energized and dying to talk to somebody about it. I knocked on the door and he opened it moments later.

"Hey man!" I said.

"Hey!" He hugged me tightly.

"So, my coworker quit today. Cissy. The white lady?"

"Yeah, I remember you telling me about her. What happened?" He closed the door behind me and I put my bag on the sofa while I paced.

"It's a long story. I mean, it's not that long a story, but it's not very interesting."

"Oh…okay…"

"Yeah, I just wanted to come talk to somebody because I was just thinking, you know? Like…I have a college degree. I have a degree from Syracuse. I should be able to do a lot with that, right?"

"Seems like it to me," he said.

"Right! And like, I might not be a director, but I know a little something about a few things. I've made programs. I've recruited volunteers. I should be able to go out there and work someplace else, right?"

"Sure," he said. "I always thought you were pretty smart."

I stopped pacing and smiled.

"Thank you," I said. I began pacing again.

"So, I don't know, maybe I should stop being scared and, you know…do something."

"Like what?" he asked, sitting on the sofa.

"I don't know! All I know is computers and whatever else needed to be done for Magdalene. But maybe there's more. Maybe I should go to grad school. Get a certification. Or, you know, maybe start up my own shit!"

"Why don't you have a seat?" he asked.

"Naw, I'm good," I said.

"I think you need to have several seats, actually."

"Why?"

"You're pacing a hole in my floor, that's why."

I smiled and sat down next to him on the sofa.

"Better?" I asked. He smiled and cuddled up next to me. He held my hand, kissed it, and calmed me down.

"Now, what is it that you actually want to do? Generally."

"I want to help people," I said.

"Do you know how?" he asked.

"I'm not sure yet. I want to help the sick, that's fine. But I really want to help people who don't have resources. People in poverty. People who left school. I just want everybody to have a chance, you know? Shit happens, but people don't need to be punished for it for the rest of their lives."

"Sounds good to me," he said. He kissed me lightly on the temple. "Just take a breath, slow down, and think about what you want to do. I'm here for you."

"I appreciate that," I said, kissing him back. "I didn't interrupt you when I came over, did I?"

"Well…"

"I can go, it's no problem."

"No. Don't go. I was working out back. But you can come help. Or watch. Whichever."

"I'll help. No problem."

We walked through his house, through the kitchen and the back door, and down the rusty iron stairs leading to the backyard.

The yard was enclosed by a tall wooden fence on all sides. There was no way you could see from outside just how large the space was. The vast majority of it was a garden. A gravel driveway led to the basement garage.

Dante led me through an old, sad looking trellis with ivy growing up it. The garden was divided into several lanes. It all looked green to me, but Dante had a ball explaining what exactly he was growing.

"Okay, over there you got some carrots, you got some chard. We got a whole row of peppers over on that side. Some chili peppers, bell peppers. All nice and colorful, right? Onions and radishes over here. That row there? Berries. Nothing but berries. And way in the back are a few avocado trees."

"And what's right here?" I asked, pointing off to my left at a wild looking patch of shrubbery that didn't even seem like part of the garden.

"Oh, those. They're just herbs."

"Just herbs?" I repeated.

"Yeah, they don't have a name. Anyway, you like it?"

"Yeah, it's cool," I said. "This keeps you pretty busy, huh?"

"Yeah man. It's fun, though. Relaxing, too. You'll see. Hey, grab some extra gloves off the porch, let's get started."

I grabbed the work gloves and helped my man weed his garden and harvest some radishes.

"Where did you learn how to do this?" I asked.

"Family," he said, throwing a radish in the basket he asked me to hold.

"Oh, okay. Were you raised on a farm or something?"

"Nah, not quite. You could say I was raised in the south. Living off the land was normal for us."

"Where in the south?"

"Louisiana. But DC is home now."

"You got brothers and sisters?"

"Brothers. A lot of 'em. All over the place."

"I have four siblings all together. They all live in New York, though."

"I see. You the baby, aren't you?"

I smiled and looked away.

"That obvious, huh?"

"Lil' bit," he replied. "But you not spoiled. Not that I can tell."

"I'm not, really. So did you go to high school here?"

"Oh, uh, naw. Back in Louisiana."

"When did you graduate?"

"19…"

"19? Dude, how old are you?"

He smiled wide.

"Old enough," he said slyly.

"I see I gotta watch you," I said with a raised eyebrow.

"I gotta watch you, too, my man." He tossed a radish at me and laughed.

We worked for a while in his plain little garden, but it was fun. I never thought in a million years that I'd actually be doing something like this with a guy I was crazy about. But I suppose stranger things have happened.

July 4

DC was hot. As in, over-a-hundred-degrees hot, with no end to the heat wave in sight. Not a cloud in the sky.

The Freemasons across the street from Magdalene House were hosting their annual Fourth of July block party despite the oppressive heat. From the Dollar General to the beauty school down the block, each storefront had a different kiosk set up with games, merchandise, and snacks.

I walked past the action to Dante's house, walked up the steps, and knocked on the door. I heard a quick series of stomps, and then a quick open of the door revealed that he was already smiling.

It was contagious.

"Hi," he said.

"Hey," I replied. I gave him a quick once-over. As usual, he was wearing a white sleeveless t-shirt, this time with red board shorts and black sandals. His feet were impeccable, as though he'd never walked a day without moisturizing them.

"You look good today," he said, checking out my khaki shorts and orange Syracuse shirt.

"Thanks," I replied. "So do you."

"Why don't you come in out the heat and come get some of this good air?"

I stepped inside and was greeted by the icy air inside the house. He closed the door behind me and grabbed me from behind. He kissed my neck, slowly opening his mouth and letting his tongue slide across my skin as he tasted me.

"Shit," I exhaled.

"I missed you," he whispered.

I turned around and kissed him on the mouth, awkwardly pressing my nose against his.

"We've seen each other like every day, fool. Now come on, let's see what this block party is all about."

We stepped back outside and the heat hit us like a wave of maple syrup. Sweat was just something I'd have to get used to if I wanted to enjoy the block party. Dante and I walked close to one another, but without daring to show any affection in public. Although times had changed immensely in the years I had lived in DC, it was still never a good idea for men to show affection to one another in neighborhoods like this one. No, things were still far too conservative, because of the corner boys and the hair stylists, and the old ladies and old men belonging to the Masonic orders.

We walked past the Afro-centric bookstore and paused to rummage through their offerings.

"Lots of good stuff here," I mused.

"Yeah, it is," Dante said. "I've read most of them."

"Really?" I asked.

Dante looked at me with an eyebrow raised.

"You surprised I read?" he asked.

"I mean…kinda."

He smirked and scanned the table, picking up a copy of Gloria Naylor's *The Women of Brewster Place.*

"Ask me about 'beige bras and oatmeal,'" he demanded. I was silent.

"How about *Roots*?" he asked, picking up Alex Haley's tome. "Whatchu know about Chicken George and Matilda? Hmm?"

"I mean, those are movies."

"Oh, a smart nigga," Dante mocked. "How about Clare and Irene in *Passing*? Passing for white or passing for heterosexual? Or *Sula*? Whatchu know about the Bottom? Something more contemporary… How about Paul Beatty, *The White Boy Shuffle*?"

"Yo…" I said. "I didn't mean to offend you."

Dante paused, then smiled.

"I'm just fuckin witchu," he laughed. "But yeah. I like to read. A lot."

I smiled back at him. We moved throughout the block and watched as the kids and some grown-ups enjoyed the makeshift games the business owners had set up.

The barbershop had a dartboard set up just outside its doors.

"Wanna play?" Dante asked.

"Oh, I'm no good at darts," I said.

"Come on," he said. "Ayo, how many darts I get for five dollars?" he asked the barber who manned the table.

"Three," he said flatly.

"And what's the prize?" Dante asked.

"I dunno man, I just give you a voucher for the prize table down there."

"Aight. Lemme hold three darts then," Dante said as he passed the man a crumpled five-dollar bill from his pocket. The barber passed him his three darts and stood back.

"Watch this," Dante said to me. I nodded and stood back.

With silent precision, Dante cocked his arm back behind his head and released the dart with a slight throw and a flick of the wrist.

Bull's eye.

Again he cocked his arm back in the same stance and repeated the throw.

Bull's eye again, with this dart landing right next to the first.

He aimed for the third time and shot the dart. This one landed on the dartboard with such force that it knocked down the other two.

"Shit," the barber said.

"Damn," I said.

"Thank you," Dante said. "I'll be taking that voucher now."

"You got it, buddy," the barber said. He gave Dante a gold sheet of paper and wrote some information on it.

"Give this to the lady at the gift table. You can pick from the first prizes."

"Thank you, man," Dante said. We walked away.

"Yo… How the hell did you learn to throw darts like that?" I asked.

"Years of practice, my nigga."

A DJ set up in the parking lot of the Dollar General was playing old soul music from the 70s. Dante's head immediately started bouncing.

"You like this?" I asked.

"Hell yeah," he said. "It reminds me of the music I used to listen to."

"You listened to old school music growing up?"

Dante paused, blinked slowly, and then spoke again.

"Yeah, man! My parents used to play this all the time."

"I see." In terms of his personality, he was definitely an odd mixture of a lot of things, but I couldn't put my finger on what, exactly.

"What kinda music you like?" he asked me.

"A little bit of everything, but mostly hip-hop. If it has a beat, I fuck with it."

"Word."

We passed the Dollar General parking lot and went to the prize table. All they had was kid's toys and Dollar General gift cards, so Dante picked the latter and immediately handed it to me.

"Naw man, that's yours!" I said.

"I know. But I'm giving it to you. You know how they used to do back in the day. Man wins his woman a teddy bear at the state fair. Well, you ain't a woman and this a block party, but I want you to have it anyway. I know you be likin' them Sprite Zeroes and shit."

I laughed and took the gift card.

"Thanks, man," I said. Just then, the DJ began to play "Boogie Shoes" and Dante's entire demeanor changed.

"Oh shit!" he exclaimed.

"What?" I asked, stuffing the gift card in my pocket.

"That's my jam! Come on!" He grabbed my arm and we hurried to the makeshift dance floor on the parking lot. We joined a dozen women and kids who had already begun a line dance.

It was easy to keep up. Right leg out, tap tap, left leg out, tap tap, cha-cha, turn, back, back, back… The fun of it all made us forget just how hot it was outside.

We spent the rest of the daylight hours playing more games—sometimes with some of the neighborhood kids—and eating some of the awesome food the street vendors had. Some of the best, ice-cold watermelon I'd ever had was at the block party that day.

"You staying for the fireworks?" he asked me, as we moseyed back down to his house.

"I can," I said.

"Do you want to?" he asked.

"I do."

"Good." He looked at me out of the corner of his eye and smiled.

"The sun's setting soon. The fireworks will be going up after that."

"Where can we see them?" I asked, as we entered the house. The air was still icy and a chill went through my body.

"The roof," he said. I nodded.

"You want some water?" he asked.

"Yes. Please." He went to the fridge and produced two bottles. We both gulped them down. I closed my eyes for a few minutes and relaxed.

"Come on upstairs," he said. I followed him up to the second floor of the house, then through another door to the attic. He easily opened the window and we stepped out onto the slightly inclined roof. We could see down either side of the block.

"You ain't afraid of heights, is you?" Dante asked me.

"Nope, I'm good," I replied. "Which way are the fireworks gonna be?"

"That way," he said pointing directly in front of us, toward the park a few blocks away.

"I'll be right back," he said. As soon as he climbed back in the window, I heard him zoom down the stairs. Less than a minute later, he was back with a blanket and a cooler.

"Sit on this," he instructed. I unrolled the blanket and put it down on the roof. We both sat down comfortably.

"What's in the cooler?" I asked.

"Beer," he said. "If you want some."

"Sounds good to me," I said. He opened the cooler and popped the top of the cold Corona bottle before he handed it to me. I thanked him.

As I sipped the beer, I looked up at the sky. For the first time in years, I actually noticed the stars.

"I like to see you looking up," Dante said.

"Literally and figuratively," I quipped.

"Yeah. You got a pep in your step like shit."

I laughed. "Your DC slang be killin' me softly," I said.

"What slang? 'Like shit?'"

"Among other things. You sound like you ain't never stepped one foot out the Beltway."

"You'd be surprised where I been," he winked. The first fireworks began to light the sky and fill the air with rapturous booms.

I had lived in DC for several years. I'd done the fireworks on the National Mall, and even though it was entertaining, I began to greatly prefer the idea of all of the neighborhood fireworks celebrations around the city. There was less congestion than down on the Mall and they created a safe environment for small communities.

The night finally began to cool down some. It wasn't too warm to lean my head on Dante's shoulder as more and more lights filled the sky, or for him to put his arm around me while the smell of sulfur filled the air.

The sky was magical. This fireworks display inspired oohs and ahs from the children and families down below, still at the block party, and from the roof, between two unlikely lovers.

Dante turned to me, my head still on his shoulder, and kissed me on my forehead.

"Isn't this sweet?"

The voice was sarcastic, crisp, and clear.

It wasn't Dante's.

Startled, I turned around to see another man sitting on the roof behind us.

"Who the hell are you?!" I stood up and positioned myself in front of Dante in a defensive stance.

The handsome, sandpaper colored man with long dreadlocks slightly tilted his head to the side, as if he were amused.

"My name is Victor Pearl," he said calmly but forcefully. He stood up and approached us.

"He my cousin," Dante said stepping from behind me. Shocked, I looked on as Dante embraced the tall and lean Victor, who was at least six inches taller than him.

"Vic, this Justin," he said, introducing me to his cousin. Still suspicious, I extended my hand to Victor. He took it into an extraordinarily tight grip. I winced.

"It's nice to meet you," Victor said.

"Aye, I'm sorry I ain't mention him before," Dante said. His entire demeanor changed in Victor's presence. His confidence seemed to melt away and he had a problem looking either of us in the face.

"He… We both own the house, sorta." Dante said.

"Our uncle left it to all of the cousins," Victor explained. "Dante is the primary caretaker."

"You're not from around here," I said.

"I'm from around everywhere," Victor said. I knew already that Victor could never be mistaken for charming. He had an arrogant air about him, the same type of aloof personality as many of the black men I went to college with–the same sort of guys I preferred avoiding at reunions.

"Enjoy the fireworks, gentlemen. I'm going to go unpack my things. And Dante, my instruments are coming in the morning. I hope the basement is as I left it?"

Dante nodded.

"Good. See you in the morning." Victor climbed back through the open window and disappeared.

"The fuck is that all about?" I asked angrily.

"Nothin. He my cousin. He lives here too. Sometimes."

"We been talking how long and I'm only just now learning about a cousin?"

"I'm sorry. He be coming through randomly. It's just how he is."

Annoyed, I sat back down on the roof and continued watching the fireworks in silence. Dante sat down next to me.

"Aye, don't be mad. He family. He cool."

I looked at Dante out of the corner of my eye.

"Mmm-hmm," I affirmed.

He sighed and looked back up at the sky.

"He's okay once you get to know him," Dante said.

"I'm not mad because he's rude. I'm just annoyed that this is how I had to find out about him."

"I'm sorry," he said. "Really."

He grabbed my hand, lightly squeezed it, and then kissed it on the inside. He then closed my palm and placed my hand back in my lap.

"You can have that when you stop being mad at me," he said matter-of-factly.

I looked at him and laughed. But I certainly didn't un-ball my fist for a little while longer, just in case that kiss were to float away.

One Door Closes

I heard the heavy footsteps of my coworker as he bounded up the stairs to my attic office.

"Hey champ," Steve said.

"What's up?"

"Boss man called a meeting in the conference room."

"What's that idiot want now?"

"He didn't say, but he looked jive sad or something."

"Well, things can't get much worse than they are right now."

"I guess," Steve said. We walked down the flights of steps and were the last people to enter the conference room. We took our seats in the corner as our boss began, his greasy face sullen and his voice nearly cracking. He glanced around the table from the irritable faces that Steve and I stopped hiding months ago, to Lana's indifferent gaze, to Teresa's perpetual cross-eyed look of pure senile craziness. Rounding out the bunch was the housing manager Tab, the life coaches Tony and Geoff, and the finance consultant LaJwanne.

Ernie sighed and began.

"Team, as you know, we've had a really hard time the past few months. We've been getting dinged left and right with our housing grants from the government and just when it seems like we've got things under control, they ding us on something else. Well, I got some really bad news today."

He paused and his bottom lip began to quiver.

"Take your time," Teresa said.

"We're closing the office today. Magdalene House will be no more by the end of the week."

Everyone in the room gasped simultaneously.

"What do you mean, Ernie?" Tony said. "We've got life skills classes planned through the end of the year."

"The Department of Housing has notified us that we are to cease and desist all housing programs. We will receive no more reimbursements for the work we provide, so the tenants will be moved elsewhere."

"Where are they going to go?" I asked.

"And aren't we responsible for the transition plan? We can't just put them out by the end of the week," Steve said.

"It's out of our hands," Ernie said, a bead of sweat trickling down his brow.

"This doesn't make any sense," Steve continued. "Ernie, what do you mean they've been 'dinging' us? There's been no sort of reports that things were terribly wrong here."

"Housing doesn't want us running this program anymore," Ernie said flatly.

"So they're just shutting us down, just like that?" Teresa asked.

"Yes," Ernie said.

"They can't do that! There are protocols which need to be followed," Teresa retorted.

"He's lying," I said. The commotion of the room suddenly came to a halt.

"Excuse me?" Ernie said.

"You're lying," I repeated.

"Listen, Justin, I know you're upset, but I am not lying about this. This is a highly political process and sometimes good nonprofits are caught in the crossfire."

"Ernie, we house women living with AIDS. There is no way in hell that politics closed Magdalene House. There is more to this story than you're saying. If this is really our last day here, then you owe it to us to tell the whole truth."

"Calm down, Justin, I know this is very stressful but you've got to get a hold of yourself."

"You know what, you are a fucking liar!" I shouted. I stood up from my chair and walked up to my executive director. To my surprise, nobody stopped me.

"You think I don't know that you've been hiring your friends to write these shitty ass grant proposals you've been submitting downtown? Dude, I run the computers here, I know what the fuck your emails say. And I know you've been hiring these two-bit con artists to score this grant money. That's why Cissy quit–you wouldn't let her write the grants. I mean, how the hell is a director of development not going to write the grants?"

"Cissy didn't quit, she was fired for insubordination. And if we weren't shutting down, you'd be getting fired, too."

"Nigga, fuck you," I said, pointing my finger in his face. "And if you think I won't tell downtown everything I know, think again."

I felt Steve touch my shoulder and try to pull me away.

"Come on, Justin, let's just get out of here. We know it's all his fault."

"What?!" Ernie exclaimed.

"That's right, we knew it was all you. We always knew your incompetence would be the death of this organization," Steve said.

"Case management hasn't had a raise in three years," Teresa said.

"Neither has life skills," Geoff added.

"And it's mighty funny how some consultants come-lately can come up in this place, get office space, and not even do shit directly helping the women we serve," I said.

"Get out of here," Ernie said.

"Oh, I will, don't worry," I said, exiting the conference room. Steve followed, as did Teresa.

"You did the right thing," she said. I thanked her and hugged her tightly, knowing it would be the last time I'd see her for a while.

We paused and glanced out of our front doors and noticed several police cars parked out front. A few men and one woman in business suits walked up to the door. I immediately opened the door when they showed their badges.

"Good morning, I'm Agent Castro. We're with the FBI. We're looking for LaJwanne Mason and Ernie Moore," the first agent said. He was tall and light brown, around his mid-forties.

Steve and I pointed to the conference room, dumbfounded.

"Thanks," he said. We peered into the conference room and watched as Agent Castro led the arrests.

"Ernie Moore, you are under arrest for embezzlement, misappropriation of funds, wire fraud, and conspiracy," an officer said.

"LaJwanne Mason, you are under arrest for embezzlement, wire fraud, misappropriation, and conspiracy. You have the right to remain silent…"

As Ernie and LaJwanne were led out in handcuffs, more people in suits walked up to our front porch.

"Who's in charge here?" asked a woman in a gray suit. She had a thick Nigerian accent and long, thin dreadlocks.

"Uh…" I paused.

"Well, the development officer quit two weeks ago, the ED got arrested… I'm pretty sure it's Justin," Steve said.

"What?" I asked.

"Justin Kena?" the woman asked.

"That's me, but…"

"I'm Agent Ifeoma. Don't worry, you're not in trouble," she said.

"Cool, but do I have a job?"

"Unfortunately not," she said.

"Oh."

"We've been investigating your boss for the better part of a year now. Only Ernie and LaJwanne seem to be involved. I know the economy is tough out here, but if you need a referral, just let us know. This will likely be in the media and anybody working here is going to have a lot of explaining to do to subsequent employers. Here's my card."

"Wow. Thank you," I said.

"Yo, son…it's really over," Steve whispered. I nodded.

The government was seizing the building, and even though we weren't in trouble, all we could leave with were our own belongings. No copy paper for the road. No spare computer parts laying around for me to tinker with at home.

I had mentally checked out of Magdalene House long ago. There was nothing in my office that I needed or even wanted. I picked up my messenger bag from the floor and turned my computer off. I didn't reminisce or get sad or anything of the sort. It was just now noon and I needed to figure out where I would spend the rest of the day.

"You good?" Steve asked me as we stood on the porch amid the rest of the staff chatting it up with the neighbors and other busybodies. I nodded.

"I'll see you around, Steve," I said, giving him dap. I glanced across the street and saw Dante sitting on the stoop of the Masonic hall with his familiar black book bag. He stared intently at me.

"Aye," Steve said to me, grabbing my shoulder.

"What?" I asked. He smiled and nodded slowly.

"Get your life!" he beamed. I smiled back, shook his hand, and pulled him into an embrace. Then I speedily walked toward busy Rhode Island Avenue in the direction of my man.

It was hot. Beads of sweat were already forming on my forehead. As the traffic lightened, I jaunted across the street and casually leaned against the glass of the bus shelter near where Dante sat.

"What's good?" he asked. I shrugged.

"I seen a lot of cop cars out there a little while ago."

I nodded.

"Was that your boss getting arrested?" he asked.

"Yeah. They got him for stealing from the organization. The city stopped funding us. The women are getting moved out and…well…I ain't got no job."

"What?" Dante squinted his eyes and looked up at me. I shrugged.

"Shit is fucked up," he said.

"Yeah." I said.

"Whatchu gonna do?" he asked me.

"I don't know."

He stood up, zipped up his book bag and slung it over one shoulder. I looked at him good for the first time today. I don't know why I felt this way about him. My mom would be so disappointed in me for falling for a common corner boy–one that sold bootlegs at that. Still, there was something clean about him, even under the sleeveless t-shirts, jean shorts, and big tennis shoes.

"Come up the block with me," he commanded. I followed him around the corner of the Masonic hall and down Thayer Street. The silence of the Woodridge neighborhood was overwhelming. Something about the tall trees and density of the houses absorbed the sounds of the street behind me.

A block away, we were at his house again. He opened the door and we walked in.

"Why don't you ever lock your door?" I asked.

"I lock it sometimes," he said.

"Aren't you afraid of somebody coming up here and stealing your shit?" I asked.

"I'm not afraid of anything," he replied, as he tossed his bag on the sofa. I gently placed mine by the door.

"Everybody's afraid of something," I said.

"Let me put it to you like this. I ain't afraid of no niggas comin' up in *here*."

"That's fair," I said. I sat down on the far end of the tattered old sofa while he went to the kitchen. He came back out with a bag of Utz potato chips and two bottles of water.

"Why are you always giving me junk food? You see how fat I am?"

"Who doesn't like junk food on a bad day? And stop calling yourself fat."

I looked at him sitting on the other side of the sofa as he gazed off into space. I looked away and opened the chips.

"Don't you know you're beautiful?" he asked, suddenly without the thick DC accent.

I looked at him again and he was already looking down on the ground.

"Thank you," I said.

"Yeah," he replied.

"Who are you?" I asked.

"I'm Dante."

"I know your name. Look at me."

His dreadlocked head turned to face me.

"Who are you…really?" I repeated.

In a manner of milliseconds, he moved close to me on the couch. I was dizzy–he moved so quickly that he was a blur. His hands caressed my face.

"Whoa," I muttered. His hands rubbed my cheeks, my lips, and my forehead. I could smell the oils he used on his hair and body. The smells, the touch, the sound of his breathing this close to my face intoxicated me. My mind became foggy and I began to find it hard to focus.

"This is who I am."

A roaring sound filled my ears and the room began to tilt.

"Dante…"

"Just listen."

Lightning flashes filled the room. My heart began to palpitate and I grabbed Dante's arms to steady myself. I was panicking, but I couldn't move.

"Relax. Listen to what I'm telling you."

I closed my eyes. With each zap of electricity I felt around me, a different image filled my head. In fact, it wasn't so much an image–more like an impression. A memory, even. Smells, sounds, feelings.

I was in the black belly of a slave ship, tossing back and forth in a storm, the lightning briefly illuminating the shackled arms and legs of my brothers.

I saw Dante's face again and he held me close to him. His heart was beating as fast as mine.

Lightning flashed, and I was on a vast African plain, blood on my hands and an antelope at my feet. I tasted vile, hot blood fresh in my mouth and felt the hot sun against my back.

His hands were against my back, caressing me as he kissed my neck.

I looked up and saw, not the ceiling, but the pedestal of a humongous statue draped by a starry sky. It had the head of a cat and the body of a woman.

His kisses turned into light nibbles on my neck as hieroglyphics detached themselves from walls and danced all about me. The roar reached a deafening volume and I felt myself falling backward into the sea, into the sand, into the grass, onto the couch, enveloped by the frigid waters of the ocean while being scorched in the burning sands.

Pain pierced my neck. As the blood left my body, the sounds gradually faded into silence and the dancing hieroglyphics disappeared into the stucco ceiling of Dante's living room. Eventually, even that faded to blackness.

The fog began to lift. My eyes could barely open, but I knew I was enveloped by some of the softest cotton sheets I'd ever felt in my life. My neck was sore.

I couldn't move my body. It was almost as though I had been drugged. My eyes fluttered open.

Dante sat on the edge of his bed, his back to me, while I lay in a catatonic state. He was arguing with Victor.

"Everything is going to be okay, why are you freaking out?" Dante asked.

"You brought this outsider to our house and showed him who we are? And fucking fed on him? You are so selfish!"

"No more selfish than you are. No matter how many times we come back, you always want to be some sort of music superstar. This time, you're on your own son. Don't you think people will be suspicious?"

"People can be suspicious all they want. Difference is I would never bring one of them into our house and tell them everything."

"I haven't told him everything…yet."

I fell back out of consciousness.

I felt Dante's strong hand shake my shoulder.

"Wake up. You gotta get something to eat."

I opened my eyes and saw him seated at my right side. My vision was somewhat blurry, but I didn't feel as drugged as I had before.

"Can you sit up?" he asked. I nodded and slowly slid into an upright position. I still had a sharp pain in my neck. I felt it and discovered that it had been bandaged.

"What did you do to me?"

"Eat some soup." He picked up a plain white bowl filled with a vegetable soup. He stirred it with a spoon and scooped some out.

"Open," he commanded.

"I can feed myself," I said, reaching for the spoon. Looking almost disappointed, he handed the spoon to me. He continued to hold the bowl. The first spoonful was strong and aromatic.

"What kind of soup is this?" I asked.

"Vegetable. Cabbage, mostly. Some other herbs in there."

"It tastes really fresh."

"You don't like it?"

"I do. It's good."

He held my bowl and allowed me to eat in silence. It really was a good bowl of soup. It seemed like my strength was returning with every helping. Before too long, the bowl was empty.

"How do you feel?" he asked.

"Okay. But I'll be even better when you tell me what the fuck you did."

He put the bowl back on his nightstand.

"Did you drug me?"

"I would never drug you, man. And how could I drug you? What was I gonna do, put PCP in a closed bag of potato chips?"

"Don't act like nothing happened."

"I know what happened."

"Will you stop beating around the bush and tell me what's going on?"

He sighed.

"I showed you who I am. I'm not from here."

"Where are you from?"

"Africa."

"Africa's a really big place."

"I am from a very small village in a remote area of what is now Nigeria."

"Okay. So why did I see a slave ship? In fact, why am I seeing things at all? Was I hallucinating?"

"You were not hallucinating. I…gave you that vision. You saw a slave ship because that's how I got here."

I blinked.

"Get the fuck out of here," I laughed. He smiled.

"I'm not joking, Justin."

"You're trying to tell me that you came to America on a slave ship? As in the transatlantic slave trade? Nigga, please. So how old are you supposed to be?"

"Centuries."

I laughed some more.

"This nigga… Okay, so I'm having some kind of psychotic episode right now, clearly."

"No, you're not. Really."

"So how can you explain the savannah? With the dead calf or whatever?"

"That was outside my village. We had to make our first kill out in the plains as our rite of passage to manhood."

"And the big ass statue?"

"Egypt. I've never been there, though."

"See, gotcha nigga! How are you going to be 'giving' me some memories of a place you've never been?"

"I didn't show you where I've been. I showed you who I am."

"Dante, for the last time. Who the fuck are you?"

He smiled again.

"My real name is Aragbaye. My people are the Razadi."

"A…aruh…who now?"

"Say it like this…ah-*rah*-gbye-yay."

"Ara-gbaye. Okay. And your people are Razadi?"

"Yes."

"And your people came over here on slave ships centuries ago and you killed and ate animals raw. But somehow, you're really from Egypt."

"In a nutshell."

"Yeah. I'm leaving." I had a lot more energy now and it was time to go. I don't know how long I had been sleeping but it was already dark outside. I found my shoes and put them on.

"Dude, it's the middle of the night. You've been asleep for like twelve hours."

"Twelve hours?! Dante…Aragbaye…whoever you are, what exactly did you do to me?"

I touched my bandage again and suddenly remembered that in between the hallucinations, Dante had kissed me. Then he bit me.

Then he sucked my blood!

"Dude! You're totally a fucking vampire!" I exclaimed.

"I am not a vampire!"

"Oh, but you are! You bit my neck, didn't you?"

"Jive like."

"And did you taste my blood?"

"Yeah."

"Dante, did you drink my blood?"

"Yeah."

"I don't know what they call that back in ancient Africa, but in the United States, in this century? That's a goddamn vampire."

He walked toward me and I threw my index fingers in front of me in the sign of the cross. He smirked.

"What's that supposed to do, homie?"

"Hey! Stay back. The power of Christ compels you!"

"Justin, I am not a vampire!"

"I said the power of Christ compels you!"

I ran past him and down the stairs, almost tripping on the last few. I grabbed my bag and bounded out the front door.

"Justin!" Dante called to me from the sloped roof.

"You stay away!" I called back.

"Justin, it's like one o'clock in the morning. Can you please come back inside?"

"Inside with a vampire?"

"Will you hush?" he hissed.

"Inside with a vampire?" I whispered back.

He rolled his eyes and leapt off the top of the building. Within a second, he was on the ground in front of me.

"How'd you…"

"You're coming with me." He grabbed me from the side with one arm and leaped straight up and forward to the roof of the house. We landed gently on the roof.

"Go in that window into the attic," he directed.

"You're going to stop talking to me any kind of way, Dante."

"I'm sorry Justin. Can you please use that window right there to go into the house? I want to show you something else that will help you understand."

"That's better. Watch your fucking tone in the future."

I climbed into the window and rolled out into the attic. It was dark and dusty, but roomy. Boxes and trunks were all over the place. A single, incandescent light bulb that hung overhead struggled to illuminate the whole room by itself.

I was scared. If he bit me once, he'd certainly do it again. I really didn't know who this guy was anymore or what I had gotten myself in to.

"You weren't ready to see what was up here." He found a big, black trunk, blew the dust off the top, and popped it open. He reached inside and pulled out an old leather bag.

I walked up beside him and looked at the bag. He gave it to me.

"Open it."

I looked at him with a raised eyebrow.

"Please?" he added. I opened up the satchel and reached my hand inside. In my hand were a stack of papers and cards: a 1984 DC driver's license belonging to Spencer Payne; a 1971 French passport of Michel Guillaume; a 1955 funeral program for Bo Williams; photographs of men in zoot suits.

These men all had Dante's face. I looked at him.

"That's really you, huh?"

"Yup. Reach further in the bag though."

I carefully put the stack to the side and reached in the satchel again. I felt something cold and hard, like a gun. I paused, looked at Dante, and then carefully pulled out the heavy metal item.

Shackles.

My eyes widened. Everything he had said was true.

"These shackles…" I stopped mid-sentence, unable to muster the words.

"They were mine. I kept them."

"So that you would never forget." He nodded. I couldn't say anything more for a long while. I put his shackles back in his bag with his photos and placed it all back in the trunk. I closed the trunk and then sat on it. He sat next to me.

"You're not anything that I thought you were," I said. "Your accent isn't even real. The slang you use…just an affectation."

"It's real. You might call it 'code switching' though."

"A couple of hundred years. That's a lot of code."

He chuckled.

"Why did you bite me?"

"I'm sorry."

"Were you hungry?"

"No. Well, kinda. It's complicated."

"Make me understand."

"Well…it was time that you knew who I was. And the way we do that is through intimacy. Touch. Giving you access to my essence, my thoughts and feelings. And in that moment, anything can happen. I didn't mean to bite you or take your blood. But it was one of those things where I felt closer to you than I'd ever been. And it just felt right. I'm sorry."

I was silent.

"Are you okay?" he asked.

"The day we first had sex…you really wanted me to fuck you raw. Intimacy?"

"Same principle," he explained.

I paused again.

"When you bit me, could I have died?"

"I wouldn't have killed you. But I need to be careful. And I won't bite you without your consent again."

"Thank you," I said.

"Oh, and one more thing. That soup I gave you? That's a family recipe. It helps you recover faster."

"It was good. And I do feel fine."

"Good."

We sat in silence for a few more moments. I put my arm around him.

"Hey," I said.

"What up?"

I laughed.

"Code switching again, I see. Anyway…yeah, um… I forgive you for lying to me about being a fake-me-out vampire and almost killing me. And…I still sorta like you in spite of all that."

He smiled.

"I'm glad. But trust and believe, I'm not a vampire. I hope you never have to meet one."

"Wait, so…" I stopped when I felt the house begin to rumble slightly with the sound of angry footsteps coming up the stairs. The attic door flew open and in a blur, I was knocked off the trunk. A force held me by the neck up against the wall, two feet from the floor. I couldn't breathe.

"Victor, stop!"

"You just couldn't keep your damn mouth shut, could you bruddah?" Victor hissed at Dante. His long dreadlocks were pulled back into a tight knot at the back of his head and his pale skin was red with fury.

"Let me tell you something, Son of Adam," Victor spat at me. "If you ever betray the secrets of my nation to another living soul, I will rip your beating heart from your chest and eat it before you die."

"Let him go, Eşusanya!" Dante shouted.

Victor dropped me to the floor and I gasped for breath, watching Dante and Victor hiss at each other. Their fangs emerged and elongated just below their flared lips.

This was really happening. I wasn't dreaming.

"Don't think I won't sacrifice one to save forty-seven, bruddah," Victor said.

"And don't think I won't sacrifice you to save him," Dante shot back.

"Please stop," I gasped. "It's not that deep."

Victor stepped over me and stormed back down the stairs.

"Are you okay?" Dante asked, as he helped me get back to my feet. I nodded, gulped, and said I'd be fine.

He pulled me into an embrace and held me there.

"So long as I live, nothing will happen to you. Do you hear me?"

I nodded. But I didn't believe him. I knew that no matter what he said, my life had changed irrevocably on that day. There was no going back now. Just then, another frightening thought popped into my head.

"Dante..."

"Yeah?"

"I ain't got no job."

He smiled, laughed and pulled me in tighter.

He thought I was cute. I knew he liked me. A lot. But what he didn't seem to understand was, no, I really didn't have a job, and whoever he really was, whether he was 500 years old or 25, if he couldn't get me a job, all the bloodsucking in the world wouldn't pay my rent.

For the rest of that night, though, it didn't matter. I fell asleep in his bed again, this time wrapped in his arms. Worries about the rent could wait until the morning.

ANOTHER DOOR OPENS

I might not have had a job, but I had savings and an appetite. Dante casually suggested that we hit up the Takoma Park Farmer's Market, and I agreed. I picked him up and we were there in no time.

The market was open on Sundays on Laurel Avenue in downtown Takoma Park, Maryland, on one city block that was shut down for the vendors. They called this place the Berkeley of the East, with its hippies and head shops and retired protestors.

Dante and I walked around the market casually. I wasn't sure what I wanted. Dante, on the other hand, came prepared with his matching reusable grocery bags.

"Oh, you serious, huh?" I asked him.

"Damn right," he said.

I watched in amazement as he haggled with the farmers over the price of the produce, picking up pieces, showing imperfections, and demanding a discount. Every time he began to walk away, the farmer would make him a deal. By the end of the morning, he had filled both of his bags to the brim with fresh fruits and vegetables.

I had a bag of apples.

"That all you want?" he said.

"I mean…I guess. I usually just go to the Safeway."

"Man, you buggin'! Always buy organic!"

"That shit is expensive."

"Man, listen. If you can't grow it yourself, buy organic. I promise you. It's better for you and it tastes better. All these pesticides they be putting in the food and shit is killing us."

"Oh, okay," I said. I was not about to have a debate with a vampire over where I purchased my food with my hard earned, if paltry, nonprofit check. Not that I'd have any more of them coming.

We grabbed some falafel sandwiches from a food truck that was parked nearby and went down the street a bit to a park.

"So, whatchu gonna do about a job?" he asked.

"I don't know," I admitted. "I guess I will start looking soon. My savings are good, though."

"Really?"

"Yeah. I got paid pretty decent for nonprofit work, so I can get by for a little while. But I'll be looking soon."

"You should be looking for leadership jobs."

"Like what?"

"I think you'd be a good Executive Director of something."

I laughed immediately.

"What could I be in charge of?"

"Anything you want!"

"Man, please…my credentials aren't that strong."

"But you have the potential. You have the vision. Believe that."

"Yeah, I guess. I do want to do something more. Something different. I don't know what, though."

I finished up my sandwich and wiped my fingers. I looked up to see Dante staring.

"What?" I asked.

"Nothing," he said. "I just like looking at you."

"I like looking at you, too," I said. "Let's go home."

"Wait. Before we go, I have a confession to make."

"I don't know if I can handle another surprise from you, man."

"Naw, this is kind of important though. I…the way my people… man, listen. It's like this. There were a couple of times that I was following you."

"Following me where?"

"One night, you were coming home from downtown. And another time down on U Street."

"Why the hell were you following me, man? That's creepy as fuck."

"It's complicated. The way my people do things. We keep each other safe. It's not about stalking. It's…man, I don't even know why I decided to tell you. It's hard to understand if you're not part of our culture."

"Let me stop you right there. So, every time that happened, you know I felt panicked, right? It's like my Spidey-sense was tingling. I knew something was off, but I didn't know what."

"Yo, man, I'm really sorry about that. I never meant to make you feel uncomfortable or anything. It's just that the minute you came into my life, I had to keep you safe. It's just how we do things. And I didn't know you that well to just show up and be your bodyguard."

"So how about this…from now on, no more stalking. You wanna make sure I'm safe? Just walk beside me. You dig?"

"I dig, man." He reached out to hold my hand. I reached back, and he brought my hand to his mouth, tenderly kissing it.

I smiled like a kid again.

At home, I knew I needed to finally tell my mom about the job so I called her up during our regular time.

"Hey ma."

"Hey sweetie! How's it going?"

"I've got something to tell you."

"Uh-oh, what's wrong?"

"I lost my job last week."

My mother gasped audibly.

"What happened?"

"Well the good news is I didn't get fired."

"So you quit?"

"Heck no."

"Laid off, then."

"In a manner of speaking. The organization closed."

"Say what?"

I laughed. "It's a long story, but basically Ernie and his goons got caught with their hands in the cookie jar."

"Stealing? From a nonprofit organization?"

"Yup. I mean, we all knew it, but nobody could prove it. Well, except the feds. Been investigating for a year until they finally got him. LaJwanne, too."

"Mmm-mm-mm," my mother said. "That's a shame. You always suspected it was something going on with them. So have you been dropping your resume anywhere?"

"I will tomorrow morning. That will be my full-time job. Wanted to take a break. Just a few days."

"Well they're always hiring IT people someplace."

"Yeah. It would be nice to work for a good nonprofit organization, though."

"I know that's what you'd prefer. But don't forget you can do just as much—if not more—if you make a great salary and join a board of directors. You don't always have to be 'in the mix' to be of service."

"You're right, ma."

"Do you need anything, though? You good on groceries?"

"Oh yeah, I'm fine. How's dad?"

"He's great. Everybody up here is fine. Ms. Thompson asked about you."

"Did she?"

"Yeah. She wants to know when you're coming up to visit. We all want to know."

"Thanksgiving, of course!"

"It would be nice to see you more than once a year."

"I know, Ma, I know. I gotta go though. I just wanted to update you on what was going on."

"Alrighty…take care. And let me know if you need anything!"

"Will do, Ma. Bye."

I clicked off my cell phone and put it on my dining room table. Dante was watching the DC United play soccer on my television in the living room. He watched intently as the ball traveled back and forth between the brown and tan legs of the players.

I sat next to him and watched. His eyebrows crinkled into knots.

"Why you so far away, papi?" he asked me, breaking from his soccer spell.

"Papi? What, you Dominican now?"

"*He vivido en decenas de lugares y puedo hablar cientos de idiomas. Este es sólo uno, mi príncipe*," he whispered in my ear.

"Uh…I don't know what you just said, but you got me!" I straddled him and he grabbed my sides. We kissed through our laughs.

He stood up and I held on. Lifting me was effortless to him and I was amazed.

"Why you look so surprised?" he asked.

"You just lifted me like it's nothing."

He slowly put me back on my feet.

"Sometimes I forget."

"Forget what? That you're always the strongest person in the room?"

"I'm not always the strongest."

"You're stronger than me."

"Maybe. But you're stronger in other ways. Promise."

I smiled.

"Think I can take you?"

Before he could answer, I planted another kiss on his lips. He opened his mouth while his arms went limp and his manhood became erect. I cradled his neck in one hand and pushed him back down to the couch with the other.

His eyes remained closed as I began to unbuckle his belt. Just then, heavy knocks rattled my door.

"Shit," I said, annoyed that my session with my man had been interrupted.

Dante sprang up from the couch and immediately went to look through the peephole.

"It's cool," he said.

"Why wouldn't it be?" I didn't wait for an answer. I went to the door and looked through the peephole. A tall, slim man with light brown skin stared back at me. He was wearing a sharp, black suit and a crisp white shirt.

"Who is it?!" I asked in my overly aggressive inner-city voice.

"Salaad."

"And who is Salaad?"

"I'm just delivering a message, sir." He held a sealed envelope in the air in front of the door.

I opened my door, which still had the chain over it. Salaad passed the envelope through and I took it.

"Thank you," I said, closing the door. I looked through the peephole and saw that he was already gone.

I looked at Dante.

"What?" he asked.

"How you just gonna look once and say 'it's cool' like you know that dude. You know him?"

"Naw. What's in the letter?"

I didn't appreciate him deflecting the subject, but my curiosity was getting the better of me. I looked down to see my name written by hand in an ornate script. There was no return address, but there was a simple logo that looked like stylized letters F, C, and J.

I tore the envelope open and unfolded the letter:

Dear Mr. Kena:

The Foundation for Community Justice requests your presence at a reorganizational meeting of Magdalene House tomorrow
at nine o'clock in the morning.

John Smith,
Chairman of the Board of Directors
The Foundation for Community Justice

I was dumbfounded.

"What's it say?" Dante asked. I passed him the letter. He read it and smiled.

"You know something."

"No, I don't. I'm just happy for you."

"I wish you wouldn't lie to me."

"I'm not lying. I'm just not saying." He kissed me on the forehead and rose.

"Where are you going?" I asked.

"I got some shit to do. See you tomorrow."

He left me feeling more confused than ever.

When I arrived at Magdalene House the next morning, the doors were wide open and a brunch buffet was waiting. The conference room was filled with the smells of bacon, eggs, bagels, freshly squeezed orange juice, and coffee.

"Hello?" I called out.

"Hey," Dante called back, emerging from the kitchen with two pitchers of orange juice.

"What the hell are you doing here?" I asked.

"Helping," he smugly said. "Do you want some breakfast?"

"What's going on? Who are you here with?"

"Relax. You'll see."

I gave him the side-eye and helped myself to a plate full of food. He had some serious explaining to do.

Victor entered the conference room. He wheeled out a flat screen television and began fiddling with the remote control.

Not this guy, too, I thought to myself.

Shortly, Steve and Cissy entered the conference room.

"Hey sweetie!" Cissy exclaimed as she embraced me. "You got a letter too?"

"Yup, got it yesterday."

"Hand delivered?" Steve asked. I nodded.

"Who are these guys? What do you suppose this is all about?" Cissy whispered.

"The shorter one is my…guy friend," I admitted in hush tones. "But I have no idea what this is about."

"Dude…your man sells…"

"I know what he sells," I interjected.

"Drugs?" Cissy asked.

"No! He sells movies."

"Bootlegs," Steve added.

"Will you shut up?" I said, embarrassed.

"I'm just saying. How does somebody go from bootleg man to… you know…whatever it is he's doing?"

"I'm telling you, I do not know."

"You think somebody bought the organization?" Steve asked.

"You can't buy a nonprofit," Cissy said. "But I'm sure Ernie tried to sell it a few times!"

We laughed heartily. Victor looked annoyed.

"Gentlemen. Ma'am." He got our attention.

"My name is Victor Pearl," he continued. "I'm a member of the Foundation for Community Justice. My uncle has a message for all of you."

Victor turned on the DVD player. A man in his thirties, or possibly forties, with a full head of long dreadlocks came on the screen. He had brown skin and a strong, wide nose.

"Greetings, ladies and gentlemen. My name is John Smith and I am the chairman of the board of directors for the Foundation for Community Justice. I'm sorry that I couldn't be with you in person today. The foundation's many interests nationwide keep me very busy here at our headquarters in Colorado and around the world. However, it became imperative to send you this message.

"The Foundation has been following with great interest the situation with Magdalene House. We were saddened to learn of the sudden closure of the facility. We had been planning all along to approach the board of directors about potentially joining up with our network of local and regional nonprofit organizations, but, unfortunately, the issues of Magdalene House proved insurmountable.

"Until now, that is. Perhaps what Magdalene House needed was to die, so that it might be reborn again. What do you think about that?" Mr. Smith paused. Cissy, Steve, and I glanced at each other. Dante handed out sealed envelopes to each of us.

On screen, Mr. Smith continued. "Mrs. Flint, Mr. Waller, Mr. Kena, I would like to make you an offer. The Foundation for Community Justice has come to an agreement with the District of Columbia government. The foundation will assume the financial liabilities of Magdalene House and will continue to provide service to women and families infected and affected by HIV and AIDS. Of the previous staff members, we have decided to retain the three of you.

"Steven, we would like you to come aboard as our Director of Programs. Your achievements in social work have gone unacknowledged for long enough. You have what it takes to develop and enhance Magdalene's programming.

"Cissy, we would like you to return to Magdalene as the Director of Advancement. We want you continue to cultivate relationships for the organization while investigating opportunities for expansion.

"And Justin, this promotion might come as a bigger surprise to you than anyone else. We thought long and hard about whom should lead Magdalene into its next phase. We wanted someone who was well respected among the staff, who was invested enough to see it succeed while maintaining the distance necessary to allow the senior staff to do their jobs. We didn't want someone with the most education or the greatest number of connections–the foundation doesn't need that. What we need—what Magdalene needs—is someone with the vision, the ideas, and the courage to take the organization further than it had ever been before. Justin, we decided that person was you."

Cissy squealed and Steve immediately patted me on the back and smiled. I was in shock.

"What?"

"If you will all kindly open the envelopes before you, you will find inside offer letters. We believe you will find the compensation to be generous as well as commensurate with your unique experiences.

"The foundation has a large board of directors. The gentlemen before you, Victor Pearl and Dante Oliver, are members of the board of directors as well. They will provide you with the tools you need to get your jobs done."

I remained speechless even as I opened my offer letter.

"This is amazing," Cissy said, under her breath.

"Holy shit!" Steve shouted. Dante smiled.

I opened my letter and skimmed to the bottom.

Six figures.

My hand began to tremble.

"Please let Dante and Victor know what your decisions are. And please know that above all else, the foundation believes in you to lead Magdalene House into the future, boldly, in service to those who need it the most. Good day."

The screen went black. Dante turned off the TV and wheeled the television out.

"Any questions?" Victor asked.

"Several," Cissy said.

"Ask away."

"Obviously the foundation is national and pretty…blessed, if you will. Where does the money come from?"

"We're a very old family foundation. We're actually all descendants from the so-called 'free people of color' in New Orleans. We're no Rockefellers, but we've done well over the years."

"And what do you all…do…now?" Steve asked.

"I'm a musician. My cousin Dante…well, he does a lot of things. But all in all, our Uncle John is the head of the family. He's something of an investment banker."

"I see," said Steve, eyeballing Dante.

"I can assure you that our family has years of experience on various nonprofit boards, even aside from our own foundation. And we're not here to interfere. We're here to get you what you need. We've been on the ground for weeks now, maybe even months, trying to figure out what's best for Magdalene, and our uncle truly believes, based on the evidence, that you all are his dream team, and that Justin is ready for this challenge."

"Are you ready?" Steve asked.

"I know he's ready!" Cissy said.

"You guys…I don't know…this is so much…" I said.

"Think of it this way," Cissy said. "You can't do any worse than Ernie."

"Nothing gets much worse than Ernie," Steve added.

I looked at the offer letter. Then at Cissy and Steve. Then at Dante, who smiled.

"Okay. If Steve and Cissy are in, then I'm in, too."

"Hot damn!" Steve said. Dante smiled and nodded in approval.

"But we've got a lot of work to do. Our brand is wrecked. We've got to change everything. Meetings after meetings. Press releases. Maybe even give this place a paint job. Have an open house. We need to let DC know that Magdalene House is under new management."

Victor smirked.

"I'll be sure to let Uncle John know all of your decisions. He hurriedly left the room. Dante followed him, but not before placing his hand on my shoulder and giving it a light squeeze.

"Nigga…" Steve whispered to me.

"What?"

"You were behind this whole thing, weren't you? From Ernie getting arrested to this takeover!"

"Like hell I was! I didn't ask for any of this man, I swear!"

"Tell me this, though. Dante…he a corner boy! How the hell does he come from a wealthy family?"

"I don't know, Steve."

"You don't know?! Y'all are dating!"

I shrugged. Annoyed, Steve turned back to his offer letter and searched for a pen to sign it with.

"Do we need to research conflict of interest policies?" Cissy whispered. "You know…I'd hate for you to lose this job if you stop dating Dante."

"I'll be fine, Cissy. Trust me."

Life was changing for me at a break-neck speed and I was fine with every moment of it.

Sunday Dinner

Dante and I were relaxing in front of the television at his place. I watched the news as I usually did, watching Annette Mitchell fill in for the regular anchor. I jotted down notes in my pad related to work while Dante peacefully read a book.

Questioning him about the events at Magdalene were fruitless. All I got from him was that his Uncle John Smith was influential and they did what he asked.

For me, it was a job—a good job—and I wasn't going to challenge that too much.

I never knew that being an executive director was what I wanted most out of life, but I loved all of the work I had to do. Assembling my new team was like casting a reality show. I wanted a Technology Director who would take over my old job, but also be responsible for rolling out a brand new training program for our clients so they could be certified in various Microsoft and Adobe products. Even if all they did was know how to design party fliers, I wanted them to be more useful to society.

I also needed an Executive Assistant. I didn't need someone who answered the phones. I wanted an ambitious, driven assistant whose sole goal was helping the organization shine. I was looking forward to diving into the stacks of resumes I received for both positions. Cissy and Steve, too, were looking forward to creating their own departments.

We were taking our time, though. Cissy was in the throes of creating a grand reopening for the organization. In a manner of weeks, Washington would know that Magdalene was back.

In the midst of my jotting notes, Victor bounded up the stairs from the basement.

"It's time for Sunday dinner," Victor announced to Dante. "And he's coming."

"Me?" I asked. "I already ate."

"It's not your meal, dumb-dumb. It's for us. I don't like to eat and drive."

Victor tossed me a set of keys.

"Where are we going?" I asked. "And I feel like you didn't say 'please.'"

"Oh, I'm sorry. George Washington University. *Now.*"

"No!" I shot back. "I'm getting tired of your funky ass attitude. I am done for the evening and I don't feel like driving across town all the way to GW to take your ass to dinner. Now maybe, if you fix your lips to say please, I might feel like it."

Victor bared his fangs.

"Please," Victor hissed.

"Okay. Maybe now I feel like it."

A little over 20 minutes later, we sat in a white van in the tony Foggy Bottom neighborhood of DC, right off of Virginia Avenue, just steps from the State Department.

"I…circle thing…B. Is this it?" I asked.

"Iota Theta Beta," Dante corrected. "Sorority."

"Why are we here?" I asked.

"Dinner," Victor answered while hopping out of the van. "Stay silent and watch."

Victor and Dante produced brown work jackets, brown caps, and clipboards. From the back, Dante got flat cardboard and swiftly popped them into empty boxes.

"Follow me," Victor said. The guys walked to the front door of the Victorian row house and rang the doorbell. Shortly, the door opened and revealed a pretty brunette girl.

"Can I help you?" she asked.

"Yeah, I got packages here for Iota Theta Beta?" Victor said.

"I'll sign for them," she said.

"Hold on, let me get a pen," Dante said. He put down the empty box and pulled a small flute-like instrument from his pocket. He put it to his lips and played four notes.

The girl froze.

"What's your name?" Victor asked.

"Lindsay."

"Lindsay, how many girls are in the house today?" Victor asked.

"Eight."

"Call them to the parlor. Tell them it's a house meeting with special guests."

"Sisters!" the girl shouted. "House meeting! Quickly, we have some guests!"

Within three minutes, the parlor was filled with puzzled girls. White, Asian, Latina. All pretty. All slender or athletic. Lindsay sat quietly with the same glazed-over look on her face.

"So, what's going on?" a blond asked Lindsay, while glancing at the three of us.

Again, Dante played his four notes. The entire room became still and silent.

"We greet thee in the spirit of Dominique Bellanger," Victor said.

"We welcome thee in the spirit of Dominique Bellanger," the girls responded in unison.

"We have traveled across burning sands and dangerous savannahs to be here today," Victor continued.

"And we have waited patiently for you."

"We have survived the middle passage and decades of danger."

"Yet we never doubted that you would return to us."

"We are your protectors, forever and ever."

"And we offer ourselves to you, the living legacy of Dominique Bellanger. We present ourselves to you: one body, one flesh. Iota Theta Beta. In the blood."

"What…the hell…" I whispered.

"Shut up," Victor hissed.

Each woman had her eyes closed, her chin up, and her neck exposed. Dante moved toward the women on one side of the room and Victor to the other. They sniffed the air around each one.

"I want those three. Maybe the one by the window," Victor said.

"Fine. I'll take these three. Not this one though," he said, pointing to a blond wearing a green t-shirt.

"HIV?" Victor asked. Dante nodded.

"I could tell as soon as I came in the house that one of them had it," Dante said.

"You can smell HIV?" I asked. Dante and Victor looked at me, puzzled for a second.

"That's right…you guys can't smell it," Victor said. "Such a pity."

"Justin, I need you to stand watch by the door, make sure nobody else comes in the house for the next twenty minutes," Dante requested. I nodded.

Victor had already buried his face in Lindsay's neck. Judging by the bob of his Adam's apple, he was drinking slowly, but deeply.

I stepped back into the hallway where I could keep watch at the door while watching Victor and Dante drink the girls' blood. I watched Dante bare his fangs and plunge them into an Asian girl's neck. She winced and exhaled slowly as he drank. He didn't caress her. Didn't hold her. Just held her head at an angle and drank. She was just a vessel to him. He didn't look at her like he looked at me. He did, however, behave with a certain grace throughout the whole process, as though he was sorry he had to do it. He always fixed the girl's hair and straightened out her shirt when he was done. Victor, on the other hand, just drank and moved on.

It took about five minutes to properly drink a girl without draining her too much. I noticed that Victor and Dante showed a lot of restraint. I knew they wanted to just drain them and be done with it, but it seemed that this set up was consensual, somehow. I made a mental note of it.

When Victor was done with his first girl, he used his fang to prick a hole in his index finger. He used his blood to heal and seal the puncture wounds he had made in his victim. Slowly, right before my eyes, the teeth marks disappeared.

In about twenty minutes, they were done, and it was time to go.

"Fare thee well, my darling sisters," Victor said. He was staggering toward the middle of the floor, trying to address the women again.

"This is the tricky part," Dante whispered in my ear as he leaned on me for support.

"Are you guys…drunk?" I asked.

Dante smiled.

"Blood drunk," he said. "Like…euphoria."

He leaned closer to my face and inhaled deeply.

"What do you bathe in? I've always wanted to ask you that."

"Soap and water," I said, looking askance.

"Like…regular soap?"

"Zest. I told you that before. Remember?"

He smiled and let his eyelids droop shut. Victor tried to continue his monologue to the ladies.

"In the name of…Dominique Bellanger…" he started, and then stopped.

"Shit, what's the words?" he said to himself. He looked down at his hands and appeared to be counting with his fingers.

"Oh yeah, okay…fare thee well, my darling sisters. In the name of Dominique Bellanger, I bid you blissful rest. Keep the lights burning for your brothers in the blood."

"Fare thee well, darling brothers. Your sisters ever wait," they responded in unison. As one unit, the women passed out.

"Oh my God," I said. "Are they okay?"

"Yup," Dante said. "Now we have about five minutes to get the hell out of here before they wake up."

"Then let's go!" I said. Me, Victor, and Dante high-tailed it out of there and were on the road back to the house in no time.

As we drove, Victor lay in the back of the van, fast asleep and snoring. Dante sat up front next to me.

"What did you think?" he asked me. His eyes were still half shut, like he had smoked a blunt.

"That was interesting."

"Did it creep you out?"

"Drinking the blood? That part? Naw. I mean, it's what you do. It's who you are. Never seen it before, but if that's how you gotta eat, then it is what it is."

He nodded.

"You know I don't like none of them girls, right?"

"I know."

"I'm serious."

"I know."

"I only like you."

I kept driving.

"I said I only like you."

"I know Dante, jeez."

"I just want to make sure you know I was just eating."

"Dante, are you apologizing for having dinner? I said it's okay, I know you gotta eat, shit! Yes, it was weird seeing your lips on those bitches, but I swear, I am good. For real."

In a flash, he slid next to me and had his nose buried in my neck.

"Dante, you are gonna make me have an accident!"

"I just wanna be next to you."

"You're being weird."

Dante put his hand on my knee and slid it up my thigh.

"Dante…"

"I just wanna…"

"Dante." In another flash, his hand unzipped my pants and pulled my penis out.

"Dante! What are you…stop that!"

I tried to move his hand, but he was too strong.

"Just want to show you who's number one. Just don't crash."

I placed both hands back on the wheel and tried to concentrate on driving while Dante gave me one of the best blowjobs of my life. His hot mouth slid up and down on my shaft, making me hard in an instant. His superhuman strength and speed led me to climax just as we pulled into the driveway.

No—I didn't crash.

Brotherly Love

"So, where are we with the development team?"

I sipped my tea slowly during my senior staff meeting with Steve and Cissy. We'd been working diligently toward our grand re-opening of Magdalene House and I was eager to hear where we stood.

"The development team has been assembled and will be ready to start after Labor Day. We've got Jules St. Jean in the communications manager role. Morehouse grad. Formerly with a charter school network. Wanted to work in the HIV sector after volunteering in Haiti for two years."

"I like him so far," I said. "And development manager?"

"Erin Rogers. Spent six years at an HIV organization in Kokomo, Indiana. Expanded their capacity from six figures to seven."

"Damn. I like that."

"Hell yeah, me too!" Cissy smiled a lot these days. She finally got the staff she needed to perform her job. I liked to see her smile.

"And your intern program?" I asked.

"Everything's good with our Georgetown partnership. These kids are just itching to learn grant proposal writing."

"Good. Definitely wish I had been as motivated at their age. Steve, what's up with the programs?"

"Everything's good. I've got five newly minted social workers ready to go: two from Howard, two from Catholic, and one from George Mason."

"I trust at least one is male?" I joked.

"Hardy har har," Steve replied. "Trust, I got the five best people, male or female. Also, I hired Mrs. Greene as the live-in house manager and Mr. Saunders and Ms. Hancock for nights and weekends."

"Excellent! I remember them from back in the day, before the big layoffs. I'm glad to have them back. We are doing big things, here. Anyway, I've decided to hire Quinn Turner to be the director of technology."

"The young lady?"

"No, the young guy fresh out of American. His portfolio was fantastic. He has a grasp on both the creative things I want done as well as the engineering. He knows his way around a database. And he also has a desire to teach and design programs. I'm a little worried he might have too much on his plate, but we have enough in the budget to hire another person in that department."

"Our budget..." Cissy said.

"Yeah," I smiled. "We're crazy rich right now!"

"It's a blessing," Cissy replied. "I'm still worried, though. What if this all goes away?"

"It won't go away, Cissy. You've seen the tax forms for the Foundation. They're filthy rich. Their money makes money. And they've given us enough to have the nonprofit of our dreams."

"And we're responsible with it, you know?" Steve added. "We're not wasting their money. We're about to build Magdalene House into something bigger and better than it's ever been. This technology thing is about to put us back on the map!"

"Okay, okay," Cissy relented. "It's just too good to be true, almost."

"I hear you," I said. "But I believe in us. The Foundation picked the right people to move us forward. And...well...I'm just happy to be able to work with my friends."

Steve and Cissy smiled with me.

After work was done for the evening, I walked over to Dante and Victor's place, where I'd taken to parking my car, since I spent so much time there. When I got there, I saw that the door was ajar. I tapped on it then walked in.

Dante and Victor were once again engaged in a bitter argument.

"I asked you to load the van hours ago," Victor said, glancing at me angrily while he berated Dante.

"I'm sorry, shit. I told you, I've been busy."

"The fuck have you been busy with?" Victor asked. "Getting fucked by this piece of meat over here?"

"Watch your fucking mouth," Dante said, baring his fangs.

"You wanna go?" Victor said, baring his fangs also. "We can rock and roll."

"Guys, please," I begged. "Can you just stop arguing for once? I'll help load the van, jeez."

Victor retracted his fangs and glared at me.

"Thanks." He disappeared in a brown and black blur of skin and dreadlocks.

"Why does he treat you so badly?" I asked Dante, as we retreated to the basement. Dante opened the back door while I picked up a set of congas.

"He's an asshole. Always has been."

"But why?" I struggled with the heavy drum and Dante took it from me.

"If you ask me, I think he misses home."

"Africa?"

"Yeah…the Razadi valley, I guess. What's left of it."

"Did something happen to your home?"

"We got conquered in one of the Oyo wars."

"What are the Oyo? Like, other vampires?"

Dante paused, stared at me, and then laughed.

"The Oyo are another tribe in West Africa. They're human."

"I really should have taken some African studies classes in college," I mused.

Dante smiled.

"It's ancient history now," he continued. "I haven't looked back since we left. Every place we've been since then has been new, different… but still, home. I'm at home wherever my brothers are."

"But your brothers treat you like shit. Victor, at least."

"You ever heard of deference?"

"Yeah. Like when a younger dude in a frat has to be nice to the older dudes in a frat, even if they don't deserve it?"

"Exactly. Victor's older than me. It's just part of our system. I'm supposed to defer to him. He defers to others."

"Your system stinks."

"Maybe. But it's just how we do things." He bent over, pushing instruments further into the van. I poked him in his sides and he turned around.

"What's up?" he asked. I sat down in the back of the van and pulled him down next to me. I rested my head on his shoulder. He placed his warm hand against my cheek.

"Tell me more," I requested.

"Like what?" he asked.

"I want to know everything," I said. "But don't do that psychic thing. That was crazy. Just tell me."

"There's so much to tell, though. Just ask me what you want to know."

"How many Razadi are there?"

"47."

"Just 47?"

"Yes. 47. There have been more. But we are now at 47, spread out all across the western hemisphere. Four are attached to DC."

"Attached? Like, live here?"

"Yeah, supposedly. Right now, it's just me and Victor."

"Where are the other two?"

He was silent.

"Dante?"

"I don't really want to talk about them right now."

"Okay."

"But I can tell you more about how we're organized. The 47 have been divided into cells. We try to stay in major cities where there's a significant African American presence."

"So you can stay under the radar."

"Right. A house full of black men in Laramie, Wyoming is gonna stick out a whole lot more than in DC, New York, or New Orleans. Our most senior member lives by himself out west, though. He's…"

"The chairman of the foundation, of course," I interrupted. "So he makes sure all the cells are properly funded and that you can survive, but everything else is on your own."

"You're smart."

"It's a brilliant set up. He's probably the only person who knows exactly where each cell is at any given moment, too. Because if you all knew, like through a network, then it could take just one person to expose the whole system."

"Right. He's the Godfather, if you will. He makes sure we have what we need to protect ourselves. But please believe if any of us went rogue, he'd make sure we were dealt with. Luckily, loyalty has never been an issue for our kind."

"Does he know where your other two cell members are?"

"I said I didn't want to talk about them." He got up from the van and went back into the basement to gather more instruments.

"Babarinde has it all under control," he said, emerging with a covered keyboard, which he handed to me. "I trust him. I believe in him more than Victor ever has. And if Baba says Orlando and John are safe, then they're safe."

Orlando and John, eh? I made a mental note of their names as I put the keyboard in the van.

"Maybe we should try to find them?"

Dante laughed.

"A human searching for a daywalker would be like looking for a needle in a haystack. Baba has a different imperative for us right now, anyway."

"And what's that?"

Dante walked back over to me and planted a quick kiss on my lips.

"The interrogation is over," he said. "Maybe another time."

I nodded. There were only 47 Razadi. I'd heard plenty conspiracy theories in chat rooms and message boards, but never anything like this. But with a group so small and diffused, of course they'd fly under the radar for centuries.

At the Go-Go

As long as I had lived in DC, I'd never liked go-go music. It was loud for no damn reason, with hood rats shouting over dissonant melodies and flat beats.

But I was going to the go-go to support Victor's debut as the headlining artist of Ol' Skool Revival Band, better known as the ORB. DC bands always wanted to be acronyms. It was crazy how many there were. But the kids always knew which band was which.

As I stood in the crowd at the renovated Ibex Theater in Northwest, I listened to the young gals in front of me gossip about the bands.

"Girrrla, it is hot than a mug in here!"

"I know, right! I'm finna sweat this mufuckin' weave out like shit. When is ORB comin' out? Shit."

"Girl, supposably they up next."

"My muhvah used to listen to the original ORB like shit. This 'bout to be wack like shit."

"Girl no it's not, neither. The original muhfucka's son is the lead singer and I heard he fine like shit."

"He betta be for all this waiting! Shit!"

Victor's plan was coming into place. Streets were already talking about the comeback of this band that nobody had seen or heard from in at least twenty years.

Dante appeared with a drink for me.

"Fuzzy navel?" he said.

"Thanks," I said. "Seems like a lot of people are excited for this."

Dante rolled his eyes.

"He's such a drama queen," he said in my ear. "Every time we cycle back through to being public, he wants to be a rock star. The fucking center of attention as usual."

"Well, we've all got something, right? If he ain't hurting anyone, might as well let him have his moment. These people aren't thinking about daywalkers."

Dante shrugged. A portly, light skinned man with about a million freckles, wearing a white t-shirt and gray sweatpants, took the stage.

"Ladies and gentlemen," he began. "I am honored to introduce to you go-go royalty. In his debut here at the Ibex, and debut before the entire go-go community, this is the son of the founder of the original ORB. For the first time in its brand new form, I introduce to you Victor Pearl and the Ol' Skool Revival Band!"

Victor and the band took the stage in silence. Each player, about eight in total, could have been no older than twenty years old. There was a full brass section as well as the standard percussion section that any good go-go band must have. Victor stood in the center of the stage wearing loose-fitting jeans and a tight white sleeveless t-shirt, his caramel muscles flexing as he gripped the microphone with both hands. His eyes glowed with intensity as his mouth opened into a sneer.

"It's about to be…" Victor sang in a whiny tenor.

"A motherfuckin' blood…bath…" the band chimed in with perfect harmony.

Bloodbath! Motherfuckin' bloodbath!
Bloodbath! Nigga, it's a bloodbath!
Bloodbath!
Bloodbath!

"It's about to be…" Victor sang again. The percussion was explosive and the brass section whined better than any band I'd heard before.

The crowd took milliseconds to be one with the rhythm. The hood chicks I had overheard earlier were quick to throw their hands up and dance. I, too, moved with the crowd with Dante at my side.

For someone who was as naturally unfriendly as Victor was, the boy was good. I could see why he took so much care in assembling his band. He not only had absolutely perfected the craft of go-go music, but his stage persona was electric. He smiled. He growled. He pointed at girls in the audience and winked. The band even had choreographed moves.

I could tell from the screams of the audience that they'd never been to a go-go like this one before.

While I lost myself in the music, I saw that Dante was just as controlled as before. Yes, he bopped around in enjoyment, but his job was still to make sure everything and everyone was safe.

After about 20 minutes of Victor's set, I noticed that Dante's gaze was on another young dude. The guy was dressed plainly in blue jeans and a gray t-shirt. He was an alright-looking dude, with thick lips and a wide nose. The odd thing about him was that he was walking around like he didn't notice the music and the dancing, as though he were confused.

Dante didn't seem to consider the guy a threat as he walked past us and toward the restrooms. I shrugged it off and kept dancing.

Drenched in sweat, Victor pulled his dreadlocks back behind his head and tied them in a knot.

"We are the Ol' Skool Revival Band. I do this in honor of my late father, Ed Pearl, who did this thirty years ago. I love you dad."

I glanced at Dante who was lightly rolling his eyes as the crowd erupted in applause. I chuckled. Victor descended from the stage and was immediately surrounded by adoring fans. The old heads approached him, shook his hand, and talked to him as he tried to walk by. Victor and I made eye contact and he smiled.

Victor never did make it back to us before it was time for his second set. This set was much mellower. Rather than the aggressive original songs of the first set, ORB performed go-go covers of the classic R&B hits of the '70s and '80s.

I noticed the young man from earlier once again wandering around the go-go. He didn't look dangerous. Just…weird. His eyes seemed empty. I didn't want to be near him.

The rest of the evening was awesome. ORB had made me a believer and now I was itching to find more quality go-go bands, even as the party ended and we helped the band load up the van. Everyone's energy was high, and for the first time ever, I saw Victor really happy. He dismissed his band mates and we finished loading up the van on our own.

"I never liked go-go before tonight," I admitted to Victor. He glanced over at me as he pushed an amp through the open back door of the van.

"Go-go reminds me of home," he said gently. In that moment, I saw a tenderness about him that I didn't know existed. The harsh fluorescent lights of the parking lot lit his face up, showing beads of sweat on his brow. In that second, I got him.

Then I noticed that the young dude who I saw at the go-go was wandering around us.

"Something's up with that dude," I told Dante, as he loaded the last horn into Victor's van. He closed the door of and hurried to my side.

The guy was unsteady on his feet and he walked closer and closer to us.

"My dude, you aight?" Dante asked, positioning himself between me and the young man.

"You aight?" he mocked in an impossibly high-pitched voice. "You aight? Yoooooouuuu aight?"

"This nigga high," Dante said to me. "Let's go."

"I'm high! I'm high! I'm high from only the best herb grown in the Razadi gardens!"

In a blur, Victor left the van and Dante approached the dude. He was unfazed: his eyes were glazed over like he had smoked weed every day for the past week.

"What did you say?" Victor hissed.

"I said…the Razadi grow the best herb this side of Yorubaland!" He laughed heartily.

"What's your name?" Dante asked.

"Puddin' tame! Ask me again and I'll tell you the same!" he replied.

With that, Victor slapped the shit out of the guy.

"Look at me," he said, grabbing him by the collar. "Tell me your name right now!"

"Mooooorlaaaasssss!" the man growled. His chest heaved up and down. Victor slowly released him.

"What do you want?" Dante asked.

"I have…what I…came for," he growled. "The boy…is mine."

"Okay," Victor said. "So…we're okay here, right?"

"The Razadi are okay with me," he said resuming his high-pitched, mocking voice.

"Alright," Victor said.

"By the way," he purred. "You might want to know something."

"What's that?" Dante asked.

"The Anubis Society…has your brother," he growled.

Victor and Dante froze.

"Aborişade?" Victor asked.

"Anubis…has him. Draining him."

"Where?" Dante asked.

The young man began convulsing.

"Oh my God," I said. He began to collapse and Dante helped him lay down on the ground.

Almost as quickly as his seizure began, it ceased. The man, seeming more like a boy with every passing second, opened his eyes. He was… different now.

"What the fuck is going on?" he asked in a quite normal baritone voice.

"What is your name?" Victor asked calmly.

"My name is Farid," he said. "Where am I? Did I pass out?"

Victor and Dante looked at each other.

"Yeah man," Dante said. "You passed out. Had a little too much to drink tonight?"

"I'm Muslim. I don't drink." He sat up on the ground

"Take it easy, buddy," Dante said.

"I'll be fine," he said. I could tell from the look on his face that he wasn't afraid. He was more upset. Almost like he was saying "not again" on the inside.

"Can we give you a ride?" Victor asked.

"No. I got it. I live nearby."

"Be careful, then," Dante said. He helped Farid to his feet. He was wobbly, but he was walking on his own.

"What the fuck?" I whispered. Dante and Victor walked back toward me.

"Get in the van," Victor barked at me, then turned to Dante. "Go around the block once, then follow him home. I don't want him to make a move without us knowing."

Dante sped away in a blur.

"Who was that, Victor?"

"The less you know, the better."

"He said his name was Farid, but before, he said his name was… Mor…Morlas?"

"Justin, seriously."

"What?"

"Stop it. You know too much as it is."

Victor pulled off. The light I seemed to see in his face for that brief moment was gone. His eyes darted back and forth and his all-too-familiar sneer crept back over his face. The sight of Farid and whatever was in him gravely concerned him, but I knew better than to try to probe.

I was supposed to be going back to my apartment, but I suppose Victor was too upset to think straight. We sped past Kennedy Street entirely and I kept my mouth shut until we got back to Northeast.

As soon as we parked, Victor wasted no time unloading all of the equipment himself with the speed of a hurricane's winds. He was done by the time I stepped out of the van entirely.

It made me wonder why he always forced those around him to work twice as hard to do the same job he could do in seconds. I guess that was just his privilege as the elder Razadi.

I followed him into the house. He poured himself a glass of water and leaned against the wall.

"Dante will be back soon enough. You don't have to worry," he said.

"I'm not," I lied. "Are you okay?"

"Yes," he said. "Goodnight."

He sped off to his room and I heard the door slam within seconds. I walked up to Dante's room and started to undress. Within seconds, I was passed out on top of his bed.

An hour later, I woke up to Dante laying down next to me in the darkness. I'd already peeled my shirt off and had my button undone on my jeans.

"Where you been?"

"Go back to sleep," he said.

"No, I'm up now. Who was that kid?"

"His name is Farid, like he said. He's…ill."

"How did he know about the Razadi?"

"He doesn't."

I paused.

"He's possessed, isn't he?"

Dante sighed.

"Yes. He's possessed."

"Mmm, mmm, mmm."

"What?"

"I'm just learning so much. But it doesn't surprise me, for some reason."

"You were meant to be part of this life."

"You think so?"

"I know. Listen, don't tell Victor I told you any of this, okay? You've got to be very careful. The being that was in Farid is dangerous to humans. They don't hurt Razadi, but they're tricky. Sometimes they work with us. Give us information. Keep us safe."

"So, they're like another race or something? What are they? Like ghosts?"

"No, they're not dead. They're Djinn. You know how the Bible says man was made from the earth? Well they say Djinn are made from smoke and fire. And what's dangerous about them—to humans, at least—is that they can appear to be just like you. Entire colonies of Djinn live in certain places of the world, indistinguishable from humans. But those ones are mostly cool. They are just humans with something extra. Powers. But some Djinn…some are just pure evil. Monsters. Demons. And they can and will possess you if you let them. Morlas is one of them."

"That Djinn… Morlas. He saw me. How do I know he won't jump into me next?"

"He won't. I won't let him. Morlas has who he wants. And thank goodness he has loose lips. We would have never known where Orlando was otherwise."

"That's right! He said some society has him?"

"The Anubis Society. But don't get worked up about it. We'll get Orlando. You just rest up."

He kissed me on my temple and, soon after, fell asleep. I lay in silence in the dark while my mind raced, struggling to come to terms with everything I'd learned in the past few hours.

A Sinister Request

"I'm so sorry I'm late, Mr. Kena! I got held up at the office with a major project. I hope I haven't inconvenienced you."

"Not at all, Ms. Esteban," I said. I'd waited for her at the swanky restaurant on the West End for twenty minutes, but at least I had the chance to tinker around on my smart phone while I waited. I rose to shake her hand and instead she hugged me.

"Please, call me Selena," she said, with the faintest Spanish accent. Selena Esteban was the Executive Director of The Friends of the Crown/ Los Amigos de la Corona, an organization of Spanish nationals located in America who donated big bucks to advance the philanthropic mission of the Spanish royal family.

"And you can call me Justin," I said while pulling her chair out. She sat down and her summery, Carolina blue dress fanned out beneath her like a dancer. Her light brown hair cascaded to her shoulders. She was an older woman, but still pretty. I couldn't tell how old she was exactly, but her refinement suggested that she had a lot of experience dealing with people.

"I was so glad to receive your letter of introduction," she said, while sipping on her mineral water.

"It was my pleasure to re-introduce Magdalene House to you."

"Mm-hmm," she said. "Where did you go to school?"

"Syracuse. I'll be coming up on ten years very soon."

"The time flies, doesn't it?"

"It does."

"Must be tough being an Orangeman in a town full of Hoyas?"

I laughed.

"I tend to crawl in a hole and hide until basketball season is over. I can't stand the rivalry."

"Not a sports fan?"

"Not so much. I was always into computers and gaming."

"You honestly don't seem like a computer geek to me," she said matter-of-factly. I smiled.

"I'm part of the new generation," I said confidently. "We don't all look like Bill Gates and Mark Zuckerberg anymore."

"Thank goodness for that. I went to university back in Spain, when dinosaurs roamed the earth. Had I not been such a party girl, I would have married one of those quiet computer guys. They're all millionaires now."

"But how do they look?" I winked.

She laughed.

"I guess money can't buy handsomeness," she admitted.

Selena recommended everything that I ate that day: the house salad, the lobster bisque soup, and a jumbo lump crab cake to die for. We chitchatted the afternoon away, and I came to really like this charming, fun, and often irreverent woman who led one of the city's most prominent foundations. We never once even chatted about work, not directly at least.

"Justin?" she asked, as she slowly ate the thick and smooth Raspberry Charlotte from her fork.

"Yes?"

"I'm very interested in your development as a nonprofit leader. Washington has a wide array of local, national, and international service organizations. Frankly, very few of them inspire us. But you...your trajectory is interesting to me. You have no advanced education. You were a computer specialist. And for some reason, the Foundation for Community Justice handpicked *you* to lead."

I smiled and chose my words carefully.

"Magdalene House, prior to its reorganization, had a noble mission and decent programming. It also had pockets of talent embedded in a bureaucracy typical of a grassroots organization in this city. I feel very blessed that the Foundation selected not just a leader, but a team of people who legitimately care about Magdalene House to make it into what it was meant to be. And it breaks my heart that the old board and most of the old staff couldn't join us for the ride, but I believe even they would be happy with the direction we're heading."

"And you're quite confident you'll be able to take Magdalene House to new heights?"

"Selena, if I can be candid. My mission is to house every homeless woman in DC who is living with HIV. But it goes beyond housing. We're talking job skills. We're talking mental health. We are talking about taking the people the city have forgotten and giving them what they need to be leaders."

She nodded.

"The Friends of the Crown will help you in any way that we can."

I smiled.

"Thank you, Selena." I never knew that the majority of my job would literally be making friends. This was a piece of cake. Raspberry Charlotte, to be exact. Rather than talking business, we continued to chat about the most random topics. She insisted that she pay our bill and I insisted on paying the next time.

As we walked down the street after lunch, a car horn honked.

"Oh, I think that's your driver," Selena said. I laughed.

"I don't have a…" I began, looking into the luxury sedan parked near the restaurant. Victor was dressed in a suit and sunglasses, standing with the door open and waiting for me to get in.

"Oh yes," I said to Selena. "My driver."

"It's been so nice getting to know you, Justin! You're going to be a great executive director, I know it."

"Thank you so much, Selena. That means a lot to me. Will I see you next week at our grand re-opening?"

"Oh, you most certainly will! The entire staff will make a day of it!"

"Thank you so much. I'll see you there."

We embraced and said goodbye. Selena put on her sunglasses and walked down the street with the confidence of royalty.

"To what do I owe the pleasure, Mr. Pearl?" I grinned.

"Just get in," he said. I complied, and he closed the door behind me. Once we got on the road toward the office, he began speaking.

"Justin, I'd like to talk to you for a moment." The lilt in his voice made the statement sound like both a question and a demand.

"Yeah?" I replied. I tried to pretend as he didn't frighten me, but he did. Not only had he once had his hand around my throat, but he was now technically one of my bosses.

"I don't like you," Victor began.

"Well thanks a lot," I said.

"No, listen. I didn't mean it like that. Well, I did. But what I want to add is that it's not your fault, exactly."

"Oh, okay. It's not my fault that you dislike me. Gotcha. Anything else?"

"Listen. The Razadi are solitary people. We don't often welcome people into our circle who are not fellow Razadi. It's dangerous to our way of life. And let's face it, Justin. Even if Dante were to stay with you for the rest of your life, you would wither away and die in what amounts to the twinkling of an eye to our kind. We stay to ourselves for our emotional health just as much as our physical safety."

"So you don't want me to be with Dante?"

"I don't care if you stay with Dante. I've had dozens of lovers over the years, women and men, who I'd give anything to see again. I understand. What I am telling you has nothing to do with you and Dante and everything to do with your place here, with us."

I crossed my legs and leaned back.

"I'm listening."

"Dante's got it in his head that he's supposed to be your bodyguard. And Uncle John wants you to lead Magdalene House. Fine. I'm cool with that. They're sold on you. But as for me, I need to see a little more."

"Like what?"

"Loyalty."

I exhaled.

"Victor, I don't know what I can do to prove my loyalty to you. I'm just a regular dude, you know? A regular dude in a crazy situation with a guy I really, really like. When it comes to Dante, I promise I'll treat him right. When it comes to your uncle and Magdalene House, I promise I'll do my very best to serve these clients. But when it comes to you, I don't know what you want from me. I've seen and heard a lot of wild shit as it is. All I can do is promise you that everything I have seen and heard stays with me all the way to the grave. I have nothing to gain by running my mouth and everything to lose. So, I mean, I don't know. What else can I say to you to prove I'm on your side?"

"There's nothing you can say. But there's something you can do."

"And that is?"

"You can't tell Dante anything I am about to tell you, but I want you to go on a reconnaissance mission for me."

"Reconnaissance? Who do you want me to spy on? That kid Farid?"

"No. Farid is on his own. Once a Djinn lays claim to a human, only the human himself can get out of it."

"So who then?"

"Nightwalkers."

"Nightwalkers?"

"Yes. Real vampires."

I stroked my goatee.

"Like the Razadi, vampires often divide themselves into smaller clans, but they are more formalized, like clubs. More like secret societies, actually. There are all these social rules and caste systems and specialized roles. Razadi, we're just laid back and observe deference. But vampires… it's like a complicated aristocracy."

"I see."

"The Djinn told us that vampires had our brother, Orlando."

"Why would they have him?"

"I don't know. Daywalkers and nightwalkers have a truce that's held up for a century. They don't bother us so we don't bother them. Hypothetically, Razadi would always have the upper hand. If they fucked with us, all we'd have to do is wait until daylight and we win. They either die in the sun or we discover their hiding places and stake them all to death."

"So why don't you?"

"We never had a reason to. And they never had a reason to come after us. There are only a few dozen Razadi and we keep to ourselves. But…"

"What?"

"It's possible that the nightwalkers took Orlando to try to learn why we can walk in the sun and they can't. We already know that they have him. We've got to find him and get him back before they kill him."

"And you're sure the vampires have him here in DC?"

"Yes. Djinn have no good reason to lie to a daywalker. If Morlas says the Anubis Society has our brother, then they probably do."

"So you want me to infiltrate the Anubis Society, stake the vampires, rescue Orlando, and bring him back?" I asked excitedly.

"No, stupid," Victor said, rolling his eyes. "I just want you to go to their mansion and scope it out. Pretend to drop off a package and get lost in their house. Take note of everything you see. Report back to me."

"This sounds hella dangerous."

"It could be. But it will be the daytime. The vampires can't hurt you then. It will probably just be some idiot rent-a-cop at a front desk who barely has a GED. Surely you can outwit somebody like that."

"Victor, why should I be the fall guy? You and Dante…you're stronger. You can actually fight a vampire."

"You want to know why, Justin? It's simple. You're not Razadi and I need to know that I can trust you anyway. That's all there is."

"And if I do this, you'll give me a break?"

"I'll be honest, man. This is about as nice as I get."

"You're nothing if not honest. Fuck it, I'll do it."

Victor nodded.

"I'm glad."

"But let's take it a step further…we can do better than just scoping out the house…"

A Dangerous Mission

"Thank you all so much for coming out today. I must confess that I am not a man of many words. In fact, I always considered myself to be fairly awkward. When I came to Magdalene House, I just wanted to use my computer skills in ways that made a difference in the community. Over the years, something happened that even I didn't expect: I fell in love with Magdalene House. What began as merely a job turned out to be a passion for serving others. The women and families that are served by this wonderful organization are forever changed for the better. We give them a roof over their heads and food in their bellies. And we've done that since the beginning of the HIV crisis, when the founders of this organization came together to assist those who had nothing and no one left to advocate for them."

I looked out into the crowd assembled on the grounds of Magdalene and saw dozens of people hanging on my every word. I'd never made a speech like this in my life. The words just flowed. Even though I'd practiced them, I still ad-libbed where I could.

This was my element now. The lawn of our modest building on Rhode Island Avenue had been perfectly manicured; the building itself had been freshly painted and all the windows washed of the grime that had accumulated over the years. Tables had been set up with plenty of refreshments for everyone, supplied by a local minority-owned caterer. I stepped back to the microphone to continue.

"Now, HIV is becoming an afterthought in our community. Because of advances in the treatment of the disease, our attention is focused on other things. But I am here to tell you that AIDS is still here and AIDS still kills—particularly the poor, particularly minorities, and particularly the members of the LGBT community.

"The Foundation for Community Justice has assumed responsibility for Magdalene House as it moves forward into a new phase of service, with a focus which expands dramatically. No longer will we just house and feed the families who come through our doors. No! We will be transforming their lives and giving them the tools they need for self-sufficiency. I am pleased to announce to all of you our newest program: The Women in Technology Initiative. From this point forward, any woman seeking training in technological careers will receive it at no cost. We have the staff. We have the support. Now, we need your help as our community partners to make those referrals to us. We want to discover the next great engineer or architect or designer. Magdalene will do that now! When you empower a woman, you change the world—and her HIV status will not be a barrier to that!"

The crowd around me erupted in applause and cheers. I was stunned. All I wanted was for Magdalene House to be great and now we were. At least, we were getting there.

Selena Esteban walked up to the porch and stood next to me. She quietly but assertively pushed me to the side as she took the microphone.

"I'm not sure that Mr. Kena was quite finished, but I just wanted to take this opportunity to respond to his challenge. The Friends of the Crown/Los Amigos de la Corona are pleased to announce our commitment to this most worthy initiative and we come bearing a check in the amount of $25,000 with a commitment for ongoing support!"

I was in shock. The crowd once again roared as Selena's assistant produced an oversized novelty check.

Cameras snapped all around me. I struggled to smile, but my mouth was still wide open, even as I held the huge check.

"I'm speechless," I said to Selena.

"He means 'thank you!'" Cissy chimed in.

"Yes, yes! Thank you!" I hugged Selena tightly and got misty-eyed. I couldn't continue at the microphone and asked Cissy to close.

"Thank you all so much for coming out to see us today. Please enjoy the refreshments and each other! And…we're just happy to be back! Tell your friends!"

I got so many congratulations as the event ended. I was sure to tell everyone that I had the greatest job on earth because all I have to do is let my team shine. And it was true. I really did have the best team that the Foundation could buy.

And I was also learning very directly that the more money you have, the more money you raise. The Friends of the Crown had little in common with us and I really never even thought I was near being able to make an "ask." But here we were, getting five figure gifts from them.

I was just a new, young executive director turning around a troubled organization. But they believed in me. They all believed in me.

I was finally becoming somebody that people respected.

"Congratulations," Victor whispered in my ear. "Now don't forget your other job."

"I gotchu," I said through my clenched-teeth smile.

Less than an hour after the close of our open house, I drove the van solo toward my destination. I had on a full brown uniform, a vase full of calla lilies, and a pocket full of magic to fulfill Victor's mission.

I drove the van down a long cul-de-sac on the edge of Rock Creek Park in Northwest DC. At the very end of the street, right against the woods, was a mansion. I couldn't believe a house so large actually existed in the city.

I got out of the van, collected the flowers and my clipboard, and walked up to the mansion. I prayed as I pressed the button on the intercom system.

"Yes?" the voice on the other end of the line said.

"Delivery man," I said.

The intercom buzzed and the door unlocked. I turned the knob and entered.

The foyer was exactly as I imagined it: covered in dark, mahogany paneling with old paintings on the walls and marble sculptures in the corners. Just feet away was a small security desk with a pudgy, brown-skinned female security guard wearing a gray uniform.

"Hey, uh, I got a package for, uh, lemme see here…Nigel Artinian?"

"I can sign for it," the guard said.

"Mmm, I dunno. This says here 'for Nigel Artinian only.'"

"Sir, Mr. Artinian is not here during the day. All packages can be left with me."

"Well, I guess I can trust a pretty lady like you." She tried to squash a smile.

"So…you think I could get your number? Maybe call you up, go get some ice cream in Georgetown? Walk around the harbor?"

"I have a boyfriend."

"What's that got to do with me?"

"Everything, if he finds out you tryin' to holla at his woman."

"Aight, aight, my bad. Well, since I can't get your number, can I at least use your bathroom?"

"They really don't like people using…"

"Aww, come on, please? I haven't had a break in like four hours, you know I'm 'bout to bust. I mean, I could pull over and go out there in Rock Creek, but look at me. You think a civilized man like me ought to be relieving hisself on a tree? Nah, I ain't think so."

"Listen, the restroom is right there down the hall, past the dining room, before you get to the kitchen. Please don't take all day and please don't funk it up. I'm not trying to hear these peoples' mouths when I get off."

"I gotchu, boo. No worries."

I hurried down the hallway, glancing at each piece of art along the way. They were humongous European scenes of fox hunting and portraits of long-dead aristocrats. Things that people looked at but never touched.

The perfect places to plant the top-of-the-line remote listening devices that I'd convinced Victor to purchase.

I didn't have much time to act. In the restroom, I ran the water and locked the door. From my pocket I produced three tiny devices, smaller than dimes. They were sound-detecting bugs that would only activate once someone was speaking, and would transmit the data via satellite to a data cloud that only I would be able to access.

I flushed the toilet and pretended to wash my hands. I peeled the paper off the back of the bugs, exposing their adhesive, and prayed they wouldn't get stuck to my hand as I tried to complete the mission. I turned the light out in the bathroom and made my way down the hall again.

I had seconds. Out of courtesy, I knew the guard would not be staring at me as I walked out of the bathroom. I pretended to make a wrong turn and entered the dining room, where I planted the first bug on the ground, next to the first grate that I saw. I immediately turned back around to the hallway, took a few steps and looked at the huge painting in front of me. I touched the bottom of the gilded frame, and stuck a bug there, totally unnoticeable.

My final destination would be trickiest. I walked up to the guard's desk and then turned around to face the sitting room.

"This house is awesome," I said. "They actually be sitting in this living room?"

"Yeah," she said, as I tiptoed in, pretending to glance around while I dropped the final bug in a potted plant by the entryway.

"Damn," I continued. "Look like a museum."

"Mm-hmm," she said. "They nice people, when I see them. But they never here during the day."

"I see. Well, thanks. Thanks, pretty lady. Maybe I'll see you next time?"

"Maybe. Have a good day!"

"You too, love."

I exhaled and hurried out of there. When I got to the van, I called Victor on the burner he gave me for the occasion.

"Yeah?" he said.

"It's done."

"Good. Very good."

"Yeah. You're welcome."

I clicked off the phone and threw it into the woods when I got to the corner.

ADMONITION

The next morning at work, I sifted through a stack of Memoranda of Understanding from our potential community partners. Now that Magdalene House was under new management, other community organizations and health providers were bending over backwards to have formal relationships with us. It was a great problem to have.

My intercom beeped and I picked up the phone.

"Good morning, Jennifer!" I said cheerfully to my executive assistant.

"Good morning, Justin! Mr. Oliver is here to see you."

"Thanks, send him up."

I continued to look over the MOUs, but within seconds, Dante was at my desk.

"So you goin' on missions now?"

"What?"

"You know what the fuck I'm talking about, nigga."

"Yo, who do you think you're talking to?"

"Somebody who almost got himself killed, that's who!"

"I didn't almost get myself killed. Everything's fine."

"Everything is not fine! You went into the heart of the Anubis Society and planted bugs in they house? You really think that's a good idea?"

"So I guess Victor told you?"

"Of course he did."

"He just told you to get under your skin."

"This ain't about him, this is about you."

"Calm down. I went in the daytime."

"Daytime my ass! They got cameras."

"I was in a UPS uniform with a hat on, they couldn't see my face on film."

"You think they can't smell you? You think they can't tell when a human they don't recognize has been in their house?"

"I did this for you."

"You didn't do this for me, sir. You did this for Victor. I didn't ask you to do this and I would never ask you to do this. What you did was incredibly stupid."

"They have your brother, Dante! If you were going to get any closer to finding him, you needed somebody—a non-Razadi—to somehow get on the inside. And I did. I don't even understand how this wasn't even on your radar."

"Are you suggesting that getting my brother back wasn't a priority? Because it was. But I follow the protocol of my tribe, and at the end of the day, I know what my prime directive is."

"And what's that?"

"To protect you!"

"I am not a fragile flower, Dante, so stop treating me like one."

"And you are also not invincible!"

Steve knocked on the door and poked his head in.

"Everything okay in here?" he asked. "Sounds like…"

"We're fine," Dante said, immediately looking Steve in the eyes. "Everything's fine here, you may leave."

"Alrighty then!" Steve happily said, as he closed the door.

"Did you just hypnotize him?"

"D'uh."

"Well excuse me. I didn't know you could do that. Anyway, don't hypnotize my staff!"

"I needed privacy!"

I turned around and looked out of the window.

"Justin."

"What?"

"Please look at me."

I turned back around and faced Dante, looking him in the eyes.

"Yeah?"

"You will not return to the Anubis Society."

"Is that an order?" I shot back.

"I said…you will not return to that mansion."

"Dude. You are totally trying to fucking hypnotize me!"

"Yeah, so?"

"But you can't?"

"I guess not."

"Ha!"

"Don't mock!"

"Ha, ha! That's what you get!"

"I'm just trying to protect you, Justin, shit!"

"Listen. I went to that house because Victor asked me to and because it was the right thing to do. Victor just wants Orlando back and I don't blame him. I was never in any danger."

"But you might be now. That's all I'm saying."

"Well. Maybe I am. Maybe I'm not. Listen, how about this: I'll promise you no more solo missions if you can promise not to bully me or lock me away in a tower for my own good."

"There's shit at play here that you just don't understand."

"Then help me understand. Let's do this as partners and friends, not as a master and slave, okay?"

"I ain't mean to make you feel that way, aight?"

"I know. Let's just do this differently moving forward. Deal?"

"That's a deal."

"And if you ever try to hypnotize me again, we're gonna have a fuckin' problem."

Proof Beyond Faith

"You want to go for a walk?" Dante asked me out of the blue one Sunday morning.

"Sure," I said. "Why not?"

"And we can grab some breakfast or something while we're out?"

"I'd like that," I said.

After showering and putting on some clean clothes, we left my apartment and stepped into surprisingly cool summer air.

"It feels amazing out here," I said.

"Doesn't it?" Dante asked. We took the back door out of my building and took the long way down to Kennedy Street, through the alley and around a massive vacant lot. Just prior to my move in, there had been an apartment building much like mine standing there, but it was a notorious tenement–a slum where the real dregs of Kennedy Street lived. But for some reason, rather suddenly, the building was haphazardly demolished, and a pile of rubble sat there in its place. It was only as a result of many complaints from the neighbors and a sassy neighborhood activist appearing on the local news that the owners did finally clean up the refuse. Now, it was just a flat mound of dirt and rocks that grass and weeds were rapidly overtaking. It might turn into a nice green space if the city would do something with it.

I paused at the corner of the vacant lot and waited for Dante to pick up his leisurely pace.

"I'm here, man. I can see you."

"But I can't see you," I laughed. "You walkin' behind me like secret service. Come on. Walk with me."

He bashfully picked up his pace and joined me. I smiled at him and looked away.

As we walked, we heard the loud argument between the two drug addicts I always saw walking up and down Kennedy Street: a black lady pushing her child in an old, ratty stroller and her partner, a sleazy white guy in need of a haircut and a bath.

She pushed her child along with no regard for the bumps and cracks in the sidewalk. The conversation was so inane, so loud and rambling, that even the kid himself seemed to beg Dante and I for a rescue.

As I stared at the baby, Dante stared at the couple with the slightest look of contempt.

Their argument was about money. It sickened me to know that they were off to score some dope with their baby in tow.

Dante and I looked at each other and shook our heads in silence.

As I looked further down the street, I saw a small herd of little old ladies in white waddling down the street toward us.

"That's precious," I said. We got closer to them and saw women of different ages, from their 40s all the way up to a wizened women of about 90, all taking their time to get up Kennedy Street, presumably on their way to church.

"Good morning, ladies," Dante said, nodding to them.

"Good morning!" they replied cheerfully. We stepped to the side and let them all pass.

"Must be on their way to communion," I mused.

"Why you think that?"

"Because they were all dressed in white. I don't know. Either that or they were the missionaries."

I sighed.

"What's wrong?" Dante asked.

"Nothing. Those ladies make me miss my grandma."

"What happened to her?"

"She died a few years ago."

"Oh. I'm sorry man."

"It's cool."

We walked in silence for a few more paces, passing several corner stores and closed liquor stores.

"You don't go to church, do you?" I asked Dante.

"Nah, I don't. You?"

"Sometimes."

"Why only sometimes?"

"I was raised in the church. Sometimes I miss it. The music. The message. But then again, I don't suppose I ever really identified with it."

"With Christianity?"

"Yeah. I find religion to be really hypocritical, especially Christianity."

"That's true. Jesus wasn't like most Christians at all."

"You say that like you knew him. Wait. Did you know Jesus?!"

"I'm not that old," he laughed.

"Well then, why you don't go to church? Because of the hypocrisy?"

"No."

"Then why not?"

"Because I don't need to."

"Why not? You got a free ticket to heaven already?"

He laughed. We turned left on Fifth Street and began walking north, up a slight hill. A Metrobus passed by us, spewing black pollution and noise into the quiet air.

"Church is for people who have faith. I don't have any."

"You don't have any faith? That's depressing."

"Why?"

"You're too young to give up on humanity."

"Humanity? Oh, no, you ain't feelin' me," he laughed. "I don't mean I don't have faith in people. I mean I don't need faith. Faith is what you hold onto when you can't make sense of the mystery of conception, the complexities of life, and the senselessness of death. Faith means an acceptance that everything happens for a reason and that it's vaguely good. It's a belief in a higher power that we presume to be benevolent. We have faith because the opposite of faith is nihilism, and maybe even insanity. I mean, what would you do if you knew for a fact there was no God? For a fact? That when you cease breathing, there's nothing else? That there is no white light or heaven or reunion with your friends or loved ones?"

"Well, I'd be really sad, to say the least. Depressed. I might not have a reason to get out of bed, maybe."

"Right. Justin, I don't need faith. I know that there is more than just humanity, that there is a before the before, and that there will be an after the after. I have proof beyond faith."

"Proof beyond faith."

"Yes."

"An interesting concept."

"Not a concept at all. It's just a fact. There is more out there. And somebody once wrote–a long time ago-that one day, everybody is just going to know. They will all have proof."

I paused for a long moment.

"If everyone has proof…beyond faith…that there is an afterlife, or God, or whatever higher power, then wouldn't everyone lose their free will at that point? Wouldn't that make right and wrong irrelevant?"

"Maybe. Or maybe it could just be the most beautiful thing in this world. Something we've been waiting for since the dawn of time."

"You should know. You were there."

"I ain't that old, nigga," he laughed. We had reached the park next to Coolidge High School. We turned to the right, taking a pathway through the park toward downtown Takoma Park, just over the DC line.

"So, what is it?" I asked.

"What's what?"

"The proof."

"Oh, well, it's like one of those things…you'll know it when you see it."

"Come on! That's no different from any other religion!"

Dante ran ahead of me in the wooded park and climbed quickly up the side of a tree. More precisely, he ran up the side of the tree with little effort or resistance from gravity.

"Dante!" I called. "Get down!" I looked around to make sure nobody had seen.

He smiled back at me.

"You don't have to believe what I believe," he said. "But I know there is more. And one day, you will know, too."

"Okay, stop being weird. Just come down."

He jumped straight down from the branch he sat on and ran directly up to my face, which he kissed.

"You'll see," he promised.

What We Learned

"First thing's first," Victor said, as he settled into his seat at the Magdalene House conference room. "How are things going here?"

"Things are excellent," I said, handing him and Dante my quarterly report. "Here are all the details. But the major things you'll want to know are that the actual housing facility is now at capacity. Thirteen families are in the building. Each of our case managers has a full caseload. As you know, we've been taking on any client who is HIV positive and needs help, not just women. This expansion allows us to stay busy and stay relevant in the HIV community here. We're quickly overtaking our competitors."

"Not that you have to compete," Victor said.

"Yes. You're right. It's not a competition. Still, I can't help but to try to measure our success against the organizations which take government funding. And frankly, guys? We're just able to do more without the red tape of the government."

"We're happy to be able to help," Dante said.

"And the training program is taking off, too. People are most excited about that. And so am I."

"Magdalene is going to do big things. I can smell it," Dante said.

"Yeah, yeah, okay, now what about the Anubis Society?" Victor said, as he pushed my report to the side.

"Glad you asked," I replied. I opened up my laptop and pushed play on the software that linked up to the recordings I had collected from the mansion.

"Now, I've gotta tell you, the batteries on these devices really only last about a week, so I doubt we get much more than what we've already heard. But I think we've heard a great deal."

At first there was static, but shortly the voices filled the conference room.

Yeah, they're going to the National Life Lab. Bethesda, like a block from NIH. No, the other side, by the library. Right. No, he's sleeping peacefully most of the time. He only fights when the morphine is low in his system.

"I'm pretty sure that was about Orlando," I said. Victor nodded.

What are we going to do about Malcolm?
There's nothing to do. He's loyal to us. Let him eat how he wants.

He's going to get us in trouble one day.

I doubt it.

"That was about Malcolm. As far as I can tell, he's the muscle. Chief of security at night."

"Go on," Victor said.

Try some.

I'm not going to try any. Nigel will kill us if he hears any of that dude's blood went missing before it got to National Life.

Just take a sip.

No!

I heard if you drink it, you can walk in the sunlight for a little while.

And I heard if you drink their blood, you get addicted worse than crystal meth. No, thank you.

"I'm not sure who those people were," I admitted. "But the guy sounded black to me. Maybe from around here. And the woman had a very slight accent. Can't tell from where. Anyway, we got bits and pieces from a lot of conversations, maybe from ten different people. I'm sure more live in the house. But the key players seem to be Nigel, Cassandra, Malcolm, and the main two servants—the black guy and the girl."

"This…" Dante began, and then he sighed. "This actually seems like really good information."

"You sound sad about it," Victor teased. "What's the matter, didn't think Justin could deliver? I had total faith in him."

"Oh, shut up," Dante said.

"Can we use this?" I asked expectantly. "Can we somehow use this information to help break Orlando out? He is in there, in the mansion. Like, right now."

"Yes. He is." Victor nodded. "But you have to understand, if we just go in there with wooden stakes blazing, it could start a war."

"Fuck war, that's your brother! If there's a war, then they started it! I don't get it, why are you guys so timid around this issue? If it was my brother, I would have been broken him out."

"There are just some things you don't understand," Dante said. "There's a whole world you still don't know about. An order to things. If we upset the balance, it could mean the end of us."

"You're talking to me like I'm a baby. I did all this for you—for both of you—and now you're just sitting on the information? Jesus Christ."

I slammed my laptop shut, stood up, and looked out the window.

"Calm your nerves, Son of Adam," Victor said. "You've done a lot for us, and we appreciate it. But just try to forget everything and let us handle the rest."

"What? Oh hell no. Whatchu think this is?"

"Listen!" Victor's voice grew loud and he came next to me, right into my ear.

"For whatever reason, we can't hypnotize you into forgetting. And we've put a lot of trust in you so far. This is about as much appreciation as I can show you. But at this point, we have to talk to Babarinde next. I have to follow his instructions. Not yours."

"Then do it!" I yelled back.

"Justin, back off," Dante said. "Please."

"I'm not afraid of either of you," I said, storming out of the room. Victor followed, brushing past me as he sped out of the door. The force of his run threw me off balance and I fell to the floor.

"I just wanted to help."

"I know," Dante said. "It's just complicated with us."

"Some things don't need to be." I picked myself up and dusted my knees off.

"Orlando left you guys on purpose, didn't he?"

Dante nodded.

"We separated. It was time."

"Well now it's time to get back together. I can't believe a human has to tell you that there is strength in numbers."

The Dressing-Down

Thanks to a contact I'd made in city hall, I was given a sneak peek at some legislation that could decrease the funding for HIV service organizations in DC. Not us, of course, because we didn't get any government funding anymore. Nor did we need it or want it. But in the event that other organizations lost funding, it would be an opportunity for Magdalene House.

I was competitive, at least when I was already winning. If Magdalene could branch out into other areas of the city, it would mean big things for our clients. I wasn't above the acquisition of another nonprofit organization.

While I was poring through the document, my Skype began to light up. I barely used the thing, so it caught me off guard.

Oh, shit.

It was Uncle John.

I answered the Skype call and sat up straight in my chair.

"Hello John! How are you?"

"I'd like to explain something to you," he said calmly.

"Yes, sir?"

"You are not a Razadi."

"I suppose you talked to-"

"Do not interrupt me. You are not a Razadi. You do not do the work of a Razadi. You do the work of a human. Your job is to run Magdalene House. That's it. Do you understand me?"

"Yes, sir."

"What you did at the request of Victor Pearl was ill-advised and reckless. You have absolutely no idea what you're dealing with here. And Victor, of all people, should have known better than to send you into a vampire nest."

"I'm sorry."

"I know. And you'll be even sorrier if this situation blows up. Be careful, Justin. You just threw a stone at a beehive."

"I-"

John ended the call and the screen went black. My heart sank. I never wanted to disappoint him. Fuck.

The End

October weather in Washington was usually mild, so my long walk with Dante down Rhode Island Avenue barely even required a light jacket. I felt safe walking with him anywhere, whether it was the tourist-filled sidewalks of downtown, or the sketchy side streets of Pleasant Hill. As the sun set, I looked at my man and knew that he had my back.

"You like these walks we be on?"

"Yeah, I do. Gets me some good exercise every once in a while."

"You look like you been losing weight."

"You think so?" I smiled.

"Yeah. I mean you looked fine the way you were."

"But it's nice to be getting in shape."

"Fuckin', walking, and drinking water. That's all you need."

"You silly."

"It's getting late," Dante said.

"And it's pretty dark out here. Damn, did we really walk all the way to North Capitol Street from Woodridge?"

"Sure did. You trying to walk down by Howard? Get something to eat?"

"Nah, we should probably head back. If I eat, I'm not going to feel like walking all the way back. Damn, I haven't walked this far since I was a kid."

Dante smiled.

"You wouldn't have made it…"

"Back in Africa?" I completed.

"Yup. All we did was walk and run in the golden valley. But it was fun. Safe and peaceful."

"You miss it."

"Sometimes. But I know that's not home anymore. You feel me? Our destiny was to be here."

"Don't you miss your family?" I asked.

"I have my family here."

"Yeah, but what about your mother? Sisters? Aunts?"

"I had all that," he smiled. "Mama Abeo."

"Abeo was your mother's name?"

"Yeah. Leader among my people. Well respected."

"Is she…still living?"

Dante shrugged.

"When we left, we left. That was it."

"You mean you nev-"

Suddenly, I was lifted from the ground and thrown across North Capitol Street, crashing through the gate at the nearby McMillan Sand Filtration Site. The wind was knocked out of me as I lay in the grass. Before I could get my bearings, I saw a dark-skinned black man towering over me with his inch-long fangs bared. He bent down and bit my neck.

Before the world went black, I noticed two things: a bloody piece of my flesh dangling from the teeth of the vampire who had just attacked me, and the look of horror on Dante's face as he approached. That's how I knew that I wasn't going to survive.

THE ZEALOT

"It's done," Malcolm said, as he glided back into the mansion on Rock Creek Park.

"He's dead?" Nigel asked.

"I don't know, I guess. Sure."

"You've got some…" Cassandra pointed to her mouth, then Malcolm's mouth.

"What? Oh." He went to the hallway mirror and investigated. He tried licking the corner of his mouth, but gave up and used a baby wipe from a hallway closet.

"He tastes…different…" Malcolm said.

"What do you mean you 'guess?'" Nigel demanded.

"I mean, I tore his neck open and rolled out."

"Was he dead when you left?" Cassandra asked.

"Not yet. He's probably dead by now, though. Unless the daywalker got him to a hospital in time."

"You were supposed to kill him!" Nigel said.

"No. *You* said to send them a message. The message was delivered: Don't fuck with the Anubis Society."

Nigel rolled his eyes and covered his face.

"Darling, who else saw you?" Cassandra asked.

"Just one daywalker. The one they call Dante. Walking around the reservoir by Howard in the middle of the night like they hadn't a care in the world. Looked like they were in love. Faggots."

"Malcolm, it's the 21st Century," Cassandra said. "Certainly, you've seen two men in love a hundred times over by now?"

"And it never gets less disgusting. I don't even drink men if I can help it. That's why I spit his ass out."

Cassandra just shook her head.

"Why didn't you kill him?" Nigel demanded.

"Because I wanted the bastards to feel the pain, Nigel! They came into our home—while we slept—and planted listening devices! They know we have their kinsman. And they ain't getting him back. It's not about killing for the sake of revenge. They need to feel pain for what they've done. Long-lasting pain."

"That isn't for you to decide, idiot. Didn't you listen to what I said about the prophecies? Justin Kena is dangerous to us. He needs to die. The daywalkers have been protecting him. This was our chance and you blew it. Fuck!"

"You and these old, stupid prophecies…Nigel, nobody believes in that old shit anymore. Vampires have always been and always will be."

Sasha and Andre Crawford shifted uncomfortably in the corner.

"Darling, I think what Nigel is saying here…" Cassandra hesitated. "When the master of this house gives you a job to do, you better do it to completion. We are the Anubis Society—not some rag-tag bunch of Razadi rebels living in foxholes. We have an order to how we do things. And if the master of this house says to go teach a human a lesson, you'd better bring his head on a fucking platter, with a side of lungs."

"Do it yourself, then. I'm not here for all these stories about ancient vampires that never existed and prophecies that will never come true. Fuck this, I'm going to go eat."

Malcolm headed to the door. Nigel flew from his seat so fast one might have heard the crack of the sound barrier being broken. Fangs bared, and with both hands around Malcolm's neck, Nigel began to scream.

"As long as you are a member of the Anubis Society, you will believe as we do: that God created vampire and left us to rule this realm under the gift of the night and the moonlight! That anything walking or crawling when the sun sets is our domain! On every single continent and in every fucking time zone!"

Malcolm's fangs retracted as Nigel's chest heaved.

"I might not have made you a vampire, but you can believe one goddamned thing: I can end you."

Nigel let Malcolm fall to the floor.

"We've got to assemble now and squash the Razadi once and for all. Andre, get the database. Sasha, draft a letter to every society, lodge, and club in the Western hemisphere."

"Nigel," Cassandra said. "Let's talk."

"About what? It's time…"

"Malcolm. Sasha, Andre…may we have the room please?"

"Yes, Miss," Sasha and Andre said in unison. Malcolm scrambled up and disappeared down the hall.

"Come sit next to me, my love," Cassandra said, as she patted the cushion of the baroque sofa.

"How long have we been together?" Cassandra asked.

"Since that night during the French Revolution, of course."

"So you know by now that after all these years, I would never steer you wrong."

Nigel nodded.

"We have Orlando. He belongs to us. We've got the best doctors that money can buy studying his blood on every level. I'm hearing they're on their way to a breakthrough. Darling, we might be on our way to unlocking the secret of Razadi blood."

"That doesn't make Justin Kena any less dangerous to us."

"Why are you focused on him? We have the upper hand. We've always had the upper hand. He's just a human. There's no way to know if he's really 'The Key' from the prophecies."

"Babarinde thinks he is," Nigel admitted.

"Babarinde is a fool. A superstitious fool."

"He might be a fool, but he's one of the few people I respect in this life. He brokered peace between vampires and Razadi. For years. But if he's found The Key, then it's the end of us."

Cassandra pursed her lips.

"Nigel, I want you to focus on Orlando. Turn your attention to the science. Oversee the doctors. Let me worry about the Razadi."

"You won't do anything."

"I will, darling! We will observe them closely and see what their next moves will be. We'll find out how injured Justin Kena is and whether he will survive. And we'll see what happens next. Of course, I have my predictions. I think nothing will happen. They know they can't beat us."

"You don't believe in the prophecies. You never have."

"Be that as it may, I believe in you. Keep a clear head. And look at it this way: if we decipher the code in the Razadi blood, even if Justin is The Key, we could defeat them anyway. Imagine, darling…a nation of nightwalkers who can finally conquer the day. And it would all be because of you."

Nigel grinned.

"I'll give it a shot, my love," he said, caressing Cassandra's neck.

He stood up and walked toward the grand foyer.

"But know this: if you're wrong about this, and we've blown our chance to eliminate Justin? A nation of nightwalkers will know that you're to blame. Not me. Not Malcolm. Our blood will be on your hands."

Nigel disappeared in a blur. Cassandra exhaled.

"Sasha!" Her maidservant appeared in nanoseconds.

"You and Andre. Track the Razadi. Tell me everything you see. But don't you dare tell Nigel first. You leave that to me. Do you understand?"

"Yes, Miss."

"Good… Sasha, tell me something."

"Yes?"

"Do you believe in the prophecies? In Nigel's fire and brimstone?"

"Truthfully…I don't know, Miss Cassandra. It's just not what my maker taught me. I never thought about it too much."

"Have you ever dreamed of walking in the daylight again?"

"Yes, Miss. I do."

"Then study the Razadi. There just might be hope for us, yet."

Sasha smiled, ever so slightly, on the inside. For the first time since she'd been tethered to the Anubis Society, she saw a glimmer of humanity in Cassandra von Croy.

Part Two:
The Coming of Ominiyi

In the Blood

It had been decades since I was last taken by surprise.

"Tastes spicy," the nightwalker hissed, as he spat out a piece of Justin's flesh.

I looked down once again at Justin. The hole in his neck spurted insane amounts of blood on the ground. His eyes looked up at me, fixated in shock. His breathing was shallow and quick.

Every ounce of my body welled up with fear and rage that exploded as I bared my fangs and charged the nightwalker.

"Watch it now," he said, pointing at me and gazing into my eyes. I froze and hissed.

"I'm going to leave now. The way I see it, you can chase me and try to kill me, or you can try to save your friend's life. Choice is yours."

In a blur, the nightwalker was gone.

"Fuck!" I screamed. He had hypnotized me. That didn't usually work between our kind, but if our guard was down, it could briefly overtake us. At least he used it to get away from me, rather than preventing me from helping Justin.

I looked down. Justin was in shock. His chest barely heaved. Blood continued to flow from his neck. He was bleeding to death.

We were three miles from the house. Shit.

I took my shirt off and placed it against his open wound. I tried hard not to panic, but the fear was setting in.

"Sweet Olódùmarè! Please let him live! Shango, give me strength!"

Dozens of lightning bolts suddenly formed out of the black, cloudless night. Thunder ripped through the sky. Lightning struck the ground all around me in huge explosions.

Runrunrunrunrunrunrunrun

I picked Justin up and held him against my body.

I ran. Ran off the site of the terrible attack, a huge pool of blood left behind.

I ran through the neighborhoods off North Capitol Street, not caring who saw me, because I wouldn't stop until I got home.

I ran all the way across Rhode Island Avenue with my man in my arms, running at speeds I had never run before.

Shango was with me.

Olódùmarè was with me.

Justin would not die. Not tonight.

The world around me became a blur, as though I were traveling through a memory of another time.

I did not stop to catch my breath. I did not stop for anything.

My man would live. God had ordained it long ago.

I reached my house and kicked in the door.

"Victor! Victor, I need you!" He appeared in seconds.

"What the fuck happened?!" he shouted.

"Hold my shirt on his neck! We gotta stop the bleeding. Here."

I laid Justin's motionless body on the floor and ran downstairs to our basement. In a far corner was a stainless steel refrigerator. I broke the lock and flung the doors wide open, grabbing as many bags of blood as I could. I raced back upstairs.

"What are you doing?" Victor asked. "You can't do that!"

"I have to!" I threw the bags to the ground and then raced to a secret compartment in the kitchen. I opened it up and found our first-aid kit: needles, tubes, pumps—everything I'd need to save Justin. I raced back to the living room.

"I can't let you do this, Dante," Victor said.

"Listen, Victor, either keep the pressure on his neck or get the fuck out of the way!"

Victor tried to grab the needle from my hand as I was preparing Justin's arm for the IV.

"Give me that," he demanded.

"No!" I shouted. My peripheral vision began to glow blood red.

"It will never work," Victor said. "Just let him die peacefully." He grabbed at my tools once more.

"I said no!" I bellowed. Without hesitation, I punched him in the face, sending him hurtling through the living room and crashing into the wooden banister leading up the stairs.

He was knocked out cold.

I placed the needle in Justin's arm and began to pump the blood into his body.

"Come on," I said. "Just hold on, Justin. Keep fighting."

While I pumped the new blood in with one hand, I sliced my wrist open with a fang and let my blood poor into Justin's open neck wound, praying that it would heal him.

"Please, God," I begged. "Let this work."

My blood covered the open wound; at first, nothing happened. Then, I could tell the wound was slowly but surely repairing itself.

"Yes. Yes. Good. Keep fighting, Justin."

I could hear rustling from the stairs. Victor rose and began walking toward me.

"Victor, I swear to Olódùmarè that I will kill you if you stop me from saving Justin."

Victor bared his fangs and continued walked to me.

"I swear it!" I yelled.

He raised his wrist to his mouth and sliced an inch-long line. He knelt by Justin's head and put his wrist to his mouth. Victor glared at me, but he said nothing. I nodded.

Justin's mouth opened and he licked his lips, taking in drops of Victor's blood. We sat in silence and in prayer.

Ten minutes later, the wound on Justin's neck had healed and the bag of blood was empty.

"Take him upstairs," Victor said, as he finally took his wrist away from Justin's mouth. "Start another IV. We'll have to do this all night. And don't forget to bind his eyes. And don't you dare tell him that I helped."

"I know," I said. Victor disappeared. Justin was breathing deeply and his eyes were still closed. He was still bad off. But he was alive.

I bent down and scooped him up with both of my arms, cradling him carefully.

"We're not going to lose you," I whispered to him. "Not tonight. Not ever."

The night was long, filled with fever and cold sweats, and Justin vomiting up the blood he was being fed to save him. And the transfusions didn't stop, either. He needed blood to replace that which he had lost in the attack; blood that would be stronger than what he'd had before. If he survived, he would be better than what he was before. He'd be stronger. He'd be faster. He would be one of us.

But he had to survive the transformation.

I picked up the phone and called Babarinde.

"Baba…something terrible happened."

"What is it?" he asked.

"Justin and I were on a walk. The nightwalkers…they got him."

I broke down into sobs.

"I told you this would happen!" he shouted. "He was to be protected at all costs."

"I know Baba…"

"I suppose he wasn't The Key after all. Damn."

"But…"

"Contact Horton's on Kennedy Street to make the arrangements. Tell Cissy and Steve. Have them notify his parents."

"Babarinde…he's not dead."

"What?"

"He survived."

"How?"

"I picked him up and I ran back home with him. We gave him our blood."

"And it's working?"

"So far."

Babarinde remained silent on the other line.

"Baba, are you there?"

"Is he awake?"

"No."

"Continue the transfusions as long as you need to. This time might be different."

"Okay," I sniffed.

"Dante. Everything is going to be okay."

Babarinde clicked off the phone and I stood still in the dark hallway. Everything would have to be okay because I couldn't imagine a life without Justin.

Changing

By the next workday, Justin was still in a coma. As a board member for Magdalene House, I had some decisions to make and Victor wasn't remotely interested in dealing with them.

"Your man, your decision, your consequences," he said as he went off to rehearse with his band on Sunday afternoon. I sat in constant vigil at Justin's bedside, waiting for him to wake up.

I decided to tell Steve and Cissy that Justin had taken ill and that he'd be out indefinitely.

"What do you mean 'indefinitely'?" Cissy asked. "What happened to him?"

"I'm afraid I can't say," I told them.

"I mean, is he sick or was there an accident?" Steve asked.

"It's nothing like that," I said.

"Is he in jail?" Cissy asked.

"Lord Jesus, he got locked up!" Steve exclaimed.

"Listen!" I shouted, my patience growing thin. Startled, Steve and Cissy looked me in the eyes.

"Justin has the flu," I said quietly, hypnotizing them into submission. They nodded.

"He will be back soon. Just needs a little while to recover. Do you understand?"

"Yes," they replied in unison.

"You will both be in charge until he comes back. The Foundation trusts you. Do you understand?"

"Yes," they replied.

"You will not ask me about Justin anymore. If anyone else asks you about Justin, what will you tell them?"

"He has the flu," Cissy said.

"He'll be back soon," Steve said.

"Good. Now get back to work...please."

Steve and Cissy quietly left the foyer of the building. I had really hoped not to have to hypnotize Justin's friends, but humans didn't often accept just anyone's words on face value. At least now I wouldn't have to worry about them worrying.

I returned to the house and sat by Justin's bedside for the remainder of the day. At around seven in the evening, Justin finally stirred. He moved his head slightly to the left, then the right. Victor entered the room silently, having heard Justin's rustling.

"Justin?" I called out to him in a firm voice and held his hands. "Justin, are you awake?"

"Where am I?" he asked.

"You're at my house. I'm here. Victor's nearby."

"Why can't I see?"

"We covered your eyes. The light will hurt."

"Take this shit offa me." He let go of my hand and then tried to take the scarf off that we had used as a blindfold.

"Justin, don't."

He removed the scarf and tried to open his eyes.

"Oh God! Oh God, it hurts!"

I took the scarf out of his hands and covered his eyes once more. I made the knot tight behind his head so it wouldn't slide off.

"I told you not to take it off."

"What happened?" he asked.

"You were attacked."

"By a vampire?" he said, slowly reaching up to touch his neck.

"Yes. A nightwalker."

"Oh God."

"I got you back here quickly."

"Am I going to turn into a vampire?"

"What? No!"

"That's how it goes, doesn't it? You get attacked by a vampire and survive, you become a vampire. Right?"

I stroked his face.

"There's only one thing we call a vampire survivor: lucky."

He dozed back to sleep. Victor disappeared.

Twenty minutes later, Justin inhaled sharply, waking himself up.

"Dante?" he called.

"Yes, I'm here."

"How did you fix me? The truth."

"I carried you back here. I started an IV with Razadi blood. And I put some in your mouth in the hopes that you'd drink it." Victor reappeared in the room and stood silently in the corner.

"Did I?"

"Yes, I'm pretty sure you did."

"Will it change me?"

"Yes. It will change you."

He looked away from me and began to sob. I touched his face and he recoiled.

"We had to do it. There was no other way to save you from the attack. Listen, before you know it, the wounds in your neck will heal. Your strength will come back, in time. I promise you."

"How could you do this to me? I don't want to be a vampire."

"You won't be a vampire. You will be greater than a vampire."

"Leave me alone."

"Listen, you ungrateful son of a bitch," Victor said. "If it wasn't for Dante, you would be dead by the side of the road. It doesn't give me great pleasure to know that my blood runs through you now, but it does. Like it or not, you're going to be one of us. That, Son of Adam, is the greatest gift a Razadi can give a human. Now, be thankful that my brotherhood has chosen you, because it could have easily gone the other way."

"But I didn't choose you…" he mumbled before he fell asleep.

I left his side. Victor followed me into the hallway.

"He's just confused," I said. "He doesn't understand how serious this was."

"I don't give a fuck," Victor said. "He's yours."

"He's ours."

"So says Babarinde," Victor retorted.

I was disappointed in Victor for being so cold and callous about everything, but my heart ached more for Justin. I knew this transformation would be long and painful, but I also knew he could do it. He, more than any human I had ever known, deserved to be more than what he was before.

I went outside into the garden and picked a basket full of vegetables: onions, garlic, sweet potatoes, red peppers, kale, and chickpeas. I also picked handfuls of the herbs that had no names.

"Wake up," I said. "It's time to eat."

Justin stirred and sat up in silence. I put the tray down on the bed and carefully picked up the bowl.

"You ready?" I asked. He nodded and opened his mouth as I spooned the soup in.

He was still angry and sad. He ate in silence until the bowl was empty.

"I need my phone."

"Why?"

"What do you mean 'why?' Am I under arrest?"

"No, it's just…"

"Then give me my fucking phone."

I produced his phone from my pocket and put it in his hand.

He fumbled with it for a few seconds. Being blindfolded, there wasn't much he could do with a touch-screen keypad.

"Who do you want to call?" I asked.

"My mom."

I opened the contacts on his phone and scrolled down to his mom. I pressed the green call button and put the phone back in his hand.

"Hi…mom?" he asked. "Hey. Nothing. I just got a little sick. Oh, I dunno. Caught the flu or something. I'll be off work for a few days. No, I'm okay. Seriously, I'm fine. Yeah, I slept through Sunday. Hope you didn't worry."

He put his head down and listened to his mother in silence.

"She did? Well, tell her I said thank you. Yeah, her daughter can send me her resume whenever. We could use help during her winter break for sure. Well mom, I gotta go. I think I want to take a nap. Of course. Tell dad I love him. And I love you, too. Thanks, mom. Bye."

He held the phone out for me to take back. I grabbed it and our fingers touched. He pulled back immediately.

"Everything okay at home?" I asked.

He nodded and lay back down on the bed, turning away from me. I picked up the tray and hurried out of the room, turning the light out as I went. In the shadows, I could see him shake in silent sobs.

Early one morning, a few days later, he began to moan.

"What's wrong?" I asked.

"My mouth hurts really bad," he said.

"That's a good sign," I said. "It won't be long now."

"What won't be long? Ouch, good God, Dante!"

Justin covered his mouth. I could see he was fiddling around with his teeth by using his tongue to push on them.

"Push 'em, that's right," I said. "Push them on out."

After a few minutes, he was ready.

"Tissue," he said. I got a napkin from his dresser and put it under his mouth.

"You ready? Push 'em out," I instructed. I saw his tongue move one last time on the right, and I heard the faintest of pops, like a knuckle cracking. One more time on the left. He spit out his two old canine teeth into my napkin.

"Good, Justin. You got it."

"What the fuck just happened?"

"Your fangs are coming in. Your old canines were loose. The new ones will be in soon. Then you can eat and protect yourself."

"Jesus," Justin said, lying back down. "When do I get to take the blindfold off? Are my corneas gonna pop out too?"

I laughed.

"Your corneas will not pop out. In a day or so, your vision will be better than ever. Trust me."

He turned away from me in silence and I left him alone once again.

"I think this process is…going better than it did in Louisiana," I said to Victor a few days after that. We sat at the kitchen table finishing up bowls of rolled oats with blackberries on top.

"LaPlace was a fucking nightmare," Victor sniped.

"Yes, I know…but this time…"

"His eyes should be mature now," Victor interrupted, abruptly throwing his spoon into his empty bowl with a clang.

"I agree. Let's do this."

Victor and I entered the room. Justin was sleeping on his side.

"Wake up, babe," I said, lightly shaking him.

"Babe?" Victor scoffed. "Why don't you just make him your *ipsaji*?"

"Must you trivialize everything? And what if he is my *ipsaji*, then what? Hmm? You'd have to finally respect him? Heaven forbid."

"What's ipsaji?" Justin asked, as he stirred awake.

"Never mind that," I said. "It's nothing. Are you ready to see again?"

"Yes," Justin said.

"Well, take the damn blindfold off," Victor said.

Justin reached around, untied the scarf, and peeled it off. He blinked several times.

"Damn," he said.

"How's your vision?" I asked.

"It's...perfect."

"As it should be."

"No, like for real. It's perfect." He blinked several more times and wiped his eyes. "I can see every detail about this room. It's...it's colorful. Like *really* colorful."

I smiled. He looked down at his hands.

"Oh gross! My hands are so...wrinkly! How the hell did that happen?!"

"Justin...your hands always looked that way."

"What?! It's like...these folds on my knuckles are fucking humongous. And look at all these triangles! Like...how the hell? This is crazy!"

"I'm telling you, that's just how hands look! You have crazy good vision right now."

"Holy shit. That's crazy. Can we go outside?"

"Sure. Let's visit the garden." I reached out for Justin's hand and he took mine. He moved slowly because he was still weak from the attack, but I was happy that he was confident enough to test out his newly reborn eyes.

"This is the first time you've smiled," I noted, as we walked down the stairs. His eyes were wide as he inspected every crack in the wall.

"I haven't had a reason to," he said.

"You're alive," I rebutted.

"Whatever."

We exited the house through the kitchen door. The sun was setting and some shadows had already cast themselves over the back yard and the alley, but some deep golden rays still slashed their way across the garden.

"Oh my God. This is beautiful."

Justin let go of my hand and walked down the rusty iron stairs to the backyard. He slowly walked through the arbor trellis that served as the entrance to the garden, lightly holding onto it for steadiness. He surveyed the small plot of land intently, taking in each portion a square foot at a time.

He slowly knelt to the ground. Soon, he was on his hands and knees, surveying the vegetation in the garden with the intensity of a prospector looking for gold.

He cupped his hand and dug it into the soil. He lifted it up into the sunlight and let the dirt slowly fall back into the ground. His human eyes would just have seen dirt. His Razadi eyes saw hundreds of shades of brown and black with crystalline specks of minerals thrown in.

"This blessed plot," I quoted. "This earth…this realm."

"What?" he said.

"Shakespeare," I replied. He nodded.

"I'm glad you can see," I said. His finger traced a path in the soil.

"So am I," he said. I placed my hand on his shoulder. He recoiled slightly and looked up at me. I could see his pupils contract to pinpoints, then dilate again. He relaxed and leaned his head against my thigh. I exhaled.

A few nights later, he moaned. Again.

"What's wrong?" I asked, as I entered the room. Luckily, Victor was out for the evening. Catering to Justin was not in his repertoire.

"My stomach is cramping. I'm really, really hungry."

"Do you want some more soup?"

"It's not filling me."

"I'm sorry."

"What am I supposed to do?" he asked me pitifully.

"Ultimately? You're going to have to get some blood."

"I know. It's like I can tell that's what my body's craving. Ever since…ever since I got attacked and woke up here…like…you know how you crave Chipotle all week and you might have like nine meals to get through before you actually go down and get your Chipotle? Well that's how I've been feeling, even though I know it's blood that I want."

"You sound sad."

"I am. I guess y'all are gonna have to take me down to the sorority house soon."

"No. I won't let your first time be with some random chick."

"What difference does it make?"

"It makes a difference. I'm yours. I should be your first blood."

I bared my fangs and sliced a thin line along my wrist. Justin sat up eagerly. I placed my wrist against his lips. He held it in place with both hands and drank the blood seeping out of my vein.

When it's done right, getting your blood sucked feels better than a blowjob.

"It's not going to fill you," I whispered. "But it will keep you healthy until you get some human blood."

Justin quietly continued sucking.

"Okay, that's it for now." I removed my wrist from his mouth, even though neither of us wanted me to. My blood would rejuvenate in short order, but a pint was about all I felt like risking right now. The last thing I wanted was to be too weak to defend him if something happened.

"When your fangs finish coming in, I'll teach you how to bite properly."

He nodded.

A few nights later, I heard Justin calling my name. I went to the door and he beckoned me toward the bed.

"Get in."

I froze.

"You not kicking me out tonight?"

"Please. Just get in bed with me. Please."

I shut the door and walked over to the bed. He was finally getting some color back into his skin. Once he got some sunshine and made his first kill, he'd be better than he ever was before.

He reached over and turned the light out on the nightstand. I took my shoes and my jeans off.

"Basketball shorts?" Justin asked. "Hot as it is outside, your nuts must be musty as hell right now."

I smiled.

"You like my authentic African musk, though."

"Gross."

I slid underneath the thin blanket next to him as he lay on his back. I took his hand in mine. He turned on his side and faced me.

"Dante."

"Yes?"

"Thank you for saving my life."

I inhaled and slowly exhaled.

"You're welcome."

He leaned in and kissed me on the forehead.

"So as it turns out, I become somewhat of a bitch when I bounce back from almost being murdered. I understand now that the only alternative to be being turned into a daywalker was my death. And let's face it: I'm not ready to die."

"I'm not ready for you to die, either."

"All my life, I've just been floating. I never felt like I made a mark anywhere. Never thought I had it in me to be important or make a difference. But surviving that attack…undergoing this transformation…I can see better. I can smell better. I can hear better. And it's like…the entire world just came out from behind a curtain. I feel the pulse of the world now. What was I doing all these years?"

"It doesn't matter what you were doing before. All these things happen for a reason. Your purpose was written before all this. Your destiny is already determined."

"Proof beyond faith."

"Proof beyond faith. You better believe it."

He nodded.

"I'm hungry," he said.

"I'm horny."

"I think we can work out a compromise," he said. We kissed and I bared my fangs.

The Lessons

The next day, Victor stormed into the room with the grace of a rabid elephant.

"Your lessons begin today," he said to Justin abruptly.

"Don't you think it's too soon?" I asked.

"No. He has our blood now. If he's going to get attacked like a Razadi, then he needs to fight back like a Razadi. And it starts with the lessons."

Justin was awake but gave Victor no acknowledgement as he tapped away on his laptop, trying to telework.

"Are you ready?" Victor asked.

"I'm working," Justin said curtly.

"Oh, excuse me," Victor said, as he began to turn away. Suddenly, he turned back toward Justin, snatched the laptop from the bed, and threw it to the ground. It made hideous crunching sounds as it hit the floor and went black.

"Are you crazy?" Justin shouted.

"I said your lessons begin today."

He snatched Justin's hand from his lap and held it, closing his eyes.

"It won't work that way," I said. "Get closer."

Victor sucked his teeth and scooted closer to Justin on the bed.

"Relax," he said, gently cupping Justin's face into his hands and leaning close enough for their foreheads to touch.

Justin immediately tensed.

"It's okay," I said. Justin loosened his shoulders and relaxed, breathing in and out slowly as Victor opened up a pathway to our memories.

I closed my eyes and tuned in to what Justin was seeing.

WEST AFRICA, 1724

"It is quite simple, Ogundiya," said the fat general. "You will accept the terms of this treaty or your people will die."

About a dozen men from each side of this war crowded into the small hut. Each side of the bloody battle was ready for it to end, but only on their own terms.

"Haruna," Ogundiya said slowly, "You have invaded the ancestral homeland of the Razadi and you dare make these demands?"

"Ogundiya," Haruna interrupted. He was a beast of a man, almost porcine in his appearance. The rolls of his stomach seemed to spill onto the table like a sack of grain. His eyes were like two beetles hidden in a cake of brown mud. Haruna took great joy in exacting revenge on the tribe that had been the bane of his existence. His whole life, he was raised to hate the Razadi for all they had. He had been taught that the Razadi had displaced his own people from the lush valleys and driven them into the barren, rocky cliffs.

"The Oyo people have not forgotten how, years ago, the Razadi forced us from the golden valley. We have simply returned to claim what is ours. We are offering a most gracious treaty in exchange for your lives."

"Your people are misguided, believing these fanciful stories," Ogundiya calmly began. Ogundiya was everything that Haruna was not. He was a slender, level-headed old man that was well known among his people for his wisdom and fairness. The crow's feet around his eyes showed both his weariness and his age. He was too old to still fight wars in the savannah when white traders threatened to encroach on their safety.

"The Razadi and the Oyo are like cousins, brothers and sisters!" Ogundiya explained. "Your people and my people all come from the valley. We did not displace you. Our division happened hundreds, perhaps over a thousand years ago. We don't even remember why, Haruna. But know this: the Razadi only want to be left alone."

"You claim to be our brothers, yet you want to be alone?" Haruna's young lieutenant stood up and yelled. "How dare you insult the Oyo with your snobbery! You know that while the Razadi live peacefully in the valley, your so-called cousins starve in the cliffs. I should slit your throat right now, old man!"

The lieutenant lunged across the table with a blade, attempting to slice the Razadi chief. Ogundiya did not even move. Before the lieutenant knew it, his blade had fallen to the ground, and the youngest Razadi lieutenant had slammed him against the wall of the hut.

"I will rip your heart out of your chest and make you watch me eat it as you die, Oyo scum," the young lieutenant said, wrapping his hands tightly around the neck of his rival.

"Let him go, Eşusanya," Ogundiya said. "He poses no threat to me."

The sandy colored Eşusanya immediately obeyed, shoving the young lieutenant away. He had fire in his eyes. He was determined to protect his kin to the death. Eşusanya wore the traditional long braids of the Razadi people.

"Ogundiya," Haruna began again. "You must face the facts. The Oyo have dammed the river. We are ready to plow salt into your fields so that nothing will grow there. We have the ability to burn your village to the ground and take what we want. You, Ogundiya, represent the most hated tribe in this region."

"Hated because we just want to be left alone," Ogundiya said.

"Wrong, old man," Haruna said. "You are hated because of the evil you represent. Our elders told us that we couldn't beat Razadi. They taught us to fear you because of the ruthlessness with which you control this area. They say you are descended from the devil, that you will even eat human flesh to stay alive if you have to."

"And do you believe those tales?" Ogundiya asked.

"No," he said. "The Razadi are formidable opponents, but your time has passed…"

Justin gasped and Victor's concentration was broken.

"Tell me what you saw," Victor sniped.

"You. Threatening somebody the same way you did me."

"Tell me more," Victor demanded.

"A war council between the Razadi and the Oyo. I don't understand why they hate you."

"They've always hated us," I said. "The Oyo lived in the cliffs, a few days' journey from us. Their land was infertile and the game was sparse. They were a poor tribe. Poor and jealous."

"Which led to desperation," Victor added. "They wanted our land, our crops, our way of life…everything."

"Why didn't they just ask?" Justin asked.

"Wasn't their way," Victor said. "They were bred to hate us and to fear us, so whatever they wanted, they felt they had to take."

Justin nodded.

"Come back in," Victor said, cupping Justin's face once more.

"We fought for days and nights until the ground was red with the blood of casualties on both sides. Even we, the youngest of our people, joined the fight. What do you see, Justin?"

"A field. I'm in a field. There are people everywhere. It's chaos out here."

"No. Not chaos. War. Look behind you. You see all those women with spears? They are our mothers and sisters. They are eager to jump in. Sometimes they do. But we usually prevent that."

"Why?"

"You kill a woman, you kill a bloodline. We can't have that."

"You're winning the fight, but the women look sad."

"Yes," Victor said, breaking the connection.

"Why?"

"That's enough for today."

Victor walked out of the room.

"Sorry about the laptop," he called from the hallway.

Justin stood up and walked over to the destroyed laptop. He tried to pick up the pieces but he had a hard time bending over.

"Can you help me?" he asked. I walked over to him, brushed against his side, and told him I'd take care of it. He walked back to the bed and sat down, exhausted.

"I want to go home," he announced when I was finished picking up the pieces of the laptop. My heart stopped for a split second.

"You're safer here," I reasoned. "Your fangs haven't grown in yet and you're still really weak."

"I want to go home. All this shit I'm learning here, I can learn at home."

"The answer is no," I said sternly. "Now that's an order from Babarinde himself."

He glared at me.

"I'm sorry…but it's just not possible right now."

"You have no idea how this feels, do you?" he asked.

"I have an idea."

"You were born a Razadi. And I suspect whatever rite of passage you went through to become a man didn't leave you feeling dead for most of the day. I feel *terrible*, Dante. I just want to be at my own place, in my own bed, with my own stuff."

"I know. And you will get that soon. But for now? You rest. There's a lot more you're going to have to learn. Mentally, spiritually, and physically. This is just the beginning."

West Africa, 1724

Word had gotten out that Justin had fallen ill, and even though he assured people he would be fine, the office was still inundated with get-well cards, flowers, and balloons. I picked them up and filled his room with them, hoping they'd cheer him up.

"I can't believe all these people care that much about me," he said. "I barely know them."

"They like you. What's hard to believe? You're a nice guy."

"I guess," he said.

"Anyway, I'll be giving you your next lesson," I told Justin gently. He nodded and closed his eyes.

"Wait," he said, quickly opening them again.

"What?"

"I have something I want to show you."

He looked at me with his mouth agape, smiling at me with his eyes. Slowly, his fangs emerged, extending just below his lips.

"That's awesome," I said, smiling.

"I got fangs, yo!"

"Baby fangs," I added. "Just wait until they get full-sized."

Justin looked away and covered his mouth.

"I can't make 'em go back in yet," he admitted.

"It's okay. Just relax. I got someplace to take you," I said, cupping his face and closing my eyes.

I sat guard outside of my mother's hut, eavesdropping on her debate with Ogundiya, our general.

"Mama Abeo," he said. "There has to be another way. We've fought for too long and too hard to give up now."

"We have never fought so hard against an enemy," she replied.

"Sorcery," he responded. "There's no other explanation. These people…they are our match. But we can defeat them."

"The soldiers are exhausted, Ogundiya. It's been months and neither side is giving up. The Oyo want this land."

"They can't have it! The scrolls say…"

"The scrolls say many things. The scrolls also say that one day we will rule without the need for force; that men will bow to us by the look in our eyes. But that day has not yet come."

My mother was a tall, regal woman, adorned in the finest fabrics and jewelry. Her tall forehead and wide cheekbones gave her the appearance of perpetual amusement. And, generally speaking, she was a happy woman, even when deadly serious. She had a peace about her that made others flock to her when the world's problems became too much to bear.

"Then we have to keep fighting!"

"To what end? Listen to yourself. This is not who the Razadi are. It is not who we are meant to be. It was always foretold that our sons would be like the airborne seeds of a flower: blown softly away from home, but sure to land in safety in another place."

"I won't leave."

"You must. You all must."

"No."

"Ogundiya. It has been twenty years since the last Razadi child was born."

"I know that."

"Olódùmarè has given us a gift. We are stronger. We are faster. We live longer."

"And with those gifts come responsibilities, Abeo. We must protect our land. We must protect our way of life. We can defeat them."

"But should we? With our gifts come the burden of the blood thirst. And we could slay and drink every Oyo that comes our way. But to what end? If not the Oyo, it would be the Ife. If not the Ife, then the Okoro. They will keep coming. Ogundiya, the scrolls have already foretold this moment. Everything we have lived for has come to this day. Our people get stronger and stronger with each generation, but what has happened? There is no next generation. My son, my darling Aragbaye, will never know what it means to be a father. How is that a gift? That, dear friend, is a curse."

"Indeed, it is a curse to live among a people that haven't heard the cries of a baby or the laughter of a toddler in decades. And it seems to me to be a curse to be able to walk in the sun for a hundred years but to never meet Olódùmarè. All things come to an end. All things get old and die."

"But we don't. Do you know how old I am?"

"I don't. You've always just been here, as long as I've lived."

"I'm three hundred fifty two."

"I wasn't aware."

"Time freezes for the Razadi. It's time to thaw it."

"Mama Abeo, but how do you know? How do you know that dividing the tribe will save us? How do you know that allowing the Oyo to live here among you, working with you, loving you, how do you know that it will work? What if you remain barren?"

"Ogundiya…it's already happened."

"What?"

"Olateju is with child. She encountered an Oyo soldier six months ago, before the war started. They love each other."

"Are we sure the baby doesn't have a Razadi father?"

"There has been no one else. We have hidden her for her safety. But she is the proof. The proof that everything we believe is coming to pass. Those systems and beliefs we hold dear, those even older than the Orishas."

"Praise Olódùmarè for the blessing of this child. But damn us all. Damn us all."

I held my breath, trying not to be heard by my mother. Eşusanya and Aborişade walked up to me quietly.

"What's going on?" Eşusanya whispered.

"It's all going to change," I whispered back, my voice cracking with emotion.

"What? What are you talking about?" Aborişade asked.

I shook my head, struggling to hold back the tears.

I stood at attention in between Eşusanya and Aborişade while my mother addressed the entire village for the final time. The sun had just risen and a cool breeze still blew over our land. The vibrant blue sky and pure white clouds were ill suited for this solemn moment.

"My brothers, my sons, my friends. I stand here before you today with a heart that is both heavy and overjoyed. It is heavy because I send you out into the world to continue our bloodlines. I say farewell to you, the builders, the soldiers, the philosophers. We will not forget your contributions to this culture. We know that wherever you go, wherever you land, you will keep the heart and soul of the Razadi with you. You will seed your communities with our tenacious spirit. Our influence will be felt all across the land because of you.

"Even though we will miss you, we know this division is necessary for the survival of us all. Even now, a new generation grows. Olateju will be known as the matriarch of the next generation of our people. May all of you be patriarchs of the worldwide Razadi empire!"

Next to her stood the very pregnant Olateju and her Oyo husband, as well as Haruna, the satisfied general of the Oyo army.

"Ogundiya and Babarinde. Come to me."

Our most senior leader and his deputy approached my mother. I could not tell what she was whispering to them, but I could see what she presented them: iron casks and two scrolls each.

Nervous whispers fell over the crowd. Were those *the* scrolls? The fundamental tenets of our beliefs and the history of our origins?

Abeo embraced each man and they rejoined the group, carefully entrusting the casks and the scrolls to their assistants. Abeo then descended into the ranks. She looked carefully into the eyes of about a dozen men, and nodded at them. She didn't speak at all.

I knew they were all her sons. So much time had passed in between our births that most of us weren't terribly close. They were no more my brothers than my peers were, as each man in our tribe respected one another the same.

She came to me and paused. Tears welled in her eyes and she leaned close to me.

"You, my youngest, are the one who will change the world."

"I don't want to go, Mama," I said, choking on my tears.

"Go. Seek the new dawn. I love you."

"I love you too, Mama."

She took her place in front of her men for the final time and uttered but one phrase.

"May Olódùmarè and the Orishas forever protect you!"

"And you!" we shouted in response.

And then, the hundred and twenty five or so of us, we walked.

And we walked.

And we walked some more.

The low men on the totem pole like me, Aborişade, Eşusanya, and Ogundiya's son, also named Ogundiya, didn't ask specific questions of our leadership. We just walked.

"What did your mother say to you?" Aborişade asked me on the first night. We lay next to each other on our thin pallets, staring up at the night sky with its thousands of stars.

"She said she loved me. She said to seek the new dawn. And she said that I'd change the world."

"She didn't say a word to the rest of her sons," Eşusanya said. "I wonder what makes you so special."

I scowled.

"He's the youngest," Aborişade said. "The youngest is always the favorite."

"It isn't like that at all," I said. "I don't know why she chose to speak to me."

"Where do you think we're going?" Eşusanya said.

"Eko," Ogundiya said.

"Who told you that?" Eşusanya asked.

"No one told me. I heard my uncle talking. We will settle in Eko."

"Well that's not bad at all," Aborişade said. "We learned about Eko. It is diverse."

"It's right on the water," I said.

"They say you can't see the other side of the great river, there's so much water," Eşusanya said.

"Is there another side?" I asked.

The four of us fell silent, staring at the stars.

The next morning we rose and we walked some more. Our leaders assured us that we would be reaching our destination soon.

Each of us carried something we would need. Seeds. Water. Spices. Weapons. Textiles. Tools. We were starting a new life with new people, whoever they would be. We would be useful to them.

I surmised that the iron casks were filled with gold and gems we'd amassed from our various conquests through time. We'd certainly need to trade some things as we reached other villages.

Night fell again and we were exhausted. The older ones pitched tents, and the younger ones slept outside on pallets.

I woke up suddenly from a deep sleep. I looked to my right and saw Eşusanya on top of Ogundiya, embracing him. Men loving each other among our tribe was nothing new, but I hadn't realized those two had a relationship. I stared for a moment, then turned over in an attempt to get back to sleep.

Almost immediately, I heard an immense clopping noise, like a herd of antelope coming right for us. We sat up and our elders began coming out of the tents. The noise got louder and louder. Soon, we were all on our feet, facing in the direction of the roar of the stampede, and waiting for the threat to show itself. We hadn't eaten in a while, and surely whatever this animal was would make a great late night feast.

"Wait…listen…" Aborişade said. We stood still.

"The noise is coming from behind us," Eşusanya said. I immediately stood back-to-back with him, assuming a stance we'd learned long ago in manhood training.

"They're coming!" Aborişade said over the deafening roar. There was no time to strategize. Only time to react.

Dust rose into the sky, obscuring the bright moon and stars, even in the darkness. The roar reached a crescendo and then stopped.

"Sweet Olódùmarè, protect us," I whispered.

In an instant, we were attacked on all sides by a force moving too fast for us to see.

"What kind of beast are you?" Aborişade yelled into the fracas of moving bodies pushing, shoving, and slicing at us.

A blade sliced at my arm and I yelped, more from surprise than from pain. I looked down and saw the flesh wound already healing itself.

"Just swing!" Ogundiya shouted.

We swung our fists into the air and every third swing landed on something. It slowed the white blurs around us down ever so slightly. I decided that, rather than punch, I would grab.

I had a handful of hair in my hand, still attached to the head of one of the monsters trying to attack us. It was soft and long.

"Lasciami andare, bastardo nero!" The monster growled at me in his foreign tongue and slowed down enough to reveal himself to me.

He looked human, on the surface. He had eyes, ears, a nose, a mouth, and fangs, just like us. But he was different. His eyes were a light brown, such as I'd only seen in the amber beads of the women in my tribe. His features were sharp, angular and angry. His nose came to a point. His brow was strong and low. And his skin…his skin was a ghostly white.

I bared my fangs and he lunged at me with both hands outstretched toward my neck. I deflected his arms and grabbed him by the waist with both hands. I could see he wore a plain white shirt with buttons, black pants, and black boots. I picked his light frame up, hoisted him over my head, and hurled him to the ground. I kicked him in the lower back in an attempt to stun him.

He merely laughed and hopped back up on both feet again.

"Si presenterà alla mia volontà!"

"I don't know what you said, but I know that you're going to be my meal," I responded.

My own body must have looked like a brown blur as I attacked the man. My lips met the vein in his neck and I bit him as hard as he could. He tried to fight me off, but I was too strong for him. My fangs sank into him and his hot blood soon filled my mouth.

It tasted like nothing I'd ever had before. I didn't like it.

I spat his vinegary blood to the ground and tossed him aside. All around me, similar fights were unfolding. And the terrorists just kept coming. Before I got a chance to pull one of them off Eşusanya, two more had overpowered me and taken me to the ground. I tried to fight them off, but before I knew it, they had placed heavy iron shackles on my feet. I tried to reach down to take them off, but each of the men twisted my arms behind my back and bound me with more shackles. The harder I fought, the more they laughed. Finally, one grabbed a stone from the ground and bashed it against my skull, knocking me out cold.

The voices swirled around me for the next few minutes, a mixture of the foreign language of our attackers and the shouts, growls, and hisses of my own people. People walked over me. I heard our elders shouting at us to remain calm.

I felt someone being thrown to the ground behind me.

"Aragbaye," he said. It was Aborişade and he was breathless. "Wake up."

"What's happening?"

"They drink blood just like we do."

"What?"

"They're soldiers of some kind. They're on a mission."

"Haruna," I said. "Haruna sent us to our deaths. This was the plan all along."

"I think so, too. Wait; quiet."

The ghostly men ran long chains through the loops in our shackles.

"We're slaves. Aborişade, they're taking our freedom!"

"We will never be slaves and we will never be their food. We will get out of this."

From where we were lying, I could see the monsters rummaging through our belongings. One opened up an iron cask and held up several jewels to the moonlight. A second pawed over one of our scrolls.

"*Rimetterlo. Gli schiavi e i loro beni sono un pacchetto,*" a third man said. The first man hissed at the third. For his insolence, he was punched in the nose by the third.

"*Ho detto rimetterlo.*"

The remaining man slowly loaded our things back on a cart. As soon as the man turned around, I saw him sneak one of our scrolls under his shirt, leaving three others behind.

"That bastard took one of our scrolls," I whispered.

"We will get it back. We will get out of this."

Before we knew it, we were being slapped on the arms and chest and forced to stand upright. We had been chained to each other in one huge coffle. I looked to my left and to my right and saw the dead bodies of several men I'd known, mostly elders. Ogundiya, the elder, was chained several rows over from me. He nodded in acknowledgement when I saw him. Babarinde was not far behind him.

The pale-faced men seemed to have a leader barking orders at them. He pointed in one direction, then pointed toward the sky. Soon, the men started cracking their whips, and we began marching across the countryside.

As we marched, they sang a song in beat with our footsteps.

A bi bo,
goccia di limone,
goccia d'arancia,
o che mal di pancia!
Punto rosso, punto blu,
esci fuori proprio tu!

Every time one of them said "*tu*" they would crack the whip and try to hit one of us in the face with its tip. They were successful more often than not. But in spite of this humiliation, our wounds healed almost instantaneously.

We would never have dared marching at night. It's not as though we were afraid of anything in particular, but there was no reason to risk being caught by surprise if we didn't have to be, whether by springing traps set by other tribes, or by waking a sleeping den of animals.

These men had no such concerns. We marched with haste through unfamiliar territory. We could handle it. We were Razadi. Our stamina was legendary.

They knew we were different. They callously and arrogantly pushed us along, laughing and taunting all the way. But who were they and why did they want us? What would happen to us?

Within time, we were actually running—shackles and all—through the savannah to get to wherever it was we were going.

Before we knew it, we were in a compound overlooking the sea. There were about a dozen short, squat, windowless buildings that had been erected out of lumber. Each had a single door with a complex system of locks on the front. I presumed that's where we'd be housed.

The men who had kidnapped us anchored us to the ground. They worked furiously, as though working on a deadline. They finally secured the last stake in the ground.

"*Affrettatevi*!" their leader shouted, pointing to the sea as the sun began to rise. The men scattered and entered their quarters while we lay shackled to the ground.

The sun's first rays reached our skin as the last bolt locked the doors of the men's quarters from the inside. Aborişade rested his head on my back and fell asleep, exhausted from the journey. I, too, was tired, but my mind was too busy to rest.

There were other settlements closer to the shore, but we were too far to see who they were or what they were all about. We needed to get away from here and get anywhere else. I felt I'd rather die than be a slave.

My mind wandered off to sleep, even as the sun heated the air around us. We thrived in the sun. We'd be energized as we slept.

I wasn't sure how much time had passed by the time I woke up, but the majority of our men were awake, alert, and ready to fight. Babarinde and Ogundiya the elder kept admonishing us to keep our wits about us, and to not do anything that would endanger the whole.

Even as the different white men down by the shore walked up to our encampment, our elders told us to be calm, to always take the path which would lead to the fewest number of lives lost. The men, more tanned than the ones who captured us, walked with long sticks of wood and metal, heavier on one side than the other.

The white men came to us and spoke to each other in a language I was only later able to translate. And so much time passed before I learned their language that much of what they said remains lost to time. But I can tell you what they did.

They talked to each other for a long time. They couldn't decide how to proceed. The word I remember being repeated was "dangerous."

They began unpinning a section of our group from the stakes we'd been chained to, and my brothers immediately rose up against them. Twelve of them broke loose from the chains and began fighting the white men down. These men were weaker than the ones who had captured us. One fell backward immediately with the force of a single punch. My brothers descended upon him and drank as much as they could.

One of the men with a stick aimed it at my drinking brother and pulled what I know now was the trigger. He was killed instantly. That's how I found out what a gun was.

My brothers who were freed were shocked to see one of their own dead and on the ground, but they rushed the men with the guns anyway. One by one, my fellow Razadi were felled by these men's bullets. Blood spattered across the grass.

The leader spoke. I don't remember all that he said, but I remember him saying something about not being afraid to kill all of us if need be.

Through whips and muskets we were subdued. There was no more fighting back if we wanted to live to see another day. Mama Abeo hadn't sent us out in the world only to be murdered by strangers. We were charged to be the seeds of our culture. And we were determined to do that, wherever we ended up.

We were forced to march over the dozen corpses of our fallen, not giving them proper Razadi funeral rites. I remember each of their names to this day and I hope their spirits torture the people responsible for their massacre.

We were divided into two groups of no particular order or importance to our slavers. My group, including Babarinde, Aborişade, Eşusanya, and Ogundiya the younger, were marched onto the beach and forced onto a ship called *La Coeur*. The shackles and chains were built for the ship. I lay down on hard wooden planks next to Aborişade and pondered whether I would have a future.

The rest of our people, about half, boarded a ship called *La Tête*. Ogundiya the elder and most of Mama Abeo's other sons ended up on that ship.

The iron casks of jewels, the seeds, and two of the remaining three scrolls came with us on board our ship. *La Tête* took the textiles, the weapons and tools, and the third scroll.

It wasn't long before the ships set sail from what we later learned was the city of Eko, a place that we thought was a hub of commerce and culture for our region of Africa, but which turned out to be nothing more than a slave trading port.

We had been tricked into slavery by the Oyo as one last "fuck you" to our people. We thought we performed a noble act by leaving, mostly willingly, to make our fortunes elsewhere, never suspecting that we would be marching to our own executions. Even now, I wonder what life would have been like in our village had we never left, if another compromise had been worked out where we'd all stay together, insulated from the evils outside our own people, always safe within each other's arms, ostensibly able to live forever, even if another child was never born among us.

Perhaps that was how it was meant to be. Perhaps Mama Abeo was wrong. Maybe the Razadi were not being punished by becoming infertile. Maybe there was just no place else to go in the gene pool. We had reached the top and there was no more reason to reproduce the way we had known.

Instead, we were made into the living seeds of the culture, spread across the world like seeds from a dandelion, spread from the puff of air that was the will of Mama Abeo herself.

And rather than being planted to grow in the next fertile ground, we were made into property, conquered by the only beings on this earth that could possibly beat us. Those terrible creatures who couldn't even face us under the light of the sun, who'd made some insidious agreement with common, weak white men who'd never have been able to take us without the treachery of the Oyo, the assent of mercenary vampires, and the gunpowder of European muskets.

This conspiracy was so twisted that it seemed like fate itself had plotted to steal us from our homeland and plant us in the western hemisphere. It was the perfect crime.

The only comfort any of us had was that we had not died—not yet—and so long as we lived, there would be a time for redemption and a time for revenge.

Loss and Liberation

Horrifying, humiliating, and demoralizing. Those are the weakest words in your language that can be used to describe the torturous middle passage. But I experienced it, just as the hundred or so surviving men in my tribe did, and as the millions of other Africans taken from the continent had, whether they were sold as prisoners of war or taken by entrepreneurial private kidnappers, as we'd been.

We feared for our lives. The sticks, which had sent invisible spears through the bodies of our kinsmen, terrified us. Indeed, they were the only things that kept us subservient. We could survive the lash or the cat-o-nine tails. But this great instrument of instant death, this "gun"–this was the thing we knew we could not surmount. There was no defense against it. There was just survival.

The slave ship was not large. It was on the small side, as was the space inside it. Small and dark and made of wood. It was too short to stand up inside. We could only lie down or scoot up to sitting position if the chains were loose enough. There were no pillows or blankets or anything to make it comfortable. It was just hard wood and our own bodies.

The darkness of the cargo hold of the ship was like nothing I'd experienced before. It was pure black. Nothing in Africa was this black, not even the backs of my eyelids. I was scared, but there was no time to turn away, nowhere to run, no possibility of fighting.

The first day at sea was bad. Several of us had been in canoes before, but the vast majority had not known what it felt like to float in deep water. The up and down motion of the ship made us violently ill. Many of us became sick to our stomachs and vomited. If we had known, we might have tried to focus and center ourselves to manage our health better, for the vomit that came out of us wasn't draining anywhere, nor was anyone going to come by and clean it up.

There were no private corners to excuse ourselves to when we had to urinate or defecate. We held it for as long as we could that first day, but when we had to go, we went. We tried our best to pull down our pants if our chains allowed us the freedom, and we aimed ourselves away from our brethren if it was possible. But it usually wasn't. We soiled ourselves and each other in the process of handling our natural bodily functions.

Every other day or so, the hatch to the holding cell would open and men with the guns would peer in. I couldn't understand it at the time, but there was one word they kept saying over and over until I came to understand it was what they were calling us:

Négro.

No, I am not *Négro.* I am Razadi.

Négro.

No, I don't know what that is, but it's not my name.

Négro.

No. No. We are Razadi. We will never answer to a name other than that one.

We had to share a jug of water to drink and pots of a disgusting, lumpy porridge to eat. That was it. The slavers considered us to be quite dangerous, so our meals were delivered to us by a contraption that was raised and lowered down to us. Only those closest to the contraption could reach it due to the chains. They passed the food and water to the people behind them. We soon determined that we'd eat only twice a day and in small quantities.

The floor soon became slick with our excrement. It was a sludge that wouldn't soon leave the cell. The hatch closed and we baked in the heat and humidity.

Sweat.

Tears.

Piss.

Shit.

Vomit.

The stench.

The wails.

We lived in hell, tossed to and fro in the ocean for weeks, called a word we had never heard before but that we knew must mean the lowest of the low.

I wanted to die. I wanted my life to end. If there had been a way for me to kill myself, I would have. We all wasted away, constantly sick from the stench and filth, unable to clean ourselves. My body itched and ached. My head was in constant pain.

Babarinde tried his hardest to comfort us. He was the ranking member of our group, as Ogundiya the elder was on the other ship. We sang sometimes. We chanted sometimes. And we prayed. We prayed fervently and often, sometimes so long and hard that we lost our voices.

But I knew that Babarinde was just as scared and lost as the rest of us. This wasn't what he'd signed up for. This hell on the ocean wasn't what any of us had signed up for.

Many weeks into the ordeal, on one of those nights we were convinced we'd just float forever, the ship tossed violently, worse than it ever had before. We could hear the wind whipping around the ship while thunder exploded around us.

"Oya!" Babarinde shouted above the din. "She has come!"

Not that it made a difference in the blackness of the hold, but we closed our eyes and prayed that Oya would liberate us. We whispered. We shouted. We tried to speak to her as one body, one mind.

Upstairs, chaos. The slavers shouted in their native language to one another in panicked tones. If they were scared, I knew we would be alright somehow.

The hatch door flapped open against the wind and we could hear the white men ever clearer. They kept saying "*La Tête! La Tête!*" which we knew was the name of the other ship. It was night, but I could see no stars, only black sky tainted gray with the storm clouds overhead and the surreal streaks of lightning slicing through the air like a spider's web.

The ship tilted suddenly to the left and one of the unarmed crew members tumbled down into our space. He screamed on the way down. His back hit the bottom with a terrible plop and he struggled to stand in the scum.

Even amid the howls of the wind, he must have heard the fifty or so sets of fangs elongate with a pop at the same time.

"*Mon dieu…*" he whispered.

The two Razadi closest to him reached out and grabbed his arms.

"*Non!*" he shouted.

My brothers dug their emaciated hands deep into the white man's arms and each tried to drag him toward their side of the ship. The man screamed over and over again, but my brothers were unrelenting. He would become our meal. His screams would have curdled the blood of ordinary beings.

Suddenly, each of his arms was torn out of their sockets. While my brothers quickly took each arm and drank from them like a gourd, the hysterical white man flailed his torso about as his blood sprayed over us. Some landed in my mouth and slid down my throat easily.

I came back to life and knew that I could defeat my captors.

"Don't let him waste any more of that blood!" Babarinde shouted. "You! Pass those arms back! Give some to your brothers. And use your strength to break these chains! Oya sent us this meal. The rest is up to us!"

The two Razadi passed the pale and bloodied arms behind them and obeyed Babarinde's order to try to break through the chains. Each of them chanted and pulled as hard as they could. They'd never be able to break the chains, but perhaps they could pull the chains from out of the iron loops built into the ship.

They pulled. The wood began to creak against their efforts.

They struggled. The creaking got louder as the wood buckled.

They prayed. As the wood began to splinter, we screamed with excitement, drowning out the sound of the wood disintegrating into kindling.

Success!

"We did it!"

"We are free!"

"We're not free yet," Babarinde said. "Help us! Break these chains. And give me that white man's body!"

Immediately, one man hoisted the now unconscious white man on his shoulders, even as blood continued to ooze out of him. The other quickly broke through the chains of more Razadi.

The white man had little life left in his body.

"We normally don't torture people before we feed on them," Babarinde said to the white man. "Nor do we eat to kill. But what you swine have done to my people deserves no mercy whatsoever. I drink you to hell, white man."

Babarinde buried his fangs into the white man's neck and drank as much as he could. More freed Razadi bit other portions of the man's body and drank as much as they could. I was passed the man's arm and sucked the open portion that had once been his shoulder. I was growing stronger by the minute.

The raging storm continued, and though we weren't nearly as strong as we had been when we went in, we knew we would not lose this battle.

"My brothers!" Babarinde yelled out. "We go up! And eat every pale faced pig that you see!"

Enraptured by the emotion of our impending freedom, we leaped straight up through the hole in the ceiling of our prison like a swarm of bees leaving a hive.

Lightning lit the sky in terrible fireworks, the likes of which we had never seen. The handful of white men on the deck of the ship gazed upon us in horror as the ship tossed back and forth. There were less than a dozen men on the ship; hardly enough to provide a true feast, but they'd have to do. Eşusanya, Ogundiya, Aborişade, and I reassembled on the deck and grabbed the nearest white man we could find. He screamed and Ogundiya snapped his neck, killing him instantly.

"Drink up," Aborişade ordered. We each found an artery and inserted our already elongated canines. The chaos on the deck around us subsided as the white men were overpowered, too fast even for them to pick up their guns, to try to do to us what they did to our brothers on the continent.

I stood up from my meal and made room for one of my fellow brothers who had not yet eaten. The lightning still lit the night sky an eerie electric blue. I turned around in a complete circle and saw nothing but ocean around me. Land could have been a million miles away for all I knew.

In the distance, I saw our sister ship. Something was wrong.

"Babarinde!" I shouted. I pointed toward our sister ship in horror. He hurried toward me and then looked out at the other ship. Each man stopped and joined us on the side of the ship.

"No. No. No." Babarinde fell to his knees.

La Tête was sinking into the ocean like a child's toy. The wind whipping around us subsided to an eerie calm and the lightning bolts faded away. Our ship stopped rocking and we all fell silent as *La Tête* disappeared into the sea.

Not a single soul jumped off to swim toward us. No rescue boat or canoe emerged from the darkness. Our brothers and their captors were all dead. We were alone.

Babarinde, for the first and only time in my life, broke down in uncontrollable sobs. Many of us did.

But I did not. I comforted Baba and all of my other brothers who were in shock. Then I immediately began to assess the crew's quarters, the galley, and the cargo holds aside from our own. Two of our scrolls and a cask of our gold were here. We had four scrolls in total, and I knew we'd lost one to theft and the other to the ocean. Two were better than none, but it was devastating to know our knowledge was lost.

There was not enough room for all of us in the cabins. We'd have to take turns sleeping, a day shift and a night shift, until we reached our destination. But we would be comfortable. And we would remain full from the blood of our captors for a while.

The sea was calm. My head spun from the stress, from the shock, and from the blood intoxication I felt. But I had to carry on.

"Baba," I said. "Baba, get up."

I pulled him up by his arm. His face was still wet with tears. His chest heaved with sobs.

"Come. Rest."

He leaned on me and I carried him to the captain's quarters. He lay down on the slim bed and was asleep in no time.

I emerged from the quarters and saw dozens of my brothers still weeping on the deck of the ship. I gestured to Ogundiya, Eşusanya, and Aborişade. They came to me.

"There aren't enough places for everyone to sleep, so we'll have to double up. Eşusanya, divide the group in half. Take the ones who need rest down below. Leave Babarinde's quarters be, but double everyone else up. Two to a bed. Put blankets on the floors. Whatever will get everyone comfortable. Aborişade, give everyone else something to do. Shutter the hatch down to the slave holding cell. I don't want to see or smell that pit ever again. Figure out how those weapons work. Search the ship for other useful things. And Ogundiya, stay with me, here by the wheel. We'll figure out how to steer this ship until we find land."

I was the youngest of the bunch but somehow I was able to take charge without question. I knew this moment wouldn't happen again anytime soon, but the glory of the position wasn't important to me. We had lost half of our tribe when we were taken from our homeland and now we'd lost half of that half. There wasn't time to cry. Only time to figure out what was next.

My friends had done what I'd asked and Ogundiya and I figured out how to work the ship. The Orishas were with us for the next few days with calm, strong winds in our sails and placid waters beneath us. Within days, *La Coeur* reached land, an island we eventually learned was called Dominica. We weren't sure what we'd see once we disembarked from the ship, but with our weapons in our hands, we knew we'd never be enslaved again.

Dominique Bellanger of Dominica

The black sand beach and green mountains lining the Dominican coast looked menacing in the first rays of the morning sun. I leaned over edge of the ship and strained my eyes to see through the fog.

"We should drop the anchor," I suggested to Babarinde. He nodded.

"Drop the anchor!" I called out. My brothers did so and the ship lurched and then steadied itself as it rocked in the water. I continued staring off into the mountains as the morning heat burned away the fog.

Soon, I saw people descending the mountain. They were brown people, like us, with dark, shiny hair. About a dozen of them carefully came down the hills and assembled on the beach. They stood in a silent formation and waited for us. Several had weapons.

"What do we do?" I asked.

"You, me, and Aborişade. We take the rowboat to the shore. And we talk to them as best we can. We'll bring the white men's weapons, but we will do them no harm as long as they mean us no harm."

I nodded and asked Sangodare to prepare the boat.

"Dagunro?" Babarinde beckoned to the lean brother near him.

"Yes, Baba?" he answered.

"If anything happens to us...destroy the scrolls."

"I will, Baba."

The boat was lowered into the water, and, with a rope, I climbed down first with a gun across my back. Aborişade came next, also with a gun, and Babarinde came last, unarmed.

"No weapon?" I asked him. "Not even a knife?"

"No," he said with finality.

We rowed the boat through the blue waters and made it to the shore. The brown men helped us out of our boat and pulled it to the safety of the beach. They rejoined the other men, forming an inverted V with their leader at the apex.

Aborişade and I raised our weapons, but Babarinde told us to stand down. We had been through too much to let more strangers violate us, and I wasn't eager to let Babarinde walk into a trap.

But these men were different. As I glared into their eyes, all I saw was concern for us. Compassion. A willingness to talk.

These men were not evil.

Babarinde approached the leader, an older man who wore a loincloth, like the men guarding him. The morning wind whipped around us. Babarinde had both hands extended, to show the brown men he was approaching in peace.

"We are Razadi," Babarinde said in our native tongue. "We come in peace."

"Razadi?" the leader repeated. Babarinde nodded. He pointed to his heart and repeated "Razadi." He walked back to Aborişade and me and once again repeated "Razadi." He nodded and again put his hands out in peace.

The brown man nodded.

"Razadi," he said softly. He then made a fist, thumped his chest and said "Kalinago."

Babarinde nodded.

"Kalinago," the man repeated, outstretching his arms as if to include his warriors in the word.

"Kalinago," Babarinde repeated.

The man walked toward Babarinde and pointed to his chest, rapidly speaking in his own language.

"I don't understand," Baba said in the language of the Razadi. "Please slow down, I can learn."

The leader shook his head vigorously and grabbed Babarinde by the shoulders. They stared at one another and focused.

"Babarinde, show him. Show him like our people do."

Babarinde nodded and took the leader by his shoulders and leaned in, touching his forehead with his own. As Babarinde transferred his memories and emotions to the leader of this tribe, I could see them both tense their muscles with the strain of this great emotion. From my vantage point, I could see a single tear fall from the tribe leader's eye.

Moments later, Babarinde released the leader, who then took several steps backward.

The ocean roared all around us. The call of birds was thick in the air. We stood still as life around us continued.

Finally, the leader nodded. He pointed to the ship, then pointed to the palm of his hand and nodded.

Babarinde shook his head and pointed to his own palm, then made a cutting movement against his neck with his hand.

The leader nodded again and then spoke three words.

He pointed at our ship and said "No."

He pointed to behind him and said "Kalinago."

He pointed to the east and said "Razadi."

Babarinde smiled, nodded, and clasped hands with the leader of the Kalinago people. The warriors broke ranks and clasped our hands as well as Babarinde's.

After countless days and nights, and what might as well have been millions of miles, the Razadi were back on peaceful soil with people who meant us no harm.

The Kalinago were a gentle, peaceful people who, like the Razadi, merely wanted everyone else to leave them alone. And we did. After they had seen what we'd been through, they gave us three simple directives: to establish our own village to the east of theirs, deep in the forests; to stay away from their village if at all possible; and to dismantle our ship. The Kalinago wanted desperately to prevent their island from becoming a port, and they somehow felt that even the presence of a ship was a beacon of evil. After some debate, we decided to comply with their wishes. We had no way of discerning our way back to our homeland anyway. The maps of the white men were useless to us, as we didn't know where we were, which way we'd come, or what they had renamed the places they had "discovered" and stolen from natives.

The natives called this place Wai'tu kubuli, and so did we, only calling it Dominica after we left. The terrain was rugged, but lush and beautiful. The Kalinago had left their previous homeland and settled here because the island was so difficult to penetrate.

We used the timber from the ship as the foundation for the village we built in the forest. Dominica was full of trees, and the Kalinago showed us which ones were best for building. They also showed us where to plant our seeds for the best harvest. But after those tips, they left us be.

Months passed, and we were comfortably entrenched in our new lifestyle. We hunted wild boar for their blood. Nothing would ever taste as rich as human blood, but we knew our neighbors could never become our meal. They had been too good to us.

Aside from the boar's blood, we were vegetarians, successfully growing things we'd brought with us from Africa as well as plants and fruits native to the island. I've never eaten as clean as I did on Dominica.

Babarinde found a way to work through his grief and properly emerge as our leader. He was often quiet and withdrawn, but every now and then, a glimpse of the old Babarinde would shine through, whether it was a joke or a song.

We hid our scrolls and other valuables in a cave deep in the forest. There was little use for jewels and gold coins on an island like ours, so we hid them and mostly forgot about them. Our surviving scrolls were of the utmost importance to us, though. When we worshipped together, our scrolls were never far away. It devastated us that one of scrolls was lost to the ocean and the powerful mercenaries back in Africa had stolen another, but we knew they'd be of no use to anyone without the whole story and the oral traditions.

As the months went by, I took up a trade or two. I became adept at fishing, and even though we didn't typically eat the blood of the fish, we were committed to making goodwill offerings to our neighbors. They would smile politely, take the offering, and then close the gates of their village, leaving us to walk back to our own village.

We had a lot of time to work, to think, and to pray. We already knew each other well as family, but during this period, many of us became friends. And when the nights were long and lonely, some of us became more than friends. Others remained celibate.

When I wasn't fishing, I also worked as a carpenter alongside a brother of ours named Ariori. He towered over me by about seven inches. His hair had grown wild and wooly over the past few months. He refused to wear it in braids or dreadlocks as many of us had done. His shoulders were broad and his arms and back were muscular. His legs were lean.

After our carpentry was done for the day, Ariori and I would go down to the beach where we first landed, to swim and to walk and play in the black sand. It was one of our favorite places. Our home village was days and days away from the coast, so enjoying the beach was still a novelty for us, even though years later we would enjoy the golden and white sand beaches of many other countries.

Ariori and I would disrobe and leave our garments on the rocks near the shoreline. He would follow me out to the water and we'd swim. We had to learn how to swim in what you might call "the old fashioned way." Most of us hadn't learned how back in the old country because the rivers were shallow, and those that weren't were teeming with crocodiles. The waters of Dominica were safe. Babarinde threw us into the water again and again until we learned how to float and how to swim. Some days, we could see the Kalinago watching us from the mountains and laughing.

Ariori had no carnal interest in me. He was one of the brethren who opted to be celibate. As for me, I hadn't yet figured out what I was or who I was interested in. As the youngest of the group and the son of Mama Abeo, the brothers had a kind of respect for me that meant I remained untouched until I decided who I wanted—not the other way around.

We played around in the water for a bit. We took turns diving beneath the surface of the water and exploring the marine life below. We were naturally stronger and more durable than humans, so it was easy for us to hold our breath for six, seven, even eight minutes at a time.

When we came above water, we were startled to see a young white woman walking toward us. We had never seen a white woman before, and hadn't seen a woman at all since we left our village. What was interesting about her was that she was wholly unafraid of us. Making eye contact only piqued the interest in her deep brown eyes.

We were startled into silence. The last time we encountered anyone of her complexion, we were shackled and thrown in the belly of a boat. But she was a woman, and she was alone. She couldn't possibly be dangerous to us, could she?

Ariori and I looked at each other while we floated in the water, then we looked at her.

"*Je m'appelle Dominique*," she said from the shore. "*Je n'ai aucune mauvaise intention*."

We swam to the shore and walked to our clothing on the rocks. The woman stared at us until we arose nude from the water. She then lowered her head and averted her eyes to provide us some privacy.

When we were clothed, we approached her and quizzed her in our own language. Who are you? Where are you from? What do you want? Why are you here? Of course, she didn't understand us and we didn't understand her. We did discover that her name was Dominique Bellanger.

Our first meeting with Dominique was brief. We ran off and prayed she didn't see which way we went. She didn't follow us at first, though we would see her every few days. She remained friendly and harmless. The more time we spent around her, the more I could tell that she and Ariori had an attraction for one another. Ariori showed a quiet, respectful restraint around her, and though she never made overt advances, I could tell by her posture and her avoidance of his gaze that she was intrigued by him.

Wherever she came from, with her long brown tresses and her dirty white gown, she was not interested in returning. Each day we spent with her seemed longer and longer; each evening she was more and more reluctant to leave us.

One day, she finally refused to leave. We tried to send her back to the west, away from our home and away from the Kalinago, but she wouldn't go. She had nothing with her besides the clothes she wore. When we tried to leave her at the beach, she followed. Ariori screamed at her to go, but she just screamed back in her own language, just as feisty and as rebellious as she wanted to be.

Dominique was strong, as we could tell by her ability to climb the craggy mountains behind us. She walked briskly with us through the thick forest. Something was terribly wrong where she came from and we knew it was better for her to come with us than to go back to wherever her home was. Besides, I knew that Ariori was falling for her, and even if I didn't agree with her joining us, I would have been out voted.

Babarinde was furious with us for bringing her to our encampment, and he tried to banish her, but Ariori was rebellious and told us all that he would disappear with her forever into the woods if she were banished. Although Baba hated being manipulated in this way, we knew it would probably be best for her safety and ours if she stayed, at least until she learned our language and could tell us what she was running from.

Over the next few months, Dominique lived with Ariori, first in the hut he shared with several others, then in a hut he built for the both of them. She taught him French; he taught her the Yoruba dialect of our people. They were very much in love and it became apparent that Dominique was with us to stay.

We learned from her that there were others on Dominica, besides us and the Kalinago. There were, indeed, white people living on the other side of the craggy rocks and dangerous terrain. The French were colonizing Dominica, already harvesting acres of lumber to make way for coffee plantations.

Dominique's family owned a trading company that was trying to exploit the island's resources for their own financial gain, but because it just wasn't built for the type of agriculture that supported cotton or tobacco, the family was losing money. Dominique's brother was sent to oversee the endeavor; Dominique was allowed to go along for the adventure and to learn the family business.

As she told us, the Frenchmen were abusing her. She did not say to what extent, but the shame was palpable. She escaped to the beach every day to avoid the Frenchmen that her brother turned a blind eye to. She decided that she would not return when she discovered us.

Not too much time had passed before Dominique became one of us, through and through. She was properly initiated in all of our religious rites. Ariori asked for her hand in marriage shortly thereafter, and she was made a bride of the Razadi.

Ariori never drank from her. He only ever drank from the wild boar we caught. His restraint is legendary, even to this day. Dominique knew exactly who and what we were, but had perfect faith that Ariori would not harm her.

There was one night when the Frenchmen came dangerously close to discovering our village. We knew the day would come when they came for Dominique, but we were prepared. We knew that the beings that had enslaved us were nowhere near and we hoped to never encounter them again. Should we be attacked by any other beings, they would become meals.

And meals they were. A dozen men came looking for a fight and they got one. The weakest of the men was bound to a tree and forced to watch as all eleven of his fellow men were drained to death by scores of Razadi. If the message given to him by witnessing the carnage was not clear enough, Dominique made it plain to him in their language: "I am safe here, but you are not. Leave and don't return. I am with my people."

The surviving Frenchman was sent back to their camp. The next morning, we carried the drained bodies on funeral pallets across the island to the fort that the French were constructing. Dominique spoke to her brother for a final time and again warned the French that the Razadi were undefeatable. Her brother consented and left us alone.

Dominique gave up everything to live among us: her family, her life in France, her immense wealth. I never quite understood why she so readily gave up her lifestyle to be one with ours, but she was still accepted. In time, she would become our matriarch, Mama Dominique, if she wanted.

Months later, a spy from our village visited the French fort only to discover that it had been abandoned. The French had left Dominica, and both the Kilanago and Razadi could now enjoy true peace. Dominique showed no emotion for the abandonment of the island by her kinfolk. She, too, was content with being alone.

Months became years and Ariori and Dominique's love only grew, as did her commitment to our people. She learned the ways of a Razadi healer and was indispensable to us when we became injured.

As would have been the case back in Africa, Dominique and Ariori were unable to conceive a child. It seemed as though whatever issues my people had with reproduction were carried along through our men. Although their love did not waver, it was plain that Dominique was disappointed that their union would produce no heirs.

Early one morning, a few years after we had landed on Dominica, a ship appeared on the horizon, the first one we'd seen coming toward our cove. Dominique immediately recognized the flags flying on the ship as her family crest. She was annoyed to have to send her family back home as soon as they had come, but she made it plain that they must not stay. Babarinde approved a small team to meet the ship down at the beach along with Dominique: Ariori, Eşusanya, Ogundiya, and me.

It took us about half an hour to get down to the beach. By that time, two unarmed white men had already rowed a boat from the ship to the shore and were waiting for us.

Dominique was livid. One of the men greeted her and she slapped him, leaving a red imprint on his face. She immediately cursed him in French, speaking faster and more furiously than I'd ever heard her speak. She pointed in his face and then back at the ship, demanding that he leave. The exchange went on endlessly. Ultimately, the men would not back down.

Finally, Dominique turned to her husband and explained what was happening.

"This man is my brother, the same one who traveled with me to this island years ago. Our parents are on the ship and are insisting to see me."

"Why don't they come off the ship?" Ariori asked.

"They're afraid, so my brother said."

"Do you want to see them?"

"Let's just go and get this over with. I need to make it clear to them that this is my home. Aragbaye, come with us please."

I agreed without hesitation. Eşusanya and Ogundiya stayed behind on the beach while Ariori and I rowed to the ship with Dominique regally looking on. Her brother and his mate stayed behind as collateral under my brothers' watchful eyes.

We rowed hard, hoping to get to the ship quickly and then hurry back. Dominique was ready to sever these ties and move on with the rest of her life and we were eager to be rid of the Frenchmen for good.

We carefully climbed up the rope ladders that the sailors lowered for us. When we reached the top, friendly Frenchmen assisted us over the guardrail.

With muskets.

"We should have brought our guns," Ariori hissed at me.

"We ran out of bullets hunting boar years ago," I said.

About a dozen Frenchmen had their rifles raised at the three of us in silence. Ariori and I sized them up as we backed against the guardrail of the ship, protecting Dominique with our bodies.

"Put me in front, they won't shoot me," she demanded.

"No," Ariori said. "Stay back."

"Where is my father?" she asked the men in French.

"Waiting for you in Nice," the leader of the dozen white men said.

"It's a trap!" Ariori shouted. We bared our fangs and instituted the offensive we hoped we'd never have to use. For as long as we'd been on the island, we knew that guns were out there and we could not fight them unless we had our own. And because we were fundamentally peaceful, we didn't seek out new guns to own. All we wanted was a quiet existence. But we knew a day could come when men with guns would come back for us.

I charged the men, aiming at their heels, rather than their hearts. We'd need to topple them, then kill them, then drink them. We could not aim for their heads or their hearts because they would protect those. We had to rely on our most animalistic instincts and tear at their tendons and joints, disabling them.

In the twinkling of an eye, I took down three of the men. Blood sprayed from their gashes I made in their shins and calves. Ariori did the same, tearing into two of the men.

In the end, only two shots were fired: one into Ariori's head and one into my shoulder. Dominique screamed as Ariori fell onto the deck of the ship. I continued on, trying to move to Dominique to protect her, but it was too late. The bullet tore into my shoulder from behind and out the front, exiting my body and sailing off into the air above the ocean.

I stumbled toward the railing, looking at Dominique one last time before the remaining Frenchmen carted her off below deck. Her screams were blood-curdling; they were the wails of grief.

I toppled over the edge of the ship and plummeted into the ocean. My left arm was practically useless—it was numb, weak, and uncooperative. My right arm and my legs kept me afloat.

Within seconds, Ariori's body was thrown over the edge, landing ten feet away from me. I swam to him, summoning every nerve I had in my body to make my left arm work again.

I screamed, pushing my body to the limits, and wrapped my left arm around my brother. The bullet wound was over his right eyebrow and it was open down to the white meat. He wasn't moving, but I could feel his heart still beating.

I wanted to save Dominique, but I had few options. The Frenchmen had guns. They shot me and Ariori. I wouldn't be able to save us all.

I swam to the rowboat and threw Ariori in. I took the oars and rowed away from the ship furiously. The Frenchmen aimed their weapons at me but did not shoot any more.

I left Dominique. Her people had come for her and had probably killed Ariori. My choice was clear. If Ariori survived, he'd be furious with me. If he died, at least we could give him a proper burial.

The ship raised anchor and began to sail away. As I approached the white men still on the beach with my brothers, I saw the horror creep over their faces.

"What happened?" Eşusanya asked.

"They ambushed us. Stole Dominique and shot Ariori!"

Eşusanya and Ogundiya bared their fangs.

"No!" Dominique's brother screamed.

Eşusanya and Ogundiya buried their faces in the necks of the abandoned Frenchmen while I pulled Ariori onto the sand and tried to revive him. I tried to breathe air into his lungs. I pounded his chest. I tried to give him blood from the Frenchmen's corpses. I tried feeding him my own blood. Nothing worked. He was dead.

Ogundiya stumbled, blood-drunk and anguished, over to his body while I wept over it. He touched my shoulder and sat next to me in silence. We said nothing for an hour as the sun climbed higher in the sky.

"She never belonged with us," Eşusanya said finally, while sitting in the sand a ways off from us, the blood intoxication finally wearing off.

"What?" I asked. "Dominique was the love of Ariori's life."

"A Razadi could never truly love a white devil."

"Watch your mouth," I said. "And have some respect for the dead."

"Fuck Dominique. We let Dominique into our village, into our way of life, and it only led to death. Another Razadi with a bullet in his brain, just like in Africa. These people are evil and ruthless. I will never trust one. If I come across more, I can assure you I will be the last thing they see."

"Dominique wasn't like them," I said.

"Yes she was! They're all alike! They happily bring death wherever they go. They steal land that doesn't belong to them. They create technology only to conquer and destroy."

I couldn't argue with him. All I knew was that Dominique really was different. She was one of us. And now she was gone and the love of her life was dead.

Another hour passed.

"We need to go back," Ogundiya said.

"Help me carry him," I asked. My arm was still sore, but healing.

"No," Ogundiya said. "You rest. I've got him."

Ogundiya bent down and scooped up Ariori's body in his arms. Immediately, his eyes opened wide in shock.

"What's wrong?" I asked.

"He's warm," Ogundiya whispered. "And breathing."

"What?" I exclaimed.

"Put him back down," Eşusanya ordered. We knelt over the now-breathing Ariori in the sand.

"Ariori!" I said firmly. "Wake up. Open your eyes."

Ariori's eyes fluttered and then clamped shut again as though he was concentrating.

"Fight, dammit!" Eşusanya shouted.

I stared at Ariori's head wound. The flesh around it began to contract and the blood evaporated. Before my very eyes, Ariori's body expelled the bullet from his head and healed itself, leaving only a slight dimple behind.

He inhaled sharply.

"You're alive!" I exclaimed.

"Where's Dominique?" he asked, his voice raspy.

"How are you feeling?" Eşusanya asked.

"I'm fine. Where is my wife?"

We fell silent as Ariori scrambled to stand up.

"Where is Dominique? Where is she? *Where is my wife?*"

To this day, I have never seen anguish and despair in the eyes of a man like I saw in Ariori's, on the day we told him he'd never see the love of his life again.

"So...he really never saw her again?" Justin asked.

"No, he didn't. The ship had been long gone by the time he woke up. We had no good way to follow them."

"That's really, really sad," Justin said.

"Ariori was devastated. He didn't even speak for weeks after that."

"What did she look like?" Justin asked.

"I told you, she was-"

"Show me."

Justin sat upright and closed his eyes. I clasped his face and brought our foreheads together. Into his mind, I projected the beautiful face of Dominique. Her face was an oval framed by a cascade of curls as brown as freshly turned earth. Her deep brown eyes smiled even when her mouth was curled into a tight frown. Her thin eyebrows curved up in an arch. Her white skin was tanned to a golden brown by the Caribbean sun.

She reached her long fingers through the fog and touched my face.

"*Je t'aime*," she whispered before she disappeared.

"Whoa," Justin said. "That was vivid."

"That was Dominique," I said.

"So tell me…how did she end up in America to found Iota Theta Beta? How did she create this ceremony that makes her sisters beholden to the Razadi?"

I kissed Justin on the cheek.

"Another story for another day, *mon chéri*. Rest up. You'll need it."

Justin rested his head on his pillow but never closed his eyes. I began to leave.

"Wait!" he said, sitting upright once more.

"Yes?" I said.

"Ariori survived the shooting…a bullet to the head. That means… you know what that means, right? The Razadi who got shot in Africa might still be alive!"

I smiled and nodded.

"They could be, indeed…if they had the time to heal. But we'll never know. Those days are long gone."

Justin nodded, rested his head again, and closed his eyes. As I walked away, I shed a tear for the memory of Dominique Bellanger and the years I'd spent with her, loving her as my sister. And I shed a tear for the dozen Africans that the white men had probably killed with their bullets on the coast of Africa. I had far less hope than Justin that they could still be alive.

TODAY, YOU LEARN HOW TO FIGHT.

"Come with me," Victor said as we entered Justin's room a few days later.

"I'm tired," Justin said. "When do I get to go back to work? It's been too long."

"You're always tired," Victor taunted. "You want to know why? Because you're fat and lazy."

"Fuck you."

"No. Fuck *you.*"

Victor grabbed the edge of the mattress and flipped it upside down, dumping Justin to the floor.

"What the fuck is wrong with you?" Justin asked. Victor leaped over the bed frame and landed at Justin's side.

"No work for you. Today, you learn how to fight!" Victor beamed.

Then he backhanded the shit out of Justin.

"What the fuck, man! Dante, are you just gonna stand there?"

"Yes," I said. Victor slapped Justin again. His brown face was turning red.

"Dude! Stop! Dante!"

"Fight back," I said calmly.

"I can't beat him," Justin said as he tried to protect his face.

"Stand up and fight back!" I barked.

Justin stood up in the corner while Victor got in the defensive stance. He tried to charge through Victor, but Victor moved to the left and Justin careened into the floor.

I couldn't help but to laugh.

"You laughing at me now?" Justin asked.

"Well, you gotta admit it was kinda funny."

"Fuck you," Justin said. As he tried to walk away, Victor bent his arm backwards. Justin yelped.

"Fight back!" Victor said, smashing Justin's face into the door.

Justin groaned.

"Stop whining!" Victor yelled, pushing Justin with such force that he flew out of the room and tumbled all the way down the stairs.

At the bottom of the stairs lay Justin's broken body. His arm was clearly out of socket and his knee was bent the wrong way. His head was face down in the shag carpet.

"Ouch," said Victor.

"Justin?" I called.

"Yes," he responded.

"Get up."

"I can't."

"Get up right now!" I shouted.

Slowly, he slid his thigh across the carpet. He lifted his leg up and popped it leg back into a straight line. He bent it a few times to make sure it worked and then he stood up. As he did, he popped his arm back into its socket.

There was terrible rug burn on his face, but even as he looked in the hallway mirror, it healed on its own.

"Wow," he said. I smiled.

Victor launched himself at Justin again. This time, Justin was ready for him, socking Victor one good time in the jaw and knocking him off balance.

"Good one!" Victor said, while caressing his jaw. Justin came at him harder, hitting him in the chest and arms, faster and faster each time until his fists were a blur. He was getting stronger every day, every moment.

"See…that Martin Luther King, peaceful hippie shit ain't gonna work when those vampires are trying to attack you again," Victor said, getting in a few choice punches where he could, pushing Justin back into the open space of the living room.

"You leave MLK's name out your mouth, bitch," Justin retorted, kicking Victor in the gut, forcing him backward.

"Come on…that all you got?"

"Oh, I got some more, bitch. Ole uppity blood sucker."

"Uppity?"

"Mmm-hmm. Ole pale face hyena."

"Hyena?" Victor said angrily. "I got your hyena!"

Victor did a flip from a standing position and kicked Justin in the chest with both feet. Both of them crashed to the floor.

"Oh, so motherfuckers want to do flips now!" Justin said from the floor. He scrambled up, prepared to continue the fight.

"Okay, that's enough for now. I said that's enough," I said, standing between them as they tried to get at each other.

"Let me at him," Justin said while Victor smirked.

"You'll get your chance," I said. "Your training will be long and complicated and bloody. But yes, you will learn how to fight just like we do. No ordinary human will ever be able to stop you."

Victor sneered and walked away.

"When I'm gonna fight you?" Justin asked me.

"I'm not going to fight you," I said.

"Yeah, you are," Justin said. "And on that day, I'ma fuck you up."

I laughed.

"We'll see about that."

A Late Night Snack

We trained with Justin for as much as twelve hours a day over the next few days. As it turned out, Justin really was a lover, not a fighter, so he came to the table with even less knowledge of how to fight than the average man might.

He was in terrible shape, but his Razadi blood as well as our vegetarian diet made him stronger and leaner. He spent hours at the recreation center lifting, took a break for lunch, then spent more hours at a top of the line boxing gym. He built muscles he didn't know he had.

I was going to miss the old Justin with the soft chest I could rest my head in, the bear-like arms that would embrace me, and the thick thighs and ass that crashed into my body when we were intimate. But I knew that the old Justin was human, with human habits and sensibilities. The new Justin was emerging as the old Justin fell away with the fat and sweat.

He still called his mom regularly to convince her he was doing okay. He also called his coworkers and stuck with the flu story. They knew not to question it.

After a long evening at the boxing gym, Justin approached me earnestly.

"I'd like to shower and sleep at my place tonight," he said.

"I don't know about that, Justin. We gotta protect you."

"You can come with me. I just really want to sleep between my own sheets tonight, you feel me?"

"Okay," I said. "We can do that."

We went back to Kennedy Street, a place I hadn't seen in weeks, and walked up several flights of stairs to Justin's apartment. I sat on the edge of the futon in his living room while he went back into his room to disrobe and shower.

I was tired. I had never successfully made anyone a daywalker before, but it was an awful lot of work. The cooking, the fighting, the planning—it was all so much. Whenever Justin was awake, I had to be awake. And when he was asleep, I had to be awake, planning for the next day.

I lay back and soon fell asleep on the couch while Justin showered.

I was awakened by loud pounding on Justin's door. I sat up and looked around, still groggy, and walked toward the door. I looked through the peephole, saw Victor, and opened the door.

"Where is he?" Victor demanded, pushing past me.

"He's taking a shower," I said.

"I told your dumb ass not to let him leave the house!" Victor yelled at me.

"Don't call me a dumb ass!" I shouted back. "He wanted to sleep in his own bed for a change. I thought he deserved that."

"Deserved that? He's one of us now, Dante! He *can't* leave. We stick together."

"Just like we stuck together when you left? When John Irons left? When Orlando left? Are you kidding me?"

"That's not the same."

"But you couldn't wait to leave, could you? *You* made the cell weak. *You* left me here by myself. Razadi stick together when it's convenient."

"Nightwalkers leave us alone when we don't seem threatening. You were always safe."

"Fuck you, Victor."

"Hey, stop it. I'm not going to apologize over and over again for doing what Babarinde allowed us to do."

"You haven't apologized at all."

"Listen. Aren't you even worried about where Justin is right now?"

I paused. I listened. No water running. No movement from the back of the apartment. I ran to Justin's room. He was gone.

"Fuck!" I shouted.

"Didn't Babarinde say you were supposed to keep him safe?"

"Shit." I nodded, in disbelief that I had somehow lost him.

"Then fucking focus so we can find him. Close your eyes."

I shut my eyes tight, seeing fireworks beneath my dark lids. I stood still. I smelled.

"He only left like five minutes ago, maybe ten."

"Dig deeper," Victor insisted. I inhaled and tried to visualize Dante.

"A street. Dark. Streetlight is busted above. He's…he sees a family. Aw, fuck, we gotta go."

We ran out of Justin's apartment, following his scent down Kennedy Street. He foolishly hadn't even taken the alleys, but he didn't know better. I knew he was looking for a meal.

At Fifth and Kennedy, we ran to the right for another block. We paused in front of one of the quiet homes and stared.

"This idiot is in their house!" Victor hissed.

"Wait…is this a crack house?" I asked.

"Hard to say," he responded.

I looked to both sides of me then sprinted to the back door of the house. Justin had left it wide open. Of course. Victor appeared next to me.

"He's in here," I said. "Let's go."

The house was pitch black except for the dim light from the street spilling in. We entered through the barren kitchen and felt our way upstairs. We could smell Justin's trail leading up there.

"Sweet Olódùmarè, please give him restraint," I prayed silently.

In the master bedroom slept a white man and a black woman, half naked, looking like life had chewed them up and spit them out. They were oblivious to our presence.

"Crackheads," Victor said.

"I've seen them around before when I visited Justin on his block. The man…he's always unfriendly. Never a smile. Surly. The woman has her good days and bad days. But when she's with her baby, she's fine."

Victor turned to me.

"There's a baby?" he asked.

"Shit."

We hurried to the next room, where we saw Justin crouched in the dirty corner, holding the cooing, sandy colored infant. The baby instinctively wrapped his little hand around Justin's finger. Justin's fangs were elongated. His nose was millimeters away from the child's scalp and he inhaled. Not at all startled by our presence, he glanced up at me and spoke.

"Hi."

"Hi," I replied. "What are you doing here?"

"Nothin'," he said, caressing the baby's cheek with his nose.

"You can't drink the baby, Justin."

"Yes, he can," Victor said with a laugh. "Babies are a 'sometimes treat.'"

"Victor! No, Justin."

"He smells so good…"

We heard shuffling coming from the other room. Footsteps came toward us, slowly but intently. The white dude who lived in the house entered the room and turned on the light. Roaches scrambled across the floor and up the dry, chalky walls covered in ancient wallpaper that practically fell off if you stared at it too hard.

The man was pale as a zombie and out of shape, that sort of skinny-fat that white dudes in America seemed to get into in the last century or so. He had dark circles under his eyes; patches of his brown hair were missing. He barely lifted his head up or opened his eyes when he talked.

"Oh," he said nonchalantly. "How y'all doin'?"

"We good," Victor said. "'Sup with you?"

"Chillin'," he said. He opened his eyes slightly to observe Justin in the corner, still holding the baby.

"That's my son," the man said.

"Yeah, we know," I said. "We're just leaving man."

"You want him?" the man asked.

"Yes!" Justin answered excitedly.

"No," I said.

"I mean, three stacks and you can have him."

The already quiet room seemed to drop ten decibels below the threshold of silence. Even the roaches on the walls seemed to be still in horror.

"What?" I asked.

"You can have him for three thousand." He scratched his stomach.

"Are you trying to sell us your son?" Victor asked. His caramel skin seemed to glow red under his collar and he inched toward the man.

"Aight, two thou. But that's as low as I can go," he said matter-of-factly.

Victor walked slowly toward the man. He inhaled deeply. He then walked over to Justin.

"Give me the boy, please," he asked, reaching for the baby. Justin hesitated for a second, and then handed over the child. Victor then smelled the baby.

"Are they really related?" I asked. Victor nodded.

"Sicko," he muttered under his breath.

"So how 'bout it?" the man asked. Victor cradled the child against his chest and walked toward me.

"No HIV. Either of them," Victor whispered. I nodded.

"We'll take him," Victor said, handing me the baby.

"How you wanna pay?" he asked.

"Justin will take care of that," Victor said. We hurried into the hallway.

"Justin," Victor called out. Justin looked up hopefully.

"Dinner is served."

Justin smiled, bared his fangs, and walked toward his victim as Victor and I left, closing the door behind us.

"Suck him down to the marrow," Victor instructed through the door. "And don't make a mess."

We took the baby back to the master bedroom where his mother was still sleeping. The man screamed, but I could tell that Justin was muffling him with one hand while his lips clamped around his neck, piercing an artery. I knew it tasted savory and hot in his mouth.

His first kill. He'll love it. He might taste the bitterness of the illegal substances in the man's system and he will remember the difference between that and the blood of a human who lives clean, un-addicted and un-diseased.

Some people deserved to die. Men who would sell their sons to strangers for drug money deserved to die. He would not be missed. His son would be better off without him.

"Your baby's father is gone. He ran off and he's not coming back. You don't know where he is. You're not worried about him. He always runs off. You'll be fine without him. Do you understand?"

She nodded her head.

"Now go to sleep," Victor instructed. "You will wake up and believe everything we said, but you won't remember us."

She lay back down.

"Thank you," she sighed as she nodded off to sleep. Her baby was still awake, gurgling happily, not having a clue that his father was dead in the next room.

"We should check on Justin," Victor said. I nodded.

I laid the baby down next to his mom, with pillows around him so he wouldn't roll of the bed. He looked up at me.

"Be great," I demanded of him. I wasn't sure if I could really hypnotize a baby, but telling one to be great certainly wouldn't hurt him.

We entered the other room and discovered the corpse of the sick addict on the floor. Justin was quietly rocking back and forth, drunk with pints of blood in his system.

"Rock Creek Park?" I asked. Victor nodded.

"Bypass the axe and the garbage bags," he instructed. "If his body is ever found, it's not like anybody will give a damn."

I agreed. I looked down on the fiend's body and knew we'd done the right thing. When Justin sobered up, he'd feel awful about it, but he'd get used to it. We all did after our first kill.

The Gym

I woke Justin up early the next morning and fed him fresh fruit to cleanse him and alleviate his blood hangover. He could barely keep his eyes open. He was largely quiet as the placed pieces of honeydew in his mouth, chewed, and swallowed.

"Did I do...what I think I did?" he asked.

"Yes," I said softly.

"I...killed somebody?"

"Yes. You did."

"Oh my goodness..."

"He was a sick fuck, Justin. He would have sold us his own son."

"That doesn't give me the right to take his life."

"One thing you're going to have to learn is that your morals are going to have to evolve right along with your body. We are advanced beings for a reason. We live in the shadows for a reason. We are older than the laws of this country. Justin...that guy you drained last night was born into this world with nothing, just like you and I were. Born with nothing, but with every opportunity to get things right every day. Every day, he woke up and decided to abuse drugs, abuse his family, and do whatever he needed to do to get his fix. We're not above the law, Justin. We're outside of it. We can fix things that the police can't fix, that social services can't fix."

"I thought I could drink him until I got full. But I couldn't stop."

"Even if you had stopped, we would have finished the job."

"I can't control it."

"Yes, you can. You will learn."

"I was so hungry."

"You will learn to control the hunger. You will learn how to survive."

"I would have killed that baby."

"But you didn't. You are getting stronger every day. Your body. Your mind. Your willpower. You will be great. And that kid will be great, too. You're still learning."

He ate the rest of his meal in silence. He didn't ask me any questions as I told him to get in the van. He didn't say anything on the half-hour drive to Mitchellville in Prince George's County. And he didn't say anything when we met with Salaad at the two-story warehouse in the remote industrial park.

"Justin, this is Salaad. He's a friend of the Razadi."

Salaad cut an impressive figure. He was tall and lean—about six feet, four or five inches—with sandy brown skin and close cut, but curly hair. Justin sized him up and spoke.

"I remember you," he said, gripping Salaad's hand. "You delivered Babarinde's invitation to me. Thank you."

"It's an honor to meet you," he said.

"Is it?" Justin asked. Salaad's smile faded.

"You're Djinn?" Justin continued.

"I see your sense of smell grows stronger every day. Come in," Salaad said. He pushed a heavy door open and we entered the dark warehouse. I hadn't seen the inside of it in years. Salaad flipped a switch and the room was filled with fluorescent light bouncing off the gray walls of the hangar-like facility. Old blue mats lined the entirely of the room, save pathways dividing the space into quarters. There were balance beams, pommel horses, ropes, and structures that looked like jungle gyms.

"Where are we?" Justin asked.

"This is our gym," I said.

"You own it?"

"No, we don't own it. But we know the owners. They're good Djinn."

"I feel like it's hard to trust Djinn," he said, looking at Salaad squarely.

"Sometimes it is. But once you have a good Djinn at your disposal, you've got a friend for life. Salaad is one of the good ones. For real."

"Unless they possess you like that poor kid we met."

"Morlas," Salaad muttered. "He's renegade. I'm not like him. Nobody in my family is like him."

"I'll have to take your word for it," Justin deadpanned.

"Listen, don't worry about that," I said, touching Justin on his shoulder blade. "This gym here? This is your playground now. You're going to learn how to run, how to jump, how to climb. How to do all that superhero shit you only read about in comic books and saw on television. You will work out seven nights a week for at least four hours at a time. You will learn wrestling, capoeira, fencing, a wide array of martial arts, and parkour."

"What's parkour?" he asked. I smiled.

"This is parkour."

I ran to the first quadrant of the room at my top speed and scrambled up the iron holds embedded in the concrete. I leapt from the top of the makeshift climbing wall onto some hanging ropes and swung myself to the first balance beam. On the beam, I forward flipped all the way to the end, launching myself onto some staggered boxes, crisscrossing them like a videogame I once played.

I flipped, jumped, climbed, and swung my way across the entirety of this make-shift obstacle course designed to mimic the very same environment that we live in from day to day. This would prepare Justin for a life in the shadows and on the run if need be. The back alleys, the dark roads—those were our domain, for the safety of our kind.

I finished my run with a flourish: a spinning jump that would have been more suitable for a figure skating event in the Winter Olympics. I landed on both feet, inches from Justin's face.

"Holy shit," he said.

"Let's get started."

You Better Run

Wake up. Eat. Run. Study. Eat. Boxing gym. Eat. Big gym. Eat. Fuck. Sleep. These were Justin's days until we felt he could fend for himself. No more resting, just lessons in our history and our traditions in between training.

"Run!" Victor barked.

"I am running!" Justin hollered.

"Faster!"

We ran through Rock Creek Park in the middle of the day, just like any other joggers.

"Keep running. If I catch you, I'm going to fuck you."

"Don't you mean fuck me up?"

"No. I mean I'm going to put my penis inside you if I catch you."

Justin sped off in a blur, the first time I had seen him do so. He was getting the hang of this transition.

"That's funny as shit," I said.

"What's funny? I fully intend to catch up to him." Victor quickened his pace.

"Excuse me?" I asked, catching up to Victor.

"What, you think I don't have needs?"

"You don't even like dudes…this century."

"It ain't no fun if the homies can't have none."

In a rage, I pushed Victor with all of my might. He flew from the jogging path, over the grass, and into Rock Creek.

Emerging from the water, he smiled.

"After centuries, you still can't take a joke?" he asked.

"Gotcha!" I said, taking off in a blur down the road.

Five miles later, we were in a clearing somewhere in Montgomery County. Justin had slowed to a jog and found a picnic area where he could rest.

"I'm thirsty," he announced.

"The creek is right there," Victor said.

"I ain't drinking that old dirty creek water," Justin said.

"First of all, the water in Rock Creek isn't all that dirty," Victor argued. "And second of all, you drank the blood of a crackhead."

"Good point," Justin admitted. He walked over to the creek, knelt down, cupped his hands, and drank from it. He paused and appeared to gaze at his reflection for a few moments. He returned, refreshed.

"You okay?" I asked.

"Yeah. I just…I thought I saw something in the water."

"A person?" I asked.

He nodded

"Was it a Djinn?" he asked. I shook my head.

"Oshun watches over the waters."

"What's Oshun?"

"'Who,'" Victor corrected. "She's a spirit."

"A ghost?" Justin asked.

"Closer to a goddess," I said.

"Jesus," Justin said, sitting in the grass and stretching in the heat. "Vampires, Djinn, goddesses walking around…this shit is crazy."

"And you killed somebody!" Victor added happily.

"Thanks for reminding me," Justin deadpanned.

"Our religion, our faith… It's old," I explained. "It's multilayered. It's full of history. At the end of the day, we believe in one god. Our god has many names to many people, but we usually call the creator Olódùmarè. From him came many other spirits that rule us. What we believe is what many West Africans believe. We brought these traditions with us just like Haitians and Dominicans and Brazilians. It's not that different. It's just that we…we brought our own flavor."

"When can I go back to work?" he asked.

"Whenever you want. You look healthy."

"I'll go tomorrow."

"But you will still work out every day."

"Okay," he said. He leaned back into the grass and stretched out his arms and legs until he looked like a starfish in the grass. He closed his eyes.

"How did you guys come to leave Dominica and get to America?" he asked.

Victor walked over to Justin and beckoned me to join him. He lay down in the grass opposite Justin, placing his head next to him. I flanked the other side of Justin and let the top of my head graze the top of his.

The sky above was one of those hazy shades of blue that were common in the inner city, nothing at all like the clean royal blue skies of Dominica. I closed my eyes and helped Victor take Justin back to the island.

"When are we?" I heard Justin's voice ask, as I recalled my life in our encampment. We were packing up our belongings from our village, which had grown in area and sophistication, but not in population.

"It's 1804. About 75 years after Dominique got taken from us," I said.

"Shit, that's a long time," Justin said.

"I know. A long time to get over it, which Victor and I did. Ariori, on the other hand, not so much. He spoke little for the first few years. But life goes on."

When we arrived on Dominica, the French were in control. Then came the British. On our corner of the island, it really didn't matter who was in charge. If they were white, they were not trustworthy, so we did not interact with them.

We observed that the whites owned African slaves—what we were meant to be had we not overcome our captors and started our own life. Although we hated the institution of slavery, we still did not interfere. There was much we had to learn about the ways of the white people. They were evil. They were deceptive. And even the good ones—like Dominique—would be somehow eliminated by them.

Years passed. We lived. We created. We harvested. Year after year, our community grew closer and closer. We established good relationships with our native neighbors. And yes, we intermingled with them. As time went by, our men and their women established relationships. They never resulted in children, of course, so we often became the second husbands after they became widows. These were genuine relationships between men and women who loved each other, but they all eventually faded away. We just didn't die.

As the island grew, and more Europeans and their slaves came, it became more and more challenging to protect our corner of the island, but we did it. We knew how to create our own weapons, and when we could, we stole weapons from the white men. Every few years, a different expedition would come "discover" us again and try to invade. Making meals of them was fun. With every failed conquest came new information about their so-called "New World." We learned much about the new country called the United States during that time, and how black people were building it up, literally and figuratively.

The white men only confessed these things to us under duress. But at night, their slaves would sneak off to worship in the ways of their people, which were also the ways of our people. By the bonfire, on the beach, we discovered our enslaved cousins from other African lands and spoke to them in French, in our own mother tongue, and after a while, English, the eventual prevailing language of the island.

We worshipped. The names may have been different, but they were our spirits, our Orishas.

At first, we did not interfere with their lives. The white presence on the island was growing and we knew that influencing the enslaved Africans to revolt would be dangerous for all of us. But by 1804, we knew this was a mistake. Rumblings of a revolt in Haiti had excited us and much talk was transpiring about how to control Dominica and expel the whites once and for all.

We talked to the slaves regularly. They gave us information. Facts. Rumors. Speculation. Haiti was changing. Free blacks were moving to a place called Orleans.

Our people were on the move. We had a chance for new lives, new opportunities beyond the forest. After 75 years, we were restless.

I came upon Babarinde on the beach one evening as a trail of ships sailed by, departing from the island for parts unknown. I sat next to him on the sand. He looked at me, then back at the ships.

"What's on your mind?" I asked.

"Leaving," he answered. I nodded.

"They say there are opportunities in Orleans. Space. Commerce. Everything."

"Free blacks, like us. I don't enjoy living hidden. I really don't."

"I know."

"I want to see more."

"So do I. But we're different."

"We can figure it out. We weren't banished from our homeland to live in hiding. Maybe, just maybe, all of this happened for a higher reason."

"And what reason would that be?" I asked.

"I don't know, exactly. We are to be seeds in the wind, not immobile rocks in the dirt."

And with that, the decision had been made, more or less. The majority of us were restless enough to make the move once more.

Over the next couple of months, we amassed supplies, sneaking into the camps of the white people on the other side of the island with the assistance of our enslaved brethren. We knew the journey would be long and rough, but if we could make it across the Atlantic in the belly of a slave ship, we could certainly traverse the Caribbean Sea on the deck of a galleon.

Babarinde met little resistance from us. We viewed the adventure as a welcome diversion from the mundane nature of our existence to that point. Seventy-five years was far too long to wait. It was time to go.

In the end, only three stayed on Dominica: Ogundadegbe, Orimolade, and Efunboláde. They were the only three still married to native women and they were content to stay with their families. There were no hard feelings, for we knew each Razadi had to follow his heart.

The plan to leave the island was simple: take one of the fishing vessels, load up, and sail off in the night. We were better armed than we had ever been before, after stealing dozens of guns and boxes of bullets over the years from various camps and farms. Our aim was perfect and our reflexes were sharp.

We also learned how to be excellent swimmers over the years. The dozen of us on the advance team were swimming in the night water like twelve brown tadpoles. We scaled the side of the vessel silently, not so much as a splash hitting the surface of the water as we emerged.

I held a blade in between my teeth and a pistol at my side, ready to use either at a moment's notice. We happened upon a white British man at the helm. He was unarmed.

He opened his mouth to scream and Babarinde raised his voice to a loud whisper.

"Stop," he ordered. The portly, gray-haired man froze. We all paused and looked at one another, uncertain of the man's paralysis.

"We are taking control of this vessel," Babarinde said. The man slowly nodded.

"How many are aboard?" Babarinde asked.

"Five," he said.

"Where?"

"Four are below, asleep."

Babarinde nodded toward Eşusanya and me. We went below and tied up the sleeping men so quickly that they didn't know what happened by the time they woke up. I found the ship's maps and brought them to Babarinde on the way back up to the deck.

"What do we do with the men? Dinner?" Eşusanya hoped aloud.

"No…" Babarinde said, musing on his newfound hypnotic power.

"Mama Abeo used to tell us that one day, we would evolve past the need to use our hands. Brothers, it would appear as though that day has come."

"And that's how we left Dominica," I said, breaking the memory chain with Justin and Victor.

"Just like that?" he asked. Victor got up and walked to the picnic shelter.

"Yup. The men on the ship were easily subdued once we hypnotized them all. Didn't have to kill them. And they tasted good, too."

"Wow," Justin said.

"It was a simple, uneventful voyage. We landed in Orleans and used our cunning and our will to establish ourselves a nice plantation. We grew a lot of things that we had on the island and back at home. We even branched into textiles. Yes, we were farmers and fashion mavens, even back then."

Justin laughed.

"But the best part? Free black people. Not everyone was free, but we could walk around among white people and not be afraid that they would put a bullet in us. We had the law on our side. We had the power of hypnosis on our side. And of course, we knew that we could overcome bullets, too. With time and patience."

"Let's go back home," Victor said. He zoomed off.

Justin turned to me.

"Did you have a wife?"

I shook my head vigorously.

"Never had the desire," I said. "I guess I always knew something greater was out there for me. Someone."

"Maybe there is," Justin said. "If you can catch him!"

He zipped away from me. I laughed and chased him back home.

The Uprising

"Welcome back, Justin!"

Cissy ran to me as soon as I got in the door and hugged me tightly.

"It's so good to see you!" she exclaimed.

The entire staff—including the interns—were in the office to welcome me back to the job. I was overwhelmed.

I put my briefcase down on the freshly carpeted floor and looked around.

"It all looks different," I said quietly. Steve nodded vigorously.

"Well, before you got sick, you told us to make the place our own. To do what we needed to do to make this look like a real office. Well… new carpet, new fixtures, fluorescent lights…we got you, boss!"

"And we can afford it," Cissy added.

"Wow," I said. The whole office had a new glow about it that it had never had before.

My director of technology, Quinn Turner, tapped me on the shoulder to get my attention. I had forgotten how handsome this dude was with his curly brown hair, chiseled face, and blue eyes.

"Let me show you your office. And the computer room," he said.

"I'd like that," I said. "We're still having our staff meeting at 9:15, guys. Status reports from everyone."

"The boss is back!" Steve exclaimed. Everyone laughed. I smiled.

Quinn took me upstairs and carried my briefcase for me.

"I can't believe how much got done," I mused.

"Well, Justin, it's been six weeks," he replied.

"Wow…I guess that is a long time, huh? Time just got away from me. I'm glad to be back, though."

Quinn opened the door at the top of the stairs. When Ernie got arrested and the Foundation took over, I opted to keep my old office in the attic rather than move to Ernie's old space. I liked the solitude and I could concentrate better. Quinn's office was just outside of mine, and I could tell that he spared no expense in getting us set up with state of the art machinery. Magdalene was rolling in dough, and I felt no need to be stingy. To be the best, we needed to have the best, from the front lines of the work with our clients all the way to the man who would run our information technology.

"That's a lot of monitors," I said.

"It's exactly to the Foundation's specifications," he said.

"The Foundation?" I repeated.

"Yes, a few weeks after you got sick, I was given instructions on how to set everything up. I was told it was the Foundation standard. I thought you were aware?"

"Oh, well, sure," I lied. "You know me, as long as it works."

Quinn smiled and opened the door to my office. It, too, had been given fresh carpeting. It was a funky, burnt orange color that was soft and thick beneath my hard-soled shoes. They had gotten rid of my old desk and replaced it with a black, extra-large desk fit for an executive. It curved outward, making a built-in conference table for small meetings. They had given me file cabinets to match. Setting off the whole room was a large Syracuse banner against the far wall.

"We didn't want to bother you while you were recuperating, so we took some risks with the orange. We figured if it had to do with Syracuse, you'd like it."

"It's perfect," I said. Quinn smiled.

"Thanks, Quinn. I'll be down in time for the meeting."

"Welcome back," he said.

I had a seat in my band new executive office chair and gave it a spin. I giggled.

I looked down at my slacks. For the first time—probably ever—they were loose around my thighs when I sat. I noticed that morning that I had to pull my belt tighter than I normally did, but seeing just how loose they were, I realized it was time to go shopping.

I played around with the settings on my chair and tilted the seat back. The leather was fresh and smelled divine. I placed my hands behind my head and closed my eyes.

My mind drifted off for a few seconds. Before me stood a tall, honey-complexioned woman in a gray dress, with her hair wrapped in a white turban. Her high cheekbones suggested a joviality that her twisted mouth and fiery eyes betrayed.

She walked toward me, slowly, hands behind her back, then she stopped. She produced the blade she was hiding and came for me.

I opened my eyes, startled—scared, actually—from the dream so vivid that it felt like a memory.

It was already 9:15. I hadn't even turned on my computer yet. I walked downstairs to see the entire staff waiting for me in the conference room, which they had also redesigned. Rather than the plain old conference room with a table straight from the 80s, we now had a sleek and sophisticated marble-topped table, state of the art audio/visual equipment, and framed posters of our various success stories from over the years: clients who beat the odds, photos from homeless walkathons, and even a senior staff photo from our open house.

I smiled, sat at the head of the table, and spoke:

"Let's get started."

As my staff members gave presentations covering the six weeks I'd been out, I found it incredibly hard to concentrate on them. As Cissy spoke, the woman from my dream materialized—knife in hand—and stood menacingly behind her.

I lowered my head and rubbed my eyes, foolishly hoping that the apparition would disappear. Instead, four more figures appeared behind my staff, each dressed in shabby clothing from an era gone by, each with a weapon: a hoe, a machete, a knife, a hammer. The shine of perspiration gave their faces and arms a glow.

I ignored them and allowed the staff to continue. They were oblivious to the visions I was having. As they concluded, I thanked them all for holding down the fort during my illness. I left the conference room in a rush and headed up the stairs.

Steve followed me, cornering me in the copy room on the second floor. All five apparitions appeared behind him, crowding us in the room.

"Justin, did you come back too soon?" Steve asked.

I shook my head.

"It was time," I said. "Been down way too long. Gotta come support my team."

"Yo, man…you lost hella weight."

"I look bad?" I asked, eyeballing the tall, dark man hovering behind Steve with the machete.

"No, actually. I gotta say you look really good. Healthy. Like, did you have the surgery or something?"

"Surgery? Like weight loss surgery?" I laughed.

"Well, did you?" Steve demanded. I laughed harder.

"Naw, man. Just a really bad case of the flu that it took a long time to bounce back from. And I hit the weight room when I could. You know how it is."

"I guess. Just…you know…if you need more time, just let me know. We can hold it down."

"Thanks Steve, but I don't need more time off. Wouldn't want to take away time you could be spending with your boo Chiyoko," I said, taking his hand into mine and pulling him into a hug. The visions I was seeing dissipated as quickly as they had appeared.

"I'll be fine," I reiterated. "I just gotta get re-acclimated. Speaking of which, I'm sure I have a ton of emails to catch up on."

"Aight player, go handle that," Steve said. I slid past him and went back into my office, closing the door behind me.

In my chair sat the first woman I had dreamed up. She stood up and walked toward me, blade in hand.

"Remember!" she shouted.

I bared my fangs at her and she disappeared.

"Jesus!" I said, reaching into my pocket and calling Dante on my phone with a trembling hand.

"Hey handsome, what's up?"

"I'm seeing ghosts," I whispered.

"What?"

"When I got to work today, I started daydreaming about these people I've never seen before. And…and they're dressed like from a hundred years ago. Like, like slaves or something. But I wasn't daydreaming. They were here. They *are* here. They won't go away. Why won't they go away?"

"Justin, relax."

"Don't tell me to relax! Tell me how to get rid of these ghosts!"

"They're not ghosts."

My heart stopped.

"Djinn?"

"No, not Djinn either. They're memories. Was one of them a tall woman with high cheekbones?"

"Yes."

"Rebekah."

"Who?"

"Rebekah Deslondes. Listen, Justin, don't panic. Sit down, relax, and let them visit with you. They are people from our past, from our history. Let them talk to you. I will be there soon."

"Okay," I said. I clicked off the phone and put it on my desk. I walked to my empty chair and sat down timidly. I closed my eyes and exhaled. The woman appeared to me once more.

I tried not to panic.

"Are you Rebekah?" I asked. She nodded.

"Do you mean me any harm?" She said nothing.

"Please…show me what you want me to see." I opened my eyes and found myself surrounded by the slave apparitions once more. They looked over me, and then walked away. Above me was not the ceiling of my office, but the blue sky and blazing sun of another time.

***

I finished my shopping at the Whole Foods in Silver Spring and hurried back across town to get to Justin. The passenger seat and floor of the van were covered with bags of beans, fruits, vegetables, tofu, herbs, spices, and bottles of water and juices. I was grateful that there were still organic options in this era. It seemed as though forces conspired against black people for generations. It was bad enough that they had to endure the horrors of slavery, but after we left the plantations and the south in general, it seemed like black folks couldn't even get a good grocery store in their neighborhoods, much less clean, organic foods.

I hurried and put the food away in our refrigerator and walked over to Magdalene to help Justin, lunch bag in hand. I knew that the fact that the memories were coming without my prompting was a good thing. I was no geneticist, but it seemed to me that the Razadi blood in him was bonding with his and reproducing. Our memories were in our DNA; our blood was now his blood.

Magdalene had never looked cleaner. Justin's staff took major pride in this place and it showed, from the polished glass doors to the smiling face of the assistant who greeted me by name.

"How can I help you, Mr. Oliver?"

"Please, just Dante," I smiled at her. She smiled back.

"Well how can I help you, Dante?"

"Your boss—Mr. Kena—left his lunch at home *again*. I was wondering if I could take it upstairs to him."

"Oh, I can do that for you-"

"I'd kind of like to surprise him. If that's okay with you, of course."

"Oh, okay, sure! That's really sweet of you!"

I smiled.

"Thanks, Jennifer," I said. The world really was changing. This evolution was more rapid than I had anticipated. Men were able to love other men openly and freely, even in black American communities. This love wasn't without its challenges, and homophobia did still exist, but at least in Justin's workplace his staff could accept who I was—and who I was to *him*—without so much as a second glance.

I carried his lunch bag up the stairs directly to his office, nodding at the technology dude and entering Justin's office without knocking.

As I thought he would be, he was lying on the floor, face up, as straight as a board. His eyes were closed, but they moved beneath the lids as though he were in REM sleep. His lips were moving with an attempt at speech, in a volume too low for me to understand.

I locked the door behind me, put his lunch on the desk, and sat on the floor beside him. He flinched as I caressed his cheek.

"Justin, can you hear me?" I asked. He lips quivered for a few moments and he finally stuttered my true name.

"A…A…Aragbaye. Aragbaye."

"Yes, good. I'm here. Tell me what you see."

"Camp. Camp. Campfire. Razadi. Slaves. Free men. Slaves. Together. Meeting."

I propped Justin up and slid behind him, cradling him in my arms and allowing him to rest comfortably. I whispered into his ear.

"You're okay. You're safe. Take me there. Take me back."

I leaned close to him until our skin touched, and I remembered.

"Bernard, I am asking you. I am begging you. Please, join us. Can't you see that this relationship between our people—between slave and free—is the only way that we can all be free? We can't do it ourselves. We don't have the access to movement that you do. Do I have to remind you of all that the white man has taken from us? Hmm? Do I have to remind you that my family is broken? Shattered and scattered across the south. I have a son who I will never see. I have parents I will never know. You have to help us, Bernard. Peace is not the answer. Not as long as the white man walks this earth. We have to conquer them. We do, you *and* I. We can do this together. Do it for our people, yours and mine, but especially mine.

"We who do not remember our true homes. We who do not know our true names. We who toil in the fields for trash who wouldn't survive here on their own. It is time. It is time for us to take the land which we till. It is time for us to rise up against our masters with our scythes. With our hoes. With our blades. With whatever we have available. It is time for us to take back our own lives, and we can't do it without the help of our brothers. Our brothers who have given us these gifts. The power. The strength. The second chance at life. We need you, brothers. Please. Join us. Join this rebellion. Join this war. Give us that gift."

Babarinde, now known as Bernard, sat in silence at the bonfire behind our plantation house, built with our own hands in the harsh Louisiana heat. We lived in LaPlace, in the Territory of Orleans, on a vast cotton plantation amid dozens of our neighbors' sugar cane fields.

Charles Deslondes, a black overseer from a neighboring sugar plantation, was pleading with Babarinde on that November evening in 1810.

"Why are you silent, Bernard?" demanded the angry woman with the high cheekbones. "Were you not aware of the monster you would create?"

"You are not a monster," he replied.

"Of course I am," she hissed. "I am stronger than my wildest dreams and the nightmares of my slavers."

Babarinde grinned.

"Ah, Bernard, you smile because you know. You know what you've done for me, the gift you bestowed on me. And you know it can't be undone."

"You had a terrible carriage accident, Rebekah. I couldn't let you die."

"What you did was more than save my life," Rebekah said, walking around the fire to get to Babarinde. She knelt at his lap and caressed his wooly hair.

"When that carriage I was driving hit that stone and tossed me clear across the road, I thought I was done. I didn't even see the horse run me over. But what you did for me…coming out of nowhere, like an angel, opening your own vein and giving me your blood to drink, pouring it in my open wounds. You gave me life. You gave me a new life."

Babarinde frowned again and stood up, shaking Rebekah's hands from him.

"I should have let you die."

"Why do you say such hateful things!" she shouted, standing up from the ground.

"Because your people are not ready! Enslaved blacks are scattered and divided. There is no central hierarchy or particular loyalty-"

"Haiti rose!" Charles said. "We could be next! And who knows, maybe your brethren somehow helped there, too."

Babarinde vigorously shook his head.

"No. It wasn't us."

"But you're not sure," Rebekah added.

"Can any of us be sure?" Ariori said. His new name was now Louis. "You all know that we are an old people—a very old people—and we know Africa. And we know the Caribbean. And maybe, just maybe, more of our people came to this hemisphere under force, or trickery, or maybe by choice, in search of us. We don't know. But Rebekah. Charles. All of you. It's just too dangerous. We don't even know how this all works."

"We don't care how it works," Charles said. "We just know that it works. You saved my sister and made her better. Now please...make us better. Let us rise up and be our own nation. Louis, Bernard, Pierre?"

He reached out his hand, gesturing toward me.

"Pierre, I see it in your eyes. You long to go back to your homeland. But you know you can't. Even if you could cross the ocean without incident, you'd surely give the white man a path directly to your ancestral secrets. So you can't come out of the shadows and let the world know what you really are. But what if you could recreate your nation here? What if out of the whiteness of our oppressors could emerge a new nation—a dark nation of brothers and sisters united in the blood?"

I looked down and then quickly up at Babarinde.

"I think I'd like that," I said in response to Charles, while making eye contact with Babarinde.

"Pierre!" Eşusanya said. He chose the name Henri for our lives in Louisiana. "You be quiet. This isn't our fight."

"Isn't it? Baba... Tonton Bernard. It's time."

Babarinde turned to me, his eyebrows raised in astonishment.

"Charles, Rebekah... Please, give us a moment." Bernard requested.

Our five enslaved guests quietly ascended the stairs into our home while the rest of us remained outside.

"Speak, Aragbaye," he said.

"Baba, we have been away from home for a long time. And we know that we can't go back. Not now. We can't risk the safety and sanctity of our families and our land. But I am tired. And I am restless. I thought that Orleans would be a new life for us. But being a free black here isn't much better than what our enslaved brethren experience. And yes, they are our brethren.

"We've lived in Louisiana for six years now. Six long years, and for what? What we saw on Dominica was nothing compared to this. Do you realize that our people are building this country? Yes, our people. African people. I am no longer comfortable sitting in this big house, in the middle of a cotton field, among dozens of plantations, when people who look just like us can't leave.

"And can we leave? Really? Can any of us truly walk about freely without fear?

"Can you, Eşusanya? How about you, Aborişade? No. None of us can. Listen...I'm not saying that we should be irresponsible. But Razadi fight for what's right—always!"

My hands trembled with excitement and I fell on my knees before Babarinde.

"This is our home now. We have to take it. For our people. Give them our gifts."

"Do you all feel the same way?" Babarinde asked slowly.

The brothers broke the circle around the campfire and approached Babarinde. One by one, they fell to their knees with me in solidarity, even Eşusanya.

"I mean, it's time we had us an old-fashioned rebellion, don't you think?" Eşusanya whispered.

"If it's good for Haiti, it's good for Louisiana," Aborişade whispered in my other ear. I smiled.

All of us were on our knees before our leader.

"Charles!" he shouted. "Get out here!"

Charles' boots could be heard clomping on our hard wooden floors as he emerged onto our porch.

"Yes, sir?" he said.

"All these men want to help in your rebellion."

"Will you allow them?" Charles asked. His sister and companions fanned out behind him.

Babarinde extended his hand over us and we all rose. He brought his wrist to his mouth and pricked a vein with his fang. Blood trickled out.

"Come. My people will help."

Charles came to Babarinde, clasped his hand, and brought his wrist to his mouth. He drank Babarinde's blood unrelentingly. Baba's eyes closed in ecstasy.

"Know this, beloved," Babarinde growled. "If this doesn't work, you're on your own. We've lost too much. We won't lose it all."

Charles nodded slowly. I bared my wrist for Rebekah, and she drank as well, gaining more power with each gulp.

Over the next few months, our plot developed. We would march to Orleans and take each plantation along the way, liberating the slaves and recruiting them for our cause.

Each night, new slaves would appear at our doorstep, traveling for miles from nearby plantations to get a sip of Razadi blood. None of us knew how it worked. All we knew was that when they drank our blood, they got powerful. They got bold. In hindsight, they got reckless. And we were all too happy to play into their recklessness, foolishly believing that we could truly overthrow the white man in his own county. Maybe we were still bitter about the kidnapping of Dominique Bellanger, who was long dead by then. Or perhaps we never quite got over being tricked and kidnapped from our own homeland.

The mild winter months came, and it was clear the same transformation that you're going through now, Justin, was happening to these slaves. They lost the taste for meat once they had a taste for blood. When their vision worsened is when I felt most sympathetic for them. What are cataracts in the eyes of slaves but an excuse for more abuse?

Their vision improved and got better than it ever had been. They grew their own fangs, hidden from their masters. They were stronger, leaner, and faster. For those few months, productivity was at an all-time high on their plantations.

We wanted to wait until the spring to launch the revolt. We wanted to be organized. We wanted to know how to take this plot of earth, this land, this Orleans for ours once and always. But Charles was impatient.

On the night of January 8, Charles and Rebekah showed up on our doorstep.

"We have to go, Pierre," Rebekah said.

"What? Why?" I asked.

"Mercredi and Amos…they killed Gilbert Andre."

"Master Manuel Andre's son?"

"Yes! They killed him with an axe! Then they came next door and got Charles and I. We've got to go. The rebellion has begun!"

"No! You're not ready!" I exclaimed.

"Ready or not, here we come," she said, bounding down the stairs of our porch.

"Baba!" I called out. I ran to our staircase and yelled his name again.

"What?" he called back. He emerged from the hallway, bare-chested and sleepy.

"The others…they…they killed Gilbert Andre!"

"Dear God," he said. "Where are they now?"

"Outside our house getting ready to march on Orleans!"

"Shit," he said. He and I ran through the house assembling dozens of our men and arming them with every weapon we had. In minutes, we were on the side of the road.

"This is very stupid, Charles!" he shouted to Charles.

"We're ready, Bernard! A new day has begun!" Charles bared his fangs for the first time.

"No, Charles. You're not ready. There is much to learn. This is not how you win a war."

"We are not stoppable, don't you see that? Hundreds of Africans have been made like you. We thirst for the blood of the white men and we will get it. To Orleans!"

We began our march to the city.

"This is wrong, Babarinde," Aborişade said. He had a look of dread on his face.

"It may be wrong," Baba replied. "But we're here. And we can't let our fellow Africans down. We will fight until we can't fight anymore."

And fight we did, all night long, liberating black people from each plantation along the German Coast, inching closer and closer toward Orleans. Charles and Rebekah Deslondes led the way, their sandy faces twisted in rage and vengeance as they flung wide the gates of the plantations, giving the blacks inside the choice to either join us and fight or stay behind and die with their masters. Whether out of fear, jubilance, or even rudimentary hypnosis, not a single slave stayed behind. Men, women, and children joined our bloody band.

For a day and a half, we marched toward the city, camping at various plantations that had been deserted by the whites at the very rumor of an insurrection. We ended up at the Bernoudy estate, a vast sugar cane plantation with some of the only hills in all of the German Coast. We marched up one hill to survey our destruction and attempt to see Orleans in the distance.

To our surprise, we found that militiamen surrounded us on all sides.

"Can we hypnotize them?" Ariori whispered to Babarinde.

"Can't get close enough to see their eyes," he whispered back.

Mercredi, standing on the front lines next to Charles, began to retch.

"What the hell is wrong with him?" Eşusanya said.

Suddenly, others were retching and vomiting blood all around us.

"What's happening?" Ariori asked.

"Something's wrong," Babarinde said.

People were collapsing all around us. None were Razadi. All were slaves.

A calm, silent whiteness fell over us like a fog. It was as though we had all been bathed in coconut milk. Through the silence, we heard a soft, but powerful voice in our own tongue:

This is not your fight.

"Obatala!" several of us shouted at once, in spiritual ecstasy.

The whiteness around us dissipated and the militia still encroached upon us.

"Run!" Babarinde said to us. We headed toward the swamps behind us as the bullets whizzed by us.

Rebekah laid on the ground beside me, doubled over in pain. She grabbed at my leg.

"Please…help," she pleaded.

I looked at her in pity and tried to speak, but the words were caught in my throat.

I ran, leaving her and the others behind, disappearing into the words, praying that Olódùmarè would somehow protect our stricken friends.

Over the next few days, we were visited several times by angry men, demanding to know our role in the slave uprising. We told them, each time, that we had nothing to do with it; that we didn't know anything about it and that we were just peaceful cotton farmers with a thriving textile business.

The power of hypnosis helped immensely during this period. I am certain that had we been ordinary men, we would have all been lynched. Although we'd lost the battle, at least we would stay alive through the power of suggestion and the stealth of our existence.

A cloud seemed to hang over our house for weeks after the strange events at the Bernoudy estate. Babarinde hushed us each time we tried to bring it up, saying only that it wasn't our fight.

In March, as we worked in the fields, we noticed a lone figure on horseback trotting his way to our plantation. We stopped our work and waited to see if this was yet another white slave owner looking to harass us about his losses in the German Coast uprising.

As the horse came closer toward us, I could tell its rider was black like us. As it came even closer, I could see who it was:

Rebekah Deslondes.

We abandoned our work and came to the front of the house to receive our visitor. We guided the horse to a post and tied it down. I stretched my hand out to help Rebekah off the animal, but she ignored me, instead using one hand to steady herself as she jumped down. Her cloak fell open and to the ground, exposing what remained of her left arm.

I gasped.

"I suppose you've never seen a woman with one arm before," she barked at me. The words got caught in my throat and I remained silent.

"Fetch Babarinde," she snarled.

"I'm here," he said from the porch. I picked up her cloak and handed it back to her.

"I didn't know there were any survivors," he said.

"If you can call this survival," she retorted.

"What happened?" he asked.

She walked toward him with a slight limp.

"You mean, what happened after you all ran away like cowards?"

Babarinde remained silent.

"Why don't you come in, get some water. Rest for a while."

"I don't want or need anything from you, Bernard. Other than the next five minutes of your life."

"I'm listening," he said, folding his arms.

"After you all left us at Bernoudy, the white men slaughtered us. It was bad enough that our bodies began rejecting your blood, your precious gift that was supposed to turn us into beings like you. We were left quivering on the ground with no one to help us but ourselves, and we were too ill to do anything.

"The men? All dead. Mercredi, Amos, everyone. Shot dead. Executed there on the spot. The women? Stripped of their children and forced to watch as they were thrown into the swamp. Some of the infants were kicked around like playthings until they were black and blue.

"They saved the worst for me and Charles. They took me—dozens of times. They beat me relentlessly. They tried to draw and quarter me to finish me off, but the first horse took off too soon. Rather than put me out of my misery, they let me wander off. I was so confused, so much in a fog, that they thought it would be a fun game to predict where I would walk off to and die. They didn't notice that I was slowly but surely healing. I suppose the last of your blood still flowed in me, allowing me to regenerate enough to stop the bleeding. Obviously, I couldn't grow my arm back. Nowadays, I wonder what would happen if the same happened to any of you. Whether I can pluck one of your limbs and have them grow back in complete order, better than before. That ever happen to you? Hmm? Didn't think so.

"Charles wasn't so lucky. In front of all of the surviving women, his hands were chopped off, one right after the other. Then they shot him in his thighs. He couldn't walk. He couldn't even crawl. Then they shot him in the chest. But before he died, they stuffed him in a sack of straw and threw him into the fire.

"Do you know he never even screamed?"

"Rebekah…I'm sorry."

"Shut up."

She shuffled back to her horse and shooed us away as we tried to hoist her up.

"I hope you enjoy your days on this plantation."

"Rebekah, I'm sorry, from the bottom of my heart," Babarinde began. "We've never tried to make one of our own before. We should have had more time to see if it would really work. Time to train you. Time to initiate you into—"

"You left us! You saw that we were ill and outnumbered and you left us! You were more powerful than everyone out there, and you still left! I will never forget this Bernard! Not for as long as I live. You and your people will never be brothers to me. Ever. One day, we'll be free. No thanks to you."

She whipped the side of the horse lightly and he galloped off toward the horizon. We never saw her again and we were forbidden to speak of it.

I cradled Justin in my arms as he gasped and came back to reality. His eyes were wide open, searching for some sort of connection to the modern world.

"It's okay," I said, wiping the sweat from his face with one of the napkins from his lunch bag. "You're back. You're in DC. You're in your own time."

"Why didn't I die?" he breathed in between gasps.

"What?"

"Why didn't I die?! I was supposed to die, but you saved me, just like you tried to save the slaves. They got sick. They died. Why didn't I die?"

"I don't know, Justin."

"The hell you mean you don't know? You mean I still might reject this blood? I could just suddenly keel over and die? Why hasn't that happened to me?"

"Because you're special," I said.

Justin clutched my arm tighter, but turned away from me.

"I don't want to be special."

"Too late," I said. I kissed him on his forehead as he closed his eyes and tried to rest.

THE SECOND COMING

Back at the parkour gym, Justin was sweating once again. It was the end of a long day of running and martial arts. He stood panting before me.

"What do you want me to do?" he asked.

"I want you to run this whole thing in less than 30 seconds," I said.

"The whole thing?" he repeated.

"Yup. I've got a surprise for you if you can do it."

"Aight then," he said. He squared up next to me on a painted line near the door.

"Ready…go!"

He zoomed off to the right, darting between steel barrels like a football star, his calf muscles tightening under his brown skin. His old workout clothes had begun falling off his body, so a steel gray compression top and black compression tights were his new uniform. This was his combine.

He leapt up twelve feet into the air and grabbed onto the bottom of iron chains suspended from the ceiling. He swung to the far wall, where he easily climbed the bricks to the ceiling, then swung from pipe to pipe until he was over a pit of cardboard boxes and rubber blocks. He fell gracefully into the pile and almost immediately popped up, running toward piles of wooden boxes. He hopped on one stack, then a higher one, then the highest, landing on the far edge of the wall with less than ten inches to walk on. He kept his balance—on his tiptoes, no less—and jumped down onto the floor. He ran at full speed at that point, flipping his way over more barrels until he landed inches from my face.

I looked down at my watch.

"Twenty-five seconds," I said.

"Let me do it again, I can get it down to twenty."

"You don't need to," I smiled. "Want your surprise?"

He nodded and smiled.

"Christiana? You can come out now."

A tall, brown girl with thin braids halfway down her back emerged from the shadows behind me.

"Who are you?" Justin asked as he wiped the sweat from his brow with a towel he had nearby.

"This is Christiana. She's a new initiate of Iota Theta Beta. She's in a trance. She won't remember meeting you."

Justin approached the tall, young, dark brown coed. If I didn't know him better, I'd think he was attracted to her.

"I didn't know Iota took black girls," he said.

"They all bleed red," I said. "Now…do you remember the words?"

He nodded vigorously.

"Well…spit 'em."

"I greet thee in the spirit of Dominique Bellanger," he said.

"I welcome thee in the spirit of Dominique Bellanger," Christiana replied.

"I have traveled across burning sands and dangerous savannahs to be here today," Justin continued.

"And I have waited patiently for you."

"I have survived the middle passage and decades of danger."

"Yet I never doubted that you would return to me."

"I am your protector, forever and ever."

"And I offer myself to you, the living legacy of Dominique Bellanger. I present myself to you: one body, one flesh. Iota Theta Beta: in the blood."

Christiana lifted her chin and turned away from Justin, exposing her neck to him. He bared his fangs and buried his face deep into the girl's neck, careful not to spill a drop. His hands gripped her slim waist and she held him in return.

"She's a meal. Not a date."

He moved his hands to her back, in a far less sexy area. I laughed.

"You're doing well," I said as I watched him drink. "You know, I guess I should tell you now…this whole series of events…you know, teaching you how to fight. Getting you in shape. Showing you how we garden. All of that? That's not just to protect you against nightwalkers. And it's not just necessary for your survival. I mean, sure, you need all of this training. But it's leading up to a fight. The fight of your life."

He ignored me as he drank.

"You hear me?" I asked. "I said you're going to have to fight. It's your initiation. You don't just become a Razadi. You have to earn it. You earn it by fighting when you're ready. And you're ready."

Justin suddenly stopped drinking and he pushed Christiana away. His knees buckled and he stumbled to the ground. I went to Christiana and whispered instructions in her ear as I pricked my finger and healed her puncture wounds with my blood.

"Drive back to school. Tell anyone who asks that you were tutoring. Take a nap and forget everything. You understand?"

"Yes," she nodded.

"Fare thee well, my darling sister."

"Fare thee well, my darling brother." She hurried away and I heard her car speed off. I then tended to Justin, whose eyes were fluttering back into his head.

"Justin, what's happening?" I asked, touching his temples with my hands.

"It's hot."

"Where are you? Go deeper."

"New Orleans. The French Quarter. A long time ago. It smells like shit. Horse shit."

"Horse shit?" I laughed. "Welcome home!"

New Orleans, to me, has looked the same for over a hundred years. At least, the good parts do. All that's really changed has been the people. Except for the remaining Razadi who still live there, of course. They are the city's constant.

In 1899, the daywalkers had been living in the Pontalba buildings in the French Quarter for over 30 years. As the city grew, so did its population of free black people, so Babarinde grew more and more comfortable with letting us mingle, in spite of the terrible shame we felt after the failure of the German Coast rebellion.

Baba became more and more reclusive after those events. Even today, I'm not sure that he fully forgave himself for deserting our friends; but what choice did we really have when Obatala himself tells us to leave?

It was Eşusanya who came to Baba with the idea of buying some apartments in the city.

"So what do you say, Baba? We can get some of those buildings the Baroness is renting out. Make a colony like the one we have here, but closer to the action. Get real jobs."

"Tending this land is a real job," he grumbled.

"Yes, yes, I know it is. We pick the cotton, we operate the cotton gin, we spin the thread, we weave the fabric. And we've done it for a century. And we're wealthy because of it! But let's strike out on our own and diversify our strengths and talents."

"Why do you want to go so bad?" Baba asked.

"I'm restless, I can admit that. But I want to learn new things, too."

"Don't you think it's dangerous? Going out there among the world? You can pretend to be just like everyone else for a while, but it's going to become obvious that you're not aging."

"I've got that worked out, too. We create new identities and give them expiration dates—say, fifteen years. Longer if we can find good disguises to make us look aged. And we just live, work, and move on back to the house when it's time."

"It could work," I interjected. "I mean, look at everything that's happened. The Civil War. Slaves are free. Things aren't perfect, but they're better. Resources are out there for us. We just have to grab them."

"Resources? We have everything we need here. Food. Commerce…"

"Baba," Eşusanya said flatly.

"Yes?"

"Baba."

"What?"

"Baba, really?"

"What?"

"We have everything we need, sure, but what about everything else? Music. Art. Sports. Laughter. Living on this plantation is no better than living in the woods of Dominica. Of course, nothing would be better than home. But if we're here, then let's be here fully, living among people. Not just our people. Any people."

"You know what, fine. Do whatever you want, Eşusanya. Just count me out. Organize the men how you want, buy whatever you want. The coffers are open to you. Just leave me out of it—me and anyone else who wants to stay here."

And we did. The first fifteen years went so well that we were loath to come back to the plantation, but we had to in order for the whole thing to work. Babarinde stayed at the plantation and literally everyone else went to the Pontalba apartments for their turn at a real life in the real world.

By 1899, my cohort was back at Pontalba. We happily said farewell to agricultural life and looked forward to ingratiating ourselves in New Orleans' thriving urban culture.

Ariori and I shared a room in one of the Pontalba houses right on Jackson Square. I found work as a blacksmith in the Quarter, while Ariori chose to study medicine at New Orleans University. We were now the brothers Forestier. He was Armand and I was Augustin. Our story was that we were descendants of New Orleans' *gen de couler libre*, or free people of color—a story that was not entirely untrue. The main difference was that our lineage was not from revolution-era Haitian refugees.

Our family—our fellow Razadi brothers—had, by this time, established itself in enough markets that we were able to spend our own money on our own businesses, whether we needed food, clothing, or services. Ariori and I walked to the French Market early one Saturday morning to pick up some groceries from our family's carrel.

"Classes going well?" I asked.

"Absolutely," Ariori said. "I'm learning so much every day."

"And what about this nutrition thing you're working on?"

"It's amazing. We've only hit the tip of the iceberg with what we know about the power of plants. These scientists out here are working with chemicals, trying to make us believe a pill can cure everything. But I'm telling you what I know: we can make a difference with things that grow right in the earth. And now that we have easier access to herbs from the Far East, there's no telling what we'll be able to do next."

"Wow. You know, it amazes me that they have colleges for Negroes. And that you can actually get the same jobs as the white men now. You're going to be a doctor."

Ariori smiled. "It's truly a blessing. We don't have to pick cotton anymore."

"Leave it to Baba, that's all we'd be doing," I laughed.

"Yeah, we'd be…picking…"

Ariori froze in his tracks. We were feet away from a cluster of white women who were inspecting some fresh fruit at one of the stands. That's when he saw her, the beautiful olive-skinned woman he fell in love with.

"Dominique!" he gasped. The young woman in the white blouse and long, slate gray skirt turned to us, pleasant looking but startled. She looked just like Dominique, from the cascade of brown curls to the slender nose and brown eyes. Even her skin seemed tan, as Dominique's skin had looked on the last day we saw her.

"Yes, sir?" she replied, looking up at his tall frame.

"It can't be her," I whispered. "That was a hundred and seventy-five years ago!"

"I'm sorry, Miss," Ariori said, his eyes threatening to well up with tears. "I had you confused for someone else."

"But my name is Dominique," she affirmed. "Do I know you?"

"No. Not at all. We must be going now."

"Sir, please…" Dominique grabbed Ariori's hand. Immediately, her eyes fluttered closed, as did his. I touched Ariori's shoulder and knew at once what was happening.

They remembered.

Scenes of Dominique Bellanger and Ariori's short life together replayed in my head as it did in theirs: secret visits on the beach; stealing away through the forest to visit each other; their wedding; the day she was stolen away from him.

"I know you…" Dominique said finally, as her eyes opened.

"What did you do to her?" Dominique's companion asked. Her round face tightened into a scowl.

"Nothing," Ariori whispered.

"I'm fine, Carmen. I'm fine." A tear rolled down her face and they stared at one another for what seemed like years.

"We should be getting back to school," Carmen said to Dominique.

"Yes, we should," Dominique agreed.

"Can we…walk you to your carriage?" Ariori asked.

"By all means," Dominique agreed. Carmen scowled harder.

We walked the women to the corner of St. Ann and Decatur, where their carriage awaited them on the edge of Jackson Square.

Like a gentleman, Ariori assisted Dominique into the carriage. I tried to assist Carmen, but she snatched her arm away and insisted that she could do it herself.

"Thank you, mister…?" Dominique said.

"Forestier. Mr. Armand Forestier. Soon to be 'Doctor.'" Ariori said. "And this is my brother Augustin."

"Pleased to make your acquaintance," she said.

"Mademoiselle, begging your pardon, but I was wondering if I could see you again someday."

The carriage began to pull away.

"Yes!" she called back.

"Then meet me at Congo Square on Friday afternoon, if you please!"

"I'll be there! Three o'clock!" she called back.

"It's not her," I said. "It can't be."

"She touched me. It's her soul. I know it."

"She can't come to Congo Square. No white woman goes there unaccompanied."

"When has Dominique ever been afraid?"

Word spread like wildfire among the Razadi that Dominique Bellanger was back and it was agreed that we would all descend upon Congo Square at the appointed time. Although Friday afternoon convocations at the square were common for people of color, this time was different. There was energy in the air that had never previously existed in New Orleans.

Babarinde showed up at our doorstep in his horse-drawn buggy about an hour before we were to meet.

"Baba…I didn't think you'd really come," I said.

He nodded.

"I need to see her for myself. Plus, I knew Eşusanya would want this tinker-toy for the occasion."

He motioned behind him to a massive object covered by a black sheet.

"What's that?" I asked.

"Jacques!" he called up to Eşusanya. "Come on down here, boy."

I heard his footsteps behind me. I turned around to see him fully dressed for the cakewalk. He smiled at the sight of Babarinde.

"Is that what I think it is?" he asked.

"Come see," Babarinde said. The horse whinnied and Eşusanya climbed onto the back of the buggy. He removed the sheet and was astonished.

"You brought the piano? All the way from the house?!"

"It's a special occasion," Babarinde smiled. "Now where's Ariori?"

"I'm here," Ariori replied. He emerged from the shadows of the walkway in his finest suit.

"You wearing that down to the cakewalk?" I asked, slipping into my New Orleans drawl like it was second nature. He grinned.

"Ain't we supposed to?"

Eşusanya sat in the back of that buggy and began playing a rag on the piano. Congo Square wouldn't know what to make of such a thing—an actual piano out there with the drums and the brass instruments. Babarinde began driving the buggy up the street, a straight shot toward Congo Square, while Eşusanya played and Ariori and I followed. After about a block, we were joined by men, women, and children who danced along behind us. By the time we reached Congo Square, we had made ourselves a nice little "second line" of a few dozen revelers. We were met at the square by a few dozen more, including our own men interspersed with the other black people there.

I nodded, waved, and shook hands with all of my brothers. I

winked at the pretty ladies who were clustered in a corner of wide-open space, surrounded by trees, waiting to be chosen for a dance. They all had on modest dresses, some black, some white, but all crisp and clean.

The men were all in slacks and crisp white shirts, but Ariori wasn't alone in his desire to wear a suit jacket. This was, after all, a cakewalk, and it was always good to be at your best at such an affair.

Ariori scanned the crowd and saw nothing but the brown faces of the black women he already knew. His disappointment was subtle, but present.

"She'll come," I assured him.

"I know," he beamed.

Eşusanya picked his rag up into high gear and a few more men began improvising a tune on their trumpets. Aborişade and I, along with a few men I didn't know, took the lead in the cakewalk. We high kicked, strutted, and pranced around the square, first alone, then marching over to the cluster of women to pick out one to partner with.

I chose a very young woman who couldn't have been more than 15. Her thick, curly hair was parted down the middle and pulled into two braids. She smiled and curtsied. I bowed, took her hand, and led her through the cakewalk.

She caught on quickly, glancing ever so slightly at me to anticipate my next move. I spun her, then brought her back to me several times over through the dance. She kept smiling the whole time. We kicked high into the air, prancing a complete circuit around the square. By the end of the cakewalk, I held her dainty hand in mine and bowed before the crowd, while she curtsied. I led her back to her friends, who giggled as I dropped her off.

I wiped the sweat from my brow and took a break while Ariori got ready for his round. The music kicked up once more and the men went around to the cluster of women to choose a partner.

Ariori was last. He peered deeply into the crowd until he saw the partner he wanted. He pointed and extended his hand through the sea of women, who parted to make way for his intended.

There, at the back of the crowd, was the fairest of them all: Dominique Bellanger.

The black girls gasped in astonishment that a white woman would even appear in Congo Square, much less respond to the beckon of a black man. But respond she did. She stepped forward and curtsied deeply before Ariori while he bowed before her.

Their dance began. Ariori clasped Dominique's hands and began to parade her around the square. Her rhythm was impeccable and her moves were graceful. In spite of their mismatched height, they were the most beautiful pair on the cakewalk, with the highest kicks and deepest backbends we'd seen thus far. All the people on the square were transfixed by the sight of a black man and white woman dancing together like professionals.

The music stopped and everyone cheered. Dominique curtsied low and her curls cascaded from the back of her head to the front. Ariori bowed deeply and they came up at the same time. He clasped her hands again and brought her over to the piano, where many of the rest of us were congregated.

"Who are you, really?" Eşusanya asked. Horn players across the square had taken it upon themselves to keep the party going while everyone outside of the Razadi continued to dance.

"Dominique Rabaut," she said.

"Does the name Bellanger mean anything to you?" Aborişade asked.

"Of course," she said. "That's my family's name on my grandmother's side. My grandmother's maiden name."

"How did you get the name Dominique?" I asked.

"Not that I have to explain anything to any of you, but Dominique has been a name in my family for years, starting with my grandmother's grandmother. She was the first to visit the new world, but she was brought back. Her grandchildren settled in America a hundred years ago. And that's how I got here. Any further questions?"

"She's feisty," Babarinde said.

"And who exactly are all of you? Why are you so familiar to me?" Dominique asked.

"Touch her," Babarinde commanded Ariori. He faced her and inched toward her cautiously.

"May I?" he asked her.

"I shouldn't…but yes."

Ariori wiped his hands on his pants and carefully cupped her cheeks in his hands. Again, her eyes fluttered and she instinctually held on to Ariori.

Eşusanya, Ogundiya, Aborişade, and I each touched a portion of Ariori's bare forearms while the rest of our brothers crowded around us in concentration. In the span of seconds, the entirety of Dominique's life on Dominica was transmitted back to her. Tears streamed down her face.

Ariori released her and stepped back. We lowered our hands and waited.

She opened her eyes.

"*Ariori, mon amour*," she sobbed. She slowly raised her arms to embrace Ariori.

"It's really you," he wept. He ran to her, embraced her, and spun her around. We all rejoiced, cheering and weeping at the same time.

"I'm back," she said in between her tears. "I'm only 19 years old and all I know is America. But somehow, I'm back. I've returned to you."

"I thought I lost you forever," Ariori said.

"I thought I lost you, too. I can't remember everything. I can't remember much at all. But all of my life, I've had these flashes, these dreams of an island and of a Negro man. And I thought it was madness. That I would ever love a black man the way I loved the man in my dream. But it wasn't a dream, it was a memory."

"You were reborn," Ariori said. "God wanted us to be together."

"That's impossible," Eşusanya said. "People can't come back to life. Once they're dead, that's it."

"I know someone who can solve this riddle," Babarinde said. "Dominique, who accompanied you here?"

"I came alone. I attend Sophie Newcombe College. My chaperone Carmen would kill me if she found out I slipped away to Congo Square."

"Then we don't have time to spare. Come with me. Eşusanya, Ogundiya, stay with the piano. Take it back to Pontalba when this is over. Aragbaye and Aborişade, come with us."

"Where are we going?" Aborişade asked.

Just twenty minutes later, we were seated in the parlor of a witch: Marie Laveau III.

Aborişade and I sat on a bench in the far corner of the parlor, suspicious of Marie and her abode. Her hardwood floors were impeccably shined, so much so that we could see our reflections in them. Candles in their holders ringed the room, but none were lit, as the early evening sun still filled the room with reddish light.

Marie Laveau III was a voluptuous and vivacious woman of about 50 years, with her long black tresses hidden by a white head wrap. Gold rings adorned most of her fingers, which she clasped politely on the table in front of her. Babarinde greeted her with a kiss on the lips, surprising all of us.

"Is he courting this woman?" I whispered to Aborişade.

"Who knows? I didn't know he ever left the plantation."

"Are you really Marie Laveau?" Dominique asked.

"Of course I am, child! I am the third Marie Laveau and the reigning Voodoo Queen of New Orleans!"

"Oh," Dominique said.

"Babarinde, what can I help you with today? I know it must be important for you to come to me unannounced and with visitors in tow."

"It is very important," Babarinde explained. "You know my people are...very old. We have seen much over the years. But we've never seen this. Dominique believes—and several of the brethren also believe—that she's been here before. And we've never encountered that before. Not sure if I believe it. But as sure as you and I are sitting here, she looks just like a woman we all knew well many years ago. Many, many years. Years before Dominique was even born."

"I see," Marie said.

"So what I'm asking is, is this girl the reincarnation of the woman we all knew so many years ago?"

"How many years did you say?" Marie teased.

"I didn't say." Babarinde winked.

Marie cackled.

"Link hands," she instructed. "Boys, you as well. Join us."

Aborişade and I rose from the bench and stood at either side of Marie. We linked hands, forming a circle around a wooden bowl of water on the table.

"You know why we're here," she said. "Show us the answers."

This was an interesting approach, I thought. If she was searching for answers, she surely didn't have much reverence.

"I said tell us something! We don't have all damn day!"

The sun disappeared and the room went dark. Wind blew from parts unknown. The table shook.

"Who is there?" Marie asked.

Obatala.

A voice filled all of our minds simultaneously.

"You lie!" Marie said, angered. "Tell me your name!"

The table shook violently once more and the bowl of water overturned.

Eshu.

The table settled once more.

"I humbly greet you, Eshu, trickster of the Orishas and messenger of all that is divine."

What do you want?

"Who is the girl present before us?"

Her body is Dominique Rabaut. Her soul is Dominique Bellanger, wife of Ariori.

Ariori looked at Dominique and they both smiled.

"Why has she been sent back here?"

This is where she belongs.

"What happened to Dominique Bellanger after she was taken from us?" Ariori interrupted.

Be grateful that she has come back to you.

"Yes, yes," Ariori said. "I am."

"Thank you, dear Eshu," Marie concluded.

The sun came out once more and the winds stopped blowing. A bird chirped out on Bourbon Street.

"You have the answers you want. Dominique is the real deal."

"I'm the real deal? But I don't even know who I am anymore, or what this all means," she said.

"Neither do I," Ariori said. "But I know that what I'm feeling now is as real as it was when I lived in Dominica. And I'm never letting you go again."

"You better not," Marie said. "Chances like this don't happen in most people's lifetimes. Make the most of it."

Over the next several weeks, Dominique and Ariori indeed made the most of their relationship. She spent her days in class, studying to become a teacher at Sophie Newcombe College and learning how to be a lady. Her chaperone, Carmen, held close watch over her since the day she had snuck off to Congo Square. However, Dominique outsmarted her by sneaking out late in the evening, under the cover of darkness, after Carmen was fast asleep.

They spent every hour of the evening together, whether dancing, talking, or just sharing stories of the years of their lives so far.

One evening, during a late supper Ariori made from the herbs and vegetables from our plantation, she confided some of her plans with us.

"I've been working with nine other girls at my school," she began. "We want to create a society."

"A society?" Ariori said, as he wiped his mouth with his napkin. "Some sort of religious order?"

"No. Have you ever heard of a fraternity?"

"Yes, I think so," Ariori nodded.

"Well, there are fraternities for women, too. Sometimes they're called sororities. We want to have a way for our girls to talk about topics of the day, safe from the faculty. School is very repressive, actually, and we want to organize better. To serve our campus and each other."

"Sounds silly," Eşusanya said.

"Easy for you to say," Dominique retorted. "All of you are already organized like a fraternity. You have a leader, rules, your own ceremonies and traditions. Why can't we have the same thing?"

"Because you haven't been through what we've been through. Our rituals keep us alive."

"And what's to say the girls in my school don't need the same sort of family? Many of us are far from our homes."

"Don't compare your little girls' club to me and my brothers."

"You don't scare me, Jacques!" Dominique sharply stood up at the table.

"Who are you talking to like that?!" Eşusanya bared his fangs. Without hesitation, Dominique threw her glass of water across the table and drenched Eşusanya. In a rage, he leaped across the table and pushed Dominique up against the wall, squeezing her throat with his hand.

He hissed at her relentlessly, but she showed no fear on her face. After a few tense seconds, they began to giggle.

"It's good to have you back, wench," he said as his fangs retracted.

"It's good to be back, you old bastard," Dominique responded.

She stood before us in the field beyond our house, her face illuminated by the full moon and the torches planted in the ground that formed a circle around all of us. Her hair was crowned with a wreath of white roses. She held hands with Ariori in front of Marie Laveau while we all looked on.

"...may Olódùmarè ever bless this union. Ariori, you may now kiss your bride."

Weeks of courtship had led to this inevitable moment between them. Their love was as strong as it had been all those years ago; even though this was a new person, her spirit was the same. They wanted to be together as soon as possible.

The ceremony had been an amalgam of our own Razadi, Voodoo, and Catholic traditions, representing the beliefs of the couple as well as the place where we now lived.

We were treated to a midnight repast of fruits, salads, and an assortment of baked goods, including a cake and bean pies. We drummed and danced in celebration. Even Eşusanya smiled at the union of our brother to our sister reborn.

Just as I got my turn to dance with the blushing bride, we heard the sound of a horse racing in the distance; it grew louder and louder.

"What's that?" she asked.

Ariori took her side and we turned around, facing the cloaked figure riding directly onto our property.

"What's the meaning of this?" Babarinde asked.

The figure jumped off the resting horse and removed her cloak. It was Carmen, Dominique's chaperone.

"You tell me the meaning, boy!" she shouted at Babarinde.

"Boy?" he laughed.

"Don't laugh at me, boy! Dominique, get on this horse right now!"

"No, Carmen. Go back home," Dominique responded.

"Right now!" Carmen shrieked.

"I am here with my husband, Carmen. Now run along home."

"Husband? No, I won't believe it. I won't believe that you've married a…a…"

"A man," Ariori said. Carmen scowled at him.

"You really did it, didn't you?" Carmen asked. Dominique slowly nodded. Carmen began to sob.

"Please, walk away from this! The law won't even recognize it!"

"Absolutely not! I am staying married, Carmen. Forever."

"How can you throw your life away like this? Where did I go wrong? Don't you know this will break your parents' hearts? And they'll kill me for letting it happen!"

"You don't have to tell them," Dominique said.

Carmen's face immediately turned from anguish to anger.

"Of course I'll tell them. I'll tell your father that you married a Negro if you don't come home right now!"

"Tell him! I don't care, Carmen! This is my life! I'm an adult now and I can do what I want!"

Carmen took a step toward Dominique and drew her hand back as though she was about to slap Dominique. I grabbed her forearm and pulled her toward me.

"I wouldn't do that if I were you, ma'am."

"Get off me!" she yelled. I let her go and she hurried to her horse.

"I am going to tell your father, Dominique! And your mother! You have shamed them! Shamed! Your life will never be the same!"

"Good!" Dominique shouted back.

Carmen hurried off into the night on the horse she rode in on. We stood around in silence.

"Well, what are we all standing here for?" Dominique asked. "Isn't this a party? Let's dance!"

We laughed and began drumming and dancing once more. Dominique was wholly unbothered by the threats of her chaperone, even though, perhaps, she should have been.

Carmen made good on her threats to snitch to Mr. Rabaut, who immediately had his daughter withdrawn from Sophie Newcombe. Soon, Dominique was alone and living with us at Pontalba fulltime, and meeting with the sisters of her society on the weekends. She never broke a sweat and adjusted well to her new routine over the next few weeks.

One day, after the sun had set, we took the buggy downtown to the pharmacy. Although we grew our own herbs based on our family knowledge, the world was discovering pharmaceutical remedies from other places. Ariori was revving up his research and hoped to discover what impact various Chinese herbal supplements would have on an African diet, particularly a Razadi diet. New Orleans University was open to his research, hoping to find the next big name to come out of the school and give it some national notoriety.

"I'll be right back," he said to us, as he hopped out of the buggy, leaving Dominique and I behind. I held onto the reins of our horse and waited patiently while Dominique read a book.

The sound of thunderous hooves soon filled the air as about a dozen horses clomped their way down the street. Horses never traveled that fast in the city. Dominique and I turned around to see the men on horses charging toward us. White hoods obscured their faces.

"Augustin?! What do we do?!" Dominique shrieked.

"Get down!" I shouted, covering her with my body. I glanced

overhead to see a single can of kerosene fly over our heads. A rag was stuffed into the opening and it had already been lit on fire.

The can crashed through the window of the pharmacy, immediately causing an explosion.

"Ariori!" Dominique screamed. Our horse bucked and neighed.

"Damn it!" I shouted, hopping out of the buggy while the men in white rode off down the street. Chaos erupted all around us as the fire quickly spread through the pharmacy. It already billowed out of the shattered glass front and the door.

"We have to go in there!" Dominique screamed.

"You can't, Dominique, stay back!" She tried to push past me, but I stopped her in her tracks.

"I said stay back! I'll run around to the back and—"

Suddenly, another explosion rocked the block and threw us both down to the ground. Glass, bricks, and wood showered down all around us. Dominique was knocked unconscious. Our horse had run down the street without us.

I looked back at the pharmacy. It was already burned down to a shell.

"Ariori?" I whispered. I began to hear nearby church bells ringing, sounding the alarm.

I picked up Dominique and carried her in my arms. I ran as far as I could to get her to safety even as the fire raged on behind me.

We reached Pontalba in minutes. Eşusanya, Aborişade, and Ogundiya were already at the corner, peering down the street to see where the fire was.

"Aragbaye! What the hell happened?" Eşusanya said.

"The Klan," I said. "They got Ariori."

"What?! What do you mean they got him?" Aborişade said.

"They firebombed the pharmacy while he was in there. I had to get Dominique to safety. We've gotta go back."

Ogundiya took Dominique from me and carried her upstairs.

"'Baye…how bad is it?" Aborişade asked.

"It's terrible," I said. My voice cracked and I began to sob.

"No you don't," Eşusanya said, grabbing my shoulder. "It ain't over yet. Let's go."

We ran back downtown to see that the New Orleans Fire Department was already on the scene, battling the blaze to the best of their ability. Some men were holding back the crowd while others held the hose in front of the building, dousing it in water.

"Let me through! My brother's in there!" Eşusanya shouted as he tossed people aside in the crowd.

"There's a body in the doorway," one of the ladies in the crowd shouted. The panicked crowd screamed and stirred as the firefighters and police attempted to hold them back.

Eşusanya and I broke through the crowd and ran to the doorway.

On the floor was a corpse, blackened to a crisp, with swaths of pink flesh peeking through the soot. On the left hand of the corpse was a gold wedding band, lightly etched with the symbols of my people.

"No," I said. "No, no, no, no, no!"

Eşusanya punched a hole in the already brittle wall.

Aborişade broke through the crowd and looked at Ariori's corpse in horror.

"No. It can't be him," he said.

"It is," I confirmed. "The ring."

"Boy, you can't be in there! This is a crime scene!" a police officer shouted at us.

"Leave me be!" Aborişade commanded. The officer immediately stepped back.

"We can't leave him here," Eşusanya said. "There's still hope."

Ogundiya appeared with our errant horse and buggy.

"Where's Dominique?" Aborişade asked as we loaded Ariori's body onto the buggy.

"At the house. Sleeping," Ogundiya said softly, observing Ariori's body.

"Good," Aborişade said. "She can't see him like this. Ogundiya, there's still hope. We've got to get him to his lab at New Orleans University. Aragbaye, try to feed him some of your blood. Now! Let's go!"

Ogundiya took off and I punctured a vein in my wrist. I put it against the place on Ariori's face that used to have lips. The blood dropped in slowly.

"Anything?" Aborişade asked. I shook my head. "He'll have equipment in his lab. Let's go, hurry!"

We reached New Orleans University in minutes, rushing past the Negro doctors and nurses. We carefully laid his body on a worktable and I searched for anything to help us make this process easier.

Breaking into a drawer, I finally found his syringes. I stabbed myself in the arm, collecting as much blood as the syringe would carry. I removed it, and blood spurted until the hole healed itself seconds later.

"Put it in his neck," Aborişade said. I tried to find a vein…anywhere.

"Just stick it in!" Eşusanya yelled. I blindly jabbed anywhere and pushed the blood through. It immediately seeped out the back of his neck, through some previously unseen hole.

"Damn!" Aborişade said. "Try it again, do me!"

I used the same syringe and gathered Aborişade's blood. This time, I injected it directly in Ariori's chest. This time, it didn't seep out.

"Now what?" I asked.

"We wait," Aborişade said.

Hours passed. Ariori didn't move.

"Go get Dominique," Aborişade commanded Ogundiya.

"No," Eşusanya said. "She can't see him like this."

"I'm already here," she announced. We turned around to see Dominique standing in the doorway to the laboratory with Babarinde.

We all backed away from the table and stood aside so that Dominique could pass. She took small steps toward Ariori. Her dress was still covered in soot from the fire and her pale face was stained by her tears. She sniffed and reached her hand out to touch Ariori's chest.

"Look what they've done to you," she whispered. "My beautiful, sweet Ariori. They've finally done it. Taken you away from me once again. Don't they know we were meant to be? You were my hero twice over. Gave me a new life on Dominica. Showed me that real love didn't need the same language, or color, or beliefs. Our only belief was in love and in each other. You made me safe. It never mattered how dangerous things might be because I was safe as long as I was with you. I'm sorry I couldn't protect you, my love. I wish I could have done more."

She bent down and placed her soft lips on his blackened remains, kissing him one last time.

"Our vengeance will be fleeting. But our love will live forever."

She pulled a sheet over his face and walked back to Babarinde.

"I will cry no more," she said. "The men who did this to my husband must be punished."

Soon after the burial of our beloved brother Ariori, Dominique devised the kidnapping of her former chaperone, Carmen. She would be the only person who knew the truth about Ariori's assassination.

"That bitch goes to mass every Sunday. She'll be there. I promise," Dominique said. It was true—she hadn't shed a single tear since she said goodbye to Ariori. Although she had been removed from school, she kept herself busy by meeting with the girls in the sorority she was creating. We weren't privy to what they discussed, but we knew it was helping Dominique get through the immense tragedy.

As for us? We just wanted revenge. And we were happy to carry it out.

At the end of the early afternoon mass, we assembled outside of St. Louis Cathedral in disguise. It was Eşusanya's idea to dress in nun's habits.

Yes, nun's habits.

Carmen exited the church with the same smug look on her pug face that she always had, with seemingly no care in the world, no thought about the murder that she had facilitated.

We quickly stood up from the bench outside and walked toward her as she walked toward Bourbon Street.

Dominique led the way. We walked through throngs of parishioners trying to make their way home and none even suspected that we were just clean-shaven men in habits.

Dominique walked next to Carmen with her head bent down. We were immediately behind them.

Carmen brushed up against Dominique.

"Excuse me, sister," she said politely.

"You're excused, you murderous cunt," she replied.

"What?" Carmen faced Dominique's sinister, smiling face.

Before she even had time to gasp, we came behind her, covered her mouth, and spirited her down an alley where our carriage was awaiting.

"Make a sound and I will fillet you, my dear," Dominque said, while producing a knife from underneath her habit.

Carmen whimpered and lay down in the carriage as we sped off.

We took her to our plantation, twenty miles from the city. Nearby, there was an open field, far from the main roads, unseen by all. There, Babarinde waited, along with several of the brothers who lived at the house.

Eşusanya threw Carmen out of the carriage and she hit the ground with a thud.

"What do you want from me?" she said, scrambling up.

"Answers," Dominique said.

"I don't have any answers for you," Carmen said. She began to run toward the road.

"I don't think so," Eşusanya said, appearing before her. She turned and tried to run again, but Eşusanya grabbed her and brought her to Dominique.

"Who arranged for my husband's murder?" Dominique asked.

"I don't know," Carmen said.

"Wrong answer." Dominique produced her knife and held it a centimeter from Carmen's face.

"Who is behind my husband's murder?" she asked again.

"I don't know," Carmen said.

"Lies." Dominique slowly cut a gash from Carmen's cheek to her chin. Blood oozed out and every Razadi salivated. Carmen screamed.

"Alright, alright, alright," Carmen said. "I'll tell you. Please don't cut me again."

"Talk," Dominique ordered.

"I wrote your father and told him about your relationship. I told him everything I knew. I asked what I should do."

"What did he say?"

"He told me to fix it. He told me to undo the damage you did."

"That's it?"

"Yes, that's it," Carmen concluded.

"Lies!" Dominique shouted, slashing Carmen's other cheek with the knife. Carmen screamed.

"I am not lying! Your father had nothing to do with what happened to Armand!"

"Then who?"

"I can't…"

Dominique punched Carmen in the nose and the blood gushed out. Eşusanya let her fall to the ground and Dominique knelt down next to her.

"If you don't start telling me details, I will begin cutting off appendages," Dominique threatened.

"I told the man I'm seeing, William Beauchamp. I told him I had to take care of the situation. And he told me not to worry."

"William Beauchamp? The janitor at Newcombe?"

"Yes."

"You're fucking that old man?" Dominique laughed. Carmen stared back.

"I love him."

Dominique spat in Carmen's face.

"And you know who I loved? My husband, you cow. Now tell me the rest!"

"William went back to his friends and explained that he had to get rid of Armand."

"Who are his friends?"

"The Knights of the White Camellia."

"Not the Ku Klux Klan?"

"No…the KKK is beneath them. They would never-"

"Names. Now."

"William. His brother Eric Beauchamp, the attorney. Stefan Archer, the pharmacist. He knew when Armand would be visiting and told the rest. Edward Jones, the insurance agent. Stefan took out a policy before they firebombed the pharmacy, so he is a very wealthy man now. And he wasn't even there when it happened. All he had to do was leave the door unlocked. Damon Porter, the chemist, made sure some highly volatile chemicals were in just the right place in the pharmacy so the whole thing would blow right on cue. Sam Barnabas, the fire chief. He ensured that the damage to the neighborhood would be minimal. And then there's Jacob York."

"And who is Jacob York?"

"He's a civil war veteran and the leader of the Knights. He's the one who recruited the seven young horsemen to ride through the streets. He's a grand old man who delights in the advancement of the white race. As should you."

Dominique grabbed Carmen's ear and sliced it off. She screamed once again. Over those screams, Dominique spoke.

"Carmen, in my previous life I was a French girl on the island of Dominica during the colonial days. And I met a man named Ariori. He was a Negro man and we fell in love. We stayed together for years, until my father stole me away from him. And then, in this life, I discovered my love once again. You know him as Armand. But his name remains Ariori. And I fell in love with him again and I married him again. And again, he was taken from me.

"I am not one of those women who claims to not see skin color. Of course I saw Ariori's skin color, just as sure as I see your crimson blood. I saw his skin color and I loved it. I loved every bit of what made him a man—a black man—my man. And you facilitated his murder."

"I was just doing what your father thought was best."

"Even if he explicitly said not to murder my husband, you would have done it. You don't have a human bone in your body."

"And evidently, neither do you, nigger-lover. Look what you've done to me!"

"Yes. Look what I've done. My masterpiece of blood. Carmen… when you meet the devil, please tell him that a white woman did this to you."

Dominique jabbed her knife into Carmen's eye socket as far as it would go. Too quick for Carmen to even scream. A sickening gasp and gurgle emitted from her throat.

"Dinner is served, my brothers," Dominique said. She stood up and walked briskly to the house, wiping her knife off on the front of her nun's habit while the rest of us feasted on the brain-dead body of Carmen until she expired.

A week later, Dominique, too, was dead. Her death was peaceful, silent, and expected by all of us.

My darling Razadi brothers, as you see by my cold body in this bed, the bed I shared with my husband Ariori, I have departed this earthly realm. My life, without my beloved, is not a life at all, much less one worth living. You have remained strong for me in my hour of bereavement. I have noticed that you have barely grieved yourself. I know that the love I felt for my husband was special, but you knew him first and you knew him longest. By my passing, you no longer have to worry about protecting me. He is protecting me now, always and forever, in whatever afterlife there may be.

Free yourselves to grieve for your brother, but do not grieve for me, for I am happy as long as I am with him.

In my hands are gifts for you.
In my right hand is the ritual for Iota Theta Beta, the sorority that I had been working so hard at creating for all of these months. These women have been my sisters as you have been my brothers. They have protected me and accepted me. And it is only fitting that I give them to you, from this day forward. So long as there is blood in the sisters of Iota Theta Beta, so shall you and your people always have life. Do not try to decode the ceremonies. Just know that the four notes, when played or whistled, will be the gateway to whatever you need from my sisters, today and for all the days of your life.

In my left hand is a list of the names and addresses of each of the men responsible for the death of Ariori. I know that your first inclination is to mete out swift and decisive vengeance. But as you gather them and decide their collective fate, I just have one final wish:

Make them suffer.

In the blood,
Dominique Rabaut Forestier

"And that was the suicide note of our sister Dominique. The women whose husband you all killed."

Babarinde addressed the conspirators as they hung on the wooden poles erected for them in our back yard. We cut a dozen trees down from a small forest on our property and piled them into a semi-circle in the ground. One by one, we nailed the criminals' hands to the tops of the poles.

All of them screamed and tried to escape as we pounded the ten-inch nails through them. They couldn't understand how we found them, how we stealthily stole them from their own homes in the middle of the night, how we overpowered them, even now. The look of anger and confusion in their faces only made us taunt them more.

Try to escape. Go on. Run. Let's see how far you can get before I catch you. Five feet? Ten feet? No, white man. I will always beat you. Now, be tacked to this log, and watch my black face as you die.

There will be no knives, white man. No swords. No guns. No weapons other than my hands, my feet, and my teeth.

This is for my brother, Ariori, who you killed just because you were asked. Ariori was somebody. He was our friend. He was our brother. He was somebody's husband, you cocksuckers.

This is for Dominique, who lived two lifetimes for Ariori. This is for her, the innocent victim who couldn't help who she loved across time and space.

This is for the slaves of the German Coast who died because they dared to fight for their freedom. This is for Rebekah Deslondes, whose arm you took to spite her. This is for Charles Deslondes, whose body you mangled because he led his people. This is for Mercredi, Babe, Amos, and all the other slaves that you wiped off the rolls of history.

This is for the millions of enslaved Africans in America. This is for their heirs.

This is for the indigenous people that you displaced.

This is for the dozens and dozens of Razadi who lay dead at the bottom of the Atlantic Ocean, spared from the atrocities of life in the Americas.

This is for the first dozen Razadi who died from insidious weapons we'd never even imagined.

This is for Africa, whom you raped and pillaged.

This is for our scrolls, stolen to parts unknown.

This is for our families that we will never see again.

Take this hate, white men, young and old. Take these scratches from my fingers. Bleed for me.

Take these bites. Bleed for me. I won't give you the satisfaction of dying. I will watch the mosquitoes and flies feast on your blood just as I do, just like the animal you believe me to be.

I do this for Dominique.

I do this for Ariori.

I do this for my people.

I feed off your terror.

I feed off your blood.

Die for me.

I gasped deeply and released Justin as he regained consciousness on the floor of the gym. It was now almost dawn.

"Are you okay?" I asked. He slowly nodded.

"What about you?" he asked.

"I'm fine."

"I'm sorry that you lost Ariori. And Dominique."

"Olódùmarè has them now. There's no doubt of that."

Justin embraced me hard. The tears silently streamed from his face and onto my neck. We remembered a lifetime of death and pain, punctuated by twelve mangled white corpses, bled dry and baking in the Louisiana sun.

THANKSGIVING

Victor had acquired a luxury SUV from some place or another and we drove it to Hamilton, New York—Justin's hometown—for Thanksgiving. I drove the truck until about the middle of Pennsylvania and switched with Justin the rest of the way. Victor, as usual, slept in the back seat.

"You drive pretty good," I said.

"Thanks," he said. "I had better. Wasn't nothing to do in Hamilton except sneak into college parties. You had to learn how to drive to get away from there."

"How did y'all end up in Hamilton?" I asked.

"Whatchu mean? We always been from there."

"Well, not always. At some point y'all were from Africa."

"Duh. I'm just saying we've been from Hamilton for as long as I could remember. My dad researched it one time and found out all that stuff. It's a small town but it's always had some sort of black presence."

"Interesting," I said. "So…would you change anything?"

"About Hamilton? Naw, it's straight. Just don't want to live there."

"I mean about us. About your transition."

"Oh. That."

"I mean, what you saw…our revenge on the Knights…"

"I don't want to talk about that," Justin said. He shifted in his seat as he drove but never let his attention wander from the road."

"It's just that-"

"It is what it is. You did what you did and it's over. If I had the powers you all had, I might have done the same."

"Okay," I said.

"You know, you don't have to be ashamed of what you went through."

"I know. It's hard, though. A lot of time has passed, but it all feels like yesterday."

"I can imagine."

"So knowing everything you know now, you're still cool. We're still cool?"

"Yes! We're good, Dante. Really, we are. This life chose me, but still, I am choosing this life. I am choosing you. Before you, before the Razadi, what did I have? Wake up, go to work, come home. Eat too much, drink too much, and sometimes fuck too much. But you guys brought a lot to my life. I've got friendships. I've got confidence. I've got power.

I've got an entirely different outlook. So, would I change anything? Absolutely not. Because if I changed anything, I wouldn't have you."

I grinned and touched his free hand as he drove.

A few hours later, we were nearly there.

"Bonney Hill Road, here we are!" Justin announced. "Wake up, Victor, we're home!"

Victor stirred in the backseat and sat up. He rubbed his eyes and sniffed.

"Cute neighborhood," he sighed. We looked out at the big houses dotting the wooded street.

"Thanks!" Justin said. "We're almost at my parent's house."

I hadn't met anyone's parents in years, much less the parents of someone I was dating. I got nervous but immediately calmed myself down by realizing how much more anxious Justin must have been to see his family post-transformation.

We rolled up the long driveway with slim, bare trees lining it. There were still a few red and orange leaves dotting the grass, but they had largely been raked up already.

"Tudor house?" I asked, noticing the steep gabled roofs, contrasting brown and beige panels, and rounded windows. "Yup. Growing up? Felt like a mansion in the forest. Now it looks smaller and smaller very time I come home."

Justin parked the car on the grass next to a long line of other vehicles. We were likely the last of the family to arrive.

"Y'all ready?" Justin asked, as he put the car keys in his pocket.

"Yup!" I responded enthusiastically.

"And Victor, I trust you'll be on your best behavior?" Justin asked sarcastically.

Victor bared his fangs and hissed in response.

"I'd expect nothing less," he laughed. "Just try not to bite my family, okay?"

Justin walked up the steps to his parents' front door and rang the bell. I could hear footsteps approaching the door. It swung open slowly.

"Hey baby!"

"Hey mama!"

Mrs. Kena was a petite woman in her late sixties with a short, natural hairstyle and bifocal glasses. Justin and his mother embraced tightly.

"Come on in, it's cold out there!"

"Ma, this is Dante. And this is Dante's cousin, Victor."

"Nice to meet you ma'am," Dante said.

"Hello Mrs. Kena," Victor said. My mom hugged them both and took their coats. I took mine off.

"Justin! You…you're skinny!"

"I am not skinny! Just toned up!"

"I don't think you've ever been this built! What have you been doing?" Her stare was one of both amazement and suspicion.

"Just working out, ma. Running. Eating right. You know, all that."

"Well, we already started eating," Mrs. Kena said. "Y'all were running so late, we couldn't wait anymore."

"I understand, ma. Where's dad?"

"Downstairs eating and watching the game with the rest of them. Help yourselves! We've got turkey, ham, greens, string beans, macaroni and cheese, stuffing, cranberry sauce, rolls, and iced tea!"

"Excellent!"

We stayed close by Justin as he made his way around the house, saying hello to his siblings, nieces, nephews, uncles, aunts, and cousins. The kids loved them some Uncle Justin. Each of them ran to him and showered him with hugs, latching on to his legs like little barnacles. He could barely walk from all the kids climbing on him.

He hugged his siblings, but I noticed there was a lack of warmth there. I already knew that Justin went home sparingly, so maybe his siblings had some resentment because he wasn't around much.

The house was beautiful. It was just as spacious as the outside suggested, with high ceilings, especially in the living room area. We walked downstairs into the finished basement to see a huge spread of food set up. Apparently, this house had an entire second kitchen just for these large events.

We met Justin's dad down there, a tall, dark and somewhat brooding man in his early seventies. His easy chair had a slight lean to the side as he watched the game.

"Hey dad," Justin said.

"Hello there," Mr. Kena said. His tumbler of whisky was nearby.

"How you doin'?" Justin asked.

"Same old, same old. How you? These your friends?"

"I'm good. This is Dante and Victor."

Mr. Kena looked at us up and down.

"'Sup?" he asked.

We smiled and extended our hands to him, only to be confronted with dap rather than a handshake.

"I'm still hip, ya little niggas," Mr. Kena laughed. We laughed along with him.

"Let's eat," Justin said. We walked back over to the serving area and got our paper plates. Victor and I loaded ours up with collard greens, string beans, yams, and bread.

"No turkey? No ham?" Mrs. Kena asked.

"We're vegetarian." Dante said.

"Kind of." Victor added.

"Oh, well, I'm sorry, Justin didn't tell me that! I would have made a casserole or something."

"Don't worry ma'am, you've got more than enough to satisfy us. It looks delicious."

"Thank you!" She smiled and walked away. Justin was loading his plate up with every kind of meat that was available.

"I wouldn't do that if I were you," Victor whispered to Justin.

"What?" he asked.

"You're not going to be able to handle dead meat."

"I've had turkey and ham all my life. I'll be fine."

"Suit yourself," Victor said.

"Aye…go easy," I told Justin. "Small bites. If it doesn't feel right, stop."

"I gotchu," he said.

We all sat down on a free sofa in the basement as the family members moved about and resettled. Justin's dad was definitely the king of the castle. He never had to get up from his seat. Instead, his children and grandchildren catered to him. They deferred to him much like my tribe deferred to Mama Abeo and the rest of our elders.

Justin laughed, talked to his family, talked to us, and laughed some more, all the while stuffing his face with delicious Thanksgiving food.

Justin's sister Sarah approached us, an hour or so later, cocktail in hand.

"Hi," she said coyly.

"Uh…hi," I said back.

"I'm just gonna sit next to you," she announced, squeezing her slender frame between Victor and I, all but popping him off the couch altogether.

"So, are you like…my brother's boyfriend?"

"Jesus, Sarah," Justin said.

"What? You've been out since practically middle school; I know you're not embarrassed."

Justin rolled his eyes and exercised his right to remain silent.

"We're together," I finally said.

"I figured it was you," she whispered. "He always liked them boys with long hair. But rough, you know? You got that streetwise look about you. Still handsome, though."

She reached out and patted my dreadlocks, which had been neatly pulled into a ponytail. I felt my face get warm with embarrassment.

"Excuse me," Justin said. He ran down the long hallway taking him to the rear of the basement. I heard a door open, a light turn on, and then the door close again.

"He okay?" Sarah asked.

"I guess something didn't agree with him."

Sarah was puzzled, but said nothing else.

After a few minutes, I decided to go check on him while the rest of the family talked to one another.

I rapped lightly on the door.

"You okay?" He moaned. I quietly turned the knob and opened the bathroom door to see Justin kneeling before the toilet bowl. I closed the door behind me.

"Stomach upset?" I asked. He nodded slowly, and then began to retch. More of his dinner erupted over his lips and into the bowl.

"Yeah. You can't eat like you used to anymore. Not dead meat, at least."

"This sucks," he said.

"I know. But hey, think of all those cows, piggies, and birds that you'll be saving by going vegetarian!"

"Dante?"

"What up?"

"I don't know if you noticed this, but we drink people."

"True! But most of the time, they live! Isn't that awesome? We are like the most peaceful, symbiotic beings on the planet."

Justin began to gag once more. He vomited again.

"Oh, God," Justin said.

"It's going to be okay."

"I'm really going to miss bacon."

I sighed and ran my fingers through his afro.

Hours later, after Justin's stomach settled, it was time to get back on the road. We watched as Justin gave his awkward goodbyes to his siblings and gave warm hugs and kisses to his nieces and nephews. He shook his dad's hand and patted him on the shoulder.

"Justin, can I talk to you a second before you leave?" Mrs. Kena asked him.

"Sure. Guys, I'll be in the car in a second."

"Aight," I said. We stepped outside but stopped on the porch so we could strain to listen to what they were saying in the foyer of the house. Our hearing was better than most, but hearing through a thick mahogany door was still a challenge.

"What's going on with you?" she asked.

"What?"

"You heard me, boy. I said what's going on with you?"

"Nothing's been going on with me, Ma."

"You lost fifty pounds."

"It's more like thirty."

"You need a haircut."

"I'm growing it out."

"You have these friends I don't know about."

"They're nice."

"You're throwing up dinner."

"Stomach bug."

"Now you tell me…"

"What?"

"What exactly is wrong with you?"

"Nothing at all is wrong with me, woman! Can't you just be glad that I'm back home?"

"It just seems odd that you lost your job and bounced back so quickly."

"The Foundation for Community Justice believes in me and gave me the pay I deserve. And I still send some back home every month."

"You do."

"Ma. I'm fine. Trust me! You know I never been big on having a whole lot of friends. These dudes are different. They watch out for me. Helped me get in shape. Gave me confidence. They're family away from home."

"You still have a family here *at* home, you know."

"I know, ma. You know I love all of y'all, right?"

"I know. Just…just be careful, okay?"

"I'm always careful. You know that. Listen, we should get on the road. I love you, Ma."

"I love you, Justin."

We hurriedly went to the car and waited for Justin as though we hadn't been eavesdropping on the whole conversation.

"He's loyal," Victor said softly.

"I know," I said. "He knows how dangerous it is for them to know."

"Y'all ready?" Justin asked happily, as he got in the car and put the key in the ignition. As he pulled off, he asked Victor how he enjoyed himself.

"It was fine," Victor sighed.

"Well, I'm glad you came, Victor. Both of you. I really am glad."

"Really?" Victor asked.

"Really. I know you, of all people, didn't have to."

"You're not all bad, Justin," Victor admitted.

"Thanks," Justin said.

"I'm still going to have to kick your ass," Victor said matter-of-factly.

"Oh, this big 'fight' y'all keep talking about," Justin laughed.

"It's not funny," I interjected. "Every Razadi boy has this moment."

"Son, I am a grown ass man," Justin sniped.

"Yes, you are, but you still have to go through this. This is the most important fight of your life. It's not just a street fight. This is a very solemn, ritualistic occasion. This is how we know whether this life has really chosen you. You won't really be one of us without it."

"Not really one of you? I'm already out this bitch drinking sorority girls and crackheads. I got all the memories. The big ones, at least."

"That's true," I said. "But you're still not feeling what I'm saying."

"So I'm going to get beat in, like a gang?" Justin asked.

"Not at all. This is like your final exam, your graduation day, your bar mitzvah. It's a rite of passage."

"Okay," Justin said softly. "I...uh...I'm sorry I didn't take it seriously."

"All this shit you've been going through, it will all come together," Victor said. "And you might not win, but you better give me one hell of a fight."

"What happens if I don't win?" Justin asked.

"You die," Victor said, yawning and laying back down in the backseat.

"Oh, is that all?" Justin asked sarcastically.

"No. He's for real," I said softly. Justin looked at me askance.

"Oh."

"Do your best. That's all I can ask."

"And I guess my best is all I can give." His frown remained on his face for a hundred more miles. When we pulled over to switch drivers, again in Pennsylvania, he pushed me up against the side of the car and put his arms around me.

"You know I love you, right?" he asked. His face was just a few inches away from mine.

"I know. I love you, too."

He kissed me tenderly.

"I want to show you something," he said.

"What?" I asked. He cradled my face in his hands, closed his eyes, and leaned into me until our foreheads touched. My body was filled with a rush of emotions and memories all at once.

He was a baby, toddling through the skinny trees on his family's property, running, tripping, falling.

He was teased by his older brothers, ignored by his sisters.

He gripped his mother's apron strings, clinging to her for emotional support and strength.

He was torn away from her by his father making him "man up."

He manned up, all the way through school, making few friends along the way.

He manned up, earning the good grades that got him through school.

He manned up, when he was molested by his camp counselor, and told no one.

He bravely came out, only for his family not to care, not to offer a word of encouragement or the investment of bigotry. Just…nothing.

He was the last to leave the house and he never came back.

He studied, he partied, he studied, he partied. He drifted.

He loved. He loved often. He loved hard. But there was never a person who gave him what he needed. Never a person who allowed him to say it, to say the words.

And then I saw myself, and all memories slowed. I saw myself on the corner, peddling bootleg movies, waiting, waiting, hoping, smiling, meeting, loving, loving, loving.

Ipsaji.

I separated from Justin and gasped.

"How'd you learn how to do that?" I asked, breathless.

"It's in my blood," he smiled.

The Initiation

I washed Justin's hair and spent the better part of the hour twisting it into baby dreadlocks in preparation for the fight of his life. He sat between my legs as I worked and I could practically hear his heart beating with anticipation. We did not use products from the store for our hair care. Everything we put onto or into our bodies came from the earth if we could help it, and directly from our garden if possible.

I anointed Justin with the natural oils that my people had used in their hair for centuries. These oils, these herbs, these roots—they were a tradition, passed on from parent to child, and now from brother to brother.

"But God, I fear nothing. But God, I fear nothing. But God, I fear nothing…"

"Justin, look into my eyes. Say it again."

"But God, I fear nothing."

"Do you believe that?" I asked. He nodded.

"Why?" I asked.

"Because I was made in God's image."

"What else?"

"Because I was destined to do great things. Because I was born a human and made a Razadi. I will win because God ordains it."

"Praise Olódùmarè," I whispered.

"Praise God," Justin replied. I patted his back and he stood up, looking at his hair in the mirror.

"Take off your clothes," I instructed. Justin complied, peeling out of his Syracuse t-shirt and unbuckling his belt. His now too-loose jeans easily fell to the floor and he stepped out of them. I grabbed the pot of warm balm from the stove and hurried to the dining room.

He stood before me in his navy blue boxer briefs. I paused just to stare at him from behind. He was a new man entirely. Lean. Defined. Upright and confident. He sensed me standing there and looked at me over his shoulder. He grinned.

"This mixture is one hundred percent natural," I said.

"What's in it?"

"Belladonna is the main ingredient. Nightshade. It's toxic to humans. But the smell of it to Razadi…well, let's just say it's a sign that you're ready to fight."

"Okay. It smells good," he exhaled. I gathered the creamy balm in my hands and rubbed some into Justin's hands. Together, we rubbed it into his skin.

"It's warm," he said.

"It's supposed to be. It will relax you."

He exhaled again. We rubbed the lotion over his entire body, recreating a ritual I had gone through myself hundreds of years ago with my kinsmen. By the time we were done, his body glistened like a bronze statue.

"What's next?" he asked.

"Your clothes." From the duffel bag I had under the dining room table, I produced our simple, pure white initiatory garments.

I wrapped a plain white swath of fabric around his waist and hips several times, tucking here and draping there. I tucked the corner in, then pinned it with a safety pin. His boxer briefs peeked out of the bottom.

"Is that it? It's awfully short."

"It's a *shendyt*."

"It's really soft."

"Egyptian cotton."

"Nice. So…is this it?"

"Just this and your cloak." I pulled it out of the bag and unfurled it. Made from the same fabric as the *shendyt*, it fell easily over his shoulders and almost touched the floor. The oversized hood obscured most of his face, except for his nose and lips.

"You're ready," I said. "Let's go."

I walked out the back door toward the driveway where the van was parked. I unlocked the deadbolt and opened the door before I noticed Justin wasn't behind me.

"Justin? You coming?"

He stood in the dining room with his cloak on. I touched his shoulder. He looked up at me.

"Are you okay? Are you ready for this?"

"But God, I fear nothing. But God, I fear nothing."

I nodded.

"Let's go. You got this."

It around three o'clock in the morning when we slowly drove up North Capitol Street and pulled a sharp left into the abandoned McMillan Sand Filtration Site. The usually closed and locked fence was wide open for us.

"Why are we here?" Justin peered out of the back window of the van.

"This is where you're going to fight Victor.""But…but this…this is where I was attacked, Dante. I'm not ready."

"Yes, you are." I pulled the van close to one of the ivy-overgrown brick buildings that resembled a short, fat smokestack.

"Justin, listen to me," I said, putting the car in park and shutting off the engine. I slid between the seats and got into the back with him. His face was still obscured by the white hood.

"There are three things you need to know and you need to know them right now. First things first. I have lived for hundreds of years, and I have to tell you I am not exaggerating when I say there has been nobody in my life quite like you. Nobody. You hear me? And I've seen the world. It is my job to take care of you. But I don't have to love my job. Justin, there's no better way to say it: I love you. I love everything about you. I love the way you blush when I compliment you. I love the way I can hear your heart beating faster when I enter the room. I love the way you smell when we make love. The way you chew, the way you brush your hair, the way you talk to your mom on the phone. I love it all. I love *you.* I *love* you."

Justin sat as still as a stone.

"You feel me?" I asked.

He vigorously nodded his head and grabbed my hand. His mouth quivered and he barely eked out a whisper.

"I love you, too."

"I'm…I'm…glad you feel the same way," I stammered. "The second thing I wanted to tell you…in the Razadi culture, there's a word we use. *Ipsaji.* It means…"

"Soul mate," Justin finished.

"You know?" I asked.

"The last time you transferred memories to me, I kept hearing the word over and over. And…I don't know…I just knew. But it's deeper… it's like a partner. For eternity."

I nodded.

"Do you believe in eternity, Justin?"

"Yes."

"What do you think about…about what *ipsaji* means?"

"There's nothing to think about. It's just a fact. You are my *ipsaji.* And I am yours."

I lost all composure and began to weep. Justin held me close to him.

"What's the third thing?" he whispered.

"This is the fight of your life. Draw your strength from God. Strange things may happen to you, but know that they are all from God. From Olódùmarè. There is nothing evil about what happens here tonight. All of this is God's will."

"I love you," he said again.

"I love you, too. You're one of us. Now stand outside for a second. I gotta change."

Justin let himself out of the van and stood by the door while I shed my shoes, socks, and jeans. In another bag, I had three items: my long, red and white ritual robes; my black cloak; and a rope.

When I emerged from the van, I felt the cool grass beneath my feet.

"Justin, I'm going to put this rope around your neck. Follow me and stay silent until you're spoken to."

He nodded.

The McMillan Sand Filtration Site was scheduled to be renovated and made into a mixture of condos and retail space. For now, however, the space looked as it had for the past fifty or more years: wide open parkland with squat towers that had been overgrown with ivy and other plant life.

We left the area near the short towers where the van was parked and I guided Justin via his cable-tow to the circle of cloaked Razadi in the middle of the field. A little more than a dozen of my brethren awaited us.

Justin was nervous, but his posture did not betray him. As I glanced back, he walked tall, his chest poked out ever so slightly. He knew this was his time to shine.

As I approached the circle, two of my cloaked brothers faced me and blocked my path.

"Who goes there?" a third member of the circle shouted.

"A brother of the great and majestic golden valley of Africa, where the legendary Razadi once thrived."

"And who is it that you bring with you?"

"A neophyte in the blood, who seeks to prove himself worthy and ready for the responsibility of our tribe."

"Does our blood course through his veins?"

"It does."

"What is your pleasure, brethren?"

"Proceed with our ancient rites," said everyone in the circle.

I walked Justin to the center of the circle.

"My brothers," I began, shouting, as was our tradition. "My name is Aragbaye, son of Abeo! In the centuries since our displacement from our homeland, we have maintained our traditions. We have survived the middle passage! We have persevered through slavery! We have worked through Jim Crow! And now we are here, living among humanity in peace. It is time for us to once again grow and thrive, and be the leaders of all living things on this planet.

"Gone are the days where we pined for the better halves that we left behind in our village. A new day has dawned upon our kind. The day when a human has become one of us.

"Behold, I introduce to you Justin Kena!"

I removed Justin's pure white hood and he stood tall in front of the Razadi with his rope intact around his neck.

"Justin Kena, son of Theresa, is The Key! I present him to you with my full endorsement!"

Justin flexed his muscles as the Razadi stared in silence.

"Why?" one of my brethren asked. "He's just a Son of Adam."

"Yes, he was born a man," I replied. "But he was a man who willingly walked into a den of nightwalkers…for us! He put himself in harm's way just to earn our trust. And because of that, he put his life on the line, almost died, not even a hundred yards from where we stand, when a nightwalker tore a hole in his neck in retaliation! Yes, brothers, he has the courage, the intelligence, and the fortitude of a Razadi."

"Is he strong?" another asked.

"As strong as any one of us."

"Tell the truth," another began. "Is he your *ipsaji*?"

"Without question he is my *ipsaji*."

"Oh. Well, excuse me." Several of my brothers chuckled. A grin crept across my face as I spoke.

"As I said, brothers, I vouch for him with every fiber of my being. I implore you to accept him as one of us."

One of my brothers slowly approached Justin and I. Underneath his cloak was an old, dusty tuxedo with a dead, red rose in the lapel. He took his black hood down and replaced it with an old top hat with a tattered silver band.

"Uncle John…Babarinde," I said, nodding in his direction. "This is him. This is Justin."

Justin and Babarinde looked at each other. My uncle cupped his face and looked deep into his eyes.

"He's The Key, Uncle."

Babarinde smiled and lightly slapped Justin on the cheek.

"I see," he replied. "Razadi men! Before you is Justin Kena, son of Theresa! He is vouched for by Aragbaye, son of Abeo. Do any among you challenge his worthiness?"

"I challenge him," Victor said, emerging from the shadows.

"I, Eşusanya, son of Nkoyo, challenge Justin in the traditional ways of our people. Though we have survived and thrived hundreds of years removed from our homeland, Justin must still be crowned and named. And he ain't getting either without coming through me."

Victor shed his cloak and revealed a crisp red and black camouflage uniform.

"Yo!" Justin hissed at me. "How the fuck does he get a full uniform and I gotta fight in my drawers? That's some bullshit!"

"Stay in your zone," I whispered.

"I'm barefoot, my nigga!"

"Get your head in the game. You have everything you need to win."

Justin exhaled and flicked out his fingers a few times.

"Justin, son of Theresa, do you accept this challenge?"

"I do," he said.

"Aragbaye, join the circle. Justin, Eşusanya. The rules are simple: stay alive."

I hurried to the circle in between two of my brothers who I knew would be rooting for Justin to win. They nodded at me as I stood between them.

"Assume your stance, gentlemen," Babarinde said.

Justin and Victor squared up. Two drummers began a slow drumroll that built up in volume and in speed.

"Ready? Go!" Babarinde shouted.

Justin and Victor bared their fangs and charged at each other with all their might. The drummers beat a mid-tempo cadence that set the tone of the fight. Victor leapt into the air with a spinning kick, and Justin immediately dodged it by dipping to the right and kicking out with his left leg, grazing Victor's body and throwing him off balance.

Victor stumbled, but didn't fall. Justin came after him with his fists raised, attempting to pummel Victor, but he missed every shot. Victor's reflexes were too quick for him, at first.

"Is that all you-"

Victor's taunt was met with a right hook to his temple. Justin's face went from anger, to disbelief that he had actually landed the punch, to fear that the fight would escalate.

In disbelief, Victor felt the lump form on his temple, which almost immediately subsided. He bared his fangs.

"You fucked up now!"

Victor launched himself upward into the sky at least twenty feet and then soared back down, aiming himself toward Justin, who performed a series of back flips to evade him.

Victor landed on the ground with a crash, shaking the earth and unsteadying Justin. As the drumming continued, their fighting intensified, with Victor on the offensive, striking out and landing most of his punches, with Justin deflecting only a few.

Each punch was horrendous, with the sound of flesh hitting flesh only intensifying. Justin was taking his licks well, but not landing many of his own. The worry crept over his face.

"Remember the formula," I called out. Justin nodded while defending himself.

He performed a roundhouse kick to Victor's torso and used the momentum to flip in midair and kick his head with the other foot. Landing back on both feet, he immediately charged again with a left hook and then a block. He changed weight, landed a right hook, and blocked again.

Victor quickly adapted to this strategy and began blocking every punch. Justin adapted as well, blocking Victor's punches and kicks and anticipating his next moves, upping the intensity and power each time.

"Go back home, Son of Adam," Victor taunted. "You can never be one of us!"

Victor gave Justin an uppercut that took him off his feet and sent him careening toward us. We broke his fall and let him slide to the ground to rest. His eye was swollen shut and his mouth was bleeding.

"Get up, Justin," I said. "Get up. You can do this."

We wiped the blood from his face and propped him back up.

"You got this."

"Dig deep."

"Pray."

"You're almost there. Pray. Fight. Pray some more!"

Justin staggered then stood up straight again, both fists in front of him. He ran toward Victor, leaned and faked a fall to the left, landing on his left hand and making a perfect right angle with his body, kicking Victor in the face. Victor fell backwards, but leapt back up instantly, head-butting Justin.

Justin, for the second time, staggered backward toward us.

"Catch him!" I shouted.

Two of my brothers caught him on each side. Justin began to chant:

"Ma fo na yi Olódùmarè. Mi o beru enikan sugbon Olódùmarè."

"You've been teaching him Yoruba?" Salako asked me.

"No," I said, bewildered. "Just a few words here and there."

Justin looked into my eyes and smiled. The swelling in his face had nearly disappeared. He winked and blew me a kiss.

"I think…" Salako began, and then stopped. Justin began to convulse.

"He's been crowned!" Makinde exclaimed.

We held hands and formed a small circle around Justin as he jerked back and forth.

"Don't fight it, Justin!" Salako yelled.

"Let it happen!" Makinde said.

Justin's convulsing stopped. He stood as still as a post.

"Are you okay?" I whispered.

Justin opened his eyes. They glowed yellow and bright like the sun.

"Tell the drummer I need something up-tempo." He put his hands on his hips and posed in a feminine posture.

"Oshun!" the three of us exclaimed. We fell to our knees. Our drummers immediately began drumming furiously and the rest of the brothers dropped to their knees except for Victor.

Justin stepped outside of our circle of protection. He touched then lightly scratched my scalp as he walked past me. I looked up to see Justin confidently strutting toward Victor.

"Thought you had him beaten, didn't you?" Justin asked in a soft and high, but stern voice. "Thought he'd never get crowned? Hmm?"

"I…I…" Victor stuttered.

"I, I, I," Justin mocked. Now let's get this over with. I said *faster*, drummer!"

Justin leaped into the air straight up, at least twenty feet. Victor was awestruck and forgot to move as Justin came back down. We practically heard the crack as Justin's elbow hit Victor's skull. He went down.

Justin put his hand on his hip and made an imaginary mirror with the other.

"Damn, I think I broke a sweat," he said.

Victor scrambled to get up. Justin kicked him hard to the chest with each foot.

"This… is what… you get… for making… me… come… down… here!"

Victor began spitting blood.

"Stand up!" Justin said. "Fight back like a man!"

Justin squatted down and grabbed Victor by the collar.

"Send your ruler here so this can be a fair fight!" Justin shook Victor violently and slapped him repeatedly.

Victor bared his fangs and wailed. The pitch of his sounds got lower and lower until it was a constant growl. His eyes, with each blink, began to glow a deep red, like that of a hot coal.

"Now we're talking!" Justin said. "Good to see you again, Papa Legba!"

"Let go of my prince, Oshun," Victor growled.

"Tell your prince to leave the king be!" Justin shrieked. He threw Victor clear across the field. The Razadi stepped aside as Justin ran in a blur toward the short towers.

Victor stood up and ran directly toward Justin. Their red and yellow blurs collided in fireworks as their arms and legs furiously struggled in mid-air. The sound of the pounding was unreal—indistinguishable from the rapid beats of the drums.

We ran toward them. Justin's punches were so quick that he looked like an octopus punishing Victor.

Not to be outdone, Victor's red-eyed fury built up and exploded in a collision of legs upon legs.

This fight was epic. We stood before them gape-mouthed and astonished. Even back in Africa, the crownings weren't so furious.

Victor grabbed a handful of Justin's hair and yanked it down hard, sending him to the ground.

"Oh, is that how you treat a woman?" Justin laughed. He kicked Victor hard in the chest, sending him careening into one of the sand bins. Bricks collapsed with a sound akin to pins falling in a bowling alley.

Justin ran toward the sand bin and we followed. By the time we got there, Victor had already been tossed about like a rag doll. He tried to fight back, but Justin was quicker and more powerful than him. Sand quickly rose everywhere, making it tough for us to see more than glowing red and gold eyes.

Justin straddled Victor's body. We could all see the red glow diminish from Victor's eyes.

"Are we finished here?" Justin asked as he caressed Victor's face.

"We'll never be finished," Victor growled as he spit blood in Justin's face.

Justin roared and pummeled Victor with his closed fist over and over again until the yellow glow in his eyes softened and disappeared entirely. I approached him from behind and quietly called his name.

"Justin...*ipsaji*... What separates the Razadi from all other beings on earth?"

Justin's fist froze in midair.

"Justice..." he said in his normal voice. He stood up and reached down to grab Victor's hand. Victor reached back.

"...and redemption." He hoisted Victor up and carried his weight as they walked toward us.

"I love you, brother," Justin said, as he kissed Victor's bloody cheek.

"I love you, too," Victor admitted. Justin handed him off to some other brothers, who took care of him.

We reformed our circle, this time without our black cloaks. Each of us had on a different set of colors, some in traditional West African robes and others in more contemporary garb. Justin stood before us, chest still heaving from the excitement.

"Brothers of the Razadi," Uncle John began. "I present to you Justin Kena, son of Theresa, now and forever more known to us as Ominiyi. This means 'Oshun has honor.' Now, take the knowledge of what you have seen here tonight and spread it through your home cells. Spread the word that for the first time since we left our homeland, a new member of our tribe has been made, named, and crowned by the Orisha Oshun herself. Let them all be made aware that Justin Kena–Ominiyi–is our brother and he has more than proven himself worthy. Justin..."

Justin looked up at Uncle John with pride.

"Ominiyi. You are one of us now. Welcome home."

The circle of Razadi erupted with applause, whistles, and chants of celebration.

Babarinde embraced Justin. Bewildered, Justin embraced him back with tears in his eyes. The entire group came in to welcome Justin, one at a time. I took great pleasure in introducing him.

"Salako, bring me his cloak, please. Justin, let me introduce you to your family. From Miami: Kosoko and Omiyomi. Omiyomi shares your crown."

"Greetings, brother," they said in unison as they embraced Justin.

"From New Orleans: Salako and Omitonade. Omitonade also shares your crown."

"Welcome to the family," Omitonade said.

"From Atlanta: Ogundele and Akinlana. From Los Angeles: Makinde and Ojonda."

"Blessings, blessings."

"And from New York: Balogun, Osundara, Oyagbola, and Iranola."

"I can't believe all of y'all came to see me…all this way," Justin said.

"You da baby bruddah," Iranola said. "'Course we gonna see you be born."

"Oshun crowned you. What an amazing gift," Osundara said. "I'm so happy to have you as part of my family."

Justin's eyes continued to water.

"I've never experienced anything like this before," he said.

"Well, I should hope not!" Babarinde guffawed. We all joined in.

"So, what now?" Justin asked.

"Now?" I bared my fangs. "Now, we eat. Who's got a taste for some Iota Theta Beta?"

The Morning After

I woke up first.

He was sleeping one of those good, deep sleeps that humans only get after two Benadryl. He was exhausted and blood-drunk.

He slept with a do-rag on to keep his baby locs in place—what good that did now after a night of fighting in the grass and dirt. He still did it, though. Everything I'd taught him was a habit.

My *ipsaji.*

I ran my fingers lightly over his bare chest. He smiled without opening his eyes and pulled me closer to him. He was snoring again within moments.

I wasn't tired one bit. I barely ate anything at all. Justin was now one of us. He didn't have to worry about being accepted. He didn't have to worry about Victor. There'd be no more sickness. Old age wouldn't happen for a very, very long time.

"Dante, I need…oh. Excuse me."

Uncle John wasn't accustomed to such practices as knocking before entering a room. On the other hand, Razadi weren't known for inhibition, either. Justin remained sleeping hard on his side of the bed.

"What's up, Uncle?"

"I need to talk to you. Can I sit down?"

"Of course." He took a seat on the ottoman.

"How's Victor?"

"Recovering. I already talked to him about this."

"Okay…"

"Victor really botched this thing."

I nodded.

"We've got a mess on our hands with the nightwalkers. We've maintained this truce for a long time, but him sending Justin to their house? Well, you saw the result of that. But at least…at least we know that they have Orlando. And if we can get Orlando back, we can find John Irons, too."

"But how do we get them back without starting a war?"

"I've done my best to negotiate with the east coast nightwalker clans. And they say they won't interfere if we are solely trying to rescue one of our own."

"Which we are. We've got no beef with nightwalkers."

"But there's a catch. Only you, Victor, and, now, Justin are allowed to go after them. If any other Razadi attacks the Anubis Society, then it will be an all-out war. And you know we will lose. Philadelphia, New York, West Virginia nightwalkers would all descend on DC like cicadas if the Anubis Society is ambushed."

"I fucking hate being a minority."

"Said every minority ever."

Justin stirred in his blood-drunk sleep.

"Even him, Uncle? He just earned his name. Just got crowned. This is hella dangerous."

"I know. But Orlando is in danger. If they've got access to laboratories and doctors, they could be attempting to clone our blood. Isolate our DNA. Who the hell knows what else? Look, if I thought there was another way, I'd propose it. We know the nightwalkers have Orlando. You, Victor, and Justin are all strong enough and smart enough to get him back."

"What if we don't succeed?"

"Aragbaye. Did you see Justin out there last night? He might have been nervous, but he wasn't scared. He had confidence. It's something I haven't seen since we were back in the village. I need you now. Your people need you. We can get Orlando and end this whole thing. Say you're on board."

"Of course I'm on board, Uncle. It's just…the last thing I want to do is let you down. Or put Justin in danger."

"The only way you would let me down is if you didn't try. And as for Justin, he's one of us now, Dante. Like it or not, he will always be in danger. From the nightwalkers. From the demon Djinn. From the government. From journalists. The rest of his life will be filled with deaths and rebirths, periods of hiding in the shadows and periods of hiding in the daylight. Surely, he knows this."

"Just as surely as he knows that he needs human blood to live."

"You really take this protector thing to heart, don't you?"

"I didn't know you were handing me my *ipsaji* on a platter, Uncle."

"Indeed. You didn't."

"But you did, didn't you? When you gave me that folder…you somehow knew."

"Maybe. Maybe not."

"I think you did," I nodded. "But if you told me, it would have changed things. I needed to discover it on my own."

Babarinde smiled knowingly.

"Act quickly, but act intelligently when it comes to the nightwalkers. We need Orlando back safely. And if we've got to shed vampire blood to get him back, so be it."

"So be it," I repeated. I gazed at Justin's snoring body while I silently prayed that he was ready for his first mission.

ENVY

"I'm really happy for them," Andre Crawford said from the back seat of the mini-van.

"I know," Sasha said. "They look happy."

Andre and Sasha had seen the entire Razadi initiation fight from the top floor of a parking deck off Children's Hospital. With the assistance of binoculars and a telephoto camera lens, their already impeccable vision allowed them to practically read the lips of the daywalkers.

"I don't know a lot of the words they're saying," Andre said. "Do you think they're all African words?"

"Maybe," Sasha said. "They're supposedly West African. One of those words was weird... ip... sahj... something. Couldn't make it out."

"Funny how they just had the entire fight out in the open like that," Andre marveled.

"Well, it was on land nobody could see from the street. In the middle of the night."

"But the drumming..."

"Wasn't that loud."

"But..."

"There were over a dozen of them. They would have hypnotized any humans that discovered them. Then drunk them."

"Yeah. You're right."

They sat in silence as the Razadi dispersed.

"Should we follow?" Sasha asked.

"No. They're probably just going to go celebrate."

"This upsets you."

"Sasha...you don't know the half of it."

"I'm sorry."

"It's not your fault."

"Do you want to...you know...run?"

"They'd stake us before we could get to safety."

"Not if we had help...protection..."

"You really think the daywalkers would have a reason to protect us? We helped keep their brother hostage. We took his blood."

"What do you want to do, then? We are tethered to the Anubis Society. Now, we either run and keep running until we get someplace where we can be left alone, or we link up with the Razadi, or we just sit there in that mansion under Nigel and Cassandra until karma deals with them."

"I don't know what we're supposed to do. I don't know who we can trust."

"I hate vampires," Andre said.

"But we are vampires!"

"So are the Razadi! Look at them. They love each other. They take care of each other. They're not worried about prophecies or science. It's just family with them. Nothing more or less. And they are vampires. They drink the same blood we drink."

"They're not vampires. Not really. They own the fucking sun. You and me? We'll never see the sun again. We can't walk down the street with sunglasses on. I can't…I can't go to the beach, take my shirt off, and feel my body getting warm just from standing there. I'll never get tan. I will literally never see the sun! We got cursed, Andre! Because not only was the sun taken from us, but we are tethered to the craziest people I've ever met. All the power that we have? The strength? The influence? It's worthless. Because we have to obey these stupid, ancient, vampire laws and pay our penance to the society."

"Look at me," Andre said. Sasha turned all the way around in her seat.

"We can have the sun again. I believe that."

Sasha looked away.

"I think you're just being sentimental because the Razadi are black."

"And what if I am? Hmm? What's the harm in having faith that we're not that much different from them? That maybe—just maybe—they could look at me and see a little bit of themselves. Because when I see them…I see a whole lot of me. I see who I was. I see who I could damn well be some day. Somebody with a family. Somebody who doesn't have to run. Now, listen. I don't trust Cassandra any more than I do Nigel. I know she doesn't want to kill Justin, but I still don't trust what she wants him for."

"And what do you think that is?"

"I don't know."

They sat in silence for a few more moments.

"Andre… We can't tell Cassandra what we saw tonight."

"Yeah."

"The less she knows, the less they all know, the better. I don't necessarily think that the Razadi can help us. But I don't think they mean us any harm. We took their brother. And then they came for us, as anybody else's family would do. If they're trying to take down the Anubis Society, then we should let them. As long as we know to run when the time comes."

Andre climbed over the seat and sat next to Sasha.

"You know I love you, right?" he asked.

"I know," Sasha said. She smiled as coyly as she had the day she met him. He pulled out the camera and deleted each photo he had taken.

"I wish you well, Razadi," he said softly. "It was a pleasure peering into your most sacred moments."

Sasha exhaled.

"What's wrong?"

"Nothing's wrong. Just nervous. Justin Kena's one of them now. For real. It's only a matter of time before they strike back for what Malcolm did to him."

"And they're going to strike back hard."

"Hopefully," Sasha smiled. Andre grabbed her hand.

"Hopefully," he repeated. They kissed and hurried back to the mansion before first light.

Part Three:
Daywalker's Delight

THE MEETING

He whipped my ass fair and square.

I can't deny it and I can't be mad about it. He did what he was supposed to do.

He's one of us now, like it or not. And I respect him. Truth be told, I honor him. We were told long ago that Razadi were born, not made. But I knew different. A real Razadi had to be made through blood, sweat, and tears, and Justin had more than paid his dues.

I didn't like him. But I loved him. And now it was time to kick some nightwalker ass.

I showered, shaved, and braided my long dreadlocks behind my head so that they wouldn't be in my face. Babarinde complained that I always styled my hair too flamboyantly, that I drew too much attention to myself. I couldn't help that I took pride in my appearance. Dante might be fine looking like an average corner boy, but when people see me, I need them to know they are gazing upon royalty. So yes, my hair was always done, my face was always clean, and my nose was just a little bit higher in the air than the average person's.

I walked down the steps of our house and joined Dante and Justin at the kitchen table where they waited for me.

"Good morning, gentlemen."

"Good morning," they replied in unison.

"So, as you know, Babarinde has given us strict directives in our rescue of Orlando," I said.

"It's just the three of us against at least a dozen vampires living in the house," Dante said.

"We can handle it," I said. "Nightwalkers have their weaknesses."

"So, give me the crash course. I'm looking forward to taking care of the vampire who tried to kill me." Justin said.

"Stakes and fire," Dante said.

"Those are the only things that can kill a vampire?"

"At night. Then of course, the sunlight."

"What about moonlight?"

"Moonlight? Nah, never heard anything about that."

"What are you thinking?" I asked Justin.

"Just trying to figure out all my options. Ultraviolet light. Solar energy. All that."

"We haven't tried everything because we haven't had a reason to. We've had a truce for a hundred years."

Justin nodded in silence. His face was still puzzled, but he was a sponge, absorbing every bit of data.

"Victor, here's what I want to know," Justin began. "Do we just go in there and get our man, police style? Or do we try to uncover the bigger story? We know he ain't in no vampire jail. That's not how they roll. We know they're up to no good, but we're doing ourselves a disservice if we don't try to find out what, exactly."

"But we tried that," I groused. "You planted a bug and everything. It's time to just get Orlando."

"I agree; let's get him. But let's get him and everything else we can find out about them."

"Fine, I can agree with that. But I am not trying to spend all winter dealing with this."

"I feel you. So, the dilemma is, do we attack during the day when they're all sleeping, but guarded, or at night, when they are likely to be out hunting?" Justin asked.

"Nighttime. They are more vulnerable by themselves. And so is their mansion," Dante said.

"I think we're missing something important here," I said.

"What's that?" Justin asked.

"If the vampires know that we made you a daywalker, we might have a problem. You could end up locked away just like Orlando."

"Then we'd better get this plan right the first time around."

Leaving New Orleans

"Brothers, tomorrow is the day we realize the destiny of our people. Today, most of you leave New Orleans and start new lives under new rules. Stay small and stay unnoticeable. Cling to each other, but participate in society. And when it's time, move on into new identities. Be reborn, just as we were here. Be the seeds that we were destined to be, floating quietly from one place to be planted in another, softly and gently."

There were no tears in this farewell. As for me, I was happy to be moving on to a new adventure. I was just anxious to know who would be in my cell.

"A large group of you will be going west, to Los Angeles. Sangodare, Akerele, Danguro…"

I fidgeted as Babarinde read the names. *Let's go*, I thought.

"Some of you will be going back to the Caribbean, but to Haiti, this time. Omidiran, Oriade…"

Good. They're boring.

The other cities were rattled off: Atlanta. New York. A growing city called Miami. Seven of us would be left in New Orleans to manage the plantation. That left Aragbaye, Aborişade, Ogundiya, and me.

"You four will be going to the nation's capital: Washington."

Yes!

"So that means you're coming with us?" Aborişade said.

"No."

"What? Why not?"

"I'm going someplace else. By myself."

"You can't do that."

"Yes. Yes, I can."

"It's dangerous by yourself, Babarinde."

"Nobody will know who I am. I'll be fine." Aborişade wandered off behind the house without another word.

"So where will you be?" I asked, following after Babarinde.

"Denver."

"Denver? Ain't no black people in Denver!" I exclaimed.

Babarinde laughed and slapped me on the back.

"There are a few. I'll be fine."

Dozens of wagons assembled outside of the plantation. We loaded them up with our belongings and said our farewells. The mood was jubilant for most of us and melancholy for only a few. By and large, we were ready.

Babarinde gave each of us boxes of important documents and wallets full of cash. The textile industry had been very good to us over the years. Babarinde also had other investments of uncertain origins that ensured our financial stability. I didn't know much about trust funds and investments, but I knew there were homes waiting for each of us at our destinations.

The box accompanying us to Washington had passports with our new names on them. He had also written detailed, one page documents for us to study on the journey. They were our histories—forged biographies to match the names he had created. We had done this time and again in New Orleans, but this time it was far more serious that we know our stories since we would only have our small groups to rely on.

"Eşusanya, please take this seriously," Babarinde said to me as we walked to the field beyond our house.

"I do, Baba. I'm just happy. Can't I be happy?"

"Yes, you can be happy. Just try not to revel in your happiness too much. We are destined for great things. Not for ourselves, but for the glory of our people. For Africa."

"For the Razadi nation," Ogundiya said. He was as quiet in his walk as he was in his speech.

"Indeed," Babarinde said. We continued walking to the edge of the field and Aragbaye caught up to us.

"I worry about you being in Denver by yourself," I admitted to Baba.

"I need the time alone," he said.

"How will we reach you?" Aragbaye asked.

"My address is among your papers."

We stopped at the edge of the field where the forest began. Aborişade was already there, kneeling.

"I put the best of you together," Babarinde said.

"Obviously," I said. Babarinde smiled at me and continued.

"There are some things I believe, that I've always believed. And I know you all may not believe as I do. We have our traditions. The Orishas. Our crowns. And then there are the scrolls that we came over with. The ones that survived. We know that one of them is lost to the ocean. And we know another was stolen by our kidnappers. But two survive. And I am taking them to Denver. Maybe I can make better sense of them there in new surroundings."

"You'll never give up the old ways, will you Baba?" I asked.

"Of course not," he answered. "The one thing I can decipher from the scrolls is The Key. The Key will deliver us. We have to be patient."

Here we go again, I thought. *Babarinde has got to be the youngest crazy old man ever.*

"You think The Key is in Washington?" Aborişade asked.

"Maybe. I don't know. The scrolls suggest something like that. And I figure if it's true, I'd better have you all there, ready. Are you up for it?"

"I am," I responded. "Not that we have a choice. But yes, yes I am ready to find The Key."

"You don't have to look for him. He might not have even been born yet. Just keep your eyes open and he'll find you."

"We will," Ogundiya said.

I looked down at where Aborişade knelt. Sectioned off by white stones were the graves of Armand Forestier and Dominique Rabaut Forestier—our beloved Ariori and Dominique.

"We cannot lose any more of our brothers and our loved ones."

"We all miss them, Baba. But as we move forward, we can and will protect ourselves. Razadi comes first. All others wait," I said.

"We protect ourselves, yes," Aborişade added as he rose from the ground. "But we have to protect the most vulnerable, also. I don't think our destiny is just survival. It's the protection of our kindred here in America. We failed terribly at Bernoudy. But we can succeed elsewhere, and in other ways. I don't know how, exactly. But I know we can. We're smart. We're strong. And if we can survive all that we have so far, we can survive anything."

"That, dear brother, is why you will be in charge of the Washington cell," Babarinde said.

"What! I am the eldest out of all four of us!" I argued.

"Baba, I can't. Not me. But Aragbaye! He's Mama Abeo's chosen one and he's been your right hand for all these years." Aborişade said.

"Fuck that!" I shouted. "I am the eldest and we've always followed the laws of deference around here. Always!"

"Aborişade is the leader of your cell. There is no further discussion."

I shut up immediately.

"Brothers, I believe in you. Go to Washington. Enjoy Washington. *Be* Washington. When the time comes, we will be reunited again. May Olódùmarè smile upon you."

He embraced each of us tightly. He got to me last and whispered in my ear.

"You'll be glad I didn't put you in charge. Mark my words."

I rolled my eyes as I patted his back. Before he left us, he knelt down before Ariori and Dominique's graves and said a silent prayer. He got up and walked back to the house with Aragbaye and Aborişade, his two obvious favorites.

I looked at Ogundiya and he stared back at me.

"What?" I asked.

"Nothing."

"Yes, it's something. What are you staring at?"

"You."

"Why?"

"Because…you're so easily angered. You didn't even stop to acknowledge that you and I didn't have to be in Washington together. But we are. Does that even make you happy?"

I scowled and walked toward him, clenching my fists. I stopped two inches from his face until he could feel my breath hitting his chin. He was a good five inches taller than me and twice as wide, but I wasn't afraid of him.

For good reason.

I smiled and threw my arms around him.

"You know 'happy' is not my default emotion. Ogundiya, I'm ecstatic to be going to Washington with you."

He wrapped his massive arms around me.

"Me too," he said softly. "A new adventure, but it's still me and you."

"Always," I said. "No matter what, no matter who, it's always back to me and you."

By the morning light, Babarinde's wagon and our wagons were the last ones out. The journey would be neither easy nor short, but we would be at our destinations before we knew it. The Razadi were releasing ourselves from the trauma of our pasts and claiming our own pieces of the American dream.

Chiyoko Kobayashi

"You're up first, lover boy," I announced to Dante at our kitchen table. "Your target is Chiyoko Kobayashi. Made a vampire in the 1970s. Sole heir to the Kobayashi Gaming Company fortune. She's the Anubis Society's tie to business interests in the Far East. Make a statement, Dante. Get all the information you can out of her and then take her out."

"Got it," Dante said.

"That's funny," Justin said.

"What do you mean?" I asked.

"I've only heard the name Chiyoko once before in my life. We had a fundraiser at a bar on U Street, and this Asian woman came in and gave us a donation. Turns out she was the bartender. And it was funny because it turned into a swinger's bar at night."

"That's her," I said.

"She's a nightwalker?"

"Did I stutter? Shit!"

"I just never thought I already met one."

"You've probably met several. You just didn't know."

"I remember something she said to me. I shook her hand and it was cool to the touch. She said she had poor circulation and laughed it off."

"Yup, that's a nightwalker for you."

"She was nice. Do we really have to kill her?"

"The only good nightwalker is a dead nightwalker, especially when it comes to Anubis! So put on your big boy fangs and cut out this sentimental bullshit. This bitch is going down tonight."

This was the dirty part of our job and Justin needed to get used to it. His precious *ipsaji* was every bit the cold-blooded killer that I was and he had to see death over and over again if he was truly going to be one of us. I wasn't from Babarinde's school of thought, not since the white man murdered Ariori.

We rode out to the bar in my favorite mode of transportation: our inconspicuous white van. Chiyoko's gig at the swinger's joint on U Street was a pretty good way to have a steady supply of food and fun. I was a little mad I'd never considered that: a place where uninhibited people trusted their discretion with the bouncers and the bartenders every single night.

It was late, but the club wasn't quite closed yet. The bouncers were still out front, letting people out but not letting anyone in.

"We need Chiyoko *alone* in the club," I told Justin. "So I want you to hypnotize the bouncers."

"Can I do that?"

"Of course you can."

"What do I need to do?"

"Look into their eyes. Deep. And tell them what you want them to do. But don't just tell them. Push that emotion onto them. Like...*push* it. Visualize them *wanting* to do it."

He hopped out of the van and I watched carefully as he went to work. I couldn't hear him over the unceasing U Street traffic, but I could tell by his stance that he was fearless. He bobbed his head around like an executive director trying to earnestly seal a donation from a major funder. Suddenly, his spine straightened and he seemed to grow more powerful by the second as the burly bouncers lost control of their own minds. They each walked down the street.

Justin looked back at us and gave a thumbs-up signal.

"Great work!" Dante said, patting Justin on the back.

"What did you tell them to do?" I asked.

"I just said they should take a walk down to the National Mall and take a nap."

"Well, that'll do it. Let's go in."

We entered the club, closed the door tight behind us, and took three steps down to the main floor, lit with soft neon lights in shades of pink and blue. We walked through the foyer and the place opened up. All the patrons were gone. Chiyoko was wiping down the bar in preparation for leaving. She looked up, noticed the three of us, and calmly put her towel down.

"It's good to see you again, Justin," Chiyoko said, combing her fingers through her long black tresses, interrupted only by the rogue blond streak.

"So you do remember me?" he asked.

"Of course I do," she replied faintly.

"Listen up. It's just us, Chiyoko," Dante said, revealing a crossbow with a wooden stake he had concealed under his long coat and aiming it directly at her heart. "What you're going to do is tell us everything we want to know."

"And after that?" she asked.

"There is no after that," Dante growled.

Chiyoko's eyes darted all over the room in a panic. She knew we had her covered and there was no way out. Her eyes began to water.

"I've never been in the inner circle of the Anubis Society. I don't know much. But I'll tell you everything I do know."

"Don't waste my time, lady," Dante said.

"Don't worry. I won't. But please, can you just relax? I'm not your enemy."

Justin pulled up a bar stool and sat down. I scowled at him.

"About twenty vampires live at the mansion," Chiyoko began. "Nigel and Cassandra are the master and mistress of the house. They're a few hundred years old, both European. They have a manservant and a maidservant. The manservant is named Andre—a black guy. The maid is Sasha Forzani."

"Why do I know that name?" Victor asked.

"She's pretty old—and she gets around. Then there's Malcolm. He's the muscle. He's ruthless and cold, and will skin you alive if he can."

"Who else?" I asked.

"Nobody of note. About half of them seem to believe what Nigel believes."

"And what's that?"

"That the Razadi are their biggest threat. And the other half think you guys could be great allies."

"What about Orlando? What are they doing to him?" I asked.

"I don't know. All I know is that he's being held captive. There are rumors that they're experimenting on him."

"And he's still at the house?" I asked.

"Yes, he's definitely at the house."

"Why did you join them?" Justin asked.

"You ask too many fucking questions!" I spat at Justin.

"No more than you. He's just a baby. Leave him alone," Chiyoko said.

"As you're well aware, my father was the innovator behind the Kobayashi Gaming System in the early 1970s," she continued. "His advances in the video game industry were genius; he was approaching his first billion by the time I was born. I wanted for nothing for the first two decades of my life.

"I got sick in 1977, a few months after my twentieth birthday. The doctors quickly determined that it was ovarian cancer. They put me on an aggressive course of chemotherapy and gave me a radical hysterectomy. I was weak, ten pounds underweight, and utterly bald. But I survived. For a time.

"Two years later, the cancer came back with a vengeance and spread fast through my body. I couldn't eat. I slept all day and lay in pain all night. I couldn't even use the bathroom by myself. It broke my father's heart to see his only child cut down in the prime of her life.

"One night, my father brought a shaman to come see me, a kind of witch doctor. I was too out of it to understand what it was they were saying, but it didn't feel right. Didn't feel right at all. Nevertheless, I was dying. We were desperate.

"A few days later, my father came into my room with a tall man. He was the handsomest man I'd ever seen. I felt self-conscious meeting him. He came to my bed and began cradling my face.

"My father told me 'Chiyoko, don't worry. Mr. Yamaguchi is going to fix you. He's going to make you all better.'

"And I asked him 'Is he a doctor?'

"My father told me, 'He's better than a doctor.' And Mr. Yamaguchi didn't even say a word. He just bared his fangs and bit me in my neck. I was too weak to scream. Everything went black.

"When I woke up, it had already been done. Mr. Yamaguchi had nearly drained me of all my blood, and fed me his own blood. He was now my maker. Not only was I beholden to him, but so was my father. In exchange for saving my life, my father sold controlling interest in the Kobayashi Gaming System to the Tsukuyomi Club of Japan—the ruling vampire organization in the country. The old fool thought he was saving my life, but what he really did was send me to an eternal hell on earth.

"It wasn't long before he realized what he had done. When he saw what I was, what I was truly capable of, he had a stroke and lingered in a coma for weeks. I played around with the idea of giving him the same curse he had unleashed upon me, but I decided against it.

"When he died, the Tsukuyomi Club thought it would be best for me to take over. And I did, serving for twenty years as the always young, always beautiful CEO of Kobayashi. I tried to age myself over the years, giving myself a white streak of hair and aging my style, but ultimately I had to give it up. But I'd be damned if I'd let the bastards who made me into a vampire take control of my family's company.

"So, I did what any other bitter nightwalker would do. I hired my local yakuzas to assassinate my board of directors, all at once. Oh, you would have loved it, Victor. Such a well-executed execution. The black sludge of evil vampires filled the boardroom like swamp scum in post-Katrina New Orleans. Anyone who escaped a staking was burned alive. And I saved the best of my vengeance for my maker, Mr. Yamaguchi. My yakuzas subdued him, tied him to an antenna on top of Kobayashi Tower, and left him there to fry in the sunrise. Of course, I couldn't be there myself, but I watch the tape of his disintegration often."

She cackled. I glanced at Justin, who remained transfixed.

"Once the board was eliminated, I took control of the Tsukuyomi Club's shares and became majority stakeholder once again. I filled the board with my most trustworthy yakuzas and directed them to appoint one of my distant cousins as the new CEO. I'm still one of the wealthiest women in Japan, even though the world thinks my cousin is."

"If you're so wealthy and powerful, why are you tending bar in America?" Dante asked.

"I'd be lying if I said it was an anthropological study. Truth is, I came here on vacation, which I shouldn't have. Nightwalkers killing each other is a big no-no in international vampire law. So when I got caught, I was tethered to the Anubis Society. Of all the lodges and societies in this hemisphere, I had to get stuck with the one that has the religious nut as the head. At least working at this club, I get to have a steady supply of upscale dinners. And seeing Steve every week has been an added bonus."

"You've been seeing Steve every week?" Justin asked.

"Of course I have. That's the way the society kept tabs on you."

"What?!" Justin exclaimed, standing straight up at the bar.

"Don't worry. He doesn't do it on purpose. I hypnotized him once I found out who you were. He really does love you as a friend. I would never have gotten him to spy on you willingly."

I could see Justin turning ill.

"I really do hate the Anubis Society, though. I'm not like them. If I could escape my tether, I would. There's only one problem: I hate daywalkers just as much as nightwalkers."

In one swift motion, Chiyoko produced a huge, partially rusted blowtorch from underneath the bar and aimed it at Dante.

"Blowtorch!" Justin yelled, as he dove to the ground.

The trigger on her weapon stalled. She tried to fiddle with it, but it was too late for her.

"Shoot her!" I screamed.

Dante pulled the trigger of the crossbow and the stake penetrated her heart in less than a second. Chiyoko screamed.

"Thank you!" she coughed, before her final death transformed her from the inside out. He skin shriveled and tightened against her skeleton and darkened like a raisin. Her body fell to the ground behind the bar. We got up and ran to the end of the bar to see what happened, and, as I expected, there was nothing left but a puddle of what looked like tar.

"Holy fucking shit," Justin said.

"And that's how a vampire dies," I said.

"She told us all of that...and was going to burn us to death anyway..." Justin mused.

"That's what vampires do," I said.

"They can't all be like that," Justin argued.

"You'll see. Now clean this up so we can get out of here."

Sasha Forzani

"I'll never understand how you pop up with a new vehicle whenever you want," Justin said to me as we got into my black Corolla.

"I guess nobody ever told you just how wealthy we are, huh?" I asked Justin, as he drove the three of us to our next target, a stakeout at the vampire mansion in Northwest. Dante silently rested in the backseat as the sun threatened to set in the early afternoon.

"Well the foundation's wealth is public information—almost three hundred million dollars in the bank. Which is crazy!"

"You think that's crazy? That's only ten percent of our wealth."

"Wait."

"What?"

"The Razadi have three *billion* dollars?"

"Yeah, I guess, something like that."

"How in the entire fuck did you guys get three billion dollars? Y'all were picking cotton in the old south!"

"An entire fuck? Not a portion of a fuck?"

"Nigga! Where the money come from?!"

"Why are you so excited?"

"Because you are richer than Oprah. Ain't no black folks richer than Oprah except Jesus."

I laughed hard. Justin was hilarious when he wasn't busy being needy.

"Our wealth comes from a lot of places. The Dominican Razadi became foresters after we left. Lumber was big business back then—still is. The business spread throughout the Caribbean and down into South America. Then we picked cotton, of course, and made fabric. Everybody needs clothes. Bought up a bunch of real estate. Made some investments. And, you know, maybe we bootlegged gin."

"So it's not exactly…legal…"

"All money is dirty, is it not?"

"Y'all didn't trade slaves, did you?"

"Of course not."

"Drug trafficking?"

"Are we counting weed?"

"Oh jeez."

"No Justin, we never trafficked drugs or people."

"That's just a lot of money."

"And we were very astute in our business dealings over the years. Just know that as the times changed, so did we. Babarinde has us all well taken care of."

"Okay," Justin said. He fidgeted with his seatbelt as we paused at a stoplight.

"Are you okay?"

"Yes."

"Are you nervous about going back to the mansion?"

"I'm anxious. Not afraid."

"You know I have your back, Justin."

He looked sideways at me as the light turned green and he accelerated.

"You don't like me."

"I don't have to like you to have your back. Anyway, what those vampires did to you was criminal and I'm looking forward to seeing you get your personal revenge."

"This isn't about me, this is about Orlando."

"You don't even know Orlando."

"But I know you. And I'm one of you. So…there's that."

We pulled up at the end of the cul-de-sac just as the sun set.

"It won't be long before they start filing out," I notified Justin. "That's how they do. It's like anybody else with a night job. They wake up with the sunset, shower, shave, whatever else, and then head out."

"Do they really sleep in coffins?"

"Yup. If even a pinpoint of light hits them, it's curtains. They sizzle, pop, and turn into that sludge you saw."

"Gross. So they're all in the basement, I guess."

"Probably so."

"They'll be on their guard since Chiyoko disappeared last night," Dante said, as he sat up in the backseat.

"I know. We'll need to trail the first one that comes out, corner him, and make him talk," Justin said.

"Again with the talking?" I asked.

"Yes. We need information, not bodies."

"Vampires don't leave bodies, stupid."

"Listen, you know what the fuck I mean. We know Orlando is in there. If we could just run in there with a battering ram and get him out, we would. But all we know about the interior is what I saw when I walked in. We don't know if Orlando is in a room or a dungeon or a closet or what-the-fuck-ever-else there is in that goddamn house. Every vampire we isolate gets us closer. And don't you want to know *why* they have him?"

"Alright bitch, damn. You over here running your mouth and don't even see the chick coming out the house."

Justin tensed up and peered out of window. A uniformed security guard and another woman walked out of the house. The small white woman wore a long black coat, a Baltimore Orioles baseball cap, and ear buds in her ears. She locked the door behind her. The guard got into the company issued sedan and sped off. The woman got on a bicycle and rolled by us at a moderate pace.

"Follow her," I ordered.

"I got this," he snapped back. He made a quick U-turn and stayed about half a block behind the woman as she pedaled through the neighborhood. She never looked back once.

We followed her through Rock Creek Park as she neared Georgia Avenue, pedaling slightly harder and slightly faster.

"She made us," I said.

"I think so, too," Justin said. He accelerated as she sped across Georgia Avenue onto Missouri, pedaling furiously.

"She's gonna make that left on Fifth Street," Dante said.

"I know," Justin replied. "Relax, we're in my territory now."

Justin was right behind her as she turned onto Fifth Street. She pedaled as fast as a superhuman could and we were on her tail. We both ran through red lights.

Justin's fangs began to elongate as he concentrated on the road.

"You hop out as soon as I go past her," he instructed.

"What?!" Dante and I said in unison.

"You hop out of this truck as soon as I pass her!"

"That's crazy!" I said.

Justin ignored us and put his pedal to the metal just as we reached Coolidge High School. We passed the woman just on the other side of the school and she hopped off her bike, running through the parkland next to the gym.

"Get her, bitch!" Justin screamed at me.

Without argument, Dante and I bailed from the truck and hit the ground, tumbling a few times but hopping right back up in pursuit of the vampire. Justin sped off down the street. Our stakes were in our hands, ready for action.

The woman was fast, but we were faster. She knew she couldn't outrun us, so she attempted to hide behind the trees. To a human eye, all that could be seen was one black blur going from tree to tree, followed by two more blurs, and the sound of the wind cutting through dead leaves.

"What do you want?" she finally asked us. She had a real terror about her, which we didn't ordinarily find among vampires. Her brown hair frizzed out from under her baseball cap and her nose twitched when she talked.

We both hissed and got into offensive stances while she cowered before us.

"Tell me what you want!" she shouted.

"An eye for an eye," I hissed.

"You're responsible for Chiyoko's disappearance last night? She's dead, isn't she?" she asked.

"Back to the sludge from which your people 'evolved.' Back where we're going to send you, too," I said.

"No, you can't!" she said, placing her hands in front of her.

"Why shouldn't we stake you?" I asked.

"Because…I know that you turned Justin. And I didn't tell Nigel or Cassandra."

"Bullshit," I said.

"I'm not lying. Cassandra dispatched us to keep tabs on you. We staked out your initiation at the McMillan Sand Filtration Site. We saw everything. We saw Justin win his fight. We saw his crowning. It was… beautiful."

"How dare you intrude on our sacred ritual?" Dante hissed.

"We were following orders from Cassandra. But we didn't give her the photographs. We deleted every last one of them and told Cassandra there was nothing worth reporting. That you had taken Justin to a hospital and he was recovering from his wounds there. That he was out of commission. A non-factor."

"Why did you do this?"

"I did it because I saw the look on my husband's face when he saw your rites. He's an African American nightwalker. He sees the Razadi and he knows what you have is a gift. He'd trade almost everything to be with you."

"You're Sasha Forzani?" I asked.

"I am."

"It's nice to meet you, Countess," I said, withdrawing my stake.

"It's nice to finally meet a Razadi face to face," she said. "Even if it had to be you."

"How did you get tied up with vampires like these? I'd always heard you and your husband were free agents."

"Let's just say we got into some trouble. Ran afoul of the vampire law. We're tethered to the Anubis Society for a while."

"That sucks," Dante said.

"What sucks?" Justin asked, as he appeared out of the blue.

"You're Justin Kena?" she asked. Justin nodded.

"I am. Who are you?" he asked.

"Sasha," she said, extending her hand. Justin looked at her suspiciously.

"It's okay. That's Countess Alexandra Forzani," I added. He shook her hand firmly.

"It's nice to meet you, Countess," he said.

"Sasha is fine. I haven't been a countess in a long time. I heard you were made a Razadi. The first in hundreds of years."

He nodded modestly.

"Yeah, that's me."

"What cologne is that you're wearing?" she asked.

"He just…yeah. That's just him," I interjected.

"Curious…" she said with a smile.

"Right."

"Listen, we need to figure this thing out," Sasha said.

"So let's talk. Is Orlando still alive?"

"Yes, very much so. He's still in the house. They won't move him. The next closest safe house for us is in West Virginia—too far away from the lab."

"Lab?"

"Victor, Nigel has commissioned a genetic study of nightwalker and daywalker DNA. He's committed to discovering your weaknesses and using them to eradicate you."

"Why? We're not at war."

"Nobody knows. He has it in his head that the daywalkers will somehow destroy all nightwalkers. He sounds like a religious fanatic."

"He follows the way of the scrolls?"

"Yes. Down to believing that Justin is The Key."

"Some of us believe that, too," I admitted.

"Do you?" Sasha asked.

"I believe in survival."

"Me too. Nigel is pure evil. He will destroy you when he gets the chance. And Cassandra is an opportunist. If either of them find out Justin has been turned, then it's all over. It's war."

"Then we've got to strike first."

"No…you need to follow the blood, first."

"What? Follow the blood?"

"You have to find out what they know about your blood. Find Dr. Zolotov. He's the one who gets Orlando's blood. From what I can gather, he knows all about the difference between daywalkers and nightwalkers. And get this: he's human. But once you dispose of him, you have to come get Orlando. They will find no use for him once you get rid of the doctor and take his research."

"You're right. Sasha…What can we do for you?"

"There's nothing you can do for me. But my husband? He wants the sun again. Find out what you can from Zolotov's work and let us know. Cassandra…she says she believes in unity between our kind, but don't trust her for a second. She'd drain you if she could."

I nodded.

"I'm really glad I finally got to meet you," I said.

"Same here. Just remember that when it all goes down, you have friends on the inside. Don't forget us."

"You have our word," I said.

Sasha smiled and was off in a flash.

"Can we trust her?" Dante asked.

"I think so," I said. "She's definitely not like the others."

"Wait. What the fuck just happened? You have me Tokyo-drifting across DC, chasing this chick through the park, and all of a sudden we just trust her? How do we know we can trust her? She could be telling Nigel and Cassandra everything right now. We have to get her!"

"That was Sasha Forzani. She's a legend among nightwalkers, man," I said.

"Legend? Why you ain't tell me?"

"I mean, who knew she was in DC for real?" Dante said.

Justin growled.

"What? Calm down," Dante said.

"How are we going to fight them and I don't even know who they are?"

"Aight…I got something for your ass. Get in the truck."

We sped off to the truck and drove to Justin's apartment, where I knew we'd have the Internet connection we'd need in order to teach him what he needed to know.

"It's musty in here. Don't you believe in Plug-Ins?" I asked.

"When's the last time I was even here?"

"True. Where's your remote control?" I asked. He pointed to an end table next to his sofa, and I discovered one of the big, good remotes with a built-in keyboard. I turned on the television and went to the Internet.

"What are you doing?" Justin asked.

"Come sit down," I said. He came to me on the couch while Dante went back to the bathroom.

I typed in a series of numbers and periods into the navigation bar.

"An IP address?" Justin asked.

"Watch," I directed. Dante emerged from the restroom and sat on the floor in between Justin's legs.

A protected page came up and I typed in the lengthy password. I was in within seconds. A single folder opened with one file. I clicked it.

Justin's television made the perfect theater.

"What's this?" he asked.

"Just watch," I said.

The opening titles were blurred, jumpy, and black and white. A white man in a plain black suit appeared on the screen and spoke words I had heard many times before.

"Greetings, and welcome to Project Corn Lily. As conflict escalates worldwide, you have been selected from among hundreds of qualified soldiers to assist with a most important project: the development of a superior weapon."

The suited man stepped aside, and the camera panned back to reveal a bare bunker with one hooded figure strapped to a chair.

"This race of foreign savages has been living among us—in secret—for decades. All we know for certain is that they are a European import. They are strong, fast, and deadly. They, my friends, are vampires—the monsters that you only thought were part of movies and folklore."

The suited man pulled the hood off his prisoner. The blond vampire was angry and hissing through his fangs.

"Dark eyes. Inch-long fangs. Unfettered rage. This thing would rip your heart out and eat it if it wasn't strapped down. But watch this."

The suit produced a foot-long, sharpened stake and a hammer. The vampire panicked and tried to get out of the chair, but it was bolted down. The man steadied the stake, and then with one quick movement, drove it into the heart of the vampire. Immediately, the nightwalker shrieked and then shriveled into a black mass, just as Chiyoko had done the night before. Justin winced.

"The rules are simple for dealing with these animals. First, they have vulnerabilities. A wooden stake will kill them. It is painful, but it is quick. Second, sunlight has a similar impact. Should you ever receive orders to abort the project, those are the only two things that will kill it.

"Our experiments here are designed to mitigate these weaknesses for the benefit of the cause of freedom. Please, let the scientists do their jobs. Protect them. With your assistance, we can revolutionize the way we fight. And we can end this war.

"One final note: the females of this species are just as deadly as the males. Never, ever look directly into their eyes, and never, ever let your guard down at night. They will use every opportunity to escape, through force and cunning.

"Thank you, soldier. God bless you and God bless America."

The tape went black and the television reverted back to the file folder.

"You know what?" Justin asked, after minutes of silence.

"What?" I asked.

"This is exactly why I don't fuck with the government."

Dante and I laughed hard.

"Dead ass!" Justin continued. "You mean to tell me nightwalkers have been here for decades? And the government basically tried to turn them into weapons? That is just fucking like America to do that shit."

"That's the only tape we could find like that," Dante said. "But there are bits and pieces of the nightwalker story everywhere. They're old. They've got their own systems and traditions. But for whatever reason, they didn't come to America until well after we did."

"Did America ever weaponize them?" Justin asked.

"Didn't seem to," I said. "There's still a lot we don't know. But the most important thing we know is that they're still here and they are dangerous as fuck."

"Then we've got to find Dr. Zolotov. And then we're getting Orlando. I don't want to wait any longer. This shit is crazy.

DR. ZOLOTOV

As luck would have it, Dr. Damien Zolotov's name was in the phone book. We took the old white van and made the journey to Bethesda, Maryland, to the private National Life Lab building, near the National Institute of Health and the Walter Reed complex. We donned our work suits and grabbed bags of tools and proceed through the front door of the building, right through the metal detectors.

"We're from Rising Sun, we're here to start some renovations to Dr. Zolotov's lab," I told the elderly security man at the front desk.

"I don't have anything on the calendar for today. Let me buzz Doctor-"

"Look at me," I said sharply. The security man turned to me.

"You don't need to buzz the doctor," I said.

"I don't need to buzz the doctor."

"We're going to go up there, do what we need to do, then leave quietly. You won't remember a thing."

"I won't remember a thing."

"Thank you, friend!" I said cheerfully.

"You're welcome, have a good evening!"

"I could get used to this," Justin said. "I can't imagine you've paid a restaurant bill in years."

"Who'd want to do that?" I said.

We boarded the elevator and pressed the button for the sixth floor. We opened our toolboxes and gripped the magnificent Glocks that Babarinde had gifted us before we left. Specially equipped for regular, silver, and wooden bullets. I secretly prayed I'd get to use them soon.

We got off the elevator and hurried down the hall. The other offices were dark, long closed for the evening. We saw light at the end of the hallway, where Dr. Zolotov's office was.

Dante arrived at the door first, saw that it was locked, and quickly jimmied it open. I went in first and Justin covered me.

The lab was one large, open space, with lab tables, chairs, and long countertops along the walls. The harsh fluorescent lights showed a lab of organized chaos: notebooks and laptops and boxes of data interspersed with microscopes and test tubes. I noticed a dozen flasks of blood on the central island. I fingered the flasks, picked them up, and smelled them. It was definitely our blood.

A tall white man with a head full of curly gray hair came out of a carrel in the back of the room with a mug of piping hot coffee. He glanced at us and we raised our pistols.

"Greetings, Dr. Zolotov," I said. He dropped his coffee to the floor and the mug shattered. He raised his hands up.

"Who are you? What are you doing here?"

"The better question is: what are you doing here? Seems to me like this blood you have here belongs to us. We'd like it back."

"What are you talking about? I am performing legitimate-"

"Don't bullshit me, old man," I said, running to the doctor in seconds flat. "I know who the fuck you're working for! Now tell me right now what you're researching!"

Dante and Justin were at either side of the doctor in moments.

"You don't work for Nigel," he surmised.

"Nope. You can consider me to be an independent contractor."

"What do you want from me?"

"Tell me everything about your experiments on our blood."

"I…I can't."

I grabbed his hand and squeezed it until I felt the bone in his thumb pop.

"Argh!" he bellowed. He fell to the floor. I squatted in front of him.

"Dr. Zolotov. As a scientist, I'm quite sure you need both of your hands daily to conduct your dirty little experiments. I get that. You're just doing your job. But I can promise you that if you don't tell me what I want to know, something else will get broken. And I don't stop at fingers or limbs. Collarbones are especially fun."

My long finger traced a line over the doctor's collarbone. I smiled as he trembled.

"I was contracted two years ago by Nigel Artinian for blood research. He told me he would supply it as long as I didn't ask any questions. At first, I was getting blood from him and his…people." The doctor paused.

"You know what his people are, right?" I asked. The doctor nodded.

"I didn't at first. I know now. Vampires."

"Continue."

"I found out on my own because of the experiments. The blood… rapidly dehydrated itself under ultraviolet light. And when I took a vial into direct sunlight, it was an almost instant reaction. All that was left was slime."

"Yeah, yeah, we know all about vampire blood. Tell me what you discovered about our blood."

"There were similar properties. Hyper-regeneration when disturbed. Resistance to stress on the molecular level. But the blood you're referring to…it's different on a genetic level."

"Go on."

"Humans, vampires, and…your kind…all have nearly identical DNA when compared. But two things are happening that make them different. First, humans lack one of the base pairs that you and the vampires have in your DNA."

"What's a base pair?" I asked.

"It's like one of those rods in the double helix in a strand of DNA," Justin said.

I stared at him.

"What? I took genetics in college."

"So, you and the vampires have a different base pair. If a human receives a transfusion of vampire blood, the vampire DNA will cause the human DNA to mutate into the dominant strand. That's how vampires are made. But with your people's blood and human blood, it never worked. The mutation never happened."

"You're special," Dante told Justin, who tried to stifle a smile.

"Oh, for the love of God. And what about when you mixed daywalker blood with nightwalkers?"

"Daywalkers?"

"It's what we call ourselves. Come on, doc. Context clues."

"Oh… Well, when we mixed those two, there was another reaction, but not a full mutation. A process occurred temporarily that produced side effects that suggested a mutation. Namely, a temporary immunity to the effects of sunlight. But it didn't last."

"Would you say your experiments failed, then?" Dante asked.

"My work has been extraordinary. I learned things and saw things I'd never see without Nigel. We had a breakthrough recently. We discovered that your daywalker blood has a binding agent that doesn't appear in humans or vampires. It's almost like a virus. It's harmless in you and in humans, but it practically disintegrates in vampires. Whatever allows you to walk around in the daylight just refuses to cooperate with vampire physiology. I call it the Redemptive Agent."

"Redemptive? Why?"

"Because it prevents your strand of vampirism from being a curse. You get all of the benefits of the disorder but you can still function in society, in the sunlight."

"The Redemptive Agent," Justin repeated.

"What now?" Dante asked me.

I pondered this new information for a moment. I stood up and walked away, glancing at shelf upon shelf of notebooks and journals.

"All this data…all this is related to your experiments?"

"Yes, it is. Groundbreaking work. Years of my life."

"You know we're going to have to destroy it, right?"

"Please, please don't."

"Dr. Zolotov, you should have never been brought into this at all. I do apologize. Hopefully, your insurance will cover this."

"Insurance?"

"Yes. You do have fire insurance, right?"

The good doctor began to weep.

"Come now, get yourself together. Nigel swore you to secrecy anyway, it's not like you were going to get a…what do you call it…Justin, that thing that Martin Luther King got?"

"Nobel Prize?"

"Yes. Doctor, you weren't getting a Nobel Prize for this."

"Sir, let me make a proposition to you. Let me work for you instead. Maybe I can figure out a way to induce mutation from daywalker to human? Wouldn't you like that?"

I laughed.

"Sir, we already have the key to that, and his name is Justin."

"Hi." Justin waved.

"But we simply cannot allow you to continue these experiments on our people. Firstly, because it's wrong. You might not have been drawing the blood, but you didn't question where it came from. You knew Nigel Artinian was sinister from the start. But because he was paying you on time, you didn't question it. Hmm? Didn't even want to know how he was getting these vials of blood or who he was torturing to get it. Did you? Did you?!"

I smashed my hand on top of the doctor's, shattering his bones. He screamed.

"Secondly, you've taught us a lot today. But your research ends here. Nigel probably wants you to stabilize the Redemptive Agent, doesn't he?"

The doctor nodded.

"I thought so. Well, we can't have that. The minute that nightwalkers can walk around in the daylight is the end of the world as we know it. Nightwalkers are evil. You think the word 'bloodthirsty' just came out of nowhere? It was meant for them. It defines their essence. You make the Redemptive Agent work for them and you've signed your own death sentence and that of your entire people. I so wish you had found us first. I wish that my people could have employed you. You might not have been as wealthy as you are with vampire money, but maybe you'd be able to sleep better at night. I'm sad that this is how you have to learn the difference between a nightwalker and a daywalker."

"What's the difference?" Dr. Zolotov spat. "You've crippled my hands and you'll destroy my practice. Everything I've worked for down the drain."

I laughed again.

"The difference between a vampire and a daywalker? A daywalker might let you live. Good day, Dr. Zolotov. Justin? Seal it with a kiss."

Justin's fangs popped down and the good Dr. Zolotov screamed. Dante stifled his mouth and Justin dug deep into the doctor's neck. His jaw raised and dropped with each gulp.

I looked around the office once more. There was more data here than we could possibly carry, but we had to take as much as possible. I couldn't make heads or tails of it, but Babarinde would appreciate it. We'd need his hard drives, too.

"Doctor?" I called out.

"He's already unconscious," Dante responded.

"Shit," I said. "Hopefully, he wasn't dumb enough to back up his data on a cloud drive. Justin? Justin!"

"Yesh?" he asked, blood dripping from his mouth.

"If we take his computer, can you hack into it? See if he backed up any data to a cloud?"

He nodded vigorously and tried to dig back into the doctor's neck.

"Don't be greedy. Let Dante have some." Dante scooted next to the doctor and took some gulps.

Within the hour, the building was burning. By the time the fire department came, Dr. Zolotov's remaining work was surely all destroyed. Yet, they found the good doctor and the security guard sleeping soundly across the street, without a clue as to how the attack had happened.

Dante and Justin snored in the back of the van among the stolen computer equipment and files. They cuddled in a spoon position that I'd often shared with Ogundiya over the years. My brother, my best friend, my lover—but not my *ipsaji*. Wherever he was now was exactly where he wanted to be: alone and introspective.

Our focus was on Aborişade. Ogundiya would be found later if he wanted to be. I hadn't seen him in years.

Goodbye

I slept on and off in my king-sized bed while Ogundiya lay next to me reading a vintage Batman comic book.

I heard a tap on the door.

"What?" I said through my pillow. Aborişade walked in.

"I need to talk to you," he said.

"Yeah?" He sat down in a chair near my bed and exhaled, clearly nervous to be having this conversation with me.

"We've had a lot of adventures since we've been in DC. Done a lot of things. Met a lot of people. *Helped* a lot of people. And I want to do more. I think that's what my purpose is in life."

"Your purpose?" I asked, sitting up in bed.

"Yes. There's more for me out there. These people…these people need me. They need us. And I want to help them somehow. I've been thinking about this a lot, and I've come to a decision: I'm leaving."

"So that's it? You're going to leave? Just like that?"

"Yes. I have to."

"So you think you can just be some goddamned superhero? Is that what it is? You wanna rescue kittens from trees? Help old ladies across the street? Well, I've got news for you, sir. We're not heroes. These frail creatures, these humans, are our food. We drink them. They don't need you to be their savior. They need a hero to protect them from you! You understand me? You are the predator. And don't you ever forget that."

"We might need human blood for our long-term survival, but our relationship is symbiotic. We've always been able to feed from them and still let them live. Always."

"You think you're so special, so altruistic…"

"I don't think that at all."

"And Babarinde always liked you best."

"Babarinde is letting me leave."

"Lies! He would never let you do something so stupid."

"He would and he did. You can call him right now if you want."

"Then he's a fool just like you!"

"I'm a fool for wanting to help? For wanting to give back?"

"These cattle have given us nothing but their blood!"

"They have given us wisdom. They've given us knowledge. And they've shown us resilience. Not to mention hope. That's probably their greatest gift to us."

"Hope?" I laughed, a genuine, hearty guffaw. "Hope? In Africa, they showed us their greed. On the slave ship, they showed us their cruelty. In Dominica, they showed us their vengefulness. In New Orleans, they showed us their callousness. And here, in Washington? Corruption. Deceit. Apathy. Even—especially—among the black people here. Do you know how tired I am of living in silence among people who have the world at their fingertips but won't get up and fight for themselves to take it? The slaves are already free, Aborişade, but they are too lazy and lost to take what they're owed. If you want to fight for *that*, be my guest."

"You act like you weren't standing there next to me in 1934 when we supported those Howard students protesting against lynching. Remember? They stood there in the winter coats with ropes around their necks in front of the National Crime Conference. Or what about the March on Washington? Weren't you moved then, when we heard Martin Luther King speak, in the flesh? We witnessed watershed moments in human history—in black history. There is hope for these people."

"What are you going to do, then? Pack a knapsack and just start hitchhiking all across the country, looking for problems to solve?"

"Maybe. I don't see why not."

"You're the dumbest fuck who ever lived."

Aborişade's face fell. He stood up and walked toward my bedroom door.

"I'm sorry you feel that way," he said. I heard him go into his room and shuffle things around.

Ogundiya stared at me from his side of the bed.

"What?" I asked.

He shook his head and turned over. I heard Aborişade close his drawers and then leave his room. His footsteps went down the stairs. I shot out of the bed and ran after him.

"You want to be their Jesus so bad. Well go, be a bloodsucking Boy Scout to them if you want to. You'll be back soon. I know it."

"Maybe I will be," he said. Ogundiya came down the stairs behind me. He reached around me and silently shook Aborişade's hand. They locked hands and nodded.

"I love you both," Aborişade said. "Please tell Aragbaye I said goodbye."

"Fuck you," I said. Aborişade softly closed the front door behind him. I went back upstairs and went to sleep. Ogundiya came in a little later and hugged me tight for the rest of the night.

A few days later, Ogundiya, too, was gone. I came home from orchestra rehearsal to find a note on my pillow.

Eşusanya,

You are the most complex man I have ever met. I know that your sharp tongue only protects a soft heart. I hope that in my travels, I can meet people as sensitive as you truly are.

You will think that I am a coward for leaving you and Aragbaye as I have. And that is true, for I cannot bear to see your disappointment in me.

But I want you to know that I, too, believe there is more for the human race, and that I am to help protect them as they evolve into what they were meant to be. I am hoping to catch up to Aborişade, but if I can't, I will go it alone.

I will write you when I reach my destination.

Ogundiya

I picked up a dumbbell and hurled it across the room, shattering my mirror into millions of pieces like stars across an African sky.

Ogundiya did write to us with regularity over the next few months, but I never wrote back. I am sure Aragbaye did. I felt no similar sense of obligation or loyalty. They left us in pursuit of some dream of saving humanity, one fragile human being at a time.

I wasn't about that life.

A few months after that, I felt it was time for me to leave also.

"I knew it would one day come down to me," Aragbaye said with a sigh, as I packed up my car.

"You can go stay with Babarinde, you know. Or transfer to another cell."

"I don't know them like I know you."

"You can get to know them."

"I like DC. Plus, Baba thinks The Key is here. Somebody's got to wait. DC has potential."

"Yeah…it does. I'll miss it. But you'll be waiting a long time for a key that doesn't exist."

"Maybe. Maybe not. Will you be back?"

"I will. One day. But there's a whole country full of girls, boys, and blood, and I hope to taste a little bit of all three for as long as I can."

"Be safe."

"I will."

"And…Eşusanya?"

"Yeah?"

"Thank you for giving me a proper goodbye."

I rushed to my baby brother and gave him a tight squeeze.

"You will be fine, I promise you. Now man up and make a life for yourself."

Aragbaye nodded and shook my hand. I carried my last bag to the car and threw it on the passenger seat. I got in on the driver's side and sped away. I didn't look back once.

I wouldn't see our house again for three years, until the day I met Justin Kena for the first time.

HELL

Sometimes, it felt like a million maggots were crawling over me, threatening to impregnate my body through my ears and my nostrils. I screamed out, but nobody came to my rescue. I would fall asleep again, even though my eyes hadn't been allowed to open in weeks, months, years?

I slept, dreaming of green grass, blue skies, my brothers and sisters, my Africa. I ran across the savannahs that I called my backyard. I saw my mother and my father once again. I was home.

I slept, dreaming of the terrible voyage that ripped me from my homeland forever, depositing me on these foreign shores that had taken so much from me, yet also had given me so much to fight for. Because of that voyage, I learned just how strong I was. Because of that voyage, I loved my brothers even more.

I slept, often dreaming of nothing at all.

I fought back every time I knew they were near, resisting their needles with every ounce of strength I had, but the nearly lethal doses of morphine they gave saved their lives.

I slept.

Demons taunted me, sometimes, their tentacles being the restraints that kept me tethered to this prison, my bed, this house.

They spoke to me, teasing me about secrets that I did not know and answers I did not have. They caressed my neck, sometimes choking it until I passed out, sometimes scratching at me, and sometimes just beating me. I slept.

Holy Mary...she came to me a blinding white light in the darkness of my madness and in the hopelessness of my bondage.

Help the miserable... she covered me like the vast wings of an eagle, protecting my mind from further descent while they poked and prodded and taunted and slapped and raped and stole.

Strengthen the discouraged... the maggots fell away to peace and quietude and stillness.

Comfort the sorrowful...pray for your people... I no longer feared the nightwalkers who controlled my body, for my mind was free. I had been locked in the belly of a slave ship. At least this place had a mattress.

May all who venerate you feel now your help and protection... I would be safe. I would be strong. Help was on the way.

Be ready to help us when we pray...and I prayed and I prayed and I remembered who I was and I prayed some more.

And bring back to us the answers to our prayers.

"Search every room!"

And bring back to us the answers to our prayers.

"Break it down!"

And the knocking of the door was really my brother's foot crashing through it.

I knew I heard them. I knew there was a crashing sound, like a window being broken down the hall. I knew it. I knew they'd come for me.

They removed the tentacles from my legs first, freeing them. I could barely move them. I could hardly understand what they were saying, but I knew things were changing, then and there, in that instant, in that moment in time. I was being freed. My body was matching my spirit.

They loosed the bonds around my wrists, freeing them, letting the blood flow freely again. They spoke, but still, I didn't understand.

They reached around my head and removed the hood. Even in the darkness of night, the light from the moon, the stars, the far off streetlight, blinded me for a second. I adjusted rapidly.

"Aborişade? Aborişade?"

I blinked several times. The face in front of me was one I didn't recognize, but I knew was a friend. His head was crowned with short dreadlocks, newly begun. I could smell the scent of my people on him.

"Yes...that's my name," I said softly. He touched my face and then my chest.

"It's nice to finally meet you. My name is Justin Kena. My crown name is Ominiyi. But we've got to get you out of here. Can you walk?"

"Ominiyi...I can try." I moved my legs off the side of the bed and tried to put my weight on my feet. I stood up and immediately stumbled. He steadied me.

"I got you. But what's this? Under the pillow?" He asked. My new friend reached under the pillow and grabbed a short strand of green and white beads.

"Hold it for me," I requested. He scooped me up in his arms and walked with me to the door, where I saw a masked figure keeping lookout.

"Where's your mask?!" said an annoyed voice.

"I took it off so he could see me. Nobody's going to get carted off willingly by a masked crazy person," Ominiyi said.

"True," the other man said. He carefully lifted his mask up to his forehead and showed me his face.

"I know you," I said. "You're Aragbaye."

He smiled.

"Eşusanya is here, too. We've got to go."

He pulled his mask back down and drew both his guns. My vision was blurry but I could see that each of them had two holsters on their hips and two more strapped to their thighs. They were dressed in black from head to toe.

"They're coming!" said another familiar voice from down the hall. I looked down as Ominiyi tried to take me to a safe corner. The tall and lithe shadow was Eşusanya, just as courageous and hotheaded as I remembered.

Two nightwalkers reached the top of the steps and were each shot by my brother. His aim was still impeccable. The tall, Asian vampire was hit right between the eyes. The red-haired vampire was hit in the chest. Both shriveled, blackened, and turned into sludge there on the stairs.

"Let's go!" he shouted as a chorus of additional footsteps traveled up the stairs.

We were nearly at the open window when shots began to ring out. Ominiyi dove to the floor and pushed me over to a corner, behind a hallway table, in an attempt to keep me safe from the onslaught. Although I knew wooden bullets had a minimal impact on us, it would be terrible if I got shot in my current state of vulnerability.

A white woman with curly black hair and a muscular black man, near her in height, were at the front of the approaching platoon of nightwalkers. Their faces looked enraged on the surface, but something curious was happening.

Their hands recoiled as though they were shooting, but no bullets were coming out. It was as though they were creating a path of safety for us.

Ominiyi, Aragbaye, and Eşusanya shot around the pair, aiming only for the outer section of the rapidly approaching platoon of multicultural nightwalkers.

When they were ten feet away, the man and woman stopped, looked at each other, nodded, and then performed a standing back flip, tumbling all the way over the six vampires behind them, creating a clear shot for the brothers.

They landed behind the half-dozen nightwalkers, paving the way for their deaths by wooden bullets. After my brothers were done, all that was left were gelatinous puddles.

"Eight down," the woman said. "Nigel is out feeding, but he will certainly be on his way back. Cassandra is downstairs."

Her companion stared at us as Ominiyi tried getting me on my feet again. I stood by myself this time.

"You must be Andre," Ominiyi said.

"Yes, I am."

"Thank you," Dante said.

"It's not over yet," Eşusanya said. "Now, come on, the window."

"No!" the woman said. "Orlando is too weak. You're going to walk right out the front door."

"But Cassandra and the others…"

"You have to take us hostage. It's the only way we can all make it out of here. Walk us straight down the stairs with your guns on us."

"Sasha, that will never work!" Eşusanya said.

"Listen! We got you in here and we saved your lives. You owe it to us to get us out of here, too! Now what we're going to do is walk down the stairs with our hands over our heads and you're going to threaten to kill us if Cassandra doesn't step aside."

"Goddamn it Sasha, if you get us killed I will fucking kill you!" Eşusanya hissed.

We began walking down the winding stairs to the first floor of the house. The menacing lady of the house was frozen at the bottom of the stairs while we descended. She was beautiful, yet frightening, in her charcoal gray pantsuit and pearls.

"Sasha! Andre, what have they done to you?" she asked incredulously.

"Mistress, we-"

"Shut up, bitch, before I put this wooden bullet through your skull like your friends back there." Eşusanya acted convincingly.

"Oh my goodness, no!" Cassandra said.

"Stay back, Cassandra," Eşusanya said.

"Victor! There's no need for further violence. You have what you want, please just let my children go."

"And there's no need for us to trust you. They're coming with us until we're far away from here."

"We could be helpful to each other, darling. Put down the gun."

"You think I'm stupid?"

"Then leave it up. Listen. I know we did you all wrong, and I'm sorry. I follow Nigel. But we took care of Orlando, I swear we did. We were always going to send him back."

"Once you drained him?" Ominiyi asked.

"You're Justin!" she exclaimed. "So they did turn you!"

"Never mind him, you focus on me. Look into my eyes. Tell me what you were going to do to him."

"Your hypnosis won't work on me darling; I'm far too old for that. But I'll gladly tell you. Nigel wanted to identify any weakness of your people so that he could destroy you. He believes that the Razadi will be the downfall of our people."

"And you?" I asked.

"I think otherwise. I think we can study your blood, your DNA, figure out what mutations allow you to walk in the daylight. Together, we can be unstoppable, Victor. Daywalker and nightwalker living together in peace. Conquering the world. All mankind serving us."

"Razadi don't want that!" Dante shouted. "We just want to live in freedom. And you shattered that when you took our brother!"

"For the betterment of us all. Listen. It's not too late. We can work together and show Nigel, show *all* of them who believe in the old ways, that *this* can be the new dawn! Not the destruction of any of us, but the birth of an entirely new nation!"

"You know nothing, Cassandra," I said, standing up tall with my hand on Ominiyi for support.

"And Orlando speaks," she said smugly.

"You think that our blood will let you walk in the sun? Well…what do you think will happen if we drink your blood instead? Hmm? Maybe we don't want to own the sun. Perhaps we want to own hell!"

My fangs elongated and I hurled myself at her, knocking her to the ground as I bit her neck and drank her sour blood.

"Aborişade, no!" they cried out. I knew I shouldn't be drinking the vile blood of a nightwalker, but I hadn't had a proper meal in months. She would have to do.

Her blood spilled out from the wounds I made in her neck. I gulped her down. I heard the roar of the ocean in my ears rather than her screams and the shouts from my brothers to stop. I grew more powerful by the second.

I stopped and looked around me, smiling. Everything was red.

"We have to go!" Ominiyi shouted in slow motion.

They grabbed me, pulling me away from Cassandra's beautiful, bloodied body, leaving her spurting and nearly lifeless. I didn't walk; I floated along with Aragbaye and Eşusanya and Ominiyi as they pulled me away from the scene. The house became a big, brown blur.

Sasha and Andre didn't follow. They were frozen, stuck for some reason over the body of Cassandra. We flew away, free to live, free to be, free to choose. Just free.

Back to Work

A few weeks after the massacre at the Anubis Society's mansion, things were back to normal. I drove my new Mercedes Benz into the gravel parking lot behind Magdalene next to Steve's car, a modest Honda Accord. We'd both done well for ourselves since ourselves since the Foundation took over.

"That's a nice ride you pushin'," Steve said.

"Thanks. Hard work pays off." I smiled.

"Indeed. Can we talk?"

"Sure, what's up?" I asked, leaning against the closed door of my car.

"Nothing…we haven't talked in a while. You know, just shoot the shit like we used to."

"Yeah. It has been a while."

"Yeah man. So, I was hot and heavy with Chiyoko for a while, but she just up and disappeared on me."

"Word?" I asked. I'd long since learned to perfect my poker face when dealing with Steve.

"Yeah. Used to see her every week at the bar, but then she was just gone."

"That sucks man, sorry to hear that."

"Yeah. I really liked her, too."

"I'm sure somebody else will come along."

"We'll see." He shifted his weight from his left leg to his right leg and put his hands in his pockets. My mind wandered to the night Chiyoko died; how Dante impaled her, making her a mass of slime on the floor.

"Are you okay, though?" he asked, snapping me back into the moment.

"Me? Yeah! Everything's fine!"

"Okay." Steve smiled.

"You don't think so, do you?"

"I mean…you changed."

"Changed? Naw, it's still the same old me. I'm still Justin Kena. No worries."

"Yeah. I know. You just…"

"I just what?"

"Justin, you've lost like 50 pounds easy. I never even see you eat anymore. And you've just been rolling with Dante and his crew since you met him. I mean, I know that's your boy and all, so it's cool. But I can't help but wonder what's really going on. I worry about you, man. Shit goes down with you personally and I don't even hear about it anymore. Those weeks that you were sick. The Foundation takeover. It's just all shady man, and I don't want you to be in any trouble. You my boy."

"Steve, I promise you…"

My mind wandered again, to the first day I'd met Dante… to the day I learned what he really was… to the day I learned about nightwalkers… to the day I was attacked… to all the memories I'd made since those days and to all the memories I received from my brothers. My first kill. My next kills.

My emotions got the better of me and I began to weep.

"Hey, it's okay man!" Steve came over and embraced me. My weeping continued as I clutched him back.

"What's wrong? You want to talk about it?"

I sniffed and wiped my eyes. My heart broke because I knew in an instant what had to be done.

"Steve…look at me," I began.

"Yeah?" he said.

"Steve, everything with me is fine."

"Everything with you is fine."

"My health and my well-being are fine."

"Your health and well-being are fine."

"There is never any need to worry about me. I am safe. I am with people who love me. I am with people who take care of me. You have never seen me happier."

"I've never seen you happier."

"You don't worry about me."

"I don't worry about you."

"Now…there's no need to remember this talk. Just remember those emotions. You understand?"

"I understand."

"Have a good day, Steve."

"You, too, Justin."

Steve turned around and walked up the pathway to our building. I remained next to my car to wipe my eyes and get myself together for work. I followed the pathway and glanced across the street, seeing Dante sitting on the stoop of the Masonic hall in his leather jacket and black kufi cap. I waved. He nodded at me and pointed to his pants pocket.

I reached in my pocket and pulled out my phone.

I LOVE YOU. HAVE A GOOD DAY.

I smiled and looked at my *ipsaji,* who was smiling back at me. He would be my protector today, and every day, for the rest of my life, if he could help it.

In the office, I waved and spoke to all of my employees. Everyone was pleased with their jobs and that suited me just fine. They thrived on their independence. Our jobs program was up and running and a formal press conference with the city would be coming soon, just in time for Christmas.

I sat in my chair and turned on both my desktop and my laptop computers. While they were warming up, my office phone rang.

"Hello?" I said.

"Hey dick breath," Victor replied. I laughed.

"What's up?"

"Just wanted to remind you I'm taking Orlando down to Charleston for the sorority board meeting."

"Okay, cool. I saw that on my calendar. How's he feeling?"

"Getting stronger. Still having trouble sleeping, though."

"Yeah, that's to be expected. Getting some Iota blood will be good for him."

"And me, too. Getting tired of this local blood."

I laughed again. "Be safe, Victor."

"You too, bruddah."

I hung the phone up and began sifting through my work emails. I saw one from Selena Esteban from the Friends of the Crown, asking for a lunch date. I replied right away, putting her on my schedule. It had been a long time since we chatted, and I would need to continue to cultivate that relationship in order to establish myself as a real nonprofit executive—not just a front man for the Foundation for Community Justice. There was more to me than what I had been through.

A few minutes later, the Skype alert on my laptop went off. It was Babarinde—so far, the only person I ever needed to Skype with.

"Hello, Uncle John! To what do I owe the pleasure?" I smiled into the camera imbedded in the laptop while I looked at Baba's smiling, chiseled brown face on my screen.

"How are you?" he asked.

"I'm good! How are you?"

"I'm fine. Good, actually. We've got a lead on Ogundiya."

"Really? Wow, I never thought we'd find him so soon. When one goes off the grid…"

"Exactly. And as quiet as Ogundiya is, I thought it would be years before we found him."

"So where is he?"

"My sources say that the Djinn have him and they're ready to negotiate."

"The Djinn? Jeez. I thought we were cool with them?"

"We were. Last week. So, how about it? Will you go get him?"

The Djinn were far more mysterious to me than any other being I'd encountered since I'd been made a Razadi. Mysterious—and dangerous, I was sure.

Things would never be back to normal ever again. And that's just the way things would be from here on out.

"I'm on it."

EPILOGUE

Nigel entered Cassandra's bedroom. She stirred in her four-poster bed. Sasha and Andre brought her upstairs every day after nightfall to give her some reprieve from her dark coffin in the basement. The attack had left her weak.

Sasha sat at the foot of her bed, waiting for instructions, while Andre stood guard by the door with a semi-automatic assault rifle.

"Hello, darling," Cassandra said from her bed.

"How are you feeling?" Nigel asked after he sat down beside her.

"Tired, but getting better."

"Good. We'll get those bloody daywalkers yet, don't you worry."

"Nigel, please…"

"If Malcolm had been here, he would have stopped them."

"Even Malcolm is no match for them."

"Andre and Sasha let eight of us die. Eight!"

"It was an ambush, Nigel, they couldn't have known. And with wooden bullets and everything! It's not their fault."

"And they destroyed millions of dollars of research! Had we even known about their sabotage when it happened, we would have known we were next. Millions of dollars of work down the drain!"

"Can you really blame them? What we did to that young man was unconscionable."

"What we did to that boy was our right! It was our destiny! This was only a taste of what we can do to them. They'll soon find out just why we're called the Anubis Society. Malcolm!"

Malcolm rushed in.

"Yes, sir?"

"Unleash the jackal!"

"With pleasure, sir."

Malcolm sped out of the room. Within seconds, they heard the sound of his engine igniting and then taking off from the driveway of the mansion.

"Oh, Nigel," Cassandra said, as she closed her eyes. The air in the room chilled and Andre and Sasha glanced at one another in terror as Nigel spoke.

"We are the guardians of the jackal. I will do whatever I have to do to ensure that we are the victors in this war. The Razadi will pay by their total extermination."

OTHER WORKS BY RASHID DARDEN

Novels:

Lazarus (2005)
Covenant (2011)
Epiphany (2012)

Poetry:

The Life and Death of Savion Cortez (2011)

Rashid Darden currently lives in Washington, DC. He may be reached at any social media outlet (@RashidDarden) or at his website, www.rashiddarden.com.

Cover design by Charlis Foster for 620 Media.

CPSIA information can be obtained at www.ICGtesting.com
Printed in the USA
LVOW01s2125020114

367801LV00034B/2210/P

9 780976 598664